Praise for bestselling author

ANIA AHLBORN

THE DEVIL CREPT IN

"A beautiful and deftly wrought horror story of mothers, sons, and the delicate bond between cousins. . . . With sympathetic attention paid to the relationships between overwhelmed mothers and the sons they can't save from evil, and prose that elegantly evokes tension while illustrating [a] rich inner world, readers will be engrossed and thrilled right through to the chewy finale."

—*Publishers Weekly* (starred review)

"Creepy . . . digs under your skin and leaves marks. You may find yourself looking over your shoulder long after the book is done."

—J. Lincoln Fenn, award-winning author of *Dead Souls* and *Poe*

"Ahlborn does a great job of making readers feel the confusion, dread, and frustration. . . . This is [her] most atmospheric work to date. It also features some of her best character work. . . . With *The Devil Crept In*, Ania Ahlborn continues her steady climb through the ranks of horror, proving once again that she's got the chops, the ideas, and the innate storytelling ability required to build a long and successful career."

—*Cemetery Dance*

BROTHER

"[A] visceral, nihilistic thriller. . . . Ahlborn's impressive writing and expert exploration of the psychological effects of systemic abuse elevate what could have been the literary equivalent of a slasher flick, and the twist in the final act is jaw-dropping. This relentlessly grim tale is definitely not for the squeamish, but it's nearly impossible to put down."

—*Publishers Weekly* (starred review)

"This story of brotherly love/hate will crush you to the core. . . . *Brother* delivers horror on all fronts. . . . The writing is so good, so precision perfect, that *Brother* may be this year's sleeper novel, certainly of the *Gone Girl* caliber, that deserves all the praise and accolades it will definitely receive. . . . An instant classic. . . . This is one book you need to get in your hands as soon as possible."

—This is Horror

WITHIN THESE WALLS

"Terrifyingly sad. . . . *Within These Walls* creeps under your skin and stays there. It's insidious. . . . The book's atmosphere is distinctly damp, clammy, overcast, and it isn't all the Washington weather: its characters' souls are gray, dimmed by failure. Ahlborn is awfully good on the insecurities that plague both aging writers . . . and oversensitive young girls . . . which leave them vulnerable to those who . . . know how to get into their heads. So grim."

—*The New York Times Book Review*

"Cruel, bone-chilling, and destined to become a classic, *Within These Walls* is worth the sleep it will cost you. Some of the most promising horror I've encountered in years."

—Seanan McGuire, *New York Times* bestselling author

"A monstrous Russian nesting doll of a book, holding secrets within secrets; the plot barrels headlong toward one of the most shocking climaxes you're ever likely to read. This one's going to wreck you."

—Nick Cutter, national bestselling author of
Little Heaven and *The Troop*

"Ania Ahlborn is a great storyteller who spins an atmosphere of dread literally from the first page, increasing the mental pressure all the way through to the terrifying, chilling ending."

—Jeff Somers, acclaimed author of
The Electric Church and *We Are Not Good People*

"Ever-mounting terror and a foreboding setting make for pure storytelling alchemy. . . . Ania Ahlborn goes for the gut with surprise twists that will stay with you for days. Not a book, or an author, that you'll soon forget."

—Vicki Pettersson, *New York Times* bestselling author

ALSO AVAILABLE BY ANIA AHLBORN

The Devil Crept In

Brother

Within These Walls

The Bird Eater

The Shuddering

The Neighbors

Seed

APART
IN THE
DARK

Novellas

ANIA AHLBORN

G

Gallery Books

New York   London   Toronto   Sydney   New Delhi

Gallery Books
An Imprint of Simon & Schuster, Inc.
1230 Avenue of the Americas
New York, NY 10020

First Gallery Books trade paperback edition January 2018

GALLERY BOOKS and colophon are registered trademarks of Simon & Schuster, Inc.

For information about special discounts for bulk purchases, please contact Simon & Schuster Special Sales at 1-866-506-1949 or business@simonandschuster.com.

The Simon & Schuster Speakers Bureau can bring authors to your live event. For more information or to book an event, contact the Simon & Schuster Speakers Bureau at 1-866-248-3049 or visit our website at www.simonspeakers.com.

10 9 8 7 6 5 4 3 2

Library of Congress Cataloging-in-Publication Data is available.

ISBN 978-1-5011-8753-7

TABLE OF CONTENTS

INTRODUCTION

The moment I stepped foot onto a university campus, I knew what I wanted to be: a psychologist. I had a love for writing, of course. By then, I was no stranger to unfinished manuscripts and half-baked plot ideas. My well-intentioned parents assured me, however, that writing—at least as a career—was a far-fetched dream. Best to take the road more often traveled, the road that led to a fancy office, a private practice, and a boatload of money.

And so, I settled on the more logical choice. Psychology made sense.

And besides, what better way to crawl inside the weird brains of even weirder people and roll around like a pig in the mud (all while getting paid to do it)? By the end of my first semester, I had put together my dream list of the strange and the broken who would grace my overstuffed patient's couch: sad goth kids with dismissive parents; angry goth kids with homicidal tendencies; overgrown goth kids who spit in the face of adulthood; Satan-worshiping goth kids who'd morphed into full-on serial killers and mass-murdering psychopaths—you know, the types of people I loved to write about. Obviously, I went through a goth phase. If you've read any of my books, you know you'd need a couple of extra hands to accurately count the amount of times I've referenced black lipstick, combat boots, and the Cure.

But back then, dammit, I was determined. I was going to be a psychologist come hell or high water. Because if I couldn't spend my time writing about these fascinatingly skewed personalities, I was going to help them instead. A defender of the weak and abused. A champion of the malcontents. An ambassador to the misunderstood. And I was going to be one hell of a head doctor because I could relate. As Lydia Deetz said in *Beetlejuice*, I myself was strange and unusual. My life was one big dark room.

It was during the second semester of my sophomore year that I took one of the most difficult classes of my college career—abnormal psychology, which I was *so* excited about. I mean, come on, *abnormal* psych! It was going to be a class full of fascinating case studies about the maniacal and deranged: a perfect introduction to my ultimate client—the clinically unhinged, the dangerously unbalanced. Unfortunately for me, the fascinating field of abnormal psychology turned out to be an abnormally huge dose of reality. Somehow, the class that I had been looking forward to with such gusto ended up draining my passion for the bizarre and the broken. And then, at my lowest point—feeling defeated, with a failed test I had crammed for staring back at me—the instructor stood in front of the class and made an announcement.

He told us that if we wanted to help people, we were going into the wrong field. To help, we should be social workers, not psychologists or psychiatrists. As doctors of the mind, we weren't there to help, but to nod and listen. We were there to give our patients an hour of our time so that they could figure out their own problems by talking it out for themselves. Advice was not allowed, because advice would get you sued. To get far in the field of psychology, you simply sat, listened, and did nothing.

My mouth turned to ash.

I walked out of that lecture feeling like the homicidal maniacs I wanted to treat. His words had cut straight through me. But now, looking back . . . I know that his weird reverse pep talk changed my life that day. That hard dose of realism completely shifted my trajectory. Do I believe what he said about the field of psychology—that those doctors do nothing? No. But in hindsight, I'm glad he said it, because the next day I found myself sitting across from my advisor, changing my major from psych to English, my first real, genuine, true love. Because if I wasn't going to be allowed to dissect the human condition as a doctor, then dammit, I'd do it as a writer. This was how I would bring my dream list of patients to life.

Every story I write is about a person I believe is out there somewhere, living and breathing and walking among us, camouflaged by the banality of our everyday lives. The monsters I create aren't ones you can escape. They're your neighbors, your family, and your friends. They're inescapable because you never see their depravity coming . . . and by the time you do, it's too late.

Family and friends are a big theme for me. I can't get away from the idea that what should be a safe haven can actually be the most dangerous place of all. That very concept of a safe space being unsafe gave birth to Nell Sullivan, the main character in *The Pretty Ones*. Nell is a mouse of a girl with a simple desire, the oh-so-human ache to fit in and find a friend. But Barrett, Nell's odd and mute intellectual of an older brother, loathes the girls that make up Nell's office pool. It's his insistence, his overbearing possessiveness, that would land Nell on my overstuffed therapy couch. And isn't that always the case? Those who hurt us the most are, at times, the ones who think they're protecting us from ourselves. It's how the savior becomes the rival. How the guardian angel becomes the demon. It's how our love for someone can sour. How our faith can turn toxic.

A similar theme of family and friendship is repeated in *I Call Upon Thee*, though in a more supernatural way. Maggie Olsen is like Nell in her loneliness; but while Nell continues to struggle with her inability to make friends well into adulthood, Maggie takes matters into her own hands as a child. In doing so, she sets the unthinkable into motion—something that her oh-so-gothic Depeche Mode–loving older sister Brynn warns her about, but that Maggie doesn't heed. Did I mention I had a goth phase? In case I didn't, there it is . . . again.

In these two novellas, you'll meet a handful of my patients. An insecure wallflower. A manipulative and arrogant sibling. A girl who's trying to put her past behind her by swallowing the pain she's convinced that she brought upon her family. A woman who can't stop weaving stories about the malevolence of the dead. You'll hear their tales and begin to dissect the causality of their disorders for yourself. Angry, flippant mothers. Jagged memories of lovelessness and trauma. Death and guilt and bitterness. These, it appears, are a few of my favorite things.

I've been told by a handful of people that my stories are some of the saddest they've read, because the characters are unafraid of reflecting a fragmented and oftentimes flawed humanity. Someone once called me the "Duchess of Despair" and, at one time, I worried that my writing was too grounded in realism, too contemplative of the human condition. But, isn't that the fundamental basis of great horror—the ability to see yourself in a circumstance that you wouldn't wish upon the world? The serial killer that wanders the streets of New York City; the kid who finds joy among cemetery graves; the lonely girl who watches her beautiful coworkers lead glamorous lives she can only dream of living; the child who turns to a Ouija board because there's no one to offer her the camaraderie she seeks. These are the broken. The weird. The lost. They are the ones who sit in the dimly lit therapist's office of my mind. The tales you find in this collection are the ones they would tell.

I gave up the idea of being a psychologist, but I've always been a writer. Somehow I've flipped the script that had once seemed like my destiny. Rather than the healer, I've become an architect of pain. And you, dear reader . . . you have the job of piecing these personalities together. And while you can't offer the characters advice, you can at least try to understand where these strange creatures went wrong. And perhaps where *you* went wrong—because, my friend, you aren't that much different from Nell or Maggie or anyone else you'll find within these pages.

Perhaps the horror isn't in the story itself as much as it is in the knowledge that these characters are really you; the terror of it is that all you can do is sit and nod and do nothing. Because you *chose* this book. You *chose* this darkness. So please, step inside my office. Let me tell you a story. Just take a seat right over there on the couch . . .

THE
PRETTY
ONES

The man who smiles when things go wrong
has thought of someone to blame it on.

—Robert Bloch

N ELL SULLIVAN WAS a mouse.
    A square.
    A big fat nobody.

Sitting at her desk with her head bowed and her gaze fixed on the keys of her IBM Selectric, she didn't need to glance at the clock to know the hour had arrived. She'd been ticking away the seconds until quitting time in her head—*one Mississippi, two*—having spent the last five minutes putting her desk in order, the same as always. Never making small talk. Not once looking up.

She squared her typewriter so it lined up with the edge of her desk, fanned out the pencils in her smiley-face mug like the feathers of a peacock. *Have a nice day!* Even the heavy glass ashtray she'd never used was meticulously placed at the corner, leaving exactly two inches around two of its four sides. Smoking, in Barrett's opinion, was a sin reserved for the weak. But Barrett's opinion didn't matter to the staff of Rambert & Bertram. Every desk in the office sported the same ashtray, as if inviting the devil to mingle within the office pool. Nell had considered removing the ashtray from her desk, if only to tell Barrett that she had. Heeding his warning would make him happy. Not happy enough to spur conversation . . . but the act was rebellious, one that the other secretaries would notice. And while Nell dreamed of being "one of the girls," she was no dummy.

Everyone knew Nell was a drag. She'd been thinking about taking up smoking for that very reason. Maybe a few puffs would make her cool like all the other girls. The ones who congregated around the water cooler, the lunch area, and on the crowded sidewalk outside the building's revolving doors. If Nell started smoking, she'd have a reason to stand around right along with them. She'd breathe the noxious fumes while listening to cabbies honk their horns. Watch hundreds of busy businesspeople march through intersections—men in pressed suits, women with their hair done up and their lips painted red. She'd inhale exhaust-laced nicotine five days a week if it meant fitting in . . . even a little.

But Barrett . . .

Her attention flicked to the ashtray. A sliver of sun shone there, lighting it up like a firework, turning cheap glass into crystal. She looked away, stared down at the extension buttons numbered one through seven beneath the dial pad of her office phone.

Rambert and Bertram, how may I direct your call? One moment, please.

Rambert and Bertram, how may I direct your call? One moment, please.

Rambert and . . .

Her coworkers, having suppressed their desire for socialization since lunch, were bubbling over with pent-up energy. They'd abandon their desks the moment the clock ticked away the last seconds of 4:59 p.m. Their voices would rise above the din of dwindling telephone conversations and the muffled blare of New York City rush hour. Five o'clock: when the people Nell wished to be a part of were at their most glorious. Excited for happy-hour cocktails. For evening reunions with husbands, boyfriends, fleeting lovers. It was the hour that reminded Nell just how little she was like them. Because no matter how hard a good Irish Catholic girl prayed, God wasn't in the business of granting good looks or social grace or—dare she even think it—the burst of passion associated with a one-night stand. Twenty-two years old and Nell had more in common with the Virgin Mary than she did with any girl on the inbound call-center floor.

Five o'clock. The girls unraveled in front of their typewriters. Some fell back in their desk chairs with muffled moans. Others pulled bobby pins from their hair and shook out their tresses in cascading waves. Nell never had much success in getting her dull hair to look remotely as good. She'd watched the Breck commercials, bought the shampoos and conditioners and dry oils that Farrah Fawcett swore by. It broke the bank, but she purchased them anyway, hiding them in her bedroom where Barrett wouldn't look. She didn't dare speak of her silly, girlish desires. He'd strike them down with a single dubious look of irritation, a look that always made her feel as stupid as she knew she was.

Brigitte Bardot.

Jacqueline Bisset.

Like she had any chance of that.

Don't think about it, she told herself, purging her mind of the thought as she straightened her sweater, grabbed her purse, and rose from her desk. With her head bowed, she made a beeline for the elevator and, coincidentally, for Mary Ann Thomas as well.

Hail Mary, full of grace.

Mary Ann was *the* girl. The goddess. The gold standard. The perfect brand of slender, graceful in the way she carried herself up and down the call-center floor. Her calf muscles were smooth and powerful beneath the hem of her Halston skirt. Her hair, freshly bleached from a light chestnut to an almost shocking white, rested on the shoulders of her tunic blouse in buoyant waves. Mary Ann's red pumps—red for sexy, for dangerous—were a proverbial stop sign: *back away, forget about it.* Girls like Mary Ann Thomas didn't cavort with people like Nell.

But Nell didn't stop. She couldn't. Mary Ann was in her path, chatting away, surrounded by a group of women not quite as pretty as her, but pretty enough for Nell to fantasize about just the same.

Nell's heart leaped into her throat when Mary Ann made eye contact. Nell forced a smile, a victory for a girl who could hardly hold a conversation; a tiny win for someone whose reflex was to pull her shoulders up to her ears and look away.

Mary Ann wasn't impressed by Nell's weary triumph. She narrowed her eyes and returned Nell's smile by way of a sarcastic red-lipsticked grin.

"A little *warm*, Nell?" Mary Ann asked, her tone tinged with disgust, dripping with sarcasm. Dripping much like the sweat that was already starting to bead up along Nell's hairline.

It was hot—the hottest summer on record in what felt like forever. So hot most people walked around half-naked, in search of relief from the heat. But not Nell. She wore her grandma's Aran sweater like a pregnant girl trying to fool her mother. She needed to lose a few pounds, sure that every single girl in the office was keenly aware of that fact. Every sideways glance convinced her all the more.

"Gross." Mary Anne uttered the word beneath her breath, but Nell heard it as clear as a Chinese gong.

Hope splintered into anger.

A flash of pain lit up behind her eyes. The seed of another migraine.

Floozy, she thought. *Tramp*.

She stopped in front of the elevator, her gaze fixed on the glowing button beside the polished steel doors. Those doors cast back a vague reflection—featureless, little more than the shade of Nell's dark-brown hair and taupe bell-bottomed slacks.

Librarian, the voice of reason chimed in. *Plain Jane. Old maid. Timid white-bread mouse.*

Anything Nell could fault Mary Ann for, Mary Ann could fire right back. Which was why Nell never stood up for herself in any situation. Whatever she could say about others, they could say about her twenty times worse.

The elevator dinged above Nell's head. The doors yawned open. She shuffled inside, pressed herself against the corner, watched chunky heels and wedge sandals congregate around her penny loafers, which were missing the pennies. Even a bit of shiny copper was too flashy for Barrett's taste.

Too poor to afford them, she'd heard a girl say on one of her first days there.

Maybe if she didn't spend her entire paycheck at McDonald's, suggested another.

Stupid bitches, Nell had thought. She hadn't been to McDonald's in years.

After overhearing that particular conversation, Nell had considered quitting this job the way she had left all the others. But she was determined to push herself to be better, to be less of a hermit, to be more like Barrett, her confident and artistic older sibling. He was sure to find the perfect girl, and then who would she have? Nobody. She'd be left to weep herself to sleep in her crooked shoebox of an apartment. Hey, look, Brooklyn, Nell's crying again.

Of course, Barrett insisted she was crazy, that he'd never leave, that he couldn't. He'd leave her sunshine-yellow notes around the house:

I love you, Nell.

You're my best friend, don't forget.

Our blood is our bond.

But his promises made no difference. His love for her was keeping him in place, but a grown man could only love his sister so much. Someday, his affections would take him in a different direction, and that's when the notes would change.

Gotta go, found someone else.

Sorry Sis, but you know how it is.

The elevator reeked of day-old hair bleach. It plunged to the ground floor, taking Nell's stomach with it. Nobody spoke to her. Nobody glanced her way. They turned their bodies so that not a single one of them faced her. She was invisible as they chattered among themselves, not an arm's length away. They talked about a new dress shop opening up on Fifth. Code, Nell was sure, for how great they'd look in their new frocks, while she was doomed to live out her life in ugly bell-bottoms and boatneck shirts.

Nobody mentioned Sam.

Nell kept her head down as she spilled onto the street, marching toward the subway station and the train that would take her home. She waited on the platform among a sea of professionals, art students, musicians, and homeless. She watched a group of tall black kids occupying too much space in the crowded terminal. They were taking turns spinning a basketball on the tips of their fingers. They dribbled it on the concrete, tossed it back and forth while ignoring the stares and snorts and high-brow eye-rolling of people "just trying to get home." Nell admired people like those basketball boys—guys who did what they wanted to do no matter how unbecoming it was to others. She inched closer to the group, taking small sidesteps to the left to close the distance. Maybe if she got close enough, a little of their unabashed passion would rub off on her. Perhaps touching that basketball, even if it was by walking into its path during a pass, would transfer some of that confident magic from them to her.

The B train arrived before she could get close enough.

Folks crammed into the cars and scrambled for available seats. Straphangers grabbed dirty strips of plastic and leaned into the up-surge of speed. Nell pressed herself into a straight-backed seat be-tween an old Hasidic Jew and a fat man in a tiny damp suit. Both were as sweaty as she was. Both smelled like they'd been slathered in cumin and sea salt.

Nell dipped into her purse and pulled a stick of Doublemint gum from its slim, green pack. She popped the gum into her mouth, then hovered the silver wrapper in front of her nose, inhaling peppermint to cut through their stink. She concentrated on the graffiti that cov-ered the walls, some of it etched into the plexiglass of the car like a patchwork quilt. Most of it was unreadable—nothing but a bunch of loops and swirls and vaguely distinguishable lettering. Some was more distinct.

REBEL SCUM.

FUCK DISCO.

YOU AIN'T SHIT, CORPRIT MAN.

NEW YORK IS DEAD.

The train screamed through the underground. The fat man and his tiny suit got off at Herald Square. The Hasid rode on to West 4th Street.

Nell sped toward King's Highway station. The side of an aban-doned factory flashed a piece of urban art she read a dozen times a week: *WHEREVER YOU GO, THERE YOU'LL BE.*

She shuffled off the train behind a string of blacks and Latinos, the only white girl dumb or crazy or poor enough to live in this part of Brooklyn. Pulling her shoulders up to her ears, she braced herself for the routine dose of harassment.

"Hey, *bibliotecaria!*" A Puerto Rican bicycle gang circled in the street just beyond the station like a wake of vultures. "Hey, you got any good books?" She didn't dare look right at them, but she knew their voices well. There were five of them, shirtless due to the heat wave. They rode bikes too small for their gangly legs. They wore shabby Dr. Js on their feet, the white leather tattered by pedal spikes. They bothered her despite their lack of ammunition, because really, what did they want from a girl like her anyway? Once, she had told Barrett she'd give them something to remember her by, but her brother had shot her a look she had easily deciphered. *Don't.* It would only make it worse. And of course, he was right. Fighting back would only make them bite harder.

"Hey, hey, *bibliotecaria!*" There was out-and-out mirth in her assailant's voice. "I heard about this book, it's called the *Karma Sutra.*" More laughter. Nell clamped her jaw tight and hastened her steps. "You wanna come back with us to our place? Wanna teach us the ancient Chinese art of fucking?" An eruption of chortles, of boys speaking in fast, clipped Spanish behind her.

She balled her hands into fists and continued to march, a trickle of sweat sending a maddening tickle down her spine.

"Hey, don't get *mad.*" One of them cruised next to her on his tiny single-speed bike.

"Hey, Marco, you better shut up, man," another advised. "You're too loud, ey. You gotta be quiet in the library."

They burst into another fit of cackling, but they stopped trailing her down East 16th Street. By the time she turned onto Quentin Road, they were gone.

"It's *Kama Sutra,*" she hissed beneath her breath. "And it's not Chinese, you morons. Why don't you go make out with your cunt girlfriends?" She muttered the question, the hushed profanity tasting sweet on her tongue. She pictured their leader canoodling with some Spanish girl just before taking a bullet to the head. That was why Mary Ann Thomas had bleached her hair from chestnut to white. It was why the entire call-center floor reeked of ammonia. Blond hair was one of the few lines of defense a girl had against the 44 Caliber Killer, the one that called himself the Son of Sam. He had sent a letter to the *Daily News* only a few weeks before.

HELLO FROM THE GUTTERS OF NYC!

Nell had read that letter, unable to shake the strange itch of envy. It was a letter written by someone who had had enough. Someone who had been pushed too far; shoved right over the line of civility and onto a path of blood-soaked freedom.

Uninhibited liberation.

A personal renaissance.

She shoved her hands into the pockets of her sweater, felt the soft edges of one of Barrett's crumpled notes.

Ignore them. Don't start trouble.

Reaching her row-house apartment on Quentin Road, she climbed up the crumbling concrete steps and pushed open the front door. She had two keys on her vinyl Snoopy key ring. One for the building's front door. The other was for the apartment. But the front door had been kicked in more than six months before, either by police or a drunk resident who had misplaced his key. Most days the front door flapped open and closed like a kid's loose tooth. People came and went at all hours, whether they lived there or not. Homeless men had taken to sleeping in the front hall, sometimes blocking the stairs Nell had to take to get to her floor. Sometimes, when she arrived home late, she'd hear people having sex behind the stairwell—women moaning *daddy* and *baby* while men puffed *You like that?* like locomotives. It turned her stomach, and yet, those were the nights she couldn't help herself. She'd wake up early the next morning and run to King's Chapel to pray, unable to shake the smell of her own body on her hands, no matter how hard she scrubbed them with Borax and bleach.

Filthy pig.

Nasty whale.

Today, there were a couple of kids playing jacks in the lobby. Their clothes were dirty and half-soaked, most likely from a romp around a curbside fire hydrant. Nell gave them a faint smile, but they only stared with their wide, stupid eyes. Tempted to ask them what the hell they were looking at, she started up the stairs instead. She paused on the second-story landing to catch her breath, then continued to the third floor. Barrett would be waiting for her behind their dead-bolted apartment door.

Barrett didn't work, but Nell didn't resent him for it. His joblessness had been her idea. He was creative, had a passion for books and words. He was a writer, and someday he'd be in print. Nell would make sure of it, even though he never let her read a single sentence he wrote.

"Barrett?" Nell stepped inside the apartment, then fastened all three dead-bolt locks behind her. The place was little more than a handful of walls, thin enough for both of them to know everything about their neighbors without ever meeting them face-to-face. Yellowed wallpaper was peeling away in places like blistered skin. The ceiling was pockmarked with stains from where the upstairs neighbor's kids regularly flooded the kitchen and bathroom. The floor, while hardwood, was so warped it was next to impossible to keep the secondhand kitchen table level. Nell had shoved two old paperbacks beneath one of the legs to keep it from leaning too far to the right. Lady Chatterley and Father Lankester Merrin were doing their best to keep plates and silverware in place. And the rest of the furniture wasn't any better. All of it had come from the Salvation Army. All of it needed some sort of support.

But despite the old furnishings and dilapidated state, the place was spotless. It held an air of scruffy hipness that lent it an almost cute quality, from Nell's potted ferns balanced on the windowsills to the miniature herb garden on the fire escape. There were always two settings on that shabby kitchen table. Matching place mats and plates surrounded a small vase of the cheapest flowers the market had been selling on shopping day. Usually they were carnations, and Nell didn't mind that one bit. Carnations lasted a long time, sometimes over a week if she kept the water fresh. Plain but hearty, just like her.

She dropped her keys into a little bowl on a side table next to the door, slid her purse off her shoulder, and shrugged out of her sweater, then folded it into fourths. When she peeked into his bedroom, Barrett was nowhere to be found. Nell frowned at that, picturing him wandering the streets of Sheepshead Bay, looking for someone more exciting than her. If that was what Barrett wanted, he was likely to find it anywhere but here, in their sorry excuse of a home.

"You'll be back." She murmured the reassurance to herself. Peeling the wet back of her shirt away from her skin, she stepped into the kitchenette and tied on her ruffle-trimmed apron with a sigh. Barrett *would* be back. He never strayed for long. Men were predictable. As soon as they got hungry, they came scratching at the door.

• • •

She tried to wait up for Barrett the night before. But after an hour of reading C. S. Lewis's *Screwtape Letters* with Beary—her teddy bear—she couldn't keep her eyes open. Barrett had always hated Beary's name. Even as a boy he'd complained that it was uncreative, that it sounded too much like *his* name, but Nell hadn't cared. She liked that it sounded like her big brother's moniker. And so Beary had stayed Beary, now her only surviving childhood memento. Sometimes, it seemed, her only friend.

Hours later, she woke with her favorite book strewn across

the floor. Beary was stuffed beneath her pillow, and the apartment was silent. Her brother's absence hung like a storm cloud over her head.

When Nell woke for work, Barrett's empty dinner plate was on the kitchen table, the only sign she had of his return. But when she searched the rooms for him, he was still missing.

She stood in the kitchenette with her arms wound across her chest, staring at his dirty dishes with a sense of doom. There was an early morning argument happening in front of the building. A drunk woman screaming *don't touch me* at her stumbling boyfriend. The yelling did little to soothe Nell's frayed nerves.

She twisted away from the kitchen table—a sorry old thing that looked like it had been salvaged from a down-and-out diner. Its rounded corners and chrome trim made her think of *I Love Lucy* and *Leave It to Beaver*, of retro soda fountains and perfect families living in perfect neighborhoods inside their mother's old black-and-white TV. That memory was the reason Nell had splurged on the red-topped table in the first place. It didn't match a thing in the apartment, and it was overpriced for what it was, especially because it was missing its matching chairs. But she had bought it with a fleeting hope. Maybe if she stuck that bit of Americana in the center of her apartment, a bit of that vintage happiness would transpose itself into her own life. It was why she kept the little vase of carnations in perpetual bloom, why she fixed dinner every evening despite her long workday. The whole thing had been a stupid idea, a ridiculous childlike notion.

Nell didn't want to accept it, but the reality of it was becoming harder to shake. They could have moved into a pastel-painted house on Magnolia Lane in a perfect little town a million miles from Brooklyn, but things would stay the same. Barrett would always hate their mother. He'd always wander and never speak. Nothing would ever be perfect, no matter how hard Nell tried. Not after what Faye Sullivan had done.

Pressing her hands to her face, Nell took a deep breath, familiar pain blooming at the back of her brain. She tried not to imagine her sibling, carousing in the seedy streets of New York City or living it up while "You Should Be Dancing" pumped through club speakers. She tried not to picture him as one of the men who took women behind staircases of unlocked buildings, pressing them up against the wall. Most days, Nell thanked God she had a brother like Barrett, but there were the occasional moments . . . moments when she wished they were only friends.

Roommates that could fall in love.

Fall into bed.

Fall into a life beyond what they had.

It was a temptation she had repressed for years. A desire she didn't dare put into words. When she heard those couples behind the stairwell, her stomach soured and twisted into a fist. But not before she saw a flash of her own face pulled into a grimace of lust. Not before she imagined his hands, *his* hands, drawing across the naked flesh of her well-rounded hips.

She squeezed her eyes shut against the thought, gritted her teeth, and exhaled a quiet, abhorrent bleat deep in her throat. When her hands fell away from her face, Barrett stood not three feet from the apartment door. He had a way of sneaking up on her. Nell may have been a mouse in appearance, but Barrett had her beat when it came to silence.

"B-Barrett." His name was a faltering greeting. "You scared me."

He raised his eyebrows at her, but didn't speak. Of course not. Had he said a word, Nell would have fallen right over, maybe even fainted from shock.

That was the thing about Barrett.

He hadn't spoken since he was six years old.

"Where were you?" Nell asked. She tightened the belt of her robe, scowled at his dirty dishes. "I waited all night. I was worried. You could have at least cleaned up after yourself, instead of leaving it for me."

Barrett gave her a level look, one that suggested that she had far more pressing issues to worry about. He reached for one of the many pads of paper strewn about the apartment and scribbled something down.

What time is it?

"Oh, *damn*," she hissed. "I'm going to miss the train!" She rushed past him fast enough to catch her shoulder on the doorframe. When she appeared from the bathroom smelling of soap, her hair still sopping wet, Barrett was lounging in his tattered wingback. He was reading Robert Louis Stevenson again. Barrett was a little rock-and-roll with his surfer-like Leif Garrett hair, a little intellectual with his forever-pensive expression. Far too cool to be her biological sibling. Way too smart to stick around. He didn't raise his eyes from his book to acknowledge her exit, only lifted an arm with two fingers held aloft in a lazy peace sign.

Later, dude.

She rolled her eyes and triple-locked the door behind her, hoping it would keep him from disappearing again.

• • •

She reached Rambert & Bertram a half hour late; a reason to panic for any employee, but an absolute nightmare for a girl who tried to blend into the beige carpet and potted plants. The elevator spit her out into an incessant ringing of telephones and chipper *please hold*s. Mary Ann Thomas glanced up from her typewriter. Her upper lip curled over her teeth just enough to suggest a sneer, as though some unspoken hope of Nell quitting her job had been dashed onto the rocks of reality. Mary Ann shot a look at Adriana Esposito, who sat to her right, as if to say *Are you seeing this?* Adriana was a beautiful girl, but she wasn't quite as pretty as Mary Ann. None of Mary Ann's friends were. Nell was fairly certain that if Mary Ann ever crossed paths with a better-looking woman, that girl would be found dead in a gutter the next afternoon.

A crime of passion.

Jealousy.

Maybe revenge.

Adriana was Mary Ann's best friend. Her right hand. A hench-girl if there ever was one. As soon as Mary Ann gave her a nod, Adriana lifted her hands from the keys of her typewriter. She rose from her seat and glided across the office floor as graceful as she'd seen Michael Jackson dance across Johnny Carson's stage. A seed of panic bloomed in Nell's stomach as she watched Adriana shimmy toward their supervisor's door. Nell's attention bounced back to Mary Ann's desk, but Mary Ann had turned her back, busy transcribing hand-written notes onto official letterhead.

Oh God.

The words wheeled their way through Nell's head.

Oh God shit goddamnit oh God.

A flash of pain. A wince between beats of her heart.

She marched down the center aisle of desks as fast as she could, just short of falling into a full run. She shoved her purse into the little cabinet attached to her desk, tore off the Selectric's cover and shoved it into the compartment along with her things. Snatching up her coffee mug, she pulled her sweater tight across her chest and made for the break room. It was against her better judgment. Logic said to sit down and get to work, but Barrett would have suggested otherwise. Act natural, he would have written. Maybe if she at least *looked* like she'd been there for a while, Misters Rambert and Bertram would let her tardiness slide—not that she'd ever met them. Men like those spent their days on the golf course, not in a city dying of heatstroke.

No matter how many times Nell had considered quitting this job, she needed it to pay the rent. Without it, she and Barrett would be sleeping in the ground-floor hallway along with the drifters. Barrett would have to find a job—but how? No matter how smart or good-looking he was, he didn't speak, only wrote notes on his little yellow pad. Maybe a night stocker at a grocery store or a mechanic at a tire shop . . . a job that didn't require him to talk to anyone, to interact with customers. And once he *did* find a place to work, he wouldn't have time for his writing. That was something Nell wasn't sure he'd ever forgive her for. Her quitting this job would mean him quitting on his dreams. And then there was the fact that he'd be pulling an eight-hour shift—that was eight hours of him realizing how much better the world was without her in it. Without his sister. The girl who had cost him everything.

Nell's hands trembled as she reached for the coffeepot, splashing brew into her Mr. Topsy-Turvy mug. Only three minutes into her shift and she was already sweating beneath the wool knit of her sweater. She stared at the orange bean of a character as she chewed on her bottom lip, wondering what she'd do if the boss sent her home early with an empty Xerox box full of her things. She'd think up an excuse. Something that would make her supervisor, Harriet Lamont, think twice before terminating her. Something that Nell couldn't have prevented. An accident. No, worse. Much worse. *A death.* Someone had thrown themselves in front of the B train, took a flying leap right off the platform and onto the rails. She'd seen it with her own two eyes. It was like something out of a nightmare. She doubted she'd ever sleep again.

Someone stepped into the break room.

Nell started, turned to see Adriana standing in the doorway. She shot Nell a smile, only making Nell want to scratch her eyes out that much more. She imagined Adriana sinking to her knees, her hands clasped over her bloodied face, crying out in agony while Nell casually walked back to her desk, took a seat, and began her day's work with blood beneath her nails.

A mauling. A vicious attack on the train. You should have seen it. I hardly made it in to work at all.

"Lamont wants to see you," Adriana said.

Nell stood silent, picturing Adriana flattened against the third rail. Her body bloodied. Her arms severed. Her guts strewn across a subway platform. People standing around, laughing, *laughing* because, man, that Adriana Esposito was a *bitch.*

Nell lifted her mug from the counter and ducked around Adriana on her way to the supervisor's office, as though stepping into Lamont's office was no big deal. She even murmured a "thanks" to the girl who'd turned her in. A criminal showing appreciation to her own executioner. A Salem witch filling her own pockets with stones.

How many more for me to hit bottom?

How many licks did it take for the Son of Sam to snap?

"The world," Nell whispered to herself, "may never know." A ghost of a smile caught at the corner of her mouth, but it disappeared just as quickly as it came.

Harriet Lamont was intimidating. She sat behind a large desk surrounded by so many plants that it made Nell think of Vietnam. And in that jungle, Harriet Lamont was the tiger, ready to pounce on any girl not pulling her weight. Nell hovered in the door while Lamont finished up a call.

"Well, I don't *care* what you have to do, Dan." She spoke into the receiver. Powerful. Confident. "Just fix it." It was the way an important person ended a phone call—with a demand and an aggravated hang up. Lamont shot a look toward the office door, steadied her eyes upon Nell, and cleared her throat. "Come in," she said. "Close the door."

Nell did as she was told, certain she was going to burst into sloppy tears long before she managed to take a seat in front of the boss's desk. She didn't give a damn about Lamont, really. But if she got fired, what would Barrett think? What would Barrett *do*?

"You know we don't tolerate tardiness around here," Lamont said, her tone flat. She retrieved a cigarette out of a little silver case, stuck it between her red lips, then lit it with the crystal Ronson tabletop lighter when a cheap gas-station Bic would have done just fine.

Nell said nothing.

"*Right?*" Lamont was waiting for a response.

"Yes," Nell stammered.

"Yes?" Lamont lowered her chin, giving Nell a look that, up until then, only Nell's mother could have pulled off. It was stern, riddled with an impressive amount of impatience. Nurse Ratched. Cruella de Vil.

"Yes," Nell said, more quietly this time. "I'm sorry. I got stuck . . ."

"Stuck." Lamont seemed to grunt the word.

"At the train station."

There was blood everywhere. Adriana was dead. I pushed her onto the—

Lamont looked both unimpressed and unconvinced. She'd heard that line a million times. "And why should I care about that?" she asked. "If I cared every time one of my girls got stuck at the train station, there wouldn't be anyone answering phones at R & B."

Nell peered down at her coffee mug. It was burning her hands, but she didn't dare put it on Lamont's desk. She sat there, clutching it as fiercely as she was clenching her teeth. Because how many Bics could Lamont have bought with the money she'd spent on that fancy lighter? Didn't that giant varnished desk and having her name on the door make her feel important enough?

"Look, Nell . . ." Lamont leaned back, took a puff of her cigarette. *Sinner.* "This is between you and me, okay? You aren't like the other girls. I gotta say I appreciate that. Dare I say, I *like it.* God knows we need more girls like you around here. But I'm going to stop appreciating it if this happens again, you understand? If I let you slide, it makes *me* look bad, and I don't like looking bad. I've got a job to do just like everyone else. Just like you."

What if Lamont said that, to keep her job, Nell had to smoke a cigarette? Had to light it with that fancy crystal thing too? What if, to keep her job, Nell had to compromise everything she stood for, everything she had promised Barrett she'd be? What if she had to become a Rambert & Bertram girl, like a Stepford Wife? Maybe that's why all the girls were so goddamn cruel. Their hearts gone. Souls empty. Brains washed. Robots. Nothing but pretty, high heel–wearing, lipstick-smeared—

"Hey." Lamont snapped her fingers. "Earth to Nell."

Nell blinked.

"Yes," she murmured.

"Yes," Lamont echoed, dubious. She exhaled a stream of smoke while studying Nell from across her desk. "I know you don't have many friends. None here, anyway."

Rub it in.

"The girls here can be a little rough, but they aren't all bad. Maybe reach out a bit more, try a little harder to make a connection."

A flash. A wince. Stress was bad for Nell's headaches. She wouldn't be surprised if she ended up nursing a migraine all night after this.

"It would make things easier," Lamont promised. "Don't you think?"

"Yes." Nell wanted to disappear into the orange and brown weave of the chair beneath her. Disappear, but not before bringing her coffee cup down on top of Lamont's skull first.

Yes, she thought. *I've thought of that. I think of that every day, you condescending—*

But she cut herself off mid-thought. Because Lamont was, in her own convoluted way, trying to be helpful. Lamont wasn't going to fire her, which she had all the right in the world to do. She wasn't going to force Nell and Barrett out onto the street. Pathetic as it was, at that moment, Harriet Lamont was the closest thing Nell had to what might be considered a friend.

Lamont sat quietly, as if waiting for Nell to say something, anything. When Nell failed to speak, Lamont shook her head and waved a hand at the door. "All right. Go on, get back to work," she said. Nell rose, moved to the door. "But Nell . . ."

She froze, the door ajar, the trill of telephones and the metallic clap of typewriter keys disrupting the hush that had fallen over the boss's office.

"I just want to make sure all my girls are happy here. I want *you* to be happy here." Lamont gave her that stern, motherly look once more.

Nell stared at her supervisor, her coffee mug continuing to scorch her hands.

"All I'm saying is, if you don't like the life you have, make the life you want."

Another zing of pain.

"Yes, ma'am," Nell whispered.

"Don't be late again."

"I won't," Nell said, her voice inaudible over the office din. She ducked out of Lamont's office before the woman decided to say more. Nell knew she meant well, but all her advice had done was make Nell feel smaller than she already did. It had done little but make her want to rage.

To tell Barrett and *rage*.

. . .

Nell couldn't get Lamont's hard-nosed advice out of her head. *If you don't like the life you have, make the life you want.* There was no doubt in Nell's mind that Harriet Lamont had done her share of clawing up the corporate ladder, and she'd made it. She was a big-time boss at Rambert & Bertram, keeping the place running while *her* bosses putted down a perfectly manicured green. Lamont was a woman who lived by her own advice, and she had a private office with a view of East 44th to prove it.

Not that Nell wanted to be the boss of anyone. But the more Barrett went out, the lonelier and more desperate she felt. Barrett never revealed where he was going or where he had been. He never bothered to leave notes. Not even a simple Be back soon. He'd simply vanish like a ghost into the shadowed alleys of Brooklyn, then ignore her pointed questions when he returned.

And yet, despite his secret rendezvous with . . . whomever, Barrett was the one who told *her* to stay away from others, to not get too close to anyone, to forget the idea of having friends and going out. Those things were for other people. People who smoked cigarettes on their lunch break and had sex in building entryways. People who weren't like them—or at least not like her. He wrote long manifestos that he'd leave on her desk while she slept. Letters that, at times, spanned half a dozen pages. The world is poison—a lion waiting to devour innocence, a whore itching to spread her disease.

Poetic.

Hypocritical.

Because despite his insistence that she stay in, he'd run off somewhere and do God only knew what. It seemed that his advice only applied to Nell, while he was free to do as he chose. It was enough to get the anxiety roiling around in her gut, the sizzle of another migraine popping behind the nerves of her eyes. If she continued to follow Barrett's rules and Barrett continued to do his own thing, Nell would be left to fend for herself. It was as though he *wanted* her to be alone.

Make the life you want.

Nell frowned down at the keys of her typewriter. She couldn't just sit back and let her world unravel. If Barrett left, if for some reason, one night, he *didn't* come back, she would be the one to lose everything. Her brother. Her only friend. Her mind. With no one to talk to, no one to run to, she'd scream herself into an early coffin, cut her own throat—no, cut her own heart out, put herself down.

If Barrett disappeared, Nell would have no one.

Even their own mother was a ghost, despite being very much alive.

Faye Sullivan was living somewhere in New Jersey. Nell guessed she was maybe only a mile or two from where she and Barrett had grown up as kids. But the last time their mother had moved, Barrett had burned the scrap of paper on which she'd written her new address. He had smirked as her phone number smoldered above the stove's gas burner and left the ashes he'd smeared across the walls for Nell to clean. Their mother was perhaps little more than an hour-long train ride away, but to them she was lost, because Nell had allowed it. She'd let their mother slip out of their lives in exchange for the love of her brother. It had been years since they had heard anything from Faye, and in those years, Barrett was happier than he'd ever been. Without her, Barrett could be himself.

But without their mother, and without Barrett, Nell was an island. Brooklyn was dangerous. If something happened to him, if someone . . .

She squeezed her eyes shut against the thought. Against the pain. *Don't even think it. If you think it, it may come true.*

If Nell only had a friend, just one friend beyond her brother's company, things would be different. She had to kill her loneliness before it made her disappear.

She glanced up from her desk as Lamont skirted the call-center floor. Lamont was the mother hen, keeping her chicks in line. She was taking mental notes of who was doing what, separating the star players from the ones that could be let go the next time layoffs came around. Nell caught her boss's eye, and Lamont gave her a slight nod, a *go on*, as though wanting to see if Nell had the ambition—the guts to take her advice.

I've got the guts, she thought. *Anything Barrett can do, I can do better.* A lie if there ever was one, but if it gave her a momentary spark of motivation, she'd make herself believe it.

Pushing her mousy brown hair behind her ears, she squared her shoulders and rose from her desk. She would show Lamont that she *was* different, that her supervisor hadn't made a mistake in giving her a second chance. Grabbing her Mr. Topsy-Turvy mug off her desk, she headed back to the break room for a fresh cup of coffee, heading straight for Mary Ann Thomas and her crew of pretty friends. Adriana Esposito was there, flanked by Savannah Wheeler and Miriam Gould.

Mary Ann was leaning against the break-room counter, picking colored sprinkles off a pink-frosted doughnut with manicured nails. She gingerly placed one sprinkle after the other onto her tongue as she chatted with her girlfriends. A sexy move. Way too sexy for the workplace.

Slut.

But as soon as Nell came within earshot, their airy giggles transformed into murmurs. Mary Ann made eye contact, and despite Nell's nerves, Nell forced a smile and dared to speak.

"Hi," she said. As soon as the single syllable left her throat, Mary Ann looked to her friends and twisted her face up in grossed-out bemusement.

The whale, it speaks!

Nell caught her bottom lip between her teeth and looked away from them.

Both Adriana and Miriam had been brunettes up until a few weeks ago, just like Mary Ann. But a few days after Mary Ann had bleached her chestnut hair nearly white, Adriana came back a red-head. Miriam chopped off her long, dark hair into a sleek, angular, redheaded bob. Now, half of the office was either a bottle blonde or had cut their hair in an attempt to squelch their fears of being shot dead on the street.

Nell was one of the last girls to sport the Son of Sam's favorite hairstyle—long and dark. Sometimes she wished he'd come. Maybe, rather than killing her, they'd fall in love and run away together instead. Maybe, if he loved her enough, she wouldn't even ask him to stop. She'd help him pick out his victims, pinpoint girls who looked a little too confident, a little too bitchy, a little too much like the type of girl that made her life a living hell.

Nell cleared her throat. She forced her gaze toward the girls again. "I was wondering . . ." Her words came out stammered, sticking to the back of her throat.

"About why you're so sweaty?" Mary Ann arched a skeptical eyebrow.

Miriam and Adriana tittered beneath their breaths.

"Yeah," Mary Ann said flatly. "We were wondering about that too."

"Um, about your hair?" Nell ignored the jab. The mention of Mary Ann's locks made the bottle blonde's expression harden to flat-out defensive. She shoved a handful of curls behind her left shoulder, exposing more of the embroidered collar that rimmed her billowing peasant blouse.

"I was just wondering how you did it," Nell clarified. "What you used, I mean. I was thinking that maybe, because of the scare . . ." Her words trailed off as Mary Ann's guarded expression eased into a false grin. Nell looked away again, splashed some coffee into her mug to busy her hands.

Mary Ann exhaled a quiet laugh. "The scare?" she asked. "Trust me, Nell, if anyone has nothing to be afraid of, it's you."

Nell swallowed against the sudden lump in her throat.

Bitch.

Adriana and Miriam snickered at their leader's witty quip.

Savannah stood with her head bowed, avoiding eye contact. "Jesus, Mary," she murmured.

". . . and Joseph," Adriana tacked on—a shared joke, for sure.

Suddenly bored with her dessert, Mary Ann dropped the dough-nut back into the box of pastries and shouldered her way out of the break room with a scoff. Savannah followed, but Adriana stalled her and Miriam's departure by nudging Nell with her arm as she passed. Coffee splashed out of Nell's mug. It sloshed onto her sweater sleeve, down the front of her blouse, across the lap of her slacks.

Nell gasped and took a backward step only to crash into the break-room counter. More coffee sloshed over the rim of her cup, scorching her hand, dulling the burn that was blooming along her stomach and thighs. Adriana pulled her face into a look of surprise, but it shifted into a full-on laugh when Miriam exhaled a dramatic "Uh-oh!" They skittered out the door, nearly knocking over Linnie Carter amid their schadenfreude.

Linnie was one of the different ones. She was a short, some-what homely girl compared to the fashion models who stomped the call-center floor. But that didn't make any difference. Nell didn't dare look at her, regardless. Embarrassed, she turned away from the break-room door to keep Linnie from seeing the wet stain that now soiled her entire front.

Idiot, she thought. *You're so stupid, thinking you could talk to Mary Ann. Thinking that you're* good *enough. You deserve it. You deserve it. You* deserve it*!*

Her bottom lip quivered. She struggled to keep her composure, her stomach balling itself into a fist. People would stare at her dirty clothes on the train. The bicycle gang at her stop would use it as ammunition.

Hey, bibliotecaria*! Next time, maybe try to swallow!*

Nell shut her eyes.

Hey, Blanca!

She squeezed them tight.

Hey, Nell!

She was so stupid. Stupid to think that she could change her life. That she could be something she wasn't.

The headache that lingered at the back of her brain speared her through with a sudden jolt. Concentrated brain freeze. She grasped the break-room counter, gritted her teeth to dampen the pain.

"Hey, um . . . Nell?"

She jumped when a hand brushed her shoulder. Linnie snatched her fingers away and held them against her chest, as if escaping a bite.

"I'm sorry, I just . . ." Linnie blinked a pair of wide-set eyes. Her face lacked symmetry, as though she had been created by Van Gogh rather than God. And yet, despite her inability to compete in looks with the likes of Mary Ann or her friends, Linnie Carter wasn't an outsider. She smoked menthols on the sidewalk while watching taxi-cabs buzz by. She laughed and socialized by the water cooler with coworkers, all of them thin and tall, with glossy curls in their hair.

They weren't the pretty ones, but they knew what to wear, what to say. Somehow, they still managed to fit in. Ugly ducklings disguised as swans.

"Are you okay? Your clothes, you . . ."

Nell twisted away from her, the throb in her brain still going strong. She didn't need fake sympathy.

And what *was* she supposed to do about her clothes? Ask Lamont for the rest of the day off after arriving late? No. Nell would be forced to endure another four hours at her desk, wearing that coffee stain the way Hester Prynne wore a scarlet letter. *L* for loser. *O* for outcast. An *N*, like her name, but rather than standing for Nell, that *N* would stand for Nothing. *Nothing Sullivan.*

"Hey . . . I'm just trying to help," Linnie said from behind Nell's shoulder.

"Help." Nell croaked out the word. Like anyone would ever help her.

Except sometimes people do help, the second voice inside her reasoned. The kinder voice, the optimist that occasionally drowned out her self-disdain. *What about Lamont? What about your second chance?*

"Here." Linnie held out a wad of napkins in a fisted hand. "I'll run across the street to the deli, get some seltzer water." Nell slowly turned toward the extended arm, then eyed the girl it was attached to. Linnie gave her a pitying, crooked smile. "My mom swears by seltzer water for any stain."

Mom.

"That and lemon juice. Maybe they'll have some of that too, but I don't know."

Nell took the napkins, still unsure of Linnie's intentions. "Really?" The question was one referring to Linnie's kindness, to the fact that Linnie was willing to run across the street just to help Nell out. But Linnie mistook the question.

"My mom used to work for a dry cleaner."

Mom.

"I'll meet you in the bathroom," Linnie said. "Back in a flash."

Nell stuck close to the wall as she made her way to the restroom, trying with all her might to blend in against a stark beige wall. She held her arms across her front in awkward angles, tugging at her sweater hard enough to make the weave creak. Attempting to hide the wet spot that stretched from the top of her bra down to her crotch, she was suddenly sick with a memory: Barrett hiding from their mother after having an accident at school.

Her brother had been six years old. Gathered with his class on the floor, they were seated in a carpeted area of the classroom for story time. It seemed like an abnormally long story that afternoon, and Barrett needed to pee. But it was an inopportune moment to raise his hand. He'd interrupt the whole class, all to embarrass himself by asking permission to use the little boy's room. His friends would gape at him. They'd laugh.

He tried to hold it.

The story dragged on.

His teacher's tempo slowed to maybe one or two words a minute. One sentence per hour. One page per day.

Barrett held his breath.

Clamped his teeth.

Nearly gasped when warmth enveloped him from the waist down, only to grow cold and wet seconds later.

After story time ended, he shimmied back to his desk along the wall just as Nell was doing now, ignoring the teacher's questions to the class about the wet spot on the floor. He spent the rest of the day thinking up an elaborate excuse for why his overalls were soaked. During recess, he "accidentally" tripped and fell into a rain puddle—a perfect cover. But it was an excuse that hadn't worked on their mom. No excuse ever did. As soon as she saw him, she'd twisted both his *and* Nell's arms behind their backs and marched them outside, where she barked:

Filthy pig.

Stupid kid.

She sprayed them with the hard jet of the garden hose to wash away the stink. It was just after Halloween. Cold. Windy. They nearly froze where they stood. Anytime Barrett did something wrong, Nell got punished for it right along with him. Anytime *she* did something wrong, their mother would spare Barrett the rod. That was just the way things were.

Nell didn't look up as she crossed what seemed like a mile of office space between the break room and the bathroom. But she could feel eyes crawling across her skin. No doubt that Mary Ann and her gang were biting back Cheshire Cat–grins. Nell imagined herself above her shoddy little apartment stove, a pot of water bubbling to a boil. And there, tied to her red diner-style table, would be Mary Ann, Adriana, Miriam, and Savannah. They'd blubber instead of giggle, their pretty faces swollen with tears, ugly from all the crying. Their knees would be raw and bloody from hours of kneeling on grains of uncooked Uncle Ben's rice. They'd look at her with pleading eyes.

Please, Nell, let us go.

Please, Nell, we love you so.

But it would be too late. Too goddamn late. Nell would stick her hands into a pair of oven gloves. Pluck the pot of boiling water from the stove. And with a pirouette as graceful as Eva Evdokimova's, she'd spin around and splash the water out of the pot in a ribbon of liquid and steam. They'd scream. Their flesh would turn to soft wax. She'd pry their mouths open with kitchen tongs and pour liquid fire down their throats, scorch their faces, and, with her bare fingers, peel back their blistered skin.

Nell ducked into the office bathroom, blinked at herself in the mirror. The polyester blouse she'd plucked off the JCPenney sale rack was ruined, but whatever. She hadn't liked it much anyway. Her sweater, however, was a different matter. The right sleeve of her cardigan was soaked. It was doubtful she'd ever manage to get the stain out.

Stupid cow.

Her skin burned beneath the wet blotch that had grown cold and a deeper shade of brown. It was almost pretty, like drying blood.

A few minutes passed before Linnie returned with a bottle of seltzer water in hand. "They didn't have lemon juice," she said, breathless and red-cheeked from her run across the street. "But this should help at least." She tore a handful of paper towels from the roll on the bathroom counter and soaked them in water that fizzed against the white porcelain sink. Nell watched wordlessly as Linnie began to blot the hem of her shirt, ignoring the wool weave of her sweater to focus on cheap polyester instead. When Linnie leaned in close, Nell breathed deep, inhaling the shampoo scent of her hair. She wondered if Linnie had a boyfriend; if, outside of the office, she was more dangerous than demure. Nell imagined her gasping in the shadowed stairwell of a decrepit apartment building, her face twisted in a mask of lust as she huffed *Nell, oh Nell . . . oh Nellett . . . oh Barrett, yes.*

"You know . . ."

Snap.

Nell could just about hear the sizzle of her own nerves.

Linnie paused, as if disturbed by Nell's dazed expression, then cleared her throat and looked back down to the hem of Nell's shirt. "You know," she repeated, her voice soft, her eyes averted, "you shouldn't let them treat you like that. They think they're pretty great, but it isn't right, the way they act. That Mary Ann . . . she's a bully. They all are."

Nell worried her bottom lip between her teeth. Barrett had teased her about that very thing once. *Lucky you don't wear lipstick, sis, or you'd wolf down half a tube every day before lunch.* Linnie wore lipstick, her mouth frosted pale pink, reminiscent of Mary Ann's forgotten doughnut. If Barrett had the chance, would he run off with a girl like Linnie Carter? Would he leave Nell behind for the girl with a cotton-candy mouth and a cubist face?

"Do they bully *you?*" Nell asked. Linnie glanced up, seemingly surprised by the question, then shook her head in the negative.

"No, but I don't think they'd bully you either if you stood up for yourself. It's a matter of self-respect."

Nell glanced down to the bit of polyester held between Linnie's fingers. She reached out, allowing her hand to brush against her newfound friend's. That's what Linnie was now. A friend. It hadn't been what Nell had intended, but somehow, in some way, her plan to change her future had worked, and it hadn't even been that hard.

Nell leaned in. She wanted to thank her new friend for her help, to brush her lips across Linnie's cheek. *I'll never forget this . . .*

But Linnie pulled away.

She cleared her throat. Flashed a nervous smile. Offered Nell the wad of wet paper towels, suddenly uninterested in offering her help.

"Anyway, just keep patting at it until it comes out." An uncomfortable pause. "I should get back to my desk before someone notices I'm gone."

Nell took the towels. She was ready to speak, to thank Linnie for her kindness, but before she could say a word, Linnie fled the bathroom quick as a thief.

Nell stared at the bathroom door for a long while, then looked down the front of her ruined shirt. A proper thank-you was most certainly in order. After all, she and Linnie were friends now, and friends always showed their appreciation.

• • •

By the time Nell returned home, she had pushed Mary Ann's cruelty to the back of her mind. Even the Puerto Rican boys hadn't riled her. Her lack of irritation made them back off. Her upright stature and quick steps down East 16th made it clear she had better things to do.

She ducked into her building, sidestepped a homeless man sleeping just shy of the stairwell, rushed up two flights, and unlocked the apartment door. Once inside, she beamed at her lazy brother. Barrett was sprawled across the couch, his arm thrown over his eyes to shield himself from life's many cruelties, or maybe just from the brightness of the room.

"Hey, Barrett. How was your day?"

No response. He didn't even bother to lift his arm from across his face. A prince, vexed by the world.

"Did you get any writing done?"

Barrett slid his forearm away from his eyes and gave his sister a tortured look.

"Well, *my* day was nice." At least partly. It had been terrible before it had turned terrific. "I made a friend." The statement left her in a rush of excitement.

Nothing.

Nell tossed her purse aside, studied the stained sleeve of her sweater before shrugging it off her shoulders. She kicked her penniless loafers off beside the door.

"Her name is Linnie Carter, and she's the kindest, most wonderful person I've ever met."

Barrett's ailing gaze settled on Nell's ruined clothes. After Linnie had left the restroom, Nell had done little to remove the coffee stain, too wound up to care about a bit of destroyed fabric. But now, with Barrett staring at the ugly blotch the way a boy would gape at a swath of menstrual blood, a pang of insecurity shot through her. She peered down at the stain, covered it as best she could with her hands.

He sat up on the couch, pushed Robert Louis Stevenson aside. Scribbled a message: I'll bet.

"Oh." She shrugged a little, as if dismissing the stain as no big deal. "I just . . . it was an accident. You know me, all thumbs. I spent half the day covered in coffee. But I'm glad, because that's how I met Linnie. I mean, I already *knew* her, though she never had a reason to stop and talk to me. But she came into the break room just as they had . . ." She paused, corrected herself. "Just as I had my spill, and she was so sweet, Barrett. She was on me in a flash, asking if I was okay, if I needed help. She even went across the street for seltzer water, if you can believe it. Her mother . . ."

The muscles in Barrett's face tensed.

". . . she knows how to remove stains, see? She worked at a dry cleaning shop, and she swears by seltzer water and lemon juice. The place across from R & B didn't have any lemon juice, so we . . ." Her near-manic soliloquy faded to nothing.

Barrett's expression was blank, as though his soul had escaped his body. Another quip: Yeah, she knows how to remove stains REALLY well.

"Well, I *know* there's still a stain," she told him. "I'm not blind. It's just that Linnie had to get back to work, and I didn't know what I was doing, really. It's my fault the stain didn't come out, not hers. I could have done a better job, but I wasn't going to spend the entire day cleaning off a cheap shirt, you know."

Barrett rose from the couch, his brown eyes level on her face.

Sometimes she hated him for his silence, but she knew it wasn't his fault. She had tried to convince herself that maybe it was a choice, but it had been so long—long enough for her to completely forget the sound of his voice. Long enough to simply accept the way things were: quiet. Choice or not, she doubted Barrett would ever speak again.

"It was on sale." She shoved her hair behind her ears and shrugged at him. "Just a cheap shirt," she murmured. "I can get another one."

He held up his notepad. I thought we were on a budget.

"We *are*, but what am I supposed to do, go to the office in my pajamas?" A laugh. "Maybe I'll buy myself a nicer shirt," she mused, eyeing the blouse that struck her as more frumpy than usual. "Something that Mary Ann could feast her eyes on, something that'll show her I'm not such a square after all. What a shock *that* would be, right?" A snort. "I can just imagine her face, the surprise; look at fat old Nell Sullivan in her pretty new blouse, and maybe even a new skirt and new shoes too." That would certainly set the snobby priss straight. "Maybe I'll get my hair cut, give myself a whole new image." Just what Harriet Lamont would have suggested.

A new image for a new life.

A better life.

One that Nell deserved.

Barrett's attention remained on her face. Nell caught his eyes and flushed. He looked aggravated. Glaring down at his notepad, he began to write in a rush.

Oh God, Nell thought. *Here it comes.* Another one of his freak-outs. Slowed by his lack of vocalization, these arguments could last hours. They were exhausting. Silent and vampiric, zapping all of her energy.

"You don't know how it is, Barrett. Those girls . . ." She tried to stall him, to make him stop writing with her memory of what Linnie had said. "They're bullies. Nobody should act the way they do. They think they're so special, so *perfect*." She frowned, then looked down to her bare feet. There was a line of road grit across their tops, the dirt a reminder of Faye Sullivan's favorite saying: *You can't shine a turd.*

You're kidding yourself. You think everyone is nice right up until they throw dirt in your face. Those chicks aren't friendly. They aren't special. They'd be just as happy if you were dead.

But Mary Ann and her friends *were* special. They were the privileged ones. The gorgeous ones. The ones that even Linnie Carter couldn't compete with. So where did Linnie get off suggesting that they weren't as amazing as they seemed? Sure, Mary Ann Thomas was less than kind. That girl could be a real *bitch*. But Nell supposed that came with the territory. Everyone wanted to be Mary Ann's friend. Surely, that sort of attention must be exhausting. Nell was only adding to the noise, to the pressure, to the suggestion that Mary Ann *had* to be perfect. Maybe Mary Ann was responding the only way she knew how: with hostility.

"Anyway." Nell gave her brother a weary smile, choosing to ignore his glare, to forget the harsh words he'd scribbled onto his small pad of canary-colored paper. "I'm going to invite Linnie over for tea."

The muscles in Barrett's jaw went rigid. No you're fucking not.

Nell raised her hands at him, shook her head. "I know you hate company, but it's rude not to do it. She helped me, and I have to show my appreciation." He started writing again, but she turned away, refusing to read whatever aggravated disallowance he was preparing to throw at her next. Her fingers brushed across the fronds of a small fern poised in the kitchen window. Its waxy leaves glowed with the late afternoon sunlight. The entire kitchenette seemed to resonate with a newfound sense of hope.

"Tea," Nell said to herself. "And a layer cake, frosted with the prettiest pink buttercream." Pink like Linnie's lipstick. "And real sugar cubes in a tiny porcelain bowl sitting next to tiny silver spoons. And I'll need a proper tablecloth, something white, maybe lace."

She spun around, gave Barrett a look. "You'll be nice, won't you?" Her tone edged on pleading. Barrett showed her his back. If she was going to ignore him, he'd return the favor. An eye for an eye. In games like these, Barrett always held the upper hand. She could disregard him all she wanted, but it was Nell who was sensitive to being shut out. Barrett couldn't have cared less.

"Barrett, *please!*"

Every time she brought up the idea of a friend outside of their two-person circle, he had a fit. He didn't trust anyone, especially not women who were too fancy for their own good. To him, Plain Jane was perfect. Those ostentatious girls were little more than sinners stuffed into expensive shoes. They reminded him of their mother. A woman who couldn't have a drink without swallowing the whole bottle. Who couldn't disagree without screaming at the top of her lungs, without shoving and clawing and turning into a lunatic.

It was the very way Faye had handled Barrett's accident in the backyard.

Nell and Barrett had been sitting in a kiddie pool among the weeds and dirt clods of their New Jersey backyard. Their mother and father fought inside, the screaming nothing new. Mom and Dad always argued. Once, Nell had seen their mom try to hit him with a frying pan. Another time, Leigh had shoved Faye against a wall and held her there by her neck while she kicked and screamed to be let go. This particular afternoon, though, four-year-old Nell and six-year-old Barrett sat in their pool and listened to tiny, glittering explosions of breaking glass. There were faint sounds of fists pounding flesh, of palms hitting skin. The argument's end was punctuated by the slap of the screen door against the jamb. Dad remained inside while Mom stumbled onto the patchy lawn. She struggled to light a crooked cigarette. Her hands were unsteady, her entire body rocking as though she was standing on the deck of a boat.

Nell crawled out of the pool and ran across the yard to go inside
and pee. The one time she had let loose in the pool, Barrett had
screamed at her that it was the grossest thing in the whole wide
world. She had taken a beating from her mother for it. *Dirty, disgusting child.* Nell was exiled to the closet, and while she had screamed
and wept and beat her fists against the door, Barrett was allowed to
watch *Gumby* and eat Trix cereal out of his favorite bowl. Had it been
Barrett who had peed, they would have both spent the afternoon
sleeping among their mom's scuffed-up pumps.

When Nell returned from the bathroom to the sun-dappled yard
a few minutes later, struggling to pull her little green peplum bathing
suit up onto her shoulders, the screaming match between her parents had found a second wind. Her father was outside now, a limp
Barrett in his arms. Their mother was wailing. Her hands shook as
though each of her fingers contained the seed of a tiny earthquake,
her cigarette gone. Nell couldn't put it together. Had Barrett stood
up and slipped as he stepped out of the pool? She'd nearly fallen on
her face a few times herself, so maybe he'd lost his footing and hit
his head? Or maybe he had gone under and swallowed water? The
scenarios were muddled, confused by a sudden burst of motion. Her
dad rushed Barrett inside while her mom followed them both, pum-
meling Leigh with her fists. Neither one of them stopped to regard
Nell on their way into the house.

Nell blinked at her mother's extinguished cigarette. It bobbed up
and down in the pool, marooned in a tiny ocean. Her mom's screams
echoed from inside the house. Amid the sepia-colored tones of Nell's
memory, she couldn't recall the screaming ever stopping that day.
That was the day Barrett lost his voice. Whether it had been trauma,
stress response syndrome, or a mental break, the doctors couldn't tell.
But Barrett was all right later. He never spoke again, but he was okay.

It was their crazed, alcoholic mother who made Barrett hate

women. And after their father died, Faye Sullivan only went from bad to worse. She'd doll herself up with lipstick and hair spray, then shove Nell and Barrett in her closet. She'd lock it from the outside and run off for the night. Barrett said that she was probably going to nightclubs, or maybe spending time in the backseat of a strange man's car. At first, Nell refuted her brother's assumptions. But it wasn't long before Faye Sullivan started bringing those strange men home.

They would listen to unfamiliar voices through the crack of the closet door. Neither of them made a sound as their mother gasped and moaned, begging for the headboard to hit the wall faster, harder, louder. Nell wasn't sure, but she was pretty confident any harder would have made the entire house shake loose.

It was only after their mom's man-friends left that Nell and Barrett were allowed to come out of hiding. Sometimes those men would spend the night. "You keep your mouth shut," Faye would tell them. "If you make a peep in here, I'll beat you within an inch." During those evenings, they were left to sleep among their mother's nicotine-scented clothes. They tried to stay quiet despite contorting their faces in anguish, their bladders threatening to burst. Faye Sullivan didn't want anyone to know she had kids, and the way Barrett recalled it, in a sense, she didn't. It took more than having children to be a mother.

Eventually, the men would leave and Faye would unlock the closet door. She'd look down upon them, her hair a wild bird's nest atop her head, her satin nightgown hanging off a single shoulder, a perpetual cigarette clinging to the swell of a rouged bottom lip. And instead of crouching in the doorway and telling them she was sorry and she loved them—*It's just pretend, my babies; it's just a game*—she'd hiss, "Go to your room."

Barrett's hate was all-encompassing. So large that it spilled out beyond their mother and soaked into the skirt hems of every woman who reminded him of her. It was why he didn't want Nell going out with her coworkers. He was afraid of Nell turning into their mom. Into a witch. Into a monster.

Standing in the kitchen, Nell studied her brother's scowling face. "I know you don't like this idea," she told him. "But you need to trust me. Everything will be fine."

Barrett said nothing, his muteness a result of whatever had happened out in the backyard that summer afternoon. His stillness was a perfect illustration of his ever-present stubbornness. Whatever had transpired out at that pool had rendered him perpetually speechless, as though the water he'd swallowed had been laced with a fairy-tale curse. Like Snow White's apple, or the beer and cigar that turned Pinocchio into a donkey boy.

"She's nice," Nell promised. "She's nothing like Mom."

Mom.

Barrett flinched, stung by the word itself. His fingers tensed against the yellow paper of his notepad.

It hurt Nell to see her sibling so vulnerable, but she stood her ground. Turning to the fridge, she pulled open the door, allowing Barrett to sulk back to the couch while she searched for dinner possibilities. Though she knew Barrett wouldn't eat a bite of what she made while she was there. He always ate his dinner when she wasn't around, as if to spite her.

• • •

The following morning, a Thursday, Nell readied herself bright and early despite having the day off. She was out the apartment door long before Barrett woke, but another one of his notes greeted her from the kitchen table.

It's my house too.

Nell exhaled a long sigh, shoved the note into the pocket of her sweater, and slipped out the door. Had he threatened to leave if she went through with her plan, she would have dropped the whole idea. The fact that he didn't gave her an inkling of hope that maybe he wasn't as opposed to Linnie's visit as it seemed. Because what kind of a boy could oppose a girl dropping in for an afternoon?

Walking the few blocks it took to get to the closest secondhand store, Nell perused the aisles for items that would spruce up their shabby kitchen. She settled on a simple white tablecloth, a couple of mismatched teacups, and a tiny porcelain creamer pitcher with a toadstool printed on the side. Then, she headed for the grocery store, referencing the shopping list she'd scrawled onto the back of one of Barrett's many notes. This one voiced his concern about Bryant Park. About dope fiends and drug addicts. About how it was just a matter of time before Nell got mugged, possibly murdered. Odd that someone so opposed to all things maternal could, at times, be a reflection of an obsessive mother figure. Always worried. Always issuing warnings about things Nell had no way to control.

When she returned home from the shops, she set to baking. The cake would be three layers tall, slathered with two cans of pink frosting and topped with sprinkles, just like the ones Mary Ann had placed one after the other upon her tongue. Nell hadn't ever baked a cake of such magnitude, but if ever there was a time to make an impression, it was now. She wanted to dazzle Linnie, not only with her baking prowess, but with the fact that she'd gone out of her way to set up the perfect tea party for her new friend. She beamed at the thought of Linnie sitting in her sunny kitchen, having white cake and tea. Linnie would be Alice and Barrett would be the Mad Hatter. Nell would stand back and watch as they sipped Earl Grey and licked frosting off the tines of forks. It was, in Nell's opinion, the perfect way to start a friendship and, perhaps, the only way to get Barrett to relax. She couldn't wait to see the spark of excitement in

Linnie's eyes when Nell extended the invitation. She couldn't wait to see the relief spread across Barrett's grimacing face when he finally saw Linnie Carter standing in front of their apartment door, pretty as a picture, decked out in pastel ruffles and an Easter hat.

But come Friday, Linnie wasn't nearly as excited as Nell had anticipated.

Nell stood in the break room, clutching her half-empty Mr. Topsy-Turvy mug to her chest. Her smile faded as Linnie blinked at the invitation, wearing a stupidly blank expression across her face.

"It's white cake," Nell explained, trying not to panic at Linnie's lack of enthusiasm. Maybe Linnie was taken aback by Nell's thoughtfulness? That could be it. "I spent all afternoon yesterday on it. It came out swell. You *do* like white cake, don't you? I couldn't decide between white or chocolate, but white seemed to go so much better with pink frosting. I mean, I guess chocolate would have been fine, but I've always liked white better. Either way, we'll have tea too. It'll be great, don't you think? A real party."

Shut your mouth, Nell, before I shut it for you . . .

"Nell . . ." Linnie's face was strangely solemn, but there was a shadow of something else playing at the corner of her eyes. Nell couldn't be sure, but it almost looked like a touch of nerves. She brightened at the realization of it. Linnie was *anxious*. She was flustered by Nell's gratitude, by the fact that Nell had put in so much thought and spent so much time on something as insignificant as cake and tea.

"It's okay," Nell said, smiling. "I didn't mind. I *wanted* to do it."

"But, Nell . . ." Linnie's frown was obvious now. She shifted her weight from one platform shoe to the other, fingering the wooden bangles around her left wrist. They clattered like xylophone keys. "I'm sorry, I just . . . I really can't."

Nell shook her head, not understanding. "You can't?"

"No, I really can't. It's very nice of you to offer, though. I'm flattered that you'd go to such lengths—"

"Well, tomorrow, then," Nell said, cutting Linnie off. "You can tomorrow, can't you? Tomorrow is Saturday." Rambert & Bertrand wasn't open on weekends. "I'll even take the train to your place to meet you if you want. You don't have to ride into Brooklyn by yourself. It'll be better if we meet somewhere and I ride in with you, if only to make sure you find the apartment okay."

Linnie cleared her throat. Her hands moved from her bracelets to worrying the hem of her orange floral-print blouse. "I can't tomorrow either."

"Well, Sund—"

"Look, Nell." It was Linnie's turn to interrupt. Her tone was abrupt, edging toward annoyed. Its hard edge demanded that Nell listen. "Not Sunday either, okay? I'm not going to Brooklyn."

Nell furrowed her eyebrows. If it was the neighborhood, she could understand Linnie's trepidation. Nobody wanted to deal with a bunch of Puerto Rican boys catcalling from their stupid bicycles. Maybe, even with Nell walking her to the apartment, Linnie didn't want to be anywhere near that part of New York. It was a rough neighborhood. Girls got harassed all the time. People got mugged. Sometimes, bodies would turn up in alleys and the police would block off entire streets. And then there was the Son of Sam . . . the one the cops had yet to catch. None of the shootings had been anywhere near Nell's place, but people were still scared to go out.

"Okay," Nell relented, and Linnie let out a breath, as though she'd been holding it for the length of their conversation. That was it, then. The neighborhood was the problem, not Nell's invitation. "Just tell me where you live and we can do it at your place instead."

Linnie's angular features went taut. She shot Nell an incredulous look. "You're really far out, you know that?" Nell opened her mouth to speak—*Is that a compliment?*—but Linnie didn't give her the chance to respond. "It's . . . creepy."

Nell shook her head. But . . .

"Listen, I don't want any cake, okay? I was being nice the other day because nobody else ever is to you. I felt bad. But you just can't take a hint."

"A hint," Nell echoed.

"We just *work* together," Linnie reminded her. "Just because I helped you get a coffee stain out of your shirt . . . What I'm trying to say is . . . I was just being nice, Nell. I'm sorry, but it doesn't mean we're friends."

Nell stood motionless, her eyes fixed on the girl who was now unable to meet her gaze. Linnie splashed coffee into a plain white mug and turned away, darting out of the break room with a mumbled "I'm sorry." Nell didn't have time to protest or cry or throw Mr. Topsy-Turvy, coffee and all, in Linnie's face. Left alone with burnt coffee and day-old doughnuts, Nell stared out the open break-room door. Beyond it, a sea of perfectly aligned desks. Typewriters. Telephones.

How may I direct your call?

Linnie Carter was a fake.

Hollow. Insincere.

A backhanded contemptible Jezebel.

A real *bitch*.

Please hold.

A pair of girls walked into the break room. They paused in their conversation, taking note of Nell as she winced next to the Bunn-o-Matic auto drip. Nell's eyes shifted to catch their judging glances. Their Janus-faced expressions. Their clown-painted eyes and mouths. She imagined them hanged by the silk scarves they had fashionably tied around their necks. Pictured their faces blue and lifeless as they swung beneath the fluorescent office lights.

Not so pretty when you're dead.

"Um, hello?" One of the girls spoke, jolting Nell out of her momentary fugue. "Wanna get out of the way, please?" She nodded toward the coffeepot, waiting for Nell to step aside. Nell's eyes darted from one girl to the other, and then, before either one of them could say something underhanded—*loser, whale*—Nell slammed her mug onto the floor. It shattered into a dozen ceramic pieces, Mr. Topsy-Turvy's bean-shaped body wrecked by the impact. Coffee sloshed across her penniless loafers, spattering the closest girl's stockings. The girls jumped, exhaling yelps of surprise.

Nell narrowed her eyes.

I don't want any cake.

Bared her teeth at them.

It doesn't mean we're friends.

And marched past them with a hiss.

• • •

Kings Highway's resident bicycle gang was parked just outside the train station. They were passing around a small cigarette, sucking in smoke and exhaling in slow, deliberate breaths. The moment they spotted Nell, they abandoned their lackadaisical post, shoved their dirty sneakers against the pedals of their bikes, and began to trail her down East 16th like a group of roving hyenas.

"Hey, *bibliotecaria*," one called out. "Hey, I lost my library card . . ."

"I've got late fees, *Blanca*," another chimed in. "I borrowed that *Karma Sutra* book to figure out what position I want to try on your dimpled ass first."

Their jeers weren't anything new. Nothing shocking or all that disturbing after dealing with them day after sweltering day. She'd spent months ducking her head between her shoulders and walking faster and faster, until she was marching just under a full run.

Shouldn't complain, you need the exercise.

She never spoke to them, never made eye contact. Barrett had warned her about doing so: If you give them an inch, there's no telling how far they'll take it. For all she knew, they'd drag her into an alleyway and rape her just for standing up for herself. Maybe she'd be one of the bodies the cops found behind a Dumpster. They'd probably shut down the street—a sad white girl found in a crappy area. Tabloid news.

But today, after Linnie's rejection, their catcalls woke something dormant and ugly deep within her guts.

The moment they had set eyes on her, the new girl on Kings Highway, they'd nicknamed her "the librarian," because she was homely. Boring. A milquetoast girl taunted for the same reason her coworkers exiled her to eating lunches alone at the office. Because God forbid anyone should eat anywhere near her, which could increase caloric intake. It all boiled down to looks, to stereotypes, to who they *thought* she was—a big girl wearing a sweater in the dead of summer—rather than having the guts to find out for themselves.

"Oh shit, man," the first boy jeered. "I think you pissed her off."

"Damn, dude," a third spoke up. "You better watch it. She's gonna lay you out with her yardstick or something."

"Like one of them Catholic school nuns," another laughed. "*La monja voladora!*"

"Yeah, she looks pretty Catholic to me," the first egged on. "You a straitlaced *chica Catolica*? You wanna teach me a lesson, slap me around with a ruler?"

"That in the *Karma Sutra*?" the third boy asked. Despite his laughter, Nell could sense his genuine curiosity.

"Yeah," the first one said. "It's in the fat-girl section, filed under 'Jesus Freak.' Get on your knees and pray to my *bicho*, baby."

Nell's legs stopped working.

Her feet refused to take another step.

She glared down at a sidewalk that was black with grime, small tar-like circles of chewing gum pockmarking the concrete like freckles among the filth. She clamped her teeth together, felt her nostrils flare. Somewhere, in the not-so-far-off distance, she could hear Italian opera filtering into the street from someone's open apartment window. All at once, the heat that Nell had become accustomed to beneath the bulk of her unseasonable sweater hit her head-on, threatening to burn her up from the inside out. Spontaneous combustion. Flash paper. Atom bomb.

She snapped her head to the side.

Shot a steely look at the group of boys on their childish bikes.

Let her upper lip curl away from her teeth.

"Oh *damn*, dude," said one. "Here we go. Rabid like a fuckin' dog!"

"Aw, don't be mad, *chica*," said another. "We like you, girl."

"Yeah," said the third, pumping his hips into the handlebars of his bike. "We *really* like you." He let his tongue roll out of his mouth and flicked it at her. Obscene.

Nell's stomach pitched.

A wallop of pain punched her between the eyes.

She turned away from them as if to run, and they laughed among themselves as soon as she looked in the opposite direction. But the celebration of their victory over pudgy Ms. Nobody was premature. Nell wasn't turning away to flee. She regarded a patch of gravel between the sidewalk and the nearest building. The rocks were a mishmash of small pebbles and larger stones. Without so much as a second thought, she swept up a handful of the rocks and looked back toward her assailants. They weren't paying attention anymore, distracted by a group of black kids on the opposite side of the street.

Nothing but two lanes of tarmac separated both gangs. Traffic was sparse. Nell could sense that, at any second, the bicycle gang would move to meet their enemies, where they would be out of her reach. The tallest of the black kids yelled something that she couldn't understand, but his tone was clear: he didn't like the bike gang either. They should get out of his neighborhood. Off his streets. Or he'd show them exactly why they should never show their faces on the corner of Kings Highway and East 16th again. There was no doubt in Nell's mind that, had the bike gang not been there, the grouping of black guys would have harassed her just like the Puerto Ricans had. But that was the way things in Brooklyn worked. Everyone was at odds with one another. Nobody was safe from scrutiny. And yet, at that particular moment, Nell felt solidarity with the boys across the street. They were conveniently distracting. Just what she needed.

As the two groups puffed up their chests and hollered back and forth at one another, she picked out the largest rock from the palm of her hand. Reeled back. Let it fly as hard and fast as she could. It hit the leader of the bike gang square in the back of the head with a muffled thud. The guy's hand flew up to the point of impact. He spun around, his eyes as wide as a wild dog's. When he spotted Nell with the handful of rocks, he looked ready to fly into a rage. But then the black kids erupted into a fit of laughter. They slapped their legs and stomped their Dr. Js against the hot concrete.

She threw another.

It bounced off his shoulder with a smack.

"Bitch!" he roared, but she kept throwing, pelting him about the head and shoulders, stoning him in the middle of the intersection.

But his anger seemed to shift to low-level panic, punctuated by what must have been jabs of humiliation as the black kids howled. She could see the realization in his eyes—he'd never be able to live this down. He'd forever be the guy who got pelted with rocks by some penny loafer–wearing white chick. And his friends all looked to be suffering from a mild case of shock, either because Nell was fighting back, or because their dear leader was now shoving his feet onto his bike pedals and fleeing the scene.

Across the street, the black kids were dying of laughter. A couple of them were doubled over, clutching their stomachs. One cried out in what sounded like pain as he collapsed against the chain-link fence behind him. He wiped tears from his eyes, unable to catch his breath.

Nell's tormentors dispersed. One after the other, they pedaled after their alpha, yelling Spanish slurs into the distance. Nell imagined them comforting their ego-wounded friend before leaving him to nurse his injuries. They'd talk behind his back as soon as he was out of earshot. *Coward. Cobarde.* Perhaps now Mr. Banana Seat would get a taste of his own medicine. Maybe now he'd get a chance to see how it felt to be the pariah. The social outcast. The laughingstock of the neighborhood. Hopefully the entire borough. The whey-faced baby of Brooklyn.

The remaining rocks rolled from Nell's hand, bouncing onto the sidewalk next to her feet.

"Fuck, man!" One of the black kids shouted at her from across the street. But rather than cajoling her, he lifted his right arm and made a fist in the air in salute. "The revolution has come!" he yelled, then dissolved into another bout of cackles, flanked by his friends.

Nell slowly turned back in the direction she had been walking. The throb in her head was subsiding, but it left her light-headed. Her nerves continued to crackle with adrenaline. But rather than being overwhelmed by furious anxiety, she hummed with carnal self-satisfaction instead. Sure, the bike kid's mortification would take a violent shift. She knew that as soon as his bruised ego healed enough to let him think straight, he'd thirst for justice. But this possibility didn't bother her. If he did come back, she'd be ready for him. If he dared mess with her again, she'd *let* him pull her into an alley, maybe even tempt him to do it. She'd kick and scream and act helpless, if only to give him a few seconds of satisfaction. And then she'd whip out the knife or scissors or box cutter tucked away in the folds of her sweater and stab him straight through his stupid heart. Or maybe she'd just give him a pretty Glasgow smile to live with for the rest of his scarred, miserable life.

The idea of his blood flowing through her fingers felt salacious.

The thought ignited a dull throb between her legs.

But those wanton thoughts of bloodletting melted in the heat. By the time she reached the third floor of her apartment building, she was holding back her sobs. In her head, Mr. Banana Seat's shock was replaced by Linnie's look of disturbed surprise. His sneered insults meshed into Linnie's disdain.

Take a hint.

We're not friends.

Unlocking the door, Nell stumbled headlong into the apartment. She slammed the door behind her and dropped to the floor with her hands slapping the hardwood. Anger rushed out of her in a stifling wail.

Barrett stepped out of his room to investigate the noise, but he kept his distance. She could sense him hovering just over her shoulder, close enough to let her know that he was concerned, far away enough to give her space.

"You were right." She choked on the words. "I was stupid to think . . . to think—" Cut off by a sharp intake of air, she curled fingers against the floorboards, trying to sink her nails in, trying to find purchase to steady her dismay. She was desperate for release but didn't want to scream. She needed liberation from her own smothering anguish, but she wasn't going to beat her head against the wall. Met with the perfect solution to her hysteria, she got to her feet and scrambled to the kitchen. She shoved the set table aside in her wake.

Tearing open the refrigerator door, she pulled her perfect pink cloud of a cake off the top shelf. Her masterpiece, made from scratch. She placed it on the counter, and smashed it with two closed fists. Her breath came in gasps as she beat the confection into pink-and-white paste. She grabbed the cake plate, threw the entire mess onto the kitchen floor, stomped it beneath the heels of her shoes. The plate cracked beneath her soles. She skidded on the frosting, tumbled to the ground, left a long pink smear from where her leg had shot out from beneath her.

Stunned by her fall, she sat in a fulmination of whipped sugar and pastry. It was only then that she looked meekly at her brother. Barrett was staring, soundless, his gaze unwavering. After a long while he moved, approaching her with slow and deliberate steps. And once he was less than a few feet from his sister, he crouched down beside her, scooped up a handful of destroyed cake, and lifted a cake-smeared hand to his lips to taste its sweet destruction.

Nell blinked at him as he licked his fingers clean. A ghost of a smile sprouted across her face when he smacked his lips together to let her know that it was good, *really* good.

"Linnie didn't deserve it anyway," she murmured. And then she laughed. It belted out of her as unexpectedly as her rage had, as wholeheartedly as the black kids had whooped and hollered across a four-lane street.

She fell back onto the sugar-smeared floor and cackled at the water-stained ceiling.

And Barrett grinned, amused by her lunacy. He grinned wider than ever before.

. . .

The weekend seemed to both race and crawl. One minute, Nell could hardly focus on the book she was reading. The next, it seemed as though hours had rushed by without her noticing at all. She slept a lot, trying to forget the goings-on of the week before, attempting to erase the malignant grins of Mary Ann Thomas and her gaggle of henchgirls. She tried to forget Linnie Carter existed, nursing the migraine that would swell behind her eyes at the mere thought of Linnie's lying, angular face.

Between bouts of hatred, she felt pity. She supposed that in their own way they were just as helpless against their shortcomings as she was. Could they help it if they had been born selfish and superior? Could anyone expect them to be kind and compassionate when, by nature, they were blind to the plight of a girl like her? Perhaps, Nell thought, she was as ignorant to their issues as they were to hers. Maybe their self-confidence, their too-loud laughter, and their compulsion to surround themselves with friends were all to cover up some deep-seated hurt Nell couldn't begin to understand. Perhaps everyone was broken in their own way.

By Monday morning, Nell felt better. She wasn't sure why, but it was as though a weight had been lifted. On the way to work, she decided that maybe friendship with her coworkers wasn't in the cards, but there was only one way to truly know. Sandwiched between a businessman and a priest, Nell squared her shoulders against the subway seat and decided to apologize to Linnie for acting so odd. *Creepy.* Perhaps Linnie would accept Nell's olive branch and apologize in turn for being so rude in her refusal. Or maybe they'd never speak again. Nell decided that it didn't matter. She'd forget the whole thing, leave it up to Linnie to decide. If Linnie didn't want to be friends after Nell said she was sorry, then Linnie was more of a bitch than she thought, and Nell certainly didn't need friends like that.

She got off at 42nd Street, avoided Bryant Park the way Barrett had warned her to, and rode the elevator up to the third floor of Rambert & Bertram with a handful of other girls. A few of them murmured Monday-morning complaints about the week they knew was ahead.

Rambert and Bertram, please hold . . .

But rather than the familiar call-center scene—girls seated in their chairs, the sound of phones being answered, the clickety-clack of typewriter keys—every desk was empty. The typewriters were still. Even the phones were unmanned, ringing off the hook despite there being no one to answer their incessant scream.

Nell followed the girls out of the elevator, trailing behind them as her eyes swept the disarmingly empty floor. It looked like a strange sort of graveyard, each desk a headstone for the girl who had once worked behind it, each typewriter an unwritten epitaph. Her attention settled upon a swarm of brightly colored polyester. A cacophony of patterns and styles. Stripes and checks mingled with skirts and cigarette pants. The entirety of the staff was grouped in a giant huddle around the break-room entrance. Harriett Lamont was nowhere to be seen—probably not in yet, or maybe in her office, calling the big bosses to tell them about the chaos outside her door.

Nell approached the backs that were turned her way, but she didn't dare get too close, imagining them all turning on her like a swarm of wasps. A couple of girls broke off from the group. They shook their heads, murmuring in low tones as they walked toward their desks. Their faces were drawn and pale despite their morning-fresh makeup. They held their arms coiled protectively across their chests, as though they'd just been told to pack up their things and go home for good.

Nell paused at the thought. Could it be possible? Had they all lost their jobs? Successful corporations went out of business on a regular basis. Greedy CEOs and Wall Street missteps could undo even the largest corporate Goliath. Gathering her sweater so that it hid her stomach, she looked back to the congregation of girls. She dared step a little closer to the group, but was almost immediately shoved out of the way by a fleeing coworker. As the girl blew by her, Nell heard her despite the breathlessness of her statement.

"Oh my *God*."

Nell frowned, her curiosity piqued. She moved closer to the huddle, paused when a second girl broke away and made eye contact. "What happened?" Nell asked. "What's going on?"

"More shootings," said the girl. "The victims survived this time. They saw a dark-haired man running away from their car. But there was another murder. . . ." The girl faltered, momentarily unable to continue.

"What?" Nell pressed.

"It was Linnie Carter." The girl looked into the distance, tears setting off the green of her eyes. "They found her in an alley a few buildings down from her apartment in Bayside."

Nell gaped. Found her? What did it mean to find someone in an alley, and who had found her? She shook her head. It didn't make sense.

The girl shot Nell a look of contempt, seemingly aggravated by her poor comprehension. "She's *dead*." Her delivery was harsh, impatient despite the obvious emotion pulling her expression tight. "Someone slashed her throat and stuffed her mouth full of dirt."

The ground shifted beneath Nell's feet. She took a step away from her coworker, shook her head again, this time in disbelief.

"Oh no . . ." The words tumbled across Nell's lips.

Barrett.

"You two knew each other?" The girl dabbed at her eyes with a tissue, then raised a skeptical eyebrow at Nell's reaction. Her tone was doubtful. Certainly, Nell couldn't have had ties with the likes of Linnie.

"Yes." Nell's response was quick, unflappable, toeing the line of insult.

Barrett.

She knew. It *had* to be.

Nell shot the girl a look, uncomfortable with the obvious suspicion drawn across her coworker's face. Why was she looking at her like that? Was Nell's terror that obvious? Was it blinking above her head like a cheap neon sign?

I know who did it.

I know.

I know . . . .

"We were friends." Nell spit out the statement. Friends, because now that Linnie was gone she couldn't protest. As far as anyone was concerned, Nell and Linnie were *best* friends. Hell, Linnie and Barrett had something going on. They were sweet on each other, and he would *never* have hurt her. Not in a million years.

She whipped up a story. Linnie had been due to visit Nell's apartment just that weekend, but she hadn't shown up and she hadn't called. Nell had been worried sick, pacing the length of her room for two days, wondering what had happened to her closest confidante while her brother scoured New York City's dirty streets. Thank God Nell had taken a photo of Linnie and Barrett together just before leaving for their most recent date. That, at least, had given Barrett something to flash at people after holding up his sad little cardboard sign. Have you seen this girl? And if the police asked about the photo? Stolen. Snatched right out of Barrett's hand by a homeless bum.

"Well, sorry," Nell's coworker said, and for the first time in what seemed like forever, a stranger reached out and placed a hand on her shoulder. "I'm really sorry," she repeated, as though her first apology hadn't been enough. She said nothing more, just pulled her hand back and walked away. Except that, this time, Nell wasn't being abandoned because *she* was the one who was awkward. The girl simply didn't know what else to say.

Elation overtook Nell's initial distress for half a beat. That hand on her shoulder . . . it enthralled her, because it had finally happened. Someone had been touched by her misfortune. Someone had looked right at her and, rather than scowling, had been shot through with an arrow of compassion. *Finally*, she thought. *I am human.* But her delight was followed by a hiccup of her heart. A misfired beat. A punch of understanding.

Linnie was dead.

It was too much of a coincidence.

Nell had lost her mind. She'd wailed in the kitchen. She'd been wronged, and Barrett had seen it all. And what did he make of it? That Linnie Carter was just like their mother.

A liar.

A fake.

Linnie hadn't wanted to eat cake, so Barrett made her eat dirt instead.

"Oh no," she whispered, because what if the cops showed up at the apartment. "*Oh no . . .*" What if they took him away and she was left alone? What if Barrett was hauled off to prison and Nell was left to navigate Brooklyn by herself? It was a death sentence. She'd never survive on her own. "*Oh no!*" The words were more pronounced now, loud enough to garner the attention of a couple of passing girls. She sensed them looking. Lifted her hands to her face for dramatic effect. Peeked through her fingers to verify that they were indeed gazing upon her with a mixture of pity and concern. Mary Ann Thomas was peering at her from across the office, sizing her up. But this was Nell's moment.

"*Oh no!*" She wept the sentiment into her palms, full volume now. Because if everyone knew she and Linnie were friends, nobody would suspect that she had anything to do with Linnie's demise. "Not Linnie," Nell cried, not caring who heard her, not caring if the entire office ended up gaping. "Not my Linnie. Not my friend!"

• • • •

Lamont refused to call it a day. Despite the tragedy, there was still work to be done. Phones had to be answered. Transcriptions had to be typed. They were all forced back into their chairs, not because Lamont was worried about how an empty office on a busy Monday would look, but because letting all the girls go would be bad for morale. Let them go, and it made Linnie Carter's death real. Let them go, and suddenly every Rambert & Bertram employee was left to sit at home, wide-eyed while watching the news, wondering if they were next.

But Lamont's insistence to carry on with the day didn't make working easy. Nell sat at her desk, wooden, hardly able to get a thing done between her racing thoughts and coworkers occasionally pausing to murmur quiet sympathies about Linnie's sudden passing. Nell had made a scene with her open weeping. One minute, she had been an outsider looking in. The next, she was the center of attention, as though *she* had been the one left for dead and humiliated in an alley littered with trash.

Poor, poor Linnie.

It was just after lunch that a shadow loomed over Nell's left shoulder. Nell turned to glance behind her, and there was Mary Ann Thomas, with her eyes narrowed into accusatory slits. Nell stared at her for a beat, then offered the blonde an unsure, wavering greeting.

"H-hey, Mary Ann." Nell produced a pathetic smile, one that read: *I'm sad about Linnie, but still happy to see you.* One that made her look like a "trouper," plodding through the day despite her broken heart.

But Mary Ann wasn't having any of it. Her glare only intensified.

"Is . . ." Nell stammered. "Is everything okay?"

That was when Mary Ann took a couple of steps forward. Her pretty pink manicure gripped the back of Nell's office chair as she leaned forward, as if to rest her chin on Nell's shoulder before cooing in her ear. But there were no sweet nothings here. Mary Ann hissed instead: "I don't know what you're up to, *Sweaty*, but you aren't fooling anyone."

"What?" Nell stared at Rambert & Bertram's It Girl. Blinked a few times for good measure. Tried not to narrow her own eyes in response to Mary Ann's hideous insult, let alone at what Mary Ann was implying.

"You weren't friends with Linnie," Mary Ann said flatly. "Everybody knows that. You aren't friends with anyone, so if you think you can just—"

"I don't know what you're talking about." Nell cut her off midsentence. Mary Ann's expression became even more incredulous, but Nell didn't let Mary Ann voice her continued suspicion. "Not like *you* would know. You're so concerned with yourself, it's a wonder you know anything about anyone." Mary Ann's eyes went wide. How dare a troll speak to a princess in such a way? But Nell didn't dare take it back. *Stick to your guns,* she thought. *If you drop it now, you'll look guiltier than ever. Not only will you be the laughingstock of the entire office, but maybe Mary Ann will call the cops and tell them you lied this morning. Then they'll come to question you, because what kind of girl does something like that?*

Nell shifted in her seat and turned back to her typewriter, her eyes fixed on the mug of pencils at the corner of her desk. The yellow smiley face grinned at her.

Have a nice day!

"Have a nice day," she murmured to the bitch just beyond her shoulder. A moment later, she heard Mary Ann Thomas stomp toward the break room without so much as another word.

Except that Mary Ann's departure didn't do much to ease the anxiety that was blooming like a dahlia within the cavity of Nell's chest. She didn't have to wonder whether Barrett had really done it. She hadn't ever been so sure of anything in all her life. And she didn't wonder why either. That was just as obvious to her as Barrett's guilt. But she did wonder *when*.

Had it been Friday night, when he had left her alone to sulk in the apartment? Had it been Saturday, when she had slept her throbbing headache—and the day—away? Or maybe it had been Sunday, when she had spent what felt like minutes but turned out to be hours sitting in Barrett's wingback chair, thumbing through an old paperback without reading a single word. And if it *had* been Friday or Saturday, how had he kept such a thing a secret? Why wouldn't he have told her? Why would he have left her to learn about Linnie's death like this, in the cold fluorescent burn of an office building?

He was punishing her. *Always* punishing her. No matter what she did, it was wrong. He was forever upset and on edge, ready to tell her that she was stupid for wanting the things she wanted, for being the way she was. But Barrett? He could do no wrong. Oh no, not her *perfect* brother with his late-night outings and his goddamn manifestos, his demands, all those damn *demands*. And yeah, maybe he did say that he would never leave Nell behind, but he still used that fear against her. He *knew* she was afraid of losing him, which is why she ended up bending to his will no matter what he asked. Friends? Forget them. Guests? Not on your life. Linnie Carter? Dead. Dead. Fucking *dead*.

"Nell?" Her name cut across the noise of the office. She just about jumped out of her seat when she heard it ebb over the ringing of her phone. Nell shot a look toward the door adorned with Harriet Lamont's name in gold foil. The boss had seen everything—Nell gasping at the tragedy, wailing about her fallen comrade in the middle of the office. Nell had met Lamont's gaze only for a second, but that second of eye contact had been enough. Something about the boss witnessing her breakdown pushed Nell to ramble over to her desk, to sit down and try to collect her nerves and thoughts. But it was easy to discard Lamont's judging glance amid the heartfelt condolences that drifted across her desk. Nell spent the day solemnly nodding her head and thanking girls she'd never spoken to for their kind words.

Thank you. Yes, it's hard, but I think I'll make it through.

Leave it to Mary Ann—*that bitch*—to ruin a perfect day.

But she couldn't ruin it completely. No, Nell wouldn't allow it. The attention was strange, oddly and wonderfully strange. It was feigning grief that was familiar. It reminded her of her mother. Of the way she had cried at their father's funeral, her sadness not once touching her eyes.

Nell and Barrett had stood shoulder to shoulder beside Faye Sullivan while their father's flower-topped casket inched into the ground. Faye wept so hard into her hands that it had scared Nell. She pictured her mom disintegrating beneath waves of grief. Disappearing right where she stood. Melting away like the Wicked Witch of the West. But a simple squeeze of the hand from Nell's newly mute brother assured her that it was an act. She was faking it. And what made that memory all the more vivid were the people who failed to console the weeping woman beside them.

Nell had craned her neck around to look at the black-clad mourners behind them. Faye Sullivan didn't have family. The congregation of sniffling, stern-faced mourners were all Leigh Sullivan's relatives. For one reason or another, they didn't want anything to do with the widow Sullivan and her overly dramatic grief.

After the funeral, momentarily separated from Barrett and her mom while clutching Beary to her chest, Nell's grandmother pulled her aside. "Don't worry, baby," she had said, her heavily ringed fingers stroking one of Beary's ears. "I'll take you away from here. Everything is gonna be all right." But Nell twisted her arm out of her grandmother's too-tight grasp. What did she mean she'd take *her* away? What about Barrett? Nell turned and ran, and for a few brief, terrifying minutes she couldn't find her brother anywhere. It was as though the crowd had swallowed him, as though their grandmother had stolen him away the way she had wanted to take Nell. Standing amid the headstones, she began to yell Barrett's name while distant family watched on. They pressed their hands to their mouths, their eyes radiating sadness that Nell tried to ignore. She was sad enough about her dad as it was. She didn't need teary-eyed adults telling her it would all be okay when, even at four years old, she knew it wouldn't be.

She found Barrett sitting alone in the shade of an elm tree, and that's where they stayed, her and Barrett and Beary. Mourners looked on with expressions of sorrow and pity until their mother yelled for them to get in the car.

From what their mother had explained, their dad had hit his head the day of Barrett's backyard accident. He had gotten so upset about what had happened that, even though Barrett had been okay, he had hurt himself over it.

He felt guilty, Faye had explained. *You understand? He felt guilty for what happened to your brother, and sometimes when adults feel guilty, they do terrible, horrible things.*

Maybe it had been Barrett losing his ability to speak that had done it. Maybe that was what had pushed their father over the edge.

"Nell." Lamont again. It seemed impossible that Nell should have been able to hear her over the clatter of phones, but her supervisor's voice carried remarkably well through the clamor.

Doom settled in the pit of her stomach. The same kind Nell had felt when she had called out for Barrett at the funeral, but he had been nowhere to be found.

Maybe Lamont had changed her mind about Nell being late last Wednesday.

Maybe, despite what had happened to Linnie, Mr. Rambert and Mr. Bertram had announced it was time for a cutback, and Nell was at the top of the list. She was one of the disposable girls.

Nell sat unmoving for a good few seconds. She held her breath, afraid to draw attention to herself. It was the complete opposite of what she'd wanted only an hour before. It was a few minutes until five now. If she sat there long enough, she could bolt for the elevator just after quitting time. Certainly, Harriet Lamont wouldn't expect Nell to stay after hours for a meeting. That would have been overtime, and overtime didn't happen at R & B.

She nearly gasped when Lamont poked her head out her door and gave Nell a pointed stare. Across a vast ocean of desks and girls, Harriet Lamont's expression was stern and unrelenting. Mary Ann Thomas swiveled in her chair, as if to witness the panic that was surely twisting up Nell's face. By the time Nell slipped into the boss's office, she was queasy with nerves. Barrett was going to be so angry, so *pissed* if she lost her job.

Harriet Lamont was seated behind her desk, lighting a cigarette with that ostentatious crystal lighter. Nell gave her boss a wary smile and crossed the office to one of the wooden-armed chairs. She slid into it, immediately uncomfortable, unable to tell whether it was the chair or the sudden tightness of her own skin.

"Nell . . ." Lamont peered at her, as if searching for the answer to a question she had yet to ask. She paused, took a drag off her cigarette, and frowned before leaning back in her executive chair. It squeaked on its castors.

Unable to stand the silence any longer, Nell blinked at her supervisor, nodded. "Yes?" She wanted out of that office, and if speaking expedited her exit, then fine. The way Lamont was looking at her made her anxious, as though she was privy to some bit of knowledge everyone else had missed.

Like maybe she knew about Barrett.

Like maybe she knew what he'd done.

Like maybe that nosy bitch Mary Ann had ratted her out, not only ruining Nell's day, but her entire life.

"Nell, honestly, I'm a little disturbed."

Nell's stomach clenched.

"Disturbed?"

"Well, the whole situation with Ms. Carter . . ."

She knows.

"Linnie." The name tumbled off Nell's tongue before she could hold it back.

"Yes," Lamont said, giving her a pointed look. "Linnie."

Nell frowned down at her hands. She wasn't sure whether to pull the same act on Lamont that she'd managed to get away with on most of the girls, or whether it was wiser to wait the whole thing out. When Lamont failed to speak, Nell squeezed her eyes shut and murmured beneath her breath.

"It's terrible. Just, really horribly, terribly awful, don't you think?"

She opened her eyes, flicked her glance upward, then looked away almost immediately. "I hope they catch him," she whispered.

"Catch whom?" Lamont asked.

Nell's heart caught in her throat.

Why would you have said that?

Because she was stupid, that's why. A stupid pig, like Porky.

Th-th-th-that's all, folks!

"I don't know." Nell shook her head, scrambling for words. "I don't know who did it."

Of course not.

"I have no idea."

Why would I?

"I just . . . who would do such a thing, Ms. Lamont?"

Nobody I know.

"Who would hurt someone as sweet as Linnie?"

Lamont said nothing, her eyes not once leaving Nell's face. Her unwavering look made Nell nervous. It was dubious, unsure—made her feel like the dirty liar she was.

Another beat of silence passed.

Maybe *she* would call the cops. Maybe that's why she'd called Nell into her office—to interrogate her. Harriet Lamont was a go-getter. She wouldn't leave ruining Nell's life to a cheap girl like Mary Ann Thomas. No way. If anyone was going to end up on the news for having helped apprehend Linnie Carter's killer, it was Lamont.

The boss exhaled a stream of smoke. She leaned forward, her forearms sliding across the top of her lacquered desk. "The world is a crazy place, Nell. I gather you *do* recall being in here last week, yes?"

Nell swallowed the wad of nerves that had gathered at the back of her throat. She managed an unsure nod. Sure, she remembered, but what did her last visit have to do with anything? "I haven't been late," she said. "Not since that morning. I've been diligent, Ms. Lamont. I've been catching an earlier train just to make sure, to not leave anything to chance. You've got to believe me, I—"

"I believe you." Lamont held up a hand, as if hoping the simple gesture of showing Nell her palm would calm her twitchy employee down. "This isn't about being late. This is about what we discussed when you were sitting across from me the same way you are now."

Nell pinched her eyebrows together. What *had* they discussed? Beyond being reprimanded for her tardiness and Lamont telling her to change her life, Nell hardly remembered a word of what had been said. Lately, the headaches had made it hard to remember much.

"You don't recall, then, that I asked you whether you had many friends?" Lamont asked.

The arteries of Nell's heart tightened—a vise squeezing it from the inside out.

"I asked you whether you have many friends, and you admitted to me that you don't, isn't that right?"

Nell glared at her hands. She wouldn't answer. Lamont would have to pry her mouth open to get her to respond.

"Nell, a few of your coworkers find the claim that you and Linnie Carter were close a little odd."

Nell peered at the crystal lighter at the corner of Lamont's desk. If she lunged for it, Lamont wouldn't have time to react. If she smashed it against her supervisor's head, she'd embed a corner of that lighter into the soft tissue of Lamont's brain. Lamont would slump back in her fancy office chair. Blood would stream down her face and onto her expensive blouse. If Nell turned Lamont's chair away from the office door, the entire secretarial pool would evacuate the building without being the wiser. Or maybe she'd tell Mary Ann that the boss wanted to see her. That hussy would discover the crime and be scarred for life. Quite possibly, she'd never be able to sleep again. End up in an asylum. Tear that pretty blond hair out one strand at a time while rocking back and forth, back and forth, Harriet Lamont's dead, glazed-over eyes forever etched into her memory.

"Nell?"

Nell snapped out of her daze, looked up at Lamont's pensive expression.

"You told me yourself that you weren't close with anyone here, and yet here we are. Frankly, I find it disturbing that you'd use her misfortune to your advantage."

No. She refused to acknowledge what Lamont was suggesting.

No, she wouldn't speak.

Not in a million years.

"Look . . ." Lamont exhaled a breath. Though, with Nell's eyes fixed on the knees of her slacks, she couldn't tell if her boss was sighing in dissatisfaction or exhaling another stream of smoke. "The last time you were in here, I said that I can tell you're different from the rest of the girls. You at least remember *that*, don't you?"

Nell nodded, not lifting her eyes.

"I told you that I could appreciate that. Now, why do you think that is?"

"I don't know," Nell whispered, though what she meant to say was *I don't care*. She didn't need to explain herself. Harriet Lamont may have been her supervisor, but that didn't mean she had the right to butt into Nell's personal affairs. And Linnie was very much a personal affair.

"You didn't bother to consider it?" Lamont asked. "That perhaps my appreciation for your differences is due in part to my being one of the different ones as well?"

Nell peered at Lamont through strands of mousy brown hair.

"You don't get to where I am by being like everyone else, Nell, especially not if you're a woman. I know it's tough for you, but what you've done today isn't right."

"I didn't do anything." It slid out of her throat, slippery, unable to be contained. "Mary Ann Thomas *hates* me, Ms. Lamont. I don't know what she told you, but . . ." Catching her bottom lip between her teeth, Nell looked down again. *Shut up,* she thought. *The more you talk the worse you'll make it.* She knew using Linnie's death was wrong, knew that turning a tragedy into a grab for attention was low. But it had simply happened; it had felt natural, as though Linnie's death had been orchestrated just for her. One second, she was standing on the outside of the group trying to hear the news, and the next she was weeping into her hands and professing her sorrow for a girl she hardly knew.

But what harm did it do? It was a little white lie. It seemed fair. Linnie Carter had hurt her—the least the unappreciative slut could do was pay her back with a bit of acclaim. So what if Linnie was dead? *Nell* was still alive.

And just who was Harriet Lamont to tell Nell what she could or couldn't do? As long as Nell did her work, Lamont didn't have a right to meddle in her affairs. Not like this, not when it came to her social life, not when it was Lamont herself who had given her the advice to make a change. Nell's gaze darted up to Lamont's face. Suddenly, Harriet Lamont's rouged cheeks and red lips looked cheap. Racy. Nell guessed that she was well into her early forties, but she looked like a two-bit tramp.

You're no different, she thought to herself. *You're just like all the rest of them. If you were different once, you're just a sheep now.*

"So, are you going to fire me?" The directness of Nell's inquiry seemed to throw Lamont for a curve. The boss fussed with her cigarette, tapped ashes into an ashtray that Nell didn't doubt was real crystal. Not like the dime-store ashtrays that dotted each desk beyond the boss's office door.

"What . . . fire you? No, I just . . ."

"I don't think I *hurt* anybody, did I?" she asked, emboldened by her own sense of entitlement. Linnie Carter had humiliated her, and why? Because Nell had spent her precious time and money on baking supplies and a white tablecloth and a little creamer pitcher with a toadstool on it. She'd done those things for *Linnie*, not for Barrett, not even for herself, really. And Linnie had thrown it back in her face. And why had Nell even tried? Because *Lamont* had advised her to change her life if she didn't like it. Nell had taken that advice to heart—she'd done something different, and now Lamont wanted to scold her for it? When *she* had been the one to suggest it in the first place?

No. This wasn't right.

Nell wouldn't allow it. She wouldn't be taken for a fool.

"Well, I suppose not, but—"

"Mary Ann hates me." Nell cut Lamont off midsentence. "I try to fit in, but it's hard, and Mary Ann doesn't make it any easier. You know how it can be. You were different just like I am, right? If anyone finds out about the thing with Linnie . . ." Mary Ann may have told everyone already, but Nell didn't care. Her coworkers could speculate all they wanted, but unless Nell confessed to lying, they'd never know for sure. "I *need* this job, Ms. Lamont. I really do. I can't pay my rent without it, and—"

"All right," Lamont said.

"—it's just a shabby old place, but it's four walls and a bed, and I really don't know where I'd go if I couldn't afford it."

"*All right*." Lamont raised a hand for a second time. "Enough, Nell. I'm not going to fire you."

"And you won't tell? Please, Ms. Lamont, don't tell the girls. If they find out I made it up, I'll never live it down. You *know* how they can be. It won't happen again. Honest, it won't. I won't ever mention Linnie's name again, if that's what you want. I won't ever even look at Mary Ann Thomas if—"

"Okay, you can go," Lamont said, waving Nell off, having had her fill for one afternoon. Nell gathered herself up out of the chair, but of course, Lamont couldn't allow her to go without a final thought. "Nell, if any of the girls *do* give you trouble, you can come tell me. You know that, right?"

Nell frowned at that. If the girls did give her trouble—at least, beyond the trouble they usually gave—what would she tell Lamont for? So her boss could give her another dose of shiny, sure-to-backfire advice? Nell responded with an unsure smile. "Thanks, Ms. Lamont, but I'll be okay." And then stepped out of the boss's office.

She scrutinized each desk, wondering which of the girls Mary Ann had told. Her eyes darted from coworker to coworker, faster now, frantic to pick out any girl who may have known her secret. It was only then that she noticed the difference: the girls weren't looking at her anymore. As a matter of fact, they were avoiding looking in her direction altogether. They were all pretending to be working or busying themselves with gathering up their things. Oh sure, it *looked* like they were all getting ready to clock out, but she knew the truth. They were ignoring her on purpose. Nell had stepped out of an office full of sympathetic girls and stepped back into one where those girls didn't know the meaning of compassion. Even eye contact was deemed too awkward.

Nell Sullivan was invisible again.

She marched back to her desk, kept her head down as she walked. Sliding into her chair, she focused on the transcription she'd been working on before Lamont had interrupted her. It had been due over an hour ago, but Nell had been too distracted to get it typed out in time. She had to finish it before she left for the day—couldn't leave anything to chance, any reason for Lamont to change her mind and tell her to get lost for good. But the throb behind her eyes was rearing its ugly head again. Squeezing her eyes shut, she began to poke at the keys of her Selectric, hysteria bubbling deep inside her gut.

I do exist, she thought. *It's Linnie who's dead, not me.*

Maybe the girls were pretending Nell was a ghost because they knew . . . knew about Barrett, about what he'd done.

No. Impossible. How could they know?

Nobody knew because nobody could prove that Nell and Linnie *hadn't* been friends. Mary Ann Thomas could tell the entire office that Nell was lying, but how could she confirm that claim? Save for the fact that Nell and Linnie hadn't ever talked at the office—and so what?—Mary Ann had nothing to back herself up. Nell and Linnie didn't talk because they had that kind of friendship. They could communicate without talking, could read each other's minds like a pair of twins. They spent hours upon hours on the phone after work, so they kept to themselves while they were *at* work. Besides, Linnie's other friends wouldn't have understood.

Nell's heart twitched.

Her *other* friends.

What if Linnie had told one of the girls about how weird Nell had been last Friday?

Oh no.

Maybe she had said something about the cake, about the invitation to Nell's apartment.

Oh God!

Her breath hitched in her throat.

Her fingers stopped dead on the keys of her IBM.

She looked at the paper that she was working on, struck by five words that appeared on a line all their own.

NELL SULLIVAN IS A LIAR.

She hadn't typed that . . . had she?

NELL SULLIVAN IS A LIAR.

No. It hadn't been her. It couldn't have been.

Someone had been messing around her desk while she had been in Lamont's office. Probably Mary Ann or one of her lackeys.

That was it. It *had* to be.

Unable to stand it, she grabbed her purse and adjusted her sweater. If Lamont wanted to fire her for leaving without finishing her work first, then so be it. Nell couldn't bear to spend another second in that building. Not without strangling every single girl around her. Because *someone* had typed out that sentence on Nell's typewriter. *Someone* knew that she had lied. *Someone* knew what Barrett had done.

"Nell?"

She reeled around to look at Savannah Wheeler. For a second, she wanted to reach out and catch Mary Ann Thomas's pretty henchfriend by her throat.

This is how Linnie felt during the last minutes of her life.

But all she did was blink.

"Hey, I know you're leaving . . . I just wanted to apologize." Savannah looked unsure of herself. She glanced over her shoulder, as if to check to see if anyone was watching their exchange, then looked back to Nell and forced a smile. "For Wednesday, you know?"

Oh yes, Nell knew.

For Adriana ratting her out.

For Mary Ann being a snitch.

For Savannah just standing there, watching her friends torment Nell without doing a damn thing about it.

"I've felt bad about it ever since, but now, after what happened this morning . . ." Her words trailed off, allowing Nell to fill in the rest of the sentence herself. *After we found out about Linnie . . .*

"Thanks," Nell said dryly. She sidestepped her desk, avoided eye contact. Despite Savannah's sudden change of heart, Nell was afraid to look at her, afraid that if she did she'd only see Savannah's pretty face bloom into a nefarious grin.

Because it's a trick. Because she doesn't really mean it.

"Listen, I . . . we're going to the Cabana Club for happy hour, if you want to join us."

Nell stopped short, sure that her ears were playing tricks on her.

"It's not a big deal . . . just drinks, you know? We thought that maybe you'd like to unwind a little. Today has been, well . . ." She paused, trying to find the right word.

Nell ogled Savannah's platform shoes, unable to look away. They were pale gray leather, open-toed, with a wooden sole at least an inch thick—shoes only a harlot would wear. At least that's what Barrett would have said, scribbling it on his yellow pad. The clothes fit the girl. No proper girl wore platform shoes or short skirts or dyed her hair and smeared garish red lipstick across her mouth.

And what about Mary Ann? She'd never hang out with the likes of Nell, not after their exchange.

It's a trick. A dirty, rotten trick.

"Don't worry . . ." Savannah offered Nell a faint smile of reassurance. "Mary Ann isn't going to be there tonight. Besides, would it matter if she was?"

Of *course* it mattered. Was Savannah that dense? And what if Mary Ann really *was* going to be there? What if Savannah was inviting her out because Mary Ann told her to, and as soon as Nell got to the Cabana Club they'd humiliate her, like in that *Carrie* book by Stephen King?

"I have to go home." Nell shouldered her way around her coworker before Savannah could argue, rushing toward the elevator doors.

"Well, if you change your mind . . . !" Savannah called out after her. Her insistence nearly pushed Nell to take the stairs instead.

Nell choked when a couple of Linnie's cohorts followed her into the elevator. She clamped her teeth together and squeezed her eyes shut, held her breath as the elevator began to make its descent.

"I just think it's really weird," the first girl said.

"Yeah," said the second. "Weird that Linnie hadn't mentioned it . . ."

"Hadn't brought up that Nell girl . . ." said a third.

"Not even once either. Not a single time."

She couldn't breathe. Couldn't move. Wanted to scream. To pound her fists against the metal walls of that metal box. *Because you would have judged her,* she wanted to spit. *Because you're all the same. A girl can't be herself, can't tell the truth, can't be anything but fake, fake, fake!*

"You're all fake." Nell breathed the words out just as the elevator hit the ground floor and the doors yawned open.

Linnie's friends slowly turned to give Nell a pointed stare.

"Ex*cuse* me?" said one.

"Nothing," Nell murmured, then shoved her way out of the elevator.

Spilling out onto the crowded street, she almost ran to the train station. And yet, the longer she waited on the platform, the more Savannah's invitation scratched at the back of her brain. Maybe Savannah had been making a genuine effort. It was true that she wasn't the first girl Nell thought of when she considered potential friends, but she'd wanted to be part of Mary Ann Thomas's group, hadn't she? *Not anymore I don't.* Nell had been daydreaming about hanging out with those pretty girls for as long as she had worked at Rambert & Bertram. Except she'd screwed that opportunity up for herself, what with how she had spoken to Mary Ann earlier in the day. And then she'd gone and shot down Savannah's invitation as though she had all the friends in the world.

You're just upset because Nell Sullivan is a liar.

Yes, that was true. Nell's friendship with Linnie was all made up.

But maybe if she tried again. Just once more, with Savannah. Maybe then everything would change. And Mary Ann? Well, if Mary Ann got in the way, Nell would tell her exactly where she could go.

. . .

"How could you?"

Barrett was in his usual spot, his legs thrown across one of the arms of his old wingback chair. He folded his book across his chest and eyed his sister from across their small living room—a room that, in its disrepair, seemed to lean a touch to the left. Nell dropped her purse onto a chair as she passed through the kitchen, only to pause and give her sibling a good, long look.

"I know it was you, Barrett," she said. "The dirt in her mouth?" She snorted, turned away from him, not wanting to see the smirk she knew would eventually settle across his lips. "Nice touch," she murmured. "You may as well have shoved a cupcake down her throat with my name on it." That was overdramatic. She knew there was no way anyone could have put together the fact that Nell had anything to do with Linnie's death. After all, she *didn't*, did she? Nell wasn't her brother's keeper. "And what if the police had come? What if they had asked *me* questions?"

Then you would have lied, Barrett scribbled.

That word made Nell tense. NELL SULLIVAN IS A LIAR. It was bad enough that someone had typed it onto her transcript, ruining her work, insulting her in the process. But now Barrett was going to join in?

"Because that's all I'm good at?" she demanded.

Barrett looked unconcerned by his sister's increasing agitation. Well, he wrote, you ARE good at it.

"Oh, fuck you, Barrett!" she yelled. But rather than shocking him with her outburst, Barrett laughed instead. Nell jerked at the sleeves of her sweater, yanked it off, and threw it to the floor. The shirt she'd worn beneath it throughout the day was soaked at the armpits. She could feel a distinct line of moisture along the length of her spine. "Anyway." She turned her back to him, trying to play it cool. "I suppose you did me a favor, if you think about it." Glancing over her shoulder, she took in his new expression—a look of sour dissatisfaction. "That's right," she said. "Because when I got to the office this morning, all the girls already knew about Linnie. She was front page news. They're blaming the Son of Sam."

Barrett's perturbed look shifted into amusement. He liked that. Perhaps he had known the police were going to point the finger at Mr. Monster rather than look for another killer all along. Because really, what were the odds?

See? he wrote. No big deal.

"No big deal?" Nell narrowed her eyes at him. "As soon as I heard about Linnie, I lost it."

Barrett arched an eyebrow at her in inquiry. Lost it?

"You could have told me beforehand, don't you think? You could have at least *warned* me to prepare myself. But you let me learn about it for myself! I kept picturing the police taking you away, and *then* who would I have left?" She was nearly yelling now. "Did you ever think of that? Did you ever stop to consider what would happen to *me* if you end up spending the rest of your life in prison?"

Barrett looked down, as if mulling that over. No, of course he hadn't considered it. But now that Nell had brought it to his attention, he looked shameful. Guilty. Nell frowned at the way his shoulders deflated. He looked undignified, and it made her feel like a wretch for disgracing him. All he'd been doing was defending her honor.

Barrett held up his notepad once more. Keep your voice down. The walls were thin. How ironic would it have been if Nell's freak-out was what brought the cops calling?

She sighed, took a seat at the kitchen table. "You had to *kill* her?" she asked, her tone low.

Research, he wrote. Wanted to see how it felt.

"For your book?" she asked.

Barrett shrugged.

"I'm not angry, Barrett," she told him, suddenly tired from all the arguing. "You did it for me. You did it because she had been improper, unappreciative. That type of behavior has its consequences, right? Sometimes, if you're rude to the wrong person, you get a taste of your own medicine."

Barrett raised his eyes to meet his sister's. She gave him a small smile, assuring him that she really wasn't mad. "Besides, what started out as a bad day turned into a good one. When I made that scene at the office, the girls turned to see what was wrong. I couldn't have very well said that I was afraid my brother was going to get himself arrested. I couldn't have said *that*. So, I said that Linnie and I were friends. It just tumbled out of me, and the strangest thing happened." Nell smiled at the memory. "You should have seen them. They were like flies on a corpse. As soon as I said we were close, everyone wanted to say how sorry they were about her death, as though *I* was the one that deserved their condolences. I guess I pulled off looking pretty sad about the whole thing. Her friends were mumbling about how she had never talked about me, but what do they know anyway? They can't prove anything. Maybe I should have been an actress."

Barrett was frowning again. He wasn't happy with Nell's confession.

"I only said the thing about me and her being friends to protect *you*, you know. And isn't that what you were doing when you did what you did? Didn't you go through with the whole thing to protect *me*?"

You should have kept your mouth shut, he wrote, then looked away from her, not sold on her reasoning.

"Well, I don't see what you have to be upset about," she said. "*I'm* the one that turned down an invitation to the Cabana Club."

It was then that Barrett's eyes blazed.

He shot up from his chair, his notepad tumbling to the floor.

She could see it in his expression, the memory of their mother dancing across the deep brown of his eyes. Their sloppy drunk mother who locked them in the closet while she pulled strange men into their dead father's bed. He wore a mask of disdain, and that's when his true intentions became clear.

Yes, Barrett had killed Linnie Carter, because Linnie Carter had made Nell cry.

Yes, he'd killed her because she was an unappreciative bitch who couldn't bother with politeness.

Yes, he had wanted to see how it felt. For his book. For his art.

But mostly, Barrett had killed her because Linnie's disregard for Nell's feelings had reminded him of their mother's disregard for her own children.

He had killed her because, at her core, Linnie Carter was a carbon copy of Faye Sullivan. And Faye Sullivan was out there somewhere, alive.

"It had nothing to do with research, did it?" Nell asked. "You did it because of Mom."

Barrett reeled around, his stare hard, wild with a rage Nell hadn't seen before. That's when the realization hit her. Nell was afraid of losing Barrett, either to a girl or the police, and Barrett was afraid of losing her too. He was afraid of Nell hanging around the girls she worked with because they were just like their matriarch. Ugly and sinful and hateful right down to their bones. But if he wiped them out, Nell didn't stand a chance of being their friend. If he killed the ones who got too friendly, they wouldn't ruin his sister, and Nell couldn't make any friends.

"You can't do that, Barrett," she said, her newfound understanding igniting a flame of resentment deep in her chest—small, but still there. "You can't just go around killing people who remind you of her, no matter how much you want her gone."

Barrett refused to look at her, his lack of eye contact assuring her that he'd do whatever he damn well pleased. Because of *course* he would. It didn't matter that his actions affected his sister. That was the whole point, after all. How was she supposed to change her life if Barrett cut down her opportunities?

"You're selfish." Her tone was hard-edged. Most of the time, all she wanted was to please him, but he'd crossed a line. After all she sacrificed for him—letting him live out his dreams of being a writer. Her working full-time, while he sat around reading his books. Having to ride the dirty subway. Enduring the snide comments and judgmental looks. Dealing with that stupid bicycle gang. The least he could do was *try* to let her find some company beyond their shitty little apartment.

"What about me?" she demanded. "What about what *I* want? What about who *I* look like?" There was a resemblance. Nell had inherited their mother's mousy brown hair. If she dropped a few pounds, the thinness of her face would reflect Faye Sullivan's sharp cheekbones and weak chin. "Will you kill me too?"

Nothing.

"Barrett."

He squared his shoulders at the sound of his name, but rather than glaring at her, he peered down at his feet. Despite his twenty-four years, at that moment he looked like a little boy. That familiar pang of guilt crawled back into Nell's guts. She was making him feel bad again, but she couldn't just shrug and forget what he'd done. There would be other girls in Nell's life now. She hadn't thought it possible at the beginning of the day, but after Savannah's invitation, she was quite sure of it. Soon, Nell would have another chance, which meant there *would* be other girls. If she didn't put a stop to Barrett's compulsion now, she wouldn't stand a chance of doing it later.

"Barrett, you have to promise me," she said. "If you get caught, I'll have no one." She knew it was strange—insane, really—that she was more concerned about the police apprehending Barrett than him killing people. But maybe that was the whole problem. Maybe she *was* crazy, spending her days imagining doing terrible things to the girls who wronged her, who made her feel less than human. At least Barrett had the courage to do what Nell could only fantasize about. At least he had the strength to take action rather than spend his life as little more than a shadow. But that kind of courage was dangerous. He feared that she would become someone other than herself, and she worried that his valor would erase him from her life completely.

"If you do something bad and the police find out, if they take you away, what will I do?" she asked, her anger diluted by the worry that gnawed at every nerve.

Barrett took a seat on the edge of his wingback chair, Robert Louis Stevenson lying between his feet, his small notepad over-turned upon the floor.

"Have you stopped to think that maybe they'll come after me too? And even if they don't, I can't live alone. You *know* I can't. What choice will I have but to try to find Mother? What choice will I have, Barrett, other than to go live with her again?"

A muted moan escaped his lips. It was a cross between agony and anger, as though the mere thought of Nell living with that woman was tearing him up inside. Severing ventricles and veins. Twisting organs like tightropes.

Nell abandoned her kitchen chair. A thin film of pink frosting still clung to the floorboard seams. She padded barefoot across the small expanse of their two-bit apartment. The boards, rough and crooked, impossible to clean completely, creaked beneath her feet. She sank to her knees at the foot of Barrett's chair and laid her head next to his knee. "You see how bad it could become?" she whispered. "If I'm left alone, I may as well die." She smiled to herself, feeling his fingers drift across the top of her head like a breeze. "And acting out of anger, out of jealousy . . ." He tensed at the word. "I know you're jealous, Barrett. Don't deny it." He removed his hand from her head. "You're worried," Nell continued. "Worried that I'll find someone else."

Barrett rocketed from the chair, pushing her away.

No, he wasn't jealous. Jealousy would have meant that *he* wanted to go out with Nell to restaurants and discos and God knew wherever else. But he didn't want anything to do with that. He didn't want *her* to have anything to do with that. That was the whole point, his whole reasoning behind his actions. He was doing his brotherly duty. Saving her from herself.

She watched him stomp across the living room for no reason other than to put distance between them. "Well, *I'm* worried that you'll find someone else!" she yelled at his back. "You're going to abandon me! You're going to leave me, and what'll happen to me then?"

He shot her a glance over his shoulder, one she'd seen a hundred times before.

I would never. I couldn't, it said. *How many times do I have to tell you? How many times before you get it through your head?*

But she couldn't bring herself to believe him. How could he *not* leave? She was a pathetic mess. A loser. The apartment was a dump. Kings Highway was like a war zone. Barrett was smart and witty and charming and talented—he couldn't speak, but he could write, and that's what was important. It was how he'd leave his mark on the world, how the universe would remember he existed. She should have been pushing him out of that apartment with both hands out of love, not trying to keep him locked away out of fear. If she found a friend or two, maybe she'd have the courage to let him go. If she managed to do that, maybe she could be the sister Barrett deserved.

It was decided, then. She'd do everything she could to slough off her current image.

She'd become someone else. For him.

Anything for him.

"Barrett." Her fingers drifted across the threadbare pad of his chair. "You have to promise me, okay? Promise me you won't do it again, no matter what."

He turned away again.

"Barrett, *please!*" She raised her voice again, not caring who heard them through the walls. "I'm trying to make things better for us. I'm trying to make our life different. Don't you want that, for things to be different?"

His body language shifted ever so slightly. His stick-straight stance relaxed just a little, as if bending beneath his own secret yearning for change.

"You just have to trust me," she told him. "Things are going to get better, you'll see. Everything will be all right. I promise. We just need to believe in each other, trust each other. And I still trust *you*, Barrett . . . even after today. I still trust you, but you need to trust *me* too."

That was a tall order for either one of them. They had spent their entire lives being overprotective. To ask for a little leeway was as good as asking to be altogether let go. But there was no way around it. If they continued to clutch at each other so fiercely, they'd choke each other to death. Barrett had already killed Linnie. It was only a matter of time before he wrapped his hands around Nell's throat and squeezed.

"I love you, Barrett," she said softly. "And I'll never leave you. Never, for anyone."

That wasn't what he wanted to hear. Leaving was one thing, but there was something more important to him, something bigger.

"And I'll never become like her," she said. "I'll never turn into Mom."

• • • •

When the sun rose on Brooklyn, Nell tied a yellow ribbon into her hair to match the daybreak. The B train squealed down the tracks. Her own image reflected back at her in the scratched-up plexiglass. That bit of graffiti—WHEREVER YOU GO, THERE YOU'LL BE—shot across her line of sight. The train blasted into an underground tunnel, sending the overhead lights into a hyperactive horror-movie flicker before they resumed their cold fluorescent buzz. A black man walked up and down the train car, shaking a metal camping cup in each rider's face. He ignored a businessman's offhanded threat of calling the cops. See? Barrett would have scribbled at her. Everyone's breaking the law. No one's afraid. The man smelled like trash-can sludge. And while Nell would have been quick to ignore his begging, she reminded herself that today was the first day of the rest of her life. Today, things were going to change, and that change would be a direct result of the effort she put in.

Drawing a small crocheted coin purse from her bag, she shook a few loose dimes into the palm of her hand, readying herself for the homeless man's cup. As Nell waited for the man to make his second and final pass of the car, she noticed the woman sitting next to her staring at the coins, as if contemplating stealing them for herself. When their eyes met, the woman—a babushka if there ever was one, a floral-print scarf tied around her white hair—shook her head in disapproval.

"You should not," she said in a heavy Baltic accent. "You give to him and he remember you. He come back again."

Nell frowned at the dimes, not sure what harm it would do to give the guy a break. She'd read a newspaper article about how many homeless men were Vietnam vets, too unskilled or traumatized by what they'd seen overseas to keep a job. That man, no matter how bad he smelled, may have been someone's brother, someone's Barrett. Her gaze drifted back to the man with the cup. She pictured him in army fatigues rather than the tattered clothes he was wearing now. He may have been handsome once, may have clutched a rifle to his chest while sloshing his way through the rice paddies. And before that? He may have lounged in a wingback just like Barrett's, poring over books, dreaming of his first novel hitting the stands. Fame. Fanfare. Now? Poverty. Desperation. The New York City subway a moving, screaming home.

"You do not know what he will do with money you give," the woman murmured beneath her breath. Despite the early hour, Nell could already pick up the faint scent of onions wafting up from the old woman's hands.

The man came closer, his cup clattering above the scream of train wheels on the tracks. *Help me*, the clamor implored.

"Maybe he eat, or maybe will drink, or maybe he buy knife and kill for more money. You don't know, you see? Do not give." The woman placed her gnarled, onion-scented fingers over Nell's hand, hiding the coins from sight as the man limped by. "You do not know," she whispered. "You only know what *you* do."

Nell pulled her hand away from the woman, but her fingers remained closed over the coins that were growing warm in her palm. She imagined the homeless man counting out change in a second-hand store, trying to haggle the price of a butterfly knife. Stress response syndrome could turn the city feral. The knife, held tight in his grasp, would be ready to strike at anything that dared come too close. Or maybe he'd take the money to a diner and buy himself a ham sandwich. Maybe he'd spend it on an ice cream cone—an extravagant luxury in the face of destitution and heat.

The man scuttled past once more. What sounded like a single coin clamored against the tin cup. Not enough for food, for weaponry, for hope.

Nell averted her gaze as he wandered by.

"*Dobra djevojka,*" the woman said. "May God keep you."

Nell considered responding to the woman's blessing, but the kerchiefed lady rose from her seat as the train approached the upcoming station. She hobbled onto the platform, only to look back at Nell before the doors slid shut. Crossing herself, her lips moved soundlessly as Nell squeezed the dimes in her hand. There was a quiet irony to the woman's advice, telling the sister of a man who'd murdered a girl in an alley to count her blessings like saved loose change. And if Nell revealed Barrett's secret? If she had leaned into the old woman ever-so-slightly to whisper into her ear: *My brother is a killer.* What would the woman have done? Would she have sage words of advice for her? Would she have blessed Nell then?

The train came to a shuddering halt at 42nd Street and Bryant Park. Nell rose, the warm coins rolling out of her palm to her feet. The endless rattle of the homeless man's cup stalled. Rather than moving on to the next car, he had taken a seat a few yards away, tired, more than likely hungry. But his hearing was sharp. Somehow, he was able to hear the ping of cupronickel against the floor over the stomping of feet. Over the pneumatic hiss of the doors opening and closing. Over the murmur of morning conversation. He rushed her like a hungry dog, as though he was about to attack. But rather than laying his dirty hands on Nell's clean blouse and office skirt, he skidded onto his knees and began to collect the coins.

Nell stepped off the train. She didn't look back.

· · ·

Savannah Wheeler stepped up to Nell's desk a few minutes before lunch.

"Hey, we were wondering if you'd like to have lunch with us." She looked over her shoulder. Miriam Gould, who stood a few feet behind her, offered up a halfhearted smile. Adriana Esposito didn't bother looking at Nell, clearly over the invitation before it was ever made. Mary Ann Thomas was nowhere to be seen.

Nell stammered, unsure she'd heard correctly. "W-what?" She had been expecting lunch with Savannah—that was why she had tied the ribbon in her hair. Plans of bravery and asking to join her for a bite to eat had circled Nell's thoughts all morning. It was, however, a surprise that Savannah beat her to the punch, extending an invitation rather than Nell having to inquire.

"Well, you're hungry, aren't you? Don't you want to eat?" Savannah shrugged, as if to say the offer wasn't that big of a deal. "We're going across the street to Moe's. They've got great pastrami on rye."

The truth of it was Nell wasn't hungry. She never was—not for breakfast or lunch. But when she had started skipping meals for that very reason, Barrett had immediately noticed. He'd left her a long note taped to her bathroom mirror about the dangers of buying into beauty ideals. He'd dropped words like *anorexia* and *purging* into his decree. Put ideas of emergency rooms and IVs into her head. Reminded her that if she ended up in the hospital, she could lose her job. Their income. Their home. Their entire way of life. Nell put aside her hope of losing a few pounds and ate anyway, despite feeling full. She'd clear off Barrett's empty dinner plate—always left on the kitchen table for her to tend to—and make herself toast and jam. She'd pack a lunch, afraid that Barrett would check the fridge for signs of what she'd taken with her in a brown paper sack, and eat that too. Because throwing out good food was unacceptable. They were on a budget. Bologna sandwiches didn't grow on trees.

Except that Nell *was* carrying extra cash today. Her sandwich was going soggy in her desk cabinet, but she'd deal with the guilt of wasting it for once. She could afford to drop a few bucks on lunch, if only today. But Adriana and Miriam, were they really okay with her tagging along? *That doesn't matter*, she thought. *Savannah invited you, not them. They don't have to come along if they don't want to.* She was set on change, and neither Adriana nor Miriam were going to deter her.

But the booth at Moe's happened to be sticky and far more uncomfortable than she had anticipated. It was as though the person who had sat in it last had slathered the table with pancake syrup and then shrunk the booth down to half its size. It reminded her of the frosting she had yet to completely get out of the kitchen floorboards. Tacky, like tiny octopus tentacles adhering to the bottoms of her bare feet.

Nell tried to read the menu while gingerly holding it between a pair of fingers, turning the thick laminated pages without touching them too much.

"Ugh, disgusting," Adriana complained, turning her own menu over with a set of French manicured nails. "We should have gone to Finnigan's. At least it's sanitary there."

"So," Savannah said, turning her attention away from Adriana's grievances and focusing on Nell instead. "How're you feeling?"

Nell watched Adriana and Miriam's faces for half a tick before settling on Savannah's concerned expression. She nearly jumped the gun and assured Savannah that she was fine, just fine. *Great* really, now that she didn't have to eat her bologna and cheese sandwich in the break room by herself. If only Barrett could see her now. He'd blow a gasket, for sure. And for some reason, picturing him freaking out amused her rather than caused the usual worry. She was in too good a mood to tarnish the afternoon with anxiety. After all, the police hadn't bothered to stop by the office to ask a single question about Linnie. The cops were looking in the wrong direction, and her brother should have been counting his lucky stars; Nell certainly was. Just another reason to shrug off tension and enjoy the moment. But the thought of Linnie made her expression fall. Surely, Mary Ann had voiced her doubts about Nell and Linnie's friendship to these girls. Mary Ann wasn't the type to keep her mouth shut about anything, especially things that weren't any of her damn business.

"Oh." She looked down to the repugnant menu before her. "I'm all right, I guess."

"It's just terrible," Savannah murmured.

"Terrible," Miriam repeated beneath her breath.

"Terrible if you *knew* her," Adriana mumbled.

The more Adriana talked, the more Nell didn't like her.

"But Nell *did* know her," Savannah said. "Right?" She raised an eyebrow at Nell.

Nell nodded.

"See?" Savannah appeared satisfied with Nell's mute reply. "Linnie and Nell were friends. Just because Mary Ann didn't know—"

The waitress cut her off.

"Here we go," she said, sliding their drinks onto the table. "Ready to order?" Nell kept her eyes fixed on a picture of a greasy hamburger and ordered first—a BLT and fries. She was mortified when all three girls ordered health-conscious salads in contrast to her own not-so-healthy choice.

Whale.

She slouched in the booth seat and sipped her Coke, wondering why she ever thought this was a good idea. Did she honestly think she could fit in with girls like these?

Pig.

They were an alien species.

They aren't human.

"Anyway, you shouldn't let Mary Ann get to you," Savannah said. "She's just freaked out like everyone else. The city's gone certifiably bananas with all this crime." She paused, gave Nell a once-over. "Are you really going to bleach your hair?"

Nell blinked up from her glass of soda, not sure what Savannah was talking about.

"Isn't that why you asked Mary Ann about her hair in the break room?"

Oh. Yes. That had been just before Adriana had made Nell spill coffee down the front of her blouse and pants.

The memory of it sent a pang of disdain down her spine. She couldn't help but shoot a glance Adriana's way, but Adriana didn't meet her gaze. She was staring out the window instead, disinterested, as though this particular lunch was the most boring one she'd ever had in her life.

"I don't know," Nell replied. "Probably not. I'd look silly as a blonde."

"But aren't you scared *not* to?" Savannah asked.

Nell shrugged. "Not really."

Mary Ann Thomas had said it best; Nell didn't need to worry. The Son of Sam only went after pretty girls. What was she supposed to be scared of, *Barrett* hurting her? Nell bit the inside of her cheek, stifling a smile.

"Miriam has family in Williamsburg," Savannah said. "They're pretty scared out there."

Nell cast a glance Miriam's way, feigning concern.

"I'm the only one in my family who's smart enough to lop off my hair," Miriam said with a smirk. "You should have heard the fuss my mother made when she saw it." She directed her last comment to Savannah rather than Nell. "My God. You'd think she'd rather me get murdered by some prowling psycho than cut my hair off to save my own skin."

"Well, I'm not letting some psycho freak ruin *my* life," Adriana chimed in, finally shooting Nell a hard look. "Last thing I'm going to do is lock myself up after dark. If I'm gonna end up dead, I want to have a good time first."

Oh, you bet, Nell thought. *The drunker the girl, the easier she is to knock off her feet.*

"The Cabana Club?" Nell asked.

"We go there after work sometimes," Savannah said. "It's a cool place. The bartender is nice."

"Really nice. Good looking too." Miriam grinned to herself. Clearly, she'd fantasized about Mr. Bartender a couple of times. "He gives us half-price drinks when his boss isn't around, and his boss is *never* around."

"You should come," Savannah offered. "I know you didn't want to before, but if you feel up to it . . ."

Nell's heart fluttered inside her chest. So her initial refusal *hadn't* ruined her chances.

"Oh God," Adriana murmured. "Next thing you know, she'll be telling everyone at the office we're all best friends."

That perturbed statement deflated some of Nell's hope.

"Anyway, it's a free country," Adriana said, her eyes fixed on Nell, as though the girl was on the verge of challenging their Plain Jane lunch companion to a duel. "Don't act so flattered."

Nell looked down at her hands. No matter how much she wanted to reach across the table and slam Adriana's face into the plate glass window, Adriana had a point. Nell didn't belong in this group, and she didn't belong at the Cabana Club, especially not in an ugly knee-length office skirt. But she had to try, for Barrett's sake.

Savannah shot Adriana a look. Nell pretended not to notice.

"I'd love to," she said, "but . . . I can't tonight." She had a few folded twenties tucked into her purse. After work, she'd miss her train and go to the shops instead. She'd pick out an appropriate outfit to meet them at the club the next time Savannah went. Maybe she'd be bold enough to chat up that nice bartender, because wouldn't *that* be a shock? Nell Sullivan, going out on the town in nice new clothes, talking to men and scoring a date? But as soon as the waitress slid Nell's BLT and fries in front of her, the voice inside her head reminded her that those ideas were insane.

Look at yourself, it said. *Look at what you're eating. They're just being nice because of Linnie. This has nothing to do with you, Nell. Nothing at all.*

"Well, okay . . . maybe some other time," Savannah said, stabbing at her salad with a fork.

"Probably for the better," Adriana muttered beneath her breath. "Best you have some time to mourn the death of your *friend*, huh? Wouldn't be that great of an idea going out to party right after finding out your pal got chopped up in an alley. I mean, it seems a little crass, don't you think?"

Nell's stomach twisted.

A pang of pain, like a bullet to the brain.

"Jesus, Adri. Cool it," Savannah said.

Maybe it hadn't been Mary Ann after all. Maybe Adriana had been the one who had typed NELL SULLIVAN IS A LIAR onto Nell's transcription. The more she considered the possibility, the more likely it seemed.

Her insides clenched and cramped. She winced, her headache coming on strong.

"Don't listen to her," Savannah muttered, but Adriana wasn't deterred.

Adriana exhaled an aggravated huff, flicked her hair over her shoulder, and fired off a question. "Where's Mary Ann anyway? Why are *we* here and she isn't?"

"Just eat your food, will you?" Miriam asked.

"This is stupid." Adriana dropped her fork onto the table with a clang and slid out of the booth. "This place is a hellhole, and we don't even like her. We didn't even like *Linnie*." Before anyone could ask her where she was going, she turned and stomped out of Moe's. The trio watched Adriana through the window as she marched across the street toward the deli at the corner.

Nell looked away from the window, stared down at her food. Suddenly, all she wanted was to disappear.

This was a mistake. You're fooling yourself. You shouldn't have come.

"Nell." Savannah placed a cool hand on Nell's arm. Nell pulled away, as though the chill it carried was burning hot instead. "She's just annoyed," Savannah said. "She doesn't like competing for attention."

Nell furrowed her eyebrows. "Competing," she said softly, not understanding how Adriana could even begin to think Nell was a worthy contender.

The table went quiet.

The girls ate their salads while Nell picked at her fries, doubt buzzing around her headache like a swarm of gnats around a piece of rotting fruit. Logic nagged her to get up. Reason encouraged her to go back to the office, to forget this whole confounded, impossible plan. *Just eat your sad sandwich by yourself,* she thought. *Choke it down, Moby-Dick.* She scratched at the fabric of her skirt, her right hand drifting closer and closer to her purse as she contemplated a semi-graceful exit. The restaurant was getting hotter, her sweater in sulating her, threatening to boil her brain. She could forget shopping for clothes after work, pay the entire bill, and tell them that she needed to get back to her desk. Linnie's death had put her behind schedule, and Lamont was riding her to catch up. *That*, at least, was true. Nell reached for her bag, deciding that it was the best course of action, but she was derailed by Miriam's quiet compliment.

"I like your bow," she said, nodding to the yellow ribbon Nell had tied into her hair. "You should wear it more often."

Nell stalled, blushed at the praise. She couldn't remember the last time someone had said something so offhandedly kind. Her fingers retreated from her purse just as the voice of doubt retreated to the back of her mind.

No, this was right.

This was what she needed.

This was *good* for her.

Straightening her shoulders, she gave the girls a questioning look. "Do you think Adriana would mind if . . ." She motioned to the untouched salad.

"Please," Savannah said. "Not like she's coming back." With that, she scooted the abandoned plate toward Nell.

Nell smiled in earnest then. She stabbed her fork into the leafy greens and pushed them into her mouth, chewing as she narrowed her eyes at her original order. Because she could do this; she could change her life for the better. Barrett would just have to deal with this the way he had forced her to deal with Linnie's death. Fair was fair, after all.

• • •

Nell stepped off the train later than usual, a plastic Gimbels garment bag draped over her arm and her fingers looped through the handles of a large paper bag. She had thirty-eight dollars left in her purse after eating lunch at Moe's with the girls, and she'd spent nearly all of it among the pretty, glittering racks of clothing that the world-famous department store had to offer. The salesgirl had been helpful. She handed Nell dress after blouse after skirt—things Nell would never have chosen for herself but that looked better than she had expected under the flattering dressing-room lights. She'd even found a pair of cork-bottomed sandals she liked, ones that didn't make her look like a tramp.

Coming off the platform, Nell immediately took notice of the all-too-familiar bicycle gang. At first they didn't look her way, too busy huddled together, the back wheels of their bikes jutting out from behind them. Nell knew there were drugs in the center of that tight cluster. When it came to that sort of thing, Kings Highway was predictable. She tried to sneak by them. The last thing she needed was their attention, especially with her arms loaded down with shopping bags. But it didn't take long for one of the boys to look up, and when he did, he didn't hesitate in pointing her out to the rest of his pals.

"Ey, *es la bibliotecaria.*"

She could hear them despite their distance. Whoever had said it sounded miffed, like she'd been the topic of more than a few conversations since the last time they'd run into each other.

"What do you want to do?" another boy asked.

The inquiry quickened her pulse.

All at once, she imagined them coming at her. Pulling her into the shadow of a building. Tearing up her new clothes and knocking her front teeth in with a brick. She fumbled with the garment bag that was flung over her right arm. Dipped her hand into her purse. Felt around for the switchblade she'd shoved into her bag after the rock-hurling incident. It had been something she'd done in passing, doubting she'd ever need to use it. So she shouldn't have been that surprised when her fingers failed to locate the weapon among the clutter of her things. Her heart shouldn't have somersaulted quite so readily. But it did.

The boys murmured among themselves, probably deciding between aggravated assault or flat-out homicide, when something completely unexpected came tumbling out of Nell's mouth.

"You don't want to do anything," she warned them, loud enough to breach the distance between them and her.

She didn't stop walking.

She didn't look their way.

"I have a gun," she said, "and you can bet your ass I'm not afraid to use it."

There was silence among the boys.

Nell's heartbeat pounded at the base of her throat.

If they called her bluff, she was dead, but they'd have to be crazy to test her. They wouldn't. Not after how she'd pelted their stupid gang leader with rocks. Not after how he'd been humiliated.

One of the boys wasn't convinced. "You don't have no gun." He snorted out his skepticism to the nervous chagrin of his peers.

Nell stopped walking.

All sense and reason screamed for her to not do whatever she was about to do. Don't, Barrett would have scrawled onto his notepad. Keep walking. Don't be an instigator. But if she continued on her way, they'd *know* she was lying, and that was something Barrett had taught her as well. If you were going to con someone, you had to ride it out all the way. If you were going to lie, you had to commit.

She turned her head, gave the group a *try me* look. "I'm pretty sure I do," she said, her tone flat and even. "And I'm pretty sure I have a rock or two with your name on it too . . . before I blow your head off."

A few of the boys grew wide eyes, stunned by her gall. The kid who had claimed she was lying gaped at her for a long while, motionless, as if carefully considering what to say or do next. Finally, he smirked and gave his gang a look.

"Eh, let's go," he said. "*Esta perra es loca.*"

Nell watched them pedal away, fascinated by the fact that they were leaving rather than getting even for the rock attack. It was a revelation. An overwhelming sense of power. The same feeling that had nibbled at the arteries of her heart after she'd told Mary Ann where to shove her presumptuous bullshit. The gang's retreat was a reassurance that, yes, she *was* in charge, that she *could* decide what did and didn't happen in her life. If she could fend off a group of harassing boys, a couple of high-maintenance girls would be a laugh. Nell glanced down to the Gimbels bag in her left hand, as though she had bought a helping of courage off a sales rack along with her new clothes and shoes.

"*Es loca,*" she repeated to herself. She didn't speak Spanish, but she knew enough of it to know that *loca* meant *crazy*. And if they thought she was crazy, all the better. Because you had to be nuts to mess with a lunatic.

· · ·

Nell unlocked the apartment door and Barrett looked up from his book. She gave him a smile, the paper of the large Gimbels bag crunching against the side of her left thigh. "Sorry I'm late." Her good mood beamed out at him. After her lunch with the girls, her mini–shopping spree, and now her success at fending off those idiot boys, she'd never felt better.

Swinging the apartment door closed with her foot, she stepped across the shabby space to the kitchen table and draped the plastic wardrobe bag over the back of a chair. The Gimbels bag went onto the top of the table as carefully as a new mother would have placed a baby in a bassinet. Those two bags, Nell was sure, held the key to her new life, to new friends and new opportunities. She gazed at them thoughtfully, then turned her attention to her brother.

What's all this? Barrett held up his yellow pad from where he sat, curious, but not quite curious enough to rise from his seat.

"I went to Gimbels," she said. "After how my shirt and pants got ruined last week, I figured I was due for a few new things anyway." Kicking off her scuffed penniless loafers, she dug in the bag for the shoebox that held her brand new sandals inside. "See?" She held one of them up by its strap, then took a seat, slipping her feet inside. Cinderella's life had been changed by a pair of shoes. Maybe she'd have similar luck.

"Aren't they cute?" She lifted both feet from the floor, turning her ankles left and then right, admiring her sandals in the dull kitchen light. She stood, pulled a pretty pink blouse from the bag on the table, and held it up against her chest for Barrett to see. "What do you think?"

I think they're fit for a hooker, he scribbled. The shirt too. He remained in his chair, staring at her as though his sister had finally lost her mind.

"Oh, shut up, brother," she murmured. "A hooker would never wear this."

Neither would a fat chick.

Nell blinked at the callous comment he had scrawled across the square of yellow paper. Barrett wasn't one to mince words—each syllable was precious when it had to be written by hand—but he was rarely this cruel.

She swallowed against the sudden lump in her throat. Looked away from the way his mouth had turned down at the corners. She frowned at the floor in return, and delicately folded the blouse into fourths before tucking it back into the bag, where two more shirts remained hidden from view.

"You know, I don't understand why you're upset," she said softly, her back to him, trying to keep her voice steady. "It isn't like I spent a million dollars, and it's not as though *you* never stay out late now and again." She paused in contemplation, her eyes fixed upon the interior of the Gimbels bag. "Sometimes I wait all night for you to come back from wherever you run off to. Sometimes it seems like you don't come back until morning, like you don't give a damn that I'm worried at all."

She listened for movement. If Barrett shifted in his chair, she'd look over her shoulder to read his body language. If he didn't, it meant he had no response, and no response was Barrett's fail-safe. He'd just drop his pad of paper onto the floor and walk away. Meaning: *This conversation is over.*

As kids, she'd been the chatterbox while Barrett had been the silent one, even when he could still talk. Their mother liked the quiet. She constantly complained about Nell's inability to keep her mouth shut the way her brother could. Barrett, on the other hand, was an expert at playing ghost. During the only road trip the Sullivans had taken as a family, both Fay and Leigh had panicked when Barrett had disappeared into the back of the station wagon—odd for them, since they weren't overly cautious parents. He was so quiet for so long, they were convinced they had left him at the gas station fifty miles back, but he'd been in the car the whole time. Sometimes, Nell wondered what it would have been like if they *had* left him, left them both—if she and Barrett had locked themselves in a gas-station bathroom and waited for their parents to drive into the sunset.

"And since you're already mad, I may as well tell you," Nell announced, still not looking his way. "I've decided that if I'm not happy, I should make more of an effort—you know, make the life I want.

So, on occasion, I'm going to start coming home late from now on. And that's on purpose." Her pointer finger drifted along the chrome seam of the table. She didn't want to see the look on his face, so she kept talking instead. "I had lunch with some coworkers this afternoon. Savannah and Miriam. At the diner across the street from the office." Unable to resist any longer, she glanced up at him, crossing her fingers that this time his expression would be one of surrender rather than determined disapproval.

No such luck.

Barrett was sitting stick straight in his seat, clutching his little note pad.

"They're *nice*, Barrett. They're not like Mom at all." Well, maybe *Adriana* was, but Nell didn't like her anyway. She didn't have to be friends with all of them, didn't have to bring up the likes of Adriana and Mary Ann Thomas at all.

"This apartment gets stifling," she said, pleading for him to understand. "Isn't that why you go out, to get away from this shabby old place?"

Nothing.

"Barrett, I wish you would *say* something! Just once, I wish you would at least try!"

She turned away, clamped her teeth tight. For a long while, there was no movement from Barrett's side of the apartment. Then, all at once, he was out of his chair, charging her. Nell blinked at him, wide-eyed. She nearly crawled onto the kitchen table to avoid him. The Gimbels bag tumbled to the floor. Her new blouses spilled onto the hardwood. The wardrobe bag slid off the back of the chair. She lunged for it, trying to save her precious new things. But Barrett was fast. He swept a couple of the blouses up in an angry fist, crushing the fabric in his grip.

"Stop it!"

Nell grabbed for her shirts, afraid that he'd tear them to shreds if it meant keeping her home. He knew better than anyone that she was self-conscious about her looks. That she'd never go out if she didn't have anything to wear. But *this* was too much for him—the new clothes, the fact that she was planning on stepping out with the girls, and regularly at that. It meant hitting a place that served drinks, and if there was ever a fitting symbol for their mother's cruelty, it was a half-empty bottle of booze. Nell was sure Barrett would kill her before he ever let her become a carbon copy of the sloppy drunk who ruined their lives. But she yanked the blouses from his grasp anyway. He let go, and she stumbled backward, crashing into the kitchen wall. A picture frame fell, cracking against the floor.

"Stop it!" she repeated, screaming it this time. "Barrett, just *stop* it! I can't live like this anymore! We're separate people, goddamnit! You can't control me like this!"

He froze where he stood, glared down the length of his nose at her in a silent challenge.

Oh, I can't control you? Watch me.

"No," she whispered, despite him not having said or written a single word. But she could see it in his eyes—the defiance, the objection, the determination to crush Nell's ridiculous whims beneath the sole of his sneaker. He was done fighting with her. It was high time he ended the whole thing with a win. Barrett turned away from her and marched out of the kitchen with his fingers balled into fists.

Nell found herself alone, clutching her new shirts in clenched hands that matched her brother's. Tears stung her eyes, ran hot down her cheeks. She let her fingers unfurl as she tried to steady her breathing. Maybe he was right. Maybe going out with the girls would turn her into something insufferable, something that she was never meant to be. Perhaps the whole idea of making friends to save herself from the pain of losing Barrett would circle in on itself. Maybe it would make Barrett leave instead. But she couldn't go on like this for much longer. If she didn't try, if Barrett took off and Nell found herself alone, what then?

It seemed as though there was no answer. Every solution she came up with was wrong.

"Oh God." She whimpered the words into the silence of the apartment. "Barrett, I'm sorry!" But Barrett didn't answer, and he didn't bother resurfacing from his room.

She tossed her wrinkled shirts onto the table and approached his door, but he wasn't there. She turned her attention to his window, the sill dotted with a couple of houseplants. He'd gone down the fire escape, his usual way of exiting the apartment. Nell rushed across the room, shoved the pane open and jutted her head out the window. "Barrett!" she yelled down to the street below, but he was long gone. All she saw was a tall, Latin woman being harassed by a couple of guys. They looked up at her with raised eyebrows, pausing their argument. "Where did he go?" she asked them. Maybe they would at least point her in the right direction. If she hurried, she could catch up to him before the city swallowed him whole. But all they did was give her blank stares before going back to their caterwauling. The Latina took the opportunity to lift her arm and smack one of the men with her giant purse.

The tears came again. Nell shoved the window closed and left Barrett's room, plucked her new things off the table, and made her way into her bedroom. But as she gathered a few hangers out of the closet, a sob hitched in her throat. One of her old shirts was crumpled in the corner, lying next to a pair of her ratty old loafers—ones that were far too old to wear to work. The stupid thing must have slid onto the floor, the filmy satin never wanting to stay in place on the thin wire hanger. She kneeled down, caught the shirt between her fingers, and swept it off the ground, only to drop it with a gasp. Taking a step back, her gaze fixed on what looked like rust-colored polka dots tarnishing the otherwise cream-colored fabric. Nell was naive, but she immediately knew what those spots were.

He was getting back at her. Those spots, they were Linnie's—

No. Don't even think it!

She pushed the shirt toward the back of the closet with her foot, turned to face the new clothes she had placed on the bed, and froze. She couldn't just leave that shirt on the floor, not without running the risk that someone would find it and put two and two together. Turning back to the closet, she started to cry again.

"Everything will be okay," she told herself as she gathered up her ruined blouse. "You can do this. You're in charge." Except, was she? "Yes, you are," she sobbed, pressing the heels of her hands into the sockets of her eyes. Reaching the kitchen, she shoved the soiled shirt into the almost-full trash can, pushed it deep into the garbage and tied the bag tight.

"He said so," she whimpered to herself as she stalked across the house to Barrett's room. "*He said so*," she murmured. She shoved the window open. Stepped out onto the fire escape. Let the bag drop from her hands to the Dumpster three stories below.

"The revolution has come."

It's what the boy in the street had yelled at her when she had asserted herself against those bike-riding bullies.

The revolution had come.

The revolution was her, and Barrett would have to deal with it, whether he liked it or not.

. . .

But, as usual, it was hard for Nell to disregard her brother's angry response. She tried to read but couldn't concentrate. She tried to eat but wasn't hungry. She folded down the sheets and prepared herself for bed. But once she lay down, she found herself staring up at the ceiling, wide awake, her head pounding like a bass drum without a beat. Eventually, she rolled out of bed, showered, put on her new skirt and sandals and one of the blouses she had bought, after ironing out the wrinkles Barrett had put in the fabric. She tied a fresh ribbon in her hair and left the apartment instead. Because if Barrett was going to go out, headache be damned, so was she. He couldn't keep bossing her around like this. She had to show him that she meant to do what she said. He couldn't keep disregarding her, couldn't keep treating her like she didn't matter.

The train she boarded was more abandoned than any that she'd ever been on. But the graffiti that flashed across the plexiglass was ever-present, lit up by the city's glow just enough to read.

WHEREVER YOU GO, THERE YOU'LL BE.

There and gone in less than a second.

Nell tucked her purse beneath her arm and got off at her usual morning stop. She walked past the office, paused her steps when she finally stood in the bright-red neon of the Cabana Club. The girls were probably long gone, but something about visiting a place they might have been felt cathartic. An ushering in of the change Nell was determined to make. A preview of things sure to come.

She stepped inside. Parliament's "Give Up the Funk" played loud enough to rattle her teeth, but the noise was good. She was tired of thinking. Always thinking. So incessantly thinking that she was about ready to crawl right out of her skull.

Taking a seat at the bar, she wondered if the bobbing and weaving guy who was drying glasses with a towel was the bartender Miriam daydreamed about. He was tall, slender, had an unmistakable John Travolta/Vinnie Barbarino look. When Nell caught his attention, his mouth bloomed into a smile that made her heart wriggle like a worm. He shimmied over to her, leaned in, and, as politely as a guy could, yelled right in her face.

"What's your poison?"

"What?" Nell leaned toward him, unable to hear him above the roar of the music.

He motioned for her to come closer, angled himself toward her ear. "What'll you have?"

"You mean, like, a drink?"

"Yeah!" He gave her a perplexed sort of grin. "What do you want?"

Nell leaned back, pondered for a moment, and finally posed a question. "Do you have iced tea?"

"Iced tea?" He peered at her like she was the cutest thing he'd seen in his life, even cuter than Miriam Gould. "Yeah, baby, I've got iced tea. One Long Island coming right up."

Baby.

Nell turned away, made like she was interested in the dance floor while hiding her blush. Parliament faded into KC and the Sunshine Band. A few couples vacated the floor while a handful of fresh faces took their place. Girls in tall shoes and sparkling shift dresses danced with guys in bell-bottoms, mouthing lyrics while KC wailed. *Shake, shake, shake . . .*

"Here you go, baby!"

Baby.

The bartender slid a tall glass across the counter. It was the fanciest iced tea Nell had ever seen, garnished with a slice of lemon, a maraschino cherry, and a little paper umbrella, like something you'd get on a tropical island. Nell smiled and slid a dollar bill his way.

"Two bucks!" he yelled, holding up his fingers in a peace sign, just like how Barrett did when she left for work. *Later, dude.*

Two bucks? Is that what a drink costs these days? She gave him an incredulous look. She could buy an entire dinner for two bucks. But she'd already ordered the stupid thing, so she pulled another dollar from her purse and forced a good-natured smile. And here she thought he was supposed to be giving these things out at half price. She supposed those were the perks of looking like Mary Ann Thomas. When you rivaled the likes of Farrah Fawcett, the drinks were practically free.

Shake, shake, shake . . .

Over and over.

Shake, shake, shake!

Nell wrapped her hands around her drink and turned back to the dance floor. *Baby.* She snorted, took a sip of the concoction that had cost her an arm and a leg, and just about choked on the taste. It was ghastly, like something only a person without a working set of taste buds could guzzle down.

"You like it?" The inquiry came from behind her. She twisted in her seat to catch Vinnie Barbarino grinning her way. Was he smiling like that because he was playing a joke on her? Did he mess up her drink on purpose? No. He was waiting for an answer.

"Yeah, sure!" She took another sip to convince him, trying her damnedest to keep a straight face. The barkeep gave her a thumbs-up and danced away, lending his attention to a guy who looked about Nell's age on the opposite end of the bar. This guy had a friendly face, a head of messy black hair. He was on the heavyset side—not fat, just rounded out, as though his mother had fed her baby boy well. Nell liked that. It made her feel less awkward, less out of place—the heavyset girl at a nightclub full of flashy, beautiful people.

When the guy turned his attention from the bar to Nell, she started and looked down at her drink.

Oh God.

Staring at the bright-red cherry that rode like a castaway on top of an ice float, she began to panic when she sensed him scooting down the bar toward her. Desperate for something to do, she took a gulp of her awful drink. He sidled up to her despite her obvious nerves, and Nell was left with no choice but to glance his way.

"Hi," he said as soon as she cast him a look. "How's it going?"

"What?" Maybe if she pretended she couldn't hear him above the music, he'd give up and go away.

"How's it going?" he boomed. "You here alone?"

Nell managed a smile and bobbed her head, continuing to play the deaf card. The guy wasn't dissuaded. He lifted his own drink—a bottle of Old Milwaukee—and took a swig.

"Dave," he yelled.

"Hi," she finally yelled back. No use looking more stupid than she already did.

"You got a name?" he asked.

"Huh?"

"Name!" He screamed it. "What's your name?"

"Nell," she told him, immediately regretting her honesty. She should have made something up. Should have said her name was Linnie or Savannah or Mary Ann, if not to keep her anonymity, then to at least have a more interesting name than the one she'd been born with.

Nell, plain from day one.

"You from around here?" he asked. Nell shook her head, her eyes fixed on the giant lapels of his yellow-and-green paisley-print shirt. "Where you from?"

She faltered at his persistence. "Uh, Queens!"

Dave looked intrigued by her answer, as though he had a particular interest in the borough. Then again, that was where someone had shot those two kids the other day. It was where the cops had found Linnie Carter, where the panic had risen to a fever pitch. Lots of people were interested in Queens these days. It was a horror show out there. A real bloodbath.

"You wanna get out of here?"

Nell blinked. Was he . . . ?

"To talk!" he yelled over the music. "Just to talk."

Yeah, right, Nell thought, but was flattered despite herself. Nobody had propositioned her before. The idea of accepting Dave's invitation sent a thrill spinning through her like a Catherine wheel. She looked down at her drink; she hated it, so why not give this guy a shot? Maybe he really *did* want to talk, or maybe he wanted more, and would that have been so bad? Sitting in his car in the dark. His hands sliding down her thighs. Her, pushed against the interior of his car door. Him pressing his mouth against her neck. His fingers grazing the elastic of her panties. Ducking beneath the fabric. Pushing her legs apart as he murmured hot against her ear: *You like that? You like that, huh, baby?*

A tremor shot through her hands. She pushed her iced tea onto the bar, afraid that if she didn't put it down, she'd end up spilling it all over her new clothes. A flash of a memory lit up the back of her eyelids. A slit of light beneath the closet door. Her mother's heavy breathing. The rhythmic banging of something against a wall. Nell and Barrett sitting in the dark, their hands pressed over their ears as they huddled together, holding their pee. A man's voice asking: *You like that? You filthy girl.*

That's what he had called their mother.

You little slut.

And she had liked it.

Yes, she had gasped. *I'm dirty. A filthy little slut.*

"I can't," Nell told him, cutting the memory off. "Sorry, I just . . ."

"Oh, come on," Dave urged, but he wasn't smiling anymore. His round face took on a distinct look of impatience. Her own expression must have shifted to something akin to alarm, because as soon as he looked at her again, his agitation scurried back into its hole. "What're you gonna do, go back to Queens on your own? That's dangerous, ain't it? I've got a car. Let me at least drive you."

"I'm waiting for a friend," she insisted. He needed to leave her alone.

"What?" Dave leaned in closer, holding a hand up to his ear.

He had to give up. Give her space.

"A friend," she yelled, but Dave had suddenly gone deaf.

His hand landed on Nell's arm as if to pull her away from the bar. Her pulse thumped up into her throat, keeping time to the music. She jerked her arm away.

"Hey, why don't you scram?" she yelled, unnerved by his persistence. "Go find some other girl to drive back to Queens."

Dave blinked at her like she'd just thrown dirt in his eye. His face shifted from stunned to incensed within a span of a second. And as Nell sat there watching him, she was sure he'd happily slash her throat the same way Barrett had cut Linnie's.

Dave took a step back, grabbed his beer, and turned away, but before Nell could breathe a sigh of relief he spun back around and hissed into her face. "Stupid bitch!"

Flecks of saliva spattered across her cheek.

She winced.

Her elbow jerked sideways, nudging her glass of disgusting iced tea along the sticky surface of the bar. When he finally turned away for good, Nell closed her eyes and tried to steady the rhythm of her heart.

If Barrett wants to kill somebody, he should kill that guy, she thought. *Garrote him with a piano wire. Ram that beer can down his throat.*

She waited for Dave to leave the Cabana Club, then stalled an extra ten minutes to make sure he wasn't lingering outside to ambush her. He seemed like the type of guy to pull something like that. But the longer she waited the more disgusted she became with herself. The thumping bass of the music had thumped its way right into her skull, vibrating her brain, reawakening her migraine. Her stomach churned around the alcohol she'd drunk for no reason other than to busy herself at a bar she should never have visited. And the recollection of how she'd pictured herself and Dave getting hot and heavy in his car made her skin crawl. Booze and strange men and impure thoughts and hanging out in bars on a weekday—the realization snapped inside her like a rubber band.

Barrett was right.

His outrage was sound.

He was worried that she'd turn into their mother, and here she was, dressed in a way she'd never dressed before. Drinking some horrible-tasting drink. Smiling and bobbing her head despite having a miserable time. Fantasizing about random strangers off the street.

She bounded off the stool, ready to march for the door and catch the next train home. But her legs went wobbly beneath her. She had to catch herself against the bar. That was when—involuntarily plopping back down onto her stool—her gaze fixed on the door she wanted to walk through so she could go home. There were Mary Ann Thomas and Adriana Esposito, stepping in from off the street, cool as a pair of cucumbers.

At first Nell was sure she was imagining them. The pair was a figment of her imagination, her deepest desire brought on by too much booze. They couldn't possibly be there, except that there was no reason for them not to be. Savannah had said the Cabana Club was their spot. Why *wouldn't* Mary Ann and Adriana be there? The club was in full swing.

Mary Ann and Adriana made no effort to approach the bar or put down their purses. They immediately shimmied onto the dance floor, falling into step with the other patrons as the Bay City Rollers spelled out S-A-T-U-R-D-A-Y.

Nell twisted away from the dance floor, mortified. If they spotted her . . .

Oh dear Lord.

Forcing herself onto her unsteady feet, she wobbled down the length of the bar toward the booths at the back of the club.

"Hey!" Vinnie Barbarino yelled after her. "Hey, baby, everything all right?"

She ignored him.

The back booths were hardly visible from the dance floor through all the cigarette smoke. They wouldn't see her there. They'd dance the night away and leave, and that's when Nell would make her exit. She'd be stuck at the Cabana Club until last call at the bar, but it wasn't like Barrett was home.

But just as the thought of her brother being out there somewhere settled heavy in her head, her attention was drawn to one of the dimly lit back booths. There was a man sitting alone in one of them, his face obscured by the shadows of the club, but she knew. She *knew*.

Here she was, worried about that weird Dave guy possibly waiting outside for her, but she'd been followed all along. Her own flesh and blood had ambushed her instead.

• • •

Nell couldn't remember how she got home. When she woke in the morning, her head was still throbbing. She was exhausted, hardly able to peel her eyes open. And as she peered at her alarm clock through sleep-blurry eyes, she figured herself lucky to have gotten home at all. At least she still had time to grab a shower before catching her train into Manhattan. If she hurried, she could stop by the coffee shop across from the station and buy a much-needed cup of joe. Otherwise, she was quite sure she'd end up falling asleep at her desk.

But all thoughts of preparation and commute were lost when her feet hit the planks of the floor. Even exhaustion dissipated into little more than fleeting fatigue. Because there, littering the hardwood of her bedroom, were her new blouse and skirt—the ones she'd worn to the Cabana Club. Despite her half-drunken state the evening before, she was sure she'd hung up her outfit in the closet after she'd come home. No, she was *certain*, because she remembered looking at the blouse's label. She recalled groaning when she discovered that, even though the thing smelled like cigarettes, she couldn't just throw it in the wash with her other things on laundry day. *Dry clean only.* She'd have to walk the eight blocks it took to get to the nearest cleaner and cough up fifty cents to get it laundered. So she had hung the thing up rather than dropping it on the hamper, hoping that the scent of nicotine would dissipate if it stayed in the closet for long enough. Hoping that she'd be able to wear it at least once more before trudging clear across the neighborhood to get it cleaned.

Except that now that option was out the window. Her blouse was crumpled on the floor, rust-colored handprints rendering it little more than a rag.

Nell covered her mouth and backed away from the clothes as though they were alive; as though, if disturbed, they'd tell her the story of the previous night.

"Barrett?"

She tried to yell his name, but it came out of her throat as a quiet squeak. She hadn't spoken to him at the club, hadn't dared look at him directly. She wasn't even sure it had really been *him* occupying one of those back booths.

Maybe her eyes had been playing tricks on her.

Maybe she'd just been paranoid.

But now she was sure. Yes, it *had* been him. He had watched her order a drink. He had seen the exchange between her and that creepy Dave guy. He had sat there for hours, watching it all play out the way he had predicted, his anger coming to a boil, building up until he had no choice but to release it onto the world. And after whatever he may have done—*What had he done?*—he'd come back home, pulled down Nell's new clothes, and wiped his hands on them to teach her a lesson. The clothes. The alcohol. The impure thoughts.

Nell reeled around, half expecting to see her brother standing in her open bedroom door with a smirk playing on his lips. The threshold remained empty, but there was a torn piece of yellow paper on top of her dresser. It was propped up against Beary's stomach, placed to make it appear as though Nell's beloved stuffed bear was the one delivering the message.

You're turning into her.

Bloody fingerprints obscured half of the first word, but his message was clear.

She backed away from the stuffed animal, horrified by the way it stared at her with its little glass eyes. She stumbled out of the bedroom, her eyes darting to Barrett's empty chair. The kitchen was deserted. He'd come and gone, and maybe this time for good.

And it was *her* fault.

Whatever he had done, *she* had driven him to it. And was it any wonder? Around every turn, Nell was sending mixed signals. She hated his possessiveness but was terrified to lose him. She wanted it to be him and her forever, all while buying fancy clothes and threatening to go out with girls he couldn't stand the thought of. She had pushed him too far. Dared him to exert his authority. She had made him snap, challenging him at every turn, ignoring his wishes, promising him that everything would be fine. But things were irreparably broken. How could she look at him the same way again? And how could he ever forgive her for turning him into a monster when he was trying to keep her from becoming one herself?

Nell sank to the floor and pressed her hands to her face, crying into the silence of that sad and crooked apartment.

"Oh *God!*" She scream-wept the words loud enough for the neighbors to hear, silencing herself by pressing a hand over her mouth.

Be quiet, her mother hissed inside her head.

Act normal.

Go get ready.

Don't be late for work.

• • • •

Déjà vu.

The elevator dinged. The doors yawned open. The call center was deserted, save for the area in front of the break-room door. But this time the huddle of girls was louder, more panicked. Lamont was in its center. "Girls, *girls!*" Her tone was frazzled amid their squawking.

Nell stopped dead at the sight. Maybe it was because she hadn't completely shaken off her fatigue from the night before, but not once had she considered Barrett's second victim was someone she may have known. And as she stood there, she couldn't figure out *why* she hadn't considered such a thing. It seemed so simple. So obvious. So appropriate. So like Barrett to bring Nell's punishment full circle. He was a poet, after all.

Nell's hands shook despite their desperate clasp on her purse. She slowly walked toward the group, her eyes wide, her mind reeling. Would he have dared the risk? This was twice in one week. It was hard to imagine that such tragedy could hit the same group of people a second time; hard to chalk it up to nothing more than a dark coincidence. The police would certainly look for him now. If they weren't at the office already, they were undoubtedly on their way.

Nell didn't stop the way she had on Monday morning, didn't dare linger or draw attention to herself in any way. She drifted to her desk, took a seat, and watched the girls from a safe distance. Her bottom lip quivered. A scream threatened to claw its way up her throat. *What have you done?* she thought to herself. *You goddamn idiot, what the hell have you done?*

"I can't . . ." It was the voice of a passing girl. "This is just . . . it's too much. It's *too much*!"

"It isn't safe," murmured another. "Whoever this is, this *freak* . . . he knows someone who works here. How can he not? It's obvious." This was, in everyone's eyes, an attack on the Rambert & Bertram girls—in everyone's eyes, especially Nell's.

"They should send us home," said a third to a fourth. "Whether they do or not, I'm leaving."

"I'm not staying either," said a fifth while passing Nell's desk, wiping at her eyes with a tissue. "I'm packing up. This job isn't worth my life."

"Better safe than sorry," said another. "I'm staying long enough to type up my resignation, and then I'm gone."

Nell tucked her hair behind her ears and gaped at her typewriter, her panic blooming into a thorn of guilt, that thorn scratching into the soft tissue of her heart. Barrett was an idiot. He'd lost his goddamn mind. But he'd done everything to protect her, but what he'd succeeded in doing was disturbing dozens of lives.

"Well, I'm waiting for the cops." Another voice. "Anything I can do to help them catch this piece of shit, I'll do it."

Nell squinted at the keys of her machine, trying her damnedest not to cry. That momentary flash of guilt was gone, panic winning out once more. Because the police, *the police* . . .

She looked to the dispersing huddle of girls. Harriet Lamont was waving them off, looking beyond frazzled. "They're on their way," she told them over and over again. "They'll be here any minute. Just sit tight. We're safe if we stick together. Everyone just sit down!" Nobody was listening. Hysteria kept them from hearing anything beyond their own terrified chattering. Their lives were in danger. The Son of Sam had stepped out of the morning headlines and materialized in the middle of their place of work.

They buzzed around the call-center floor while Nell sat frozen at her desk. What, exactly, had happened last night, and to whom? Whose blood was all over the clothes she had shoved into a trash bag and dropped into the Dumpster below Barrett's window? What if the police showed up and dug through the trash? What if one of the homeless bums had discovered them and reported their find? What if the cops were already at the apartment? What if Barrett had run . . . had run and they had drawn their guns, drawn and shot, shot and hit him, hit him and killed . . . *killed* . . .

She pressed her hand tight over her mouth, holding back a cry, but it tore free from her throat when a hand grazed her shoulder. Nell jumped, exhaled a strained yelp. Savannah stood over her, wiping her nose on a tissue.

"Oh God, Nell . . ." Her voice was strained with emotion. "What are we going to do?" Nell mutely shook her head. She had no idea what they were going to do; all she knew was that she had to get home. Savannah tipped her eyes up to the ceiling. She was trying not to cry, though it was clear from the puffiness of her face that she'd done plenty of crying already. "I just can't believe it. Adriana . . ."

Adriana.

That little slut had come into the Cabana Club just before Nell had meant to leave.

"And Mary Ann."

Nell's lungs deflated, emptying like a punctured balloon.

And Mary Ann? Both of them in one night?

"Oh no . . ." Nell whispered.

"And so far apart from each other. They must have been followed, don't you think?"

Nell said nothing. Numb. Hardly hearing a word.

"They said they were going to the Cabana Club last night." Savannah sniffled, trying to hold it together. "They invited me, but I had to . . . I . . ." Overwhelmed, she pressed the tissue over her mouth and squeezed her eyes shut. Tears streaked down her cheeks. "Oh my God, what's happening to this city? How can anyone keep living here after this?"

How could Nell and Barrett stay in their same apartment? How could Barrett avoid capture after what he'd done? They would find him. The police would question Nell, and they'd see it written all over her face. Maybe they'd see it all over *her*. She had left the apartment in a dazed rush. She hadn't bothered checking for stains on the clothes she'd ripped from their hangers. What if Barrett hadn't only soiled the clothes she'd found on the floor but wiped his hands on *all* her things and she hadn't noticed?

Nell shot up from her seat. She needed to get out of here, go back home. But just as Nell was about to excuse herself so she could check her clothes in the bathroom, Miriam stalled her exit when she appeared next to Savannah. "It's not the city, Vanna, it's this goddamn office. Someone is picking us off." She shot Nell a look, and while she couldn't have known who had committed last night's crimes, Nell felt accused. Because why was Miriam looking so aggravated? Did Miriam know that Nell had been at the Cabana Club too? What if Mary Ann had spotted her and called Miriam from the pay phone outside?

Guess who's here. Sweaty old Nell is cozying up to your bartender. Uh-huh. He's about to set sail on the U.S.S. Sullivan.

"Whether you stay or go is up to you," Miriam told Savannah. "But I'm cutting out of here, packing a bag, and driving up to my folks' place in Montauk until they catch this goddamn loon."

Savannah dabbed at her eyes with a nod.

"Come with me," Miriam insisted. "We'll take the train to your place first, then go to mine and take my pop's car. There's no splitting up. You'd have to be crazy . . ."

"But the police . . ." Savannah blubbered.

"We'll stay for the police," Miriam said. "Lamont's bound to have a fucking heart attack if we don't. But then we're out of here."

"We'll get fired," Savannah concluded.

"Jesus, *good*!" Miriam scoffed.

Nell's focus drifted from Savannah to Miriam and back again, waiting for an invitation to join them. She was their friend now, after all. They had invited her to lunch, to happy hour. Miriam had complimented her on her hair ribbon, and Savannah had come up to Nell's desk just now, searching for solace. Certainly they'd be concerned for *her* safety too. It was just as dangerous for Nell as it was for anyone else.

But Nell couldn't go to Montauk. She had to make sure Barrett was okay, that the police hadn't found him. He needed to know that she wasn't mad at him. She wouldn't leave him. No. Despite what he'd done, she never would. Maybe she could talk him into an impromptu vacation. Just a few days down the coast, until the cops tossed these murders into the pile with all the others. Most crimes that happened in the city never got solved, right? With four to five murders per day, it was easy for the police to throw their hands up in surrender, and for the most part, it seemed like that's just what they did. A few days away would do the trick, it *had* to, but she had to get to Barrett first.

"I have to do something before I leave town," Nell told them, an excuse at the ready. "But I can—"

"Come on, Vanna," Miriam cut her off, pulling Savannah away from Nell's desk by her elbow. "We'll see you later."

"If I don't see you before you leave, be safe, Nell," Savannah pleaded, her voice still warbling with unshed tears.

Nell opened her mouth to say something, but she was struck dumb as they both turned away. Miriam's arm was around Savannah's shoulders. Savannah slunk along like a petulant child. *Be safe.* Was that all Nell was worth, some halfhearted warning? Some fleeting hope that she wouldn't be the next one to get chopped up in a Brooklyn alley?

She swallowed the saliva that had gone bitter in her mouth.

And someone had had the audacity to call *her* a liar?

The memory of that statement, typed up on her transcription, gave her an emotional zing somewhere between sadness and rage. Savannah and Miriam were supposed to be different. She had convinced herself that they actually cared. But no. They were fake, just like the rest of them.

Like Adriana.

Like Mary Ann.

Frauds, just like Linnie Carter.

Nell looked down at her hands, which were balled into tight fists. She stared at the keys of the typewriter, her eyes fixed upon the H—H for hurt. For hate. For hopelessness. *H* for Harriet Lamont, the woman who had claimed to be like her. Who had told her to change what she didn't like. Who had told her to step out of her comfort zone and make some friends; if Nell just did that, things would be better. Well, Nell had taken that advice, she'd *tried* to make friends, and now everything was ruined, all because Harriet Lamont thought she and Nell were somehow alike.

Cunt.

That rageful voice slithered through her mind.

Stupid know-it-all bitch.

Why was Nell blaming herself for everything that had happened? She was a gutless nobody, a little brown mouse who would *never* have done the things she had done if it hadn't been for her boss putting crazy, impossible ideas in her head.

This was all Harriet Lamont's doing.

She was the one to blame, telling Nell that she had to change her life for the better.

Nell couldn't sit still a minute longer. She let her fingers unfurl just shy of her typewriter before rising from her chair. She pivoted on the soles of her new sandals—shoes that she had considered cute less than a day before but that now made her feel stupid and out of place. With her head pounding to the rhythm of her heart, she caught sight of Lamont out of the corner of her eye. The boss looked about ready to tear out her hair as the phones rang off the hook, not a single call being answered. She waved her hands at the occasional girl. *Sit down, sit down, be calm.* Nobody wanted to be calm. The whirlwind of panic made it the perfect time to duck into the elevator and get back to the apartment. That steel box would sweep her down to street level without a single person noticing. It would unleash her on the world, let her get back to what was important: her brother.

She gathered herself up, pulled her sweater tight across her chest, and walked to the elevator. Jabbing her finger against the down button, she closed her eyes, steadied her breathing. But rather than being washed over with calm, the memory of Lamont dragging her into her office blazed bright against her eyelids. She would tell the police about Linnie Carter, about Nell's lie. Like a wolf hunting the weakest sheep, Harriet Lamont had singled her out before, and she'd do it again.

Lamont was the worst one of all.

Nell shot a look over her shoulder, her fingernails biting into the meat of her palms. There wasn't a single girl within a hundred feet of her. Lamont's door was less than a few steps away. She bit her bottom lip, cast another look about, and ducked into the office with Lamont's name stenciled in gold upon the door. She had to make things right with Barrett, and she knew exactly how to do it.

Less than a minute later, Nell snuck out of the boss's office in time to see a pair of detectives step out of the elevator.

"Nell?" Harriet Lamont gave Nell a curious glance as she rushed to meet the police. Why was Nell standing outside of her office door?

Nell swallowed hard and nodded. "Ms. Lamont, I have some information about Adriana and Mary Ann . . . ," she said. Nell would be the first to grant those detectives an interview, the first to give them a lead. The girls had invited her to the Cabana Club, after all, an invitation Nell had passed on because she had some shopping to do. They had warned her about that creepy guy Dave, the one who frequented the bar. Dave was the guy the police needed to focus on. Maybe he was the guy who had killed Linnie Carter too.

. . .

Nell sat on the edge of Barrett's wingback chair, waiting for him to return home. Her attention was fixed on her favorite childhood photo of the both of them. It had been taken in the summer of '58, only a few weeks before Barrett stopped talking. And while Nell adored the photo of them standing together with their arms draped across each other's shoulders, Beary clutched to her chest, it never failed to bring up bitter memories of their father's funeral. Of the way their grandmother had whispered that she was going to take her away.

Their mother hadn't seemed the least bit sad about their father's death until they arrived at the cemetery. She had hissed at them in the car, craning her neck to glare at them from the front seat. "You keep your big mouths shut," she had warned. "And don't talk to any of those people. You hear me?" She spit the word *people* out like it was tainted with something foul. As though their father's family wasn't good enough for her. As though they had never been good enough and she was relieved that she'd never have to see their faces again. "They never liked us, and they aren't going to start doing that now that your father is gone."

Stone-faced, Faye Sullivan stepped out of Leigh's old car. She pulled the door open for Nell and Barrett and turned toward a small black-clad group that was already gathered on the cemetery's grass. It was only upon seeing Leigh's family standing together that Faye's emotions came flooding out. Nell and Barrett had been crying together in their room for what felt like weeks, while their mother hadn't shed a tear—not a single one until right then.

Clasping hands, Nell and Barrett decided that adults handled sadness in strange and confusing ways. Perhaps when they grew older, their sadness would come in fitful, manic bursts as well.

Now, thumbing the soft edge of the photo in her hand, Nell realized that, as a grown-up, emotions hit her in a similar way to how they had come over their mother. Faye Sullivan had always been erratic. She was happy one minute, screaming the next, collapsed in a fit of anguished tears moments after that. Nell remembered nights when their mom would weep while their dad held her tight in his arms.

"I don't know what's wrong with me, Leigh!" she'd cried. "It's like I'm two people. It's like I have no control over the things I do!"

That had been back when Faye was still herself. But the longer her emotional highs and lows continued, the less she thought there was something wrong with *her* and the more she was sure the problem lay with everyone else. That's when she started smelling like booze and sleeping until three in the afternoon. Those were the days when Nell and Barrett would listen to the television through paper-thin walls at all hours of the night. Their mom had no regard for the fact that it was bedtime, that they had to get up for school, that the TV was keeping them up.

Those mornings were tough. Sometimes, when Nell dozed off in class, she'd get a ruler across the tops of her hands. Once, when she had fallen asleep, her third-grade math teacher, Mrs. Brannigan, had shoved her awake. The bitch made Nell put on a rubber pig nose and stand on top of a desk like a flamingo for the rest of the hour. Ten minutes before the bell, old No Shenanigans Brannigan had to take a call in the front office. She left the classroom after warning Nell that if she moved a muscle, she'd be in even bigger trouble than she already was. As soon as she was gone, Nell's classmates pelted her with spitballs and oinked with glee. *Hey, pig!* Nell moved all her muscles. She ran out of the room sobbing, only to crash chest-first into Brannigan's trunk-like legs. That prompted Brannigan to call Faye Sullivan, complaining about Nell's inability to focus and follow instructions. Brannigan had even revealed her tactics for keeping Nell awake, as if satisfied that she'd humiliated Nell with her unorthodox punishment. But instead of Faye Sullivan raging at the instructor for disgracing her daughter, she had grabbed Nell by the arm and dragged her out to the car. In the parking lot, she slapped her across the face before shoving her into the backseat.

"They all saw up your dress," she yelled on the way home. "You stood there like a dunce while all those boys were looking at your panties. You probably liked it, didn't you? Filthy."

Filthy.

Filthy pig.

Faye's mood swings had been swift and terrifying. Sometimes Nell felt that she was falling into the same pattern as her mother, and that's exactly why Barrett kept her close, why he had done all those terrible things. He was protecting her from what at times seemed like an inevitable destiny. Perhaps Nell had been born to repeat history. To become a carbon copy of the monster that had spit her out wet and naked unto the world. It was no coincidence that Faye was a single letter shy of *fate*.

Nell frowned at the photo, wishing that, by some sort of magic, she and Barrett had remained in that marginally happier time. At least back then she had someone to talk to, someone who would answer back. Barrett had been funny. Every other sentence that came out of his mouth was a joke, something to amuse his kid sister. Even during the hard times, he knew how to make her smile. But Barrett had recently grown into his own kind of monster—one sculpted by anger and a need for vindication. He wanted reprisal, fantasized about squaring accounts with a woman he cared nothing for. His was a blood feud, and if he couldn't have it with their mother, he'd settle on the blood of someone else, even if it cost Nell her sanity.

Barrett appeared in the apartment as silently as always, having climbed up the fire escape just outside his bedroom window. Nell found herself looking into the eyes of her stern and looming brother. Her only friend and confidante. For half a second, she wanted to scream at him, wanted to demand an explanation for Adriana and Mary Ann. She had begged him not to repeat what he'd done to Linnie, had implored him to trust her, to let her make things better for the both of them. He'd purposefully ignored her wishes. She had every right to be enraged. And yet, rather than waiting for a scribbled apology, she murmured "I'm sorry" before he ever reached for that small yellow pad.

She looked down at the photograph balanced on her knee. No explanation was necessary. She knew why he had done it. She knew it was partly her fault.

"I guess I should have seen this coming," she murmured. "I should have talked to you at the club, told you why I was there." She peeked up at him. He appeared unmoved, his arms rigid at his sides. "I saw you. I know you followed me there. I was angry for a minute. I felt betrayed that you'd do that, that you'd tail me like some . . ." Her words trailed off. She didn't want to finish her sentence, didn't want to call it the way she saw it, no matter how true it was.

"Anyway, I talked to the police . . . at the office, I mean. Because Lamont had sent for them and nobody was allowed to leave until they gave a statement. I don't think they'll come here, but we should leave regardless."

Barrett's expression flickered between blank and dissatisfied. Nell wasn't surprised. She had predicted his response.

"But I know that if we leave without you finishing what you started, things will get worse rather than better," she told him. "I know that you have to do this, that this is your way of working through the hurt. But I know how to fix it, Barrett. I know how to make it right for you."

Barrett stood by, waiting for Nell's big reveal. She rose from the chair, moved across the apartment to her purse, and brought out a folded rectangle of pale yellow paper. She unfolded it and narrowed her eyes at the name in the top left-hand corner: HARRIET LAMONT. It was a blank check. They could make it out for a hundred thousand dollars if they wanted. But Nell hadn't stolen it to hack into Lamont's finances. It was for the few lines that followed Lamont's name. There, printed in crisp black ink, was her boss's home address.

"This is what you want," she said, extending her arm for him to take the check from her fingers. "She's the source of all of this, the seed of everything you hate."

Because if Barrett wanted to kill a mother figure, there was no better surrogate than the one who sat behind a shiny oak desk.

• • •

Harriet Lamont lived in a turn-of-the-century colonial on a tree-lined street in Sheepshead Bay. Nell and Barrett took a cab rather than the train to avoid being spotted, the both of them staring out the window like a pair of wide-eyed kids. Nell gave the cabbie an address a few numbers away from Lamont's place to keep him from stopping in front of the house. That, and it would be better he not have Lamont's exact address in his log book. The last thing they needed was to be fingered by some washed-up taxi driver looking for his fifteen minutes of fame.

The cab rolled to a stop a little after nine p.m. Nell paid the driver without so much as a thank-you, then slid out of the backseat behind Barrett. The street was darker than it should have been, a handful of streetlights burnt out overhead. The one across the street from Lamont's house looked as though it was on its last leg, shining a pale yellow circle onto the pavement, not bright enough to illuminate much of anything beyond its sad saffron glow. Barrett motioned for Nell to follow him. Across the street and a couple of houses down from Lamont's place, they took up a hiding spot in the middle of a thicket of pines in someone's front yard.

Lamont's house looked nothing like the one Nell and Barrett had grown up in, but there was something about the pitch of the roof, about the way the interior light filtered through sheer curtains in the front windows that reminded them both of the dark closet they'd spent so much time in as kids. It wasn't their home, but sometimes stand-ins were unavoidable. Sometimes the significance of an act was more important than the person or thing being acted upon.

They had been halfway to Sheepshead Bay when Nell started to understand what she had set in motion. This particular crime wouldn't be another senseless alleyway killing. This victim wouldn't be just another pretty face. Harriet Lamont was a successful businesswoman, an executive working for a prestigious Manhattan firm. Adriana and Mary Ann were already plastered across the front page of the papers, and Linnie didn't go without mention in those articles.

They were calling it a triple homicide, a hit on Rambert & Bertram, a series of murders that had office girls across the city in a panic. Because if a place like R & B could be targeted, that meant every other office was just as vulnerable. But Lamont? Her death would be splashed across the news cycle as inevitably as her blood would fan all over the interior walls of her home. The police would question every R & B girl again, this time far more thoroughly. They'd interview every girl's boyfriend and husband and family member in their frantic search for leads. And Nell wasn't sure if she was quite as good of an actress as she had thought.

And then there was the fact that Nell had somehow been transported to the scene of this future crime. Barrett had become a whirlwind of movement after Nell had handed him Lamont's address and somehow she had ended up in the cab right next to her brother. It may have been that, without handing over Lamont's address, scribbled on a scrap piece of gold paper, Barrett wouldn't have been able to communicate where it was he wanted to go; and that scrawled address would have been evidence.

Or maybe it was because Nell had initiated this chain of events herself—something that, up until now, she had nothing to do with at all. Linnie Carter's death had come as a shock. Mary Ann Thomas and Adriana Esposito had sent her into a panic. But Harriet Lamont's murder was all her idea. If anyone had been surprised by the suggestion, it was Barrett. Though his surprise had quickly melted into a full-on grin.

The Sullivan siblings were going to have themselves a proper family outing. It seemed as though the last time they had gone anywhere together, it had been to bid their dead father farewell.

But now, sitting among the scratchy pine branches with her eyes fixed on Harriet Lamont's lovely whitewashed home, Nell was starting to lose her nerve. Who was she kidding? She wasn't brave like Barrett. She was a spineless office worker who didn't have two friends to rub together. A social outcast who was happy to read the same book over and over in a silent apartment rather than go out to places like the Cabana Club.

She was invisible.

A figment of her own imagination.

Nell Sullivan did not exist.

"Barrett." She whispered his name, but despite her hushed tone, he shot her an angry look.

Shut your yap. He didn't have to write it. She could read his scowl. *Someone might hear you.*

Nell bit her bottom lip and looked down at her hands. "I don't think I can do this. I mean, *you* can do this. You need this. She deserves it . . ." Her whisper tapered off to nothing.

The bitch deserves it, she thought. *Putting me down, making me feel like less of a person.*

Barrett could spend months cutting down every girl in Rambert & Bertram, every alleyway kill increasing his chances of being caught. But if you took down the queen, you destroyed the hive. If Lamont was dead, all those pretty, brainless sheep would realize that even the powerful could be killed. That even leaders were susceptible to destruction. They would learn that their tall shoes and fancy clothes, their pretty faces and perfect hair, didn't count for a damn thing. If someone wanted them dead, they were dead. It was a perfect lesson to jam down their throats, but that didn't mean Nell could stomach watching her boss get killed.

"Maybe you should do it on your own." She whispered the suggestion, breathing it out from the corner of her mouth. "Don't you get it? I'll just screw it up. And we *can't* screw it up. If something goes wrong, she might see us, and then . . ."

And then it would all be over. Done. And Barrett wouldn't be the

only one they carted off to prison. They'd appear side by side on the
news, the bloodthirsty Sullivan siblings. Everyone would gasp.

He was such a quiet boy.

She was such an unremarkable nobody.

Such a mouse.

*Nobody ever suspected that he could . . . that she would . . . that her
brother had . . . oh dear, oh my, oh goodness, oh God.*

But her protest didn't sway Barrett's resolve; it only made him
more determined to have her accompany him inside. They just had
to wait for the front-room lights to snap off. And would it be so
bad? Nell was yearning for excitement, for some sort of change, and
what bigger change could someone make than to become a member
of a murderous duo? They'd be like Bonnie and Clyde, drifting from
city to city, from state to state. She'd pick up an odd job here and
there to make ends meet, while he hunkered down in cheap roadside
motel rooms to write. That, and murder had its financial advantages.
Heck, she had Lamont's check tucked into the pocket of her skirt,
and surely such a fancy dame had cash and jewelry they could pawn.

It would be great.

Exciting.

They'd be inseparable.

Bound by blood.

"Fine," she whispered, "I'll look for things we can sell while you
go after Lamont. You *do* understand that we'll have to leave after
this, right?" She shot him a look, desperate to see acknowledgment in
his eyes. "We can't stay in Brooklyn if we do this, Barrett. We have to
go, make a better life somewhere else, or they'll figure it out."

Barrett stared at her with an expressionless face, and for a moment Nell was afraid that he was going to laugh. Was she acting
crazy? Was she being completely paranoid? Did Barrett think blowing out of New York was a stupid idea?

No. She wasn't nuts. This was all part of the plan, part of what *had* to be done. She hadn't considered it before, but maybe making the life she wanted included getting out of Brooklyn. Getting out of New York. Possibly leaving the entire Eastern Seaboard behind.

But what if Barrett shook his head and refused? What if, despite it all, he told her that she could go if she wanted, but he was staying in Brooklyn because he had found a girl? What if he brought that girl back to their apartment and locked Nell in the closet and made her listen, listen, listen to her own headboard bang against the paper-thin apartment wall, hot tears searing her cheeks, Barrett's name sputtering past her lips in broken whispers as their mother cried out in ecstasy, as their father rotted in his coffin, as her brother fucked a girl, if only to remind Nell that it could never be, would never be, her?

Barrett's hard glare softened. He shook his head at her, as though reading her mind.

They aren't going to figure it out.

No, they wouldn't. Because Barrett knew what he was doing. He didn't make mistakes.

But she had to go inside with him, if not to make sure he was okay, then to prove to him that she loved him more than anyone else. To prove that she was willing to do anything to keep him close. She'd watch him slaughter her supervisor if it made him happy, if it made him whole, if it made them one.

Lamont's front light blinked off.

Both Nell and Barrett turned their attention back to the house, staring at the darkened windows. They would wait another half hour, and within the passing of those thirty minutes, Nell would convince herself that this was no longer a choice. This was something she *needed* to do, if not to prove her love to her brother, then to confirm that she was the opposite of what she'd been raised to believe herself to be.

She wasn't worthless. She was strong.

She wasn't a burden. She was an accomplice.

Barrett sprang from behind the branches of the tree and dashed across the street without so much as a nod of warning. Nell gasped when he broke away from her. Before she knew what she was doing, she was stumbling across the road, trying to catch up to him, if only to avoid being left alone. She dashed around the side of Lamont's house, mimicking his movements. She kept close to the clapboard and ducked beneath the windowsills, just in case someone still lingered in the rooms beyond the glass.

When they reached the back-door steps, Barrett froze, then shot a look over his shoulder at Nell. His expression was incredulous, as though Nell had just sucked in air and screamed, alerting the entire neighborhood to their whereabouts. Nell shook her head, not understanding why he was looking her that way. It was then that her gaze faltered on a pet flap cut into the bottom of the back door. She stammered into the silence, not having even considered the possibility of a dog. And what if Lamont had a husband? What if he had a gun? Nell just about choked on those details, things that hadn't crossed her mind until it was far too late.

But before she could picture Barrett getting mauled by a rabid Doberman or being shot by a man in his pajamas, Barrett rolled his eyes at her stupid mistake and motioned for her to come forward. Sure, there might be a dog, but at least getting in the house would be easy. And yeah, there might be a spouse sleeping inside one of the rooms with a pistol at arm's length, but as soon as Barrett wrestled the gun away, the Sullivans would be more dangerous than ever.

Nell exhaled and crouched in front of the pet door, expecting the flap to stay put, kept in place by an interior plastic locking cover. But the thing gave way as soon as Nell brushed her fingers across it. Lamont had left it unsecured.

Crazy. Barrett's face was easy to read. *You'd think there wasn't a serial killer on the loose.*

Nell nearly bellowed out a laugh, but covered her mouth with her free hand, trying to contain her sudden pang of amusement. She stuck an arm inside the house, shoved her shoulder up against the top of the pet door, and, after a few seconds of fumbling for it, threw the lock.

Barrett edged into the kitchen, not touching a thing. It was Nell who, in passing, pulled a knife from the butcher block on the kitchen counter. She wasn't sure whether Barrett had brought any sort of weapon. Better safe than sorry—that's what their father used to say.

Nell slunk through Lamont's kitchen, searched for a dog's water bowl, for chew toys or a bag of dry food or a pet bed. The pet door was big enough for her to unlock the door without much trouble, meaning the dog was big enough to attack an intruder. But there were no signs of any animal, be it a dog or otherwise. Lamont probably bought the place with the doggie door already installed and never bothered getting it replaced. Again, Nell was struck by the urge to laugh. If that was true, it was a fantastic bit of luck; that bossy hag of a supervisor could just as easily have left the door wide-open for them to come in.

Successful, but stupid, Nell thought. *Probably slept her way to the top.*

Creeping through the living room, Nell allowed her attention to drift over Lamont's various trinkets. There was a crystal table lighter like the one she had in her office. It was perched on top of a few magazines in front of the TV. A smattering of porcelain figurines depicting Rockwellian children and cherubic angels dotted various pieces of furniture. Those reminded Nell of their grandmother's house, though they never did visit much. The walls sported framed still-life paintings. One was of a bowl holding a bushel of red apples, a single green one among the others. *You aren't like the other girls.*

Another was of a vase full of sunflowers. They weren't the kind of paintings you could buy secondhand; more like student work, maybe by a high school–age kid with the fleeting hope of becoming the next da Vinci. Or maybe Picasso, like Linnie Carter's cubist face.

Nell leaned in to read the signature on the apple painting. A pair of initials: LL. The year next to the initials read '73. It was there, beneath the apple painting, that Nell spotted yet another detail she had failed to consider. Poised on top of a side table among a few figurines and a wicker basket full of waxed fruit was a framed photograph. In it, Harriet Lamont hugged two girls who looked strikingly similar to her. One looked about Nell's age, while the other was younger, maybe ten or eleven. *Daughters,* she thought. *Harriet Lamont has daughters.*

Struck by the detail, Nell reeled around, searching for Barrett, and for half a second she wanted to scream. *No, we can't do this. She has a family. We'll find another mother figure, someone else.* But that half second was long enough to let that sliver of perfection embed itself beneath her skin—a festering splinter of unrivaled faultlessness. Because what mother *didn't* have a family?

Only their own.

Nell squeezed her eyes shut against the slow bloom of familiar pain opening up behind her right eye. She clamped her fingers around the hilt of the knife she'd drawn from the butcher block and continued through the darkness of the house. Barrett climbed the stairs ahead of her. They were silent beneath his feet, as though he had somehow become weightless, but they breathed an occasional groan beneath her shoes.

Every time the risers whined, Barrett shot her a wild, wide-eyed look.

Shut up! he screamed without sound.

Quit your crying, Faye Sullivan hissed into her ear. *Or I'll give you something to cry about!*

More art lined the upstairs hall. On one side, mountain scenes and the high-rise buildings of New York City. A stream cutting through a forest of aspens. On the other, a child's renditions of a more human experience. A group of crooked friends holding hands in a crooked circle. A house with puffs of chimney smoke and pink cotton-candy trees behind a white picket fence. A picture of a two-dimensional girl and boy, both seeming as though they should have been closer together, yet they had been drawn unnervingly far apart.

Cry for the rest of your life, Nell. But you do it in your room. I don't want to hear it, you understand me? You're alone, and so what?

She looked away from the drawings, a pang of something indefinable twisting her insides into tight, springlike coils.

There was something wrong with this house.

Something haunted.

Something that was drawing out her own forgotten ghosts.

Her father with blood dribbling down his face.

Her mom with a short-handled baseball bat held fast in her hands.

Her brother sleeping on the couch in his wet bathing suit, not the least bit disturbed by their mother's high-pitched screams or the way she bolted from room to room, in search of something, before grabbing the phone and yelling into the receiver.

Help, please help!

Nell standing silent, motionless on the threshold of the open back door.

Oh God, oh God, oh God, someone help me!

Nell regarded the dark hall, her eyes stopping on the little girl who stood in her open bedroom doorway. She looked like a phantom in her pale pink ruffles. A figment of Nell's imagination? Was this girl a reflection of what she had once been? Young and unspoiled, innocent with untamed hopes. All at once, Nell wanted to rescue her childhood ghost from that house, wanted to save herself from the inevitable fate that awaited her. The girl's blond hair framed a milk-white face, her eyes wide with choking surprise. That pretty face, the brilliant hair, the girlish flounce of her rose-colored sleeper. The sadness that had unspooled within Nell's chest settled into cloying disgust. Because who would she be saving? This girl was already tainted. She was destined to become just like the others. No, this girl was not a figment. She was real.

Harriet Lamont's young daughter stood frozen on the threshold of her open bedroom door, chewing air, ready to scream.

All at once, Barrett came bounding down the hall.

Nell's grip on the kitchen knife increased.

As soon as she felt him rush by her, her migraine bloomed bright enough to render the hallway black. But she could hear the screaming.

Just like her mother. Crying. Shrieking. Wailing as paramedics rushed into their New Jersey home.

Oh God, she had wept. *My baby, my angel.*

Late night had emptied the train car of nearly everyone. Those who rode along in the same space as Nell kept their distance. She felt eyes on her—*they're staring*—but every time she looked up, the riders averted their eyes to read the graffiti scratched onto the windows, scrawled onto the walls: WHEREVER YOU GO, THERE YOU'LL BE.

She was almost back at the Kings Highway station. She just had to keep it together for a few more minutes. Keep it together so that no one would know what Barrett had done.

She had blacked out, sure she hadn't seen a thing. But bits of recollection were coming faster now.

A pink nightgown turning red.

Harriet Lamont's hysterical screams. Barrett embedding the blade of the kitchen knife Nell had pulled from the block into the soft spot just below her boss's throat.

Nell had lost her nerve. She had turned and run.

She had abandoned her brother, too frightened by what was happening. Too terrified to stop and realize that she was doing to him exactly what she'd feared he'd do to her. And now, on a train hurtling back toward King's Highway, she could hardly keep from shrieking at what was playing out within her mind.

Because somewhere back in Sheepshead Bay, Barrett was covered in blood.

Somewhere back there, they would find him, and they'd take him away.

"Oh God." The whisper escaped her throat as she stared down at the photo of the two of them. Somehow, it had made it into her pocket along with Harriet Lamont's blank check. Now, the edges of the black-and-white print were tarnished with sticky rust, smeared with the blood that must have splashed up and onto her hands while Barrett was carving Lamont's little girl a bright new smile.

"Oh God," she whispered again, because there was no coming back from this. This was too much. It would have been safer to travel in the opposite direction of home, to go to Coney Island and figure out what the hell to do next. But there she was, running toward the first place the police would look. And if Barrett didn't come home, if he stayed out because he was upset she'd abandoned him the way she had, there would be no time to run. She'd start packing as soon as she got to the apartment. She'd wait forever, for as long as it took. But Nell knew it was only a matter of time. The cops would find their way there.

She studied the old photograph, did her best to ignore the eyes that were crawling across her skin. The brakes of the B train squealed as it came to a jerking halt. The automatic double doors hissed open. The hollow jingle of a single coin rattling inside a tin cup sounded from the opposite side of the car. One train stop shy of her own, it began its incessant clatter. Nell closed her eyes and tried to block it out. But it got louder; it came closer, underscored by the shuffling of feet.

"Please." The black man murmured around his own sloppy drunkenness.

"Please." It seemed to be the only word he knew, that single syllable as sour as his stink.

"Please."

You give to him and he remember you.

This was the beggar's subway line. She'd given him money once, and now he wanted more.

Maybe he buy knife and kill . . .

The homeless man stopped in front of her. The rattle of his cup came to a curious halt.

Do not give to him.

He watched her for a long moment, as though recognizing her in kind—the receiver regarding the giver. He jingled his cup again, but his action was preoccupied, distracted, a shadow of what it had originally been. He remained fixed on her for a beat longer before he made a sudden move, his free hand catching her by the arm.

"Help," he croaked. "*Help.*"

Nell started at the contact. She tried to pull away from his grimy touch.

"Get away from me," she cried, but his grip was tight.

"Help!" He was insisting now, not willing to take no for an answer. Nell's eyes went wide. She couldn't believe it. Of all nights, she was about to get mugged.

"Stop it!" she yelled. "Let go!"

"Help!" he bellowed back, his breath stinking of booze and rotten teeth.

The people on the opposite side of the train were gaping now, but not a single one of them made a move to offer aid. They looked at one another as if unsure of the scene that was clearly an assault. *Losers!* The word hissed through Nell's head. *Stupid idiot rubbernecking losers! He could kill me and they wouldn't care! It could be Sam and they'd watch him slash me up!*

Nell tried to shove the man away, but he refused to release her arm. His dirty fingers groped at the weave of her sweater sleeve, continuing to croak *help* and *please* like a spastic parrot. Nell struggled against him and eventually managed to reach into her purse. As soon as the homeless man saw her hand disappear, he let go and took a few stumbling backward steps, his hands held up in apology, as though *she'd* been the one who had assaulted *him*.

"Take it!" she yelled, then reeled back and threw loose change in his face. The coins bounced off his filthy clothes and tinged against the metal floor.

The homeless man didn't move. He gaped instead.

The train began to slow. Nell bounded off the plastic subway seat. She shoved her way past him, squeezed through the automatic doors before they were fully open, and ran full-sprint through the station until she was out on the street. Half a block from the station, a few members of the Puerto Rican bicycle gang sat on a curb smoking cigarettes and drinking beer out of cans. Their bikes lay beside them like sleeping horses. One lifted an arm to point her out to his friends. They sat in relative silence as she bolted past them. One of them murmured "*Que carajo?*" as she ran by. She glanced over her shoulder, noticed a couple of them rising, looking after her as though ready to give chase.

Nearly tripping over a crack in the sidewalk, she kept running, and crossed her fingers that, by some unexplained miracle, Barrett would already be at the apartment waiting for her, if not to assure her that he was okay, then to fend off the boys she was sure were following her home.

You should have seen this coming, she thought, pushing herself as hard as she could. *You shouldn't have thrown those rocks. You should have left them alone.*

"Hey, *bibliotecaria*!" one of them yelled from behind her.

They were on their bikes now. She could hear the clicking of their freewheels as they advanced, getting closer.

She just about leapt up the crumbling concrete steps of her building and tore open the door that led into the lobby. There was a man sleeping at the base of the stairwell. She was moving too fast to avoid him. One of her loafers came to a stop against his thinly T-shirted abdomen. "You!" he screamed as she leapt over him. "Look at what you did! Shame on you!" His voice bellowed in the cavernous apartment lobby. "*Shame* on you, girl!"

Reaching the second-story landing, she whipped around the rickety newel post and up the final flight of stairs. She scrambled to find her keys, surprised that she still had her purse after everything that had happened. Half its contents spilled around her feet in her haste. Bills and receipts, a pack of Wrigley's Doublemint, and Barrett's small yellow notepad. *What? Why . . . . ?* But there was no switchblade, even though she was sure she had dropped it into her bag. Sure, at least, that she'd had it the night she had met Dave at the Cabana Club.

"You see a girl come in here?" A Spanish accent.

"Yeah! She kicked me!" The man downstairs.

"Yo, where'd she go, man?" Another voice, another gang member.

"She tried to kill me!" the man insisted. "Put her foot straight into my gut! I got cirrhosis! I'm a dyin' man!"

"*Bibliotecaria!*" a third voice boomed. "Hey, *chica*! We just wanna talk!"

Nell managed to unlock her door with a trembling hand. She stumbled inside the dark apartment, kicking a few of her spilled items inside. She slammed the door behind her, threw all the locks into place. With her back flush against the door, she looked around her dilapidated home for signs of her brother.

Was he here?

Had he returned?

Was he still at Lamont's place?

Someone must have heard Lamont scream. It had only been for a few seconds, but someone *must* have heard it, someone *must* have called the cops.

Nell closed her eyes, the distant wail of a police siren curdling her blood. Above it, a man sang opera out an open window, trying to blot out the underlying harmonies of the Jackson 5 coming from a few doors down.

Her eyes fixed themselves on Barrett's empty chair. He had abandoned his book on the threadbare cushion—the same book, the *only* book he ever read. Beary was sitting in her brother's place, as though waiting for the both of them to return.

Barrett was just like their dad. Leigh Sullivan had read and reread *The Velveteen Rabbit* to them what seemed like a hundred times. They had had an old wingback chair at home too, one that looked remarkably similar to the one Barrett had picked out at the secondhand store. Nell shut her eyes against the memory of his casket glinting in the summer sun. She tried to block out her mother's hysterical weeping. Tried to look elsewhere in the recollection she had played over and over inside her head for so long.

Look away.

She strained to do it, urging her four-year-old self to avert her gaze. To block out their mother's cries—only to spot a difference she hadn't noticed until now. There, in her mind's eye, just beyond her father's casket, was an identical coffin, save for its size. Present-tense Nell and her four-year-old shadow simultaneously gasped. She pushed herself away from the apartment door. Shook her head, not understanding that newly excavated shred of memory.

But it was only Daddy.

It was only him.

She twisted where she stood, letting her attention settle for a second time onto a chair that looked so much like their father's. Her old bear continued to stare at her, its glass eyes blank, soulless, horrible rather than comforting. She grabbed the toy off the chair, her mother's wailing echoing inside her head like a scream in an empty room.

My baby, my angel, my sweet little . . .

"Barrett?" The name slid past her lips in a whisper.

She turned away from his chair, numb.

Because it didn't make sense. Why wasn't he here yet?

Because he's dead.

Bullshit. He was alive. There was no way the cops would have gotten to Lamont's house so fast, no way he would have sat down and waited for them.

Nell stumbled into her room, dazed by the things she was imagining as if they'd really happened. The little casket beside her father's looked real enough in her memory, but that memory was false. A lie. Only one life had been memorialized that day—her father's. *Their* father's. Nell and Barrett had stood hand in hand together as the coffin had been lowered into the ground.

Except it hadn't been his hand.

The suggestion slithered into her brain.

Four-year-old Nell squinted against the glare of the sun while present-day Nell squinted at her own reflection in the full-length mirror that hung on her wall.

It hadn't been his hand—it had been something else.

There was a bang on the door.

"Hello? Miss?" someone yelled through the wood.

Both little Nell and grown-up Nell looked to their right hand. A fuzzy teddy bear hung limp at their side.

Except grown-up Nell's palm was smeared with blood that continued up, up, up her arm to the crook of her elbow, to her biceps, clear across the front of her blouse and down her shirt.

Nell Sullivan gaped at herself in the mirror, Beary at her side, hardly recognizing the woman she saw before her.

Help.

Covered so completely in blood, it was a wonder she'd managed to get home.

Please, you help.

The looks on the subway.

The homeless man repeating *help, help* as though he had needed it instead of trying to offer it to the girl who had aided him by giving him change.

Bang bang! The door.

"Miss? Hello? Are you okay in there?"

It had been Nell all along.

Linnie. Mary Ann. Adriana. Harriet Lamont and her daughter.

Nell's fingers flexed. Beary fell to the floor, soundless like her brother.

"Ma'am? We're going to call the police!"

It had all been her.

That's why her clothes had been scattered along the floor.

How Barrett had known to find her at the Cabana Club that night.

Because he hadn't been there, yet he was *always* there.

Always inside her head.

"But I *saw* him!" The words tumbled out of her in a sudden, incredulous yell. "He was there! It was him! I know it was!"

Suddenly, she was tearing at her clothes. Balling them up and throwing them into the hamper surrounded by scribbled yellow notes, most of them in Barrett's handwriting, some of them in her own. I won't ever leave you. I can't. It's impossible. Impossible. Impossible . . .

Half-naked, she stumbled out of her bedroom and across the rough planks of the living room into the kitchenette. Her fingers fell onto the handle of the biggest knife in the block, the same type of knife that had been used on Harriet Lamont. She drew it out, the metal hissing against wood. Staring at the blade, she choked on her sobs.

If Barrett was dead, she didn't want to live.

If Barrett was dead, it meant she was crazy.

If Barrett was dead, she had to be dead too.

She pointed the blade toward herself, taking the handle in both hands.

"Barrett?" She whispered it into the empty space of their home. "Tell me it isn't true."

When no reply came, she clamped down her teeth and roughly drew the blade across her skin. The flesh of her abdomen parted like a hungry mouth just before she dropped the knife and cried out in pain. It skittered across the floor, slid beneath the stove and out of sight. She screamed as blood gushed from her self-inflicted wound. Her hands pressed against the gaping cut, smearing her own blood over the blood of Harriet Lamont and her dead daughter.

The door rattled on its hinges.

"I saw you," she wept. "You were there."

Someone was kicking at it, trying to force it open. It groaned against each of its three locks.

"You were there!" she cried, curling up on the kitchen floor. "It was you!"

The door flew open with such force that it slammed against the adjacent wall. Nell's tear-warped gaze drifted to a few pairs of dingy high-tops. They gathered around her, their owners chattering in incoherent sentences, yelling at each other, a pair of feet running out of the apartment as quickly as they had come in. But Nell didn't care. She wanted to bleed out. If Barrett wasn't there to save her, she didn't want to be saved at all.

"Hey, girl, don't worry." A Puerto Rican boy with a kind face knelt over her. "I've got you. We're gonna get you some help."

Nell turned her head away.

Not him, not my angel, my love, my baby boy . . .

That's what her mother had screamed.

My baby boy.

It was then that she saw him—not all of him, just his shoulder and shoe.

Barrett was there, standing in Nell's room.

A gasp escaped her throat.

"Was it that guy?" the boy asked.

Nell's eyes jumped to the boy's face, certain that he had spotted Barrett peeking out from behind the bedroom door. But the kid's attention was fixed on her. He was distracted by Nell's wound, not quite deep enough to kill. Barrett was too smart to be seen, too clever to be found.

"Hey, was it him?" the kid asked. "You know, the killer? Was it that psycho Son of Sam? You think it was him that did this to you?"

Nell gave him a blank look, then turned her attention back to the bedroom.

"Yes," she whispered. "It was him."

It was all him. *He* had killed the girls. Had killed Lamont. Had tried to kill her in the end.

Barrett's eyes flashed.

He was grinning.

You should have dyed your hair, he thought.

She could hear him inside her head now. It had worked. Lamont's death had brought them closer together. Closer than ever.

And it took all of Nell's strength not to bellow out a laugh.

Because everything was going to be okay now.

Everything was going to be okay.

I CALL
UPON
THEE

To the ghosts that haunt us.

ONE

WHAT THE HELL was that?!" Dillon bolted upright, his hair a perfect Albert Einstein emulation. She could practically hear his heartbeat thudding straight out of his chest.

Maggie peeked an eye open despite herself. Personally, she wasn't concerned about the oncoming storm. Having grown up on the Georgia coast, she'd lived through dozens of tropical depressions far worse than this. But Dillon was a different story. A Maine transplant, he was unshakeable when it came to blustering nor'easters. But toss him into the path of a potential hurricane, and the man lost his everloving mind.

The sheets were pooled around Dillon's waist, mimicking the way rainwater was inevitably doing so just beyond Maggie's front doorstep. There was a divot in the brick walkway, a perfect spot for a miniature lake to form every time it rained. And it was pouring now—diagonal sheets that pounded against the windows like a madman trying to break in. It streaked silver across the light that filtered in through the bedroom window. There was a gas street lamp not more than a few steps from the door, forever casting the apartment in a warm amber glow.

Dillon—bare-chested and undeniably scrawny—scrambled to

retrieve his glasses from atop a knee-height stack of Maggie's magazines: *Popular Mechanics*, *Popular Science*, and *Discover* among the majority, though half of them had yet to be read. The maelstrom continued to beat against glass, plaster, and wood, determined to rouse them both. But Maggie refused to be rattled. No, she wouldn't move. After all, it was just going to get worse.

A peal of thunder led to a bang against the outside of the building, like God had plucked a giant bird from the sky and tossed it against the exterior wall.

"Maggie!" Her name escaped Dillon in a near squeal. A death grip seized her arm.

Another bang. Perhaps another unfortunate bird. Or Atlas throwing small boulders against the building's bricks.

"Christ, what *is* that?!" Dillon was ready to jump out of his skin. He was the polar opposite of the ultramasculine beefcakes who traipsed around campus—biceps flexed, strutting across the concourse in pastel polo shirts and board shorts—but he was still a guy. Maggie didn't want to bruise his ego. And so, rather than lying there and laughing as her boyfriend squirmed against the rumble of thunder, she rolled toward the edge of the bed.

"Relax," she said, extended an arm, and snapped on the bedside lamp.

"I know you say it's no big deal . . ." He was stammering; he always did this when he was scared. "But it sounds like, like . . ."

Bang.

"Fuck! *What is that?!*"

"Probably a killer." Maggie sat up, her feet hitting the nondescript raglan rug she'd bought at Target when she moved into the place. When she stood, Dillon's expletives were immediately silenced. She could feel his eyes following her across the bedroom, his gaze roving along the curve of her backside as she adjusted her boy-short-style underwear.

"Or maybe just a broken shutter." Turning to the window, she unlatched the pane and opened it wide despite the wind and sideways rain, then yanked the damaged storm shutter inward. She'd complained about that broken latch to the super at least a half dozen times, but the mountain of a Croatian man couldn't have cared less. *You want feex, you feex.* Surely *his* storm shutters at home were fine. If the little American girl got slashed to ribbons by exploding glass thanks to a hurricane, this apartment complex was hot property, especially with those pretty gas lamps and the UNC campus a mere ten minutes away. Her place would be rented out by another student in five seconds flat, probably by one of those pastel 'roided-out dudes with perfect hair and way too many abs. Arms the circumference of her thighs. CrossFit every day after class. Cheat days spent at Momma's table, filling up on barbeque shrimp and stone-ground grits.

"Y-you should get that fixed," Dillon stammered.

She turned away from the window, her rear brushing against the sill, and rolled her neck—a habit born of chronic pain that had abated years before, thank God. During her last semester of high school, she was handed an official diagnosis: fibromyalgia. Pain meds had done little, probably because of the stress at home. It was only after she left Savannah that she'd started feeling normal again.

"Yeah, I should," she said. But Croatia. Apparently, there was some sort of language barrier. *Feex.* Whatever. It wasn't worth the hassle. She let her hand fall from her neck and cast a glance Dillon's way. He was staring, and he *was* scrawny. The first movie they'd watched together was *Particle Fever*, about the origins of matter. He only ever indulged in three shows: *Cosmos*, of which he was currently on his eighth viewing cycle; *Dexter*—sometimes Dillon would do the monotone soliloquy thing, which she found both odd and sexy; and *Bob's Burgers*, which he quoted on an unconscious loop. Annoying, but endearing. Nerdy, but hilarious. He kept her grounded, stopped her from losing herself inside her own head, especially when that nagging guilt hit her hard. Because Dillon knew about Maggie's parents, and she assumed that was why he belted out made-up show tunes on her worst days. He even bought a tiny domed barbeque grill for her miniature patio so that he could make burgers and dogs when their research papers got to be too much. He was, as her mother would have put it, *a fixer*. (*You feex*, ha-ha.) And yet, Maggie was still surprised he'd stuck around as long as he had.

She moved back to the bed. That shutter would loosen itself again before sunrise, sooner if the wind kept up, but it currently held its place. Dillon was still staring, because Maggie's tank top was lying crumpled on the floor on his side of the bed. He had tossed it aside a few hours ago, during one of their romps. He'd been talking like Dexter again. Sometimes, she couldn't resist.

"Better?" she asked once she reached the mattress.

"Uh-huh." His response was dazed, a pubescent boy at a topless variety show.

"That's good," she said, one knee pressing into the sheets, then another. Before he knew it, Maggie was doing a slow crawl toward her skinny-armed beau. Sultry. Seductive. Dillon leaned back while the ends of her hair traced a trail across his chest. "Know why?"

"Nuh-uh." She hated it when he responded in grunts—it seemed that even the smartest boys regressed to Cro-Magnons when aroused—but she let it go. He was studying to be a mechanical engineer, not a poet laureate.

"Because I have an exam tomorrow," she said, ignoring the fingers that were now grazing her right breast. "First thing. And unless Wilmington floods overnight—"

"Which it might," he cut in.

"—which I *doubt*," Maggie continued, "I have to pass my phytoplankton exam."

"Phytoplankton," Dillon echoed. *Talk dirty to me.*

"And you know how I'm going to make that happen?"

"By clearing your mind and gaining new focus?" He grabbed her hips and pulled her down against the bulge beneath the sheets.

"By sleeping until the sun comes up," she said. "Like a baby. Because these storms? I love 'em." She rolled off him, snapped off the light, and pretended she didn't hear the muffled *awh man* escape his throat.

"Fine," he said, relenting. "But can you at least flip your cell onto its screen? It's been lighting up the place for the past half hour."

"What?" She'd been sleeping while Dillon had clearly been wide awake, probably anticipating the moment Maggie's apartment was torn from its foundation and flung up into the sky, *Wizard of Oz*–style. Maybe, if she had been as jumpy as he was, she would have noticed the room light up bright blue, but she'd been sleeping like a baby. The sound of the rain comforted her. The louder, the better. Louder meant she couldn't hear herself think.

Reaching over, she grabbed her cell off the bedside table and squinted at the screen. Nearly four in the morning and three missed calls. One voicemail. Her phone was set to automatically go silent at midnight, so she hadn't heard them come in.

Rubbing the sleep out of her eyes, she brought up the call log.

ARLEN OLSEN-DORMER, MOBILE, 13 MIN. AGO.
ARLEN OLSEN-DORMER, MOBILE, 19 MIN. AGO.
ARLEN OLSEN-DORMER, MOBILE, 22 MIN. AGO.

Her eldest sister's photo smiled out at her from a list of previously made and received calls: a high and messy ponytail, a stretched-out Reebok tank with a faded graphic of a pink ocean sunset, Arlen posing with a group of strangers in what looked to be a yoga studio.

Maggie had snagged that photo off her sister's Facebook page years ago, mesmerized by the visage of a woman she felt she hardly knew, secretly delighted to see Arlen looking like a real honest-to-God sweaty human being rather than the uptight perfectionist Maggie had grown to know. *Real Housewives of Savannah*, Brynn, Maggie's middle sister, had snorted. *Stepford Wives two-point-oh.*

"Important?" Dillon asked.

"Maybe," Maggie said. But *certainly* was more like it, because a text every now and again was as close to communication as she and Arlen ever came. Neither one blamed the other for lack of trying. Maggie and Brynn had been close as kids, but Maggie and Arlen? Never. A nine-year difference was as good as kryptonite to a sisterly bond.

Seeing those missed middle-of-the-night calls made Maggie's heart twist in her chest. She vacillated for half a second—she could leave it until after her test; that damn ecology class had given her hell all summer.

Just turn it off, avoid whatever's going on.

But her gut instinct overrode her desire for a stress-free morning. She dialed into her voicemail. The message was breathless, heaving, aggravated, straight out of Georgia.

"Goddammit, Maggie . . ." Arlen's Southern drawl. "I know it's late, but answer your phone!"

No explanation. No assurance of not needing to panic. Just a demand, and then an angry hang-up.

Maggie sat motionless, her cell in her hand, the wind heaving another blustering roar. The broken shutter vibrated against the gale, threatening to come loose once again. If this storm—they were calling it Florence—turned into a full-blown hurricane, she'd have to nail a board across the outside to keep it in place—*you want feex, you feex*—and even then, she doubted class would be canceled. Her professor was relentless. It was a summer course, and if she didn't pass, she'd be shy of graduating by three measly credits. All those applications she'd put in for grad school would be rendered useless. A total waste of time. But . . .

"Hey." Dillon. "You okay?"

"Sure." *No.*

She looked back to the now-sleeping phone in her hand. Maggie hadn't texted her oldest sister in at least half a year—Christmas, she thought, or had it been New Year's Eve? But actually spoken? More than three years ago, the day Maggie's niece Hayden had been born. That day, she and Arlen had exchanged pleasantries and congratulations. *I bet she's adorable*, Maggie had said, and even *that* had been awkward, because Arlen knew: Maggie wasn't a fan. She had made a point of letting the world know she would never have a snot-nosed kid of her own. And yet, there she was, trying to scrounge up at least *some* enthusiasm for her sister's thirdborn child.

Another gust blasted against the side of the building. The broken shutter escaped its latch, flew open, and slammed hard against the exterior wall. Maggie winced at the crash, then nearly jumped out of bed when the phone lit up bioluminescent blue. Her big sister smiled out from its screen. Arlen Olsen-Dormer, glistening with sweat, perfectly imperfect.

A lump formed in Maggie's throat. Something was very wrong.

"What the hell!" Dillon scrambled out of bed and pulled on a T-shirt as he made a beeline for the window. "You need to call your super, Maggie. This is bullshit." His footfalls were a little too aggravated, loud enough to rouse the neighbors if they weren't already awake from all the noise. But she said nothing, too preoccupied with the memory of the midnight call she had gotten from Brynn years before.

She's gone, Mags.

She meaning their mother. Brynn hadn't been crying, but Maggie heard the ragged edge to her otherwise stoic sister's voice.

But this time it was Arlen, the sister who wouldn't call unless it was an emergency. Unless it was something devastating.

The room suddenly felt devoid of air. Dillon pulled open the window and yanked the shutter back toward its ruined latch. She almost yelled for him to leave it open, nearly tossed the phone aside and bolted out of bed toward the wind, the rain, and the thunder that was inside her apartment rather than outside where it should have been. This place had always felt safe, an asylum from her otherwise grim and mournful past. A salvation to her pain. Except, now, that sense of safety was gone. Her phone was still ringing.

It's bad. So bad. It's happening again.

Maggie's jaw tensed. Her fingers tightened around the rubber case that protected her cell.

"Maggie . . . ? You getting that?" Dillon was watching, concerned, suddenly striking her as ridiculous in his wrinkled white T-shirt with a roaring T-rex riding a Segway printed across the front. If she didn't answer the call, he'd ask what was wrong. She'd be left floundering, suffocating, squelching the emotions she worked so hard to ignore. *I don't want to talk about it, okay?* It would lead to an argument. Angry, Dillon would do what he always did when he was pissed—stomp off into the tiny living room and stream another round of *Cosmos* until Maggie was ready to relent. Way too much drama for a casual relationship. Hell, they didn't even live together. Dillon only slept over whenever he had an early morning because his apartment was miles away. This was more convenient. Maybe that's why he was sticking around.

She tapped the green answer button, then pressed the phone to her ear.

"Arlen?"

There was no reply, at least not for a while, but she could hear people in the background. The blip of what sounded like a walkie-talkie. She clutched the phone. Began to tremble despite the apartment's muggy heat.

Finally, Arlen spoke. "Maggie." She paused, as if carefully considering her next few words. Maggie looked up from the pattern of her bedsheets—tiny cartoon dolphins that, upon purchase, had struck her as adorable but now only made her feel sick. She thought about hanging up, but it was too late to deny the inevitable.

She knew.

On the line, Arlen pulled in a breath, and Maggie braced herself for what was coming.

"There's been an accident."

She wanted to scream.

"I'm sorry, Maggie . . . but you have to come home. Right now."

TWO

BY THE TIME Arlen pulled up to the arriving flights area, Maggie had fielded a dozen texts from Dillon—HOW DO YOU FEEL? HOW WAS THE FLIGHT? DO YOU WANT TO TALK? MAYBE YOU CAN GET A RETEST. She had sweated halfway through her T-shirt despite the storm clouds overhead, and had streamed the entirety of Depeche Mode's *Violator* on her phone, trying to keep her mind off the exam she had surely failed—if only Dillon would stop bringing it up. She glanced up from her phone when a new red Chrysler Pacifica pulled up along the curb, the minivan's side door slid open, and the nerve-rattling screech of children poured out onto the pavement.

GOTTA GO. She typed out the message rapid-fire and hit send. She could only handle one thing at a time, and Arlen was—and always would be—an undivided-attention kind of gal.

Out in the van, two kids whined at each other, seemingly at the tail end of a bitter argument. A toddler screamed in the background. And there, in all her perfect Southern glory, was Arlen: pink chino capris, a white silk pussy-bow blouse, her blond hair done up in a bouffant. If there ever was a spitting image of Maggie's mother before she'd gone off the deep end, it was that woman's firstborn child. Maggie only hoped that Arlen would never see such a bad end. Pills strewn everywhere. A bathroom rug tangled around bare feet. An overflowing bathtub washing the blood away.

Arlen carried herself as though her minivan were a limousine. She flashed Maggie a dazzling smile—one that was far too wide, all things considered.

"Maggie." She came in for a hug, hesitated upon noticing the glisten of sweat across her baby sister's arms and neck, but eventually offered a curt embrace regardless, leaving her youngest sibling enrobed in a wave of sweet perfume. Arlen had always been the girly one, the prom queen, the stereotype every girl who wasn't head cheerleader loved to hate. And nobody had hated a Mean Girl more than Brynn.

"Hey," Maggie greeted, returning Arlen's half-hearted embrace.

"Sorry I'm late," Arlen twanged, then took a step back and gave Maggie a bereaved look: *Jesus, why did I have so many kids?* "It never stops," she said, tossing a look over her shoulder at the cacophony behind her. "But God bless them, they're mine."

Maggie forced a smile toward the car. There, inside its confines, were a boy and two girls. Harrison was the firstborn son and pride and joy of Savannah's own Howie Dormer, quarterback extraordinaire. Maggie didn't know a damn thing about football—hell, she hardly knew anything about Howie, come to think of it—but from what she'd heard, he'd been Mr. Incredible on the college gridiron, so good he should have gone to the NFL but didn't, because wasn't that always the case?

Hope—Arlen's second child, born halfway through Maggie's last year of high school—had been a running gag among the boys in Maggie's senior high school class. She never heard the end of it.

Hey, Maggie, say hi to my baby mama for me.

Hey, Maggie, tell your sister I miss her.

Only once did she lose her temper. *Hey, pervert, are you getting arthritis in that right hand yet?* Cruel irony: Maggie had spat the question just as the assistant principal had passed her in the hall. After-school detention, two days. Arlen hadn't found it the least bit funny. Brynn, on the other hand . . .

It's like the goddamn Breakfast Club, she had cackled. *Except you'd be the nerd who brought the flare gun to school.* Brynn, of course, would have been the girl sitting at the back of the room, eating Pixy Stix for lunch and setting books on fire.

The screaming toddler was Hayden, and a niece Maggie had yet to meet. Arlen could have pushed harder for Maggie to come home for the holidays, and Maggie certainly could have made more of an effort. But neither of them did. Brynn had been the one to plead. *Just come home, Maggie, please.* For a weekend. For some turkey. For presents under the tree. Maggie turned down all open invitations despite her middle sister's appeals. Three years gone, and it didn't feel like nearly long enough. It was, Maggie supposed, appropriate that had it not been for Brynn, she wouldn't have been standing next to Arlen right now.

"Harry, Hope . . . come say hi to your Aunt Maggie." It wasn't a request. Arlen gave the command and, within an instant, a boy and girl leapt onto the curb and fell in line next to their mother, *Sound of Music*–style. Harry, once nothing but a tiny child, was now a premonition of his future self. Tall. Handsome. Light-brown hair grown out like a hotshot surfer, his hairstyle perfectly coupled with a bright Billabong T-shirt and scuffed-up Vans—the kind of guy Maggie imagined herself falling head over heels for in San Diego despite Dillon's broken heart. That was, if she was accepted into the grad program there. Fat chance of that now, though. The thought of those goddamn phytoplankton made her want to cry.

Hope hadn't yet turned two when Maggie had seen her last. Now, the five-year-old stood lean and graceful beside her brother,

her blond hair pulled up in a bun, her stick-skinny frame encased in a pink dance leotard, pink tights, and matching ballet shoes—a Southern cupcake, already on her way to becoming a clone of her mom. Arlen offered up an apologetic smile, as if embarrassed by her kid's getup. "I just swept her up from dance class," she explained. "No time to change, right, sugar?" She extended an arm, dragged a thumb across Hope's cheek as if to wipe away invisible dirt. "I'm trying my best to keep things normal around here, but . . ." Her words trailed to nothing, but Maggie understood. She'd been trying to keep things normal for the past decade herself. There would be no mention of that struggle, however, of that awful inescapable guilt, especially not in front of the kids.

"Heya, Harry," Maggie said, stepping up to give her nephew a hug.

"Hi, Aunt Maggie," Harrison murmured beneath his breath—already in the throes of preteen angst at the tender age of eight. She released him, and could sense his relief as soon as her arms fell back to her sides.

Hope watched the exchange with curiosity, her expression flickering between interest and gravitas. And then she stepped up to the aunt she hardly knew, leaned in, and spoke with a solemnness beyond her years. "Auntie Magdalene, I'm sorry for your loss. But we're trying to keep things normal around here." And then, as if having planned it all out in advance, she wrapped her arms around Maggie's waist in a viselike embrace and whispered, "I missed you."

This from a child Maggie didn't know at all. And all she could do was whisper back, "I missed you, too."

• • •

The Pacifica was so new it still smelled like plastic and glue. Blasting the air-conditioning on high and pushing fifty down a rural highway that suggested half that speed, Arlen said nothing about the unfolding events that had clearly thrown a wrench in the schedule of a busy working mom. The airport wasn't exactly close to home—roughly thirty minutes northwest of where they had grown up, which Brynn had lovingly called *the middle of fucking nowhere*, and Arlen hadn't moved away from because the schools were good and the crime was low. *That, and she knew that as soon as Mom kicked off, the house was for the taking,* Brynn had said during one of their many conversations, full of vitriol. *I swear, Mags, among the three of us, you got all the brains. With my luck, Len will keep poppin' em out and I'll end up a fucking wet nurse in my own home.*

At the time, Maggie had laughed. Brynn, born too weird for words, completely bizarre by the time she was fifteen; Brynn, with her box-dyed black hair and blunt-cut bangs, her skin powdered to a ghostly white and lips painted a gory maroon; Brynn, who had lived alone in that giant house for a good three months after their mom had died right there in the master bathroom, growing comfortable with the solitude, until Arlen swept in with Howie, the kids, and a newborn baby to make the house their own. *That* Brynn—a creepy Mary Poppins to her sister's kids. *Just a spoonful of arsenic.* It was a ridiculous notion. Hilarious. Insane.

But Arlen had every right to move in. Their mother's will left the house to all three of the girls, and not because she loved them all equally. No. Toward the end of her life, Stella Olsen had been the type of woman to throw a scrap of meat to the wolves and watch them fight. The house had been granted to all her children not because she was being magnanimous, but because not choosing was far more dramatic. And oh, the quarrel it had caused . . .

Maggie sold off her share to Arlen without a second thought. All that money would afford her a comfortable lifestyle in Wilmington—close to the UNC campus, not an hour's worth of gridlock away. Not a cheap option. And after Maggie graduated and it came to her master's degree, that cash would grant her the opportunity to go to any school she wanted, *hopefully* on the West Coast, if they would have her. Selling had been a no-brainer. She didn't need much motivation to avoid setting foot anywhere near their childhood backyard swimming pool. That late-night memory was still vivid, still crippling in its pain. The pool tarp, nothing but a jumble of plastic floating upon the surface of the water. The pool light, still on, as if to suggest that Maggie had just missed the action.

Brynn, on the other hand, had been home, and yet she was the one to stubbornly hold on to her share of the house. As a result, Arlen and Brynn butted heads more often than not, and Arlen's kids ended up with an overgrown goth girl as a live-in aunt.

Brynn bitched and moaned about the house being monopolized by Arlen and her brood every chance she got, but Maggie had been the only one to leave Georgia. She hadn't bothered to consider the Skidaway Institute of Oceanography, no matter how close to home it might have been. She packed up her things and left for North Carolina the summer she'd graduated high school, no longer willing to share space with their stumbling, slurring drunk of a matriarch. But it was only a few weeks into freshman year that Maggie was forced back to Savannah. A result of Brynn's midnight call.

Maggie chewed a fingernail as Arlen drove. Meanwhile, Dillon continued to text: DID YOU GET THERE OKAY? Maggie left his queries unanswered. A response would only encourage another question, and another after that. Responding would prompt Arlen to ask who she was texting, or what was so important, or shoot off their mom's favorite barb: *I bet that* can't *wait.* Maggie couldn't handle that. Not now. Not while stuck here in the car.

"Florence is fixing to be a real problem." Arlen tried for conversation over the blast of the A/C. "The wind is going to pick up this afternoon. One more day and they would have probably delayed flights, shut the whole airport down." Maggie's outbound flight had been stuck on the tarmac for more than an hour, giving Maggie hope that Florence would, perhaps, make an emergency trip home next to impossible. After all, it was stronger in Savannah. But no such luck.

Maggie said nothing as she stared at the fifty-foot cross made of white painted pipe that loomed over the highway. At its foot, a marquee warned drivers that THE _EVIL IS _ _ON_ US, SAVE YOU_ SO_ _. That cross had been there for as long as Maggie remembered. Every time they passed it as kids, Brynn would spin stories of a towering Jesus figure, sacrificed on that very spot.

He died for your sins, she had said. *He spilled blood enough to fill Daddy's pool.*

I ain't got no sins, Maggie had scoffed. She couldn't have been more than six or seven years old.

"I don't have any sins," their mother had corrected from the front seat. *Ain't isn't a word. And cool it with the stories back there.*

But Brynn had rolled her eyes and whispered into Maggie's ear. *Everyone's got sins, dummy. Even little kids like you. Maybe I'll tell you about it one day, when* she *ain't listenin'.* Brynn had made good on her promise, and she'd done it with her typical dramatic flair.

With Arlen's Chrysler leaving that cross in the rearview, Maggie wondered if sitting through an occasional Sunday service would have restored some semblance of normalcy to her and Brynn's oddly dark childhoods. If they had prayed the way their mother had taught them rather than faking it, if Maggie had turned to God, perhaps things would have been different. Better. Not like they were now.

Arlen cleared her throat against the relative silence. The kids were busy with their tablets; the backseat sounded like an arcade. "Anyway, as for the service . . . I left most of it up to Father John. You remember him. He organized for Mom. I just, I–I mean . . ." Arlen stammered, the first crack in her pristine facade.

Brynn would have wanted Maggie to protest. *Father John? That old pedophile?* If she could have reached out from beyond the veil, she'd have slid her hand down Maggie's throat to coax out the words: *A church service? Over my dead body. Oh, wait.* But what alternative would Brynn—a girl who was never satisfied with anything—be happy with? A black-clad procession down the cobblestone streets of medieval Bruges? A boys' choir echoing through the empty chambers of Dracula's Transylvanian castle? Jackals pulling her rotting corpse onto an English hillside before devouring her beneath a full moon?

Maggie covered her mouth and snorted out a laugh.

"What?" Arlen perked, immediately defensive.

"Sorry, nothing," Maggie said. She dropped her hand to her lap and looked out the window.

"I don't see what's funny about any of this," Arlen protested. "Do you know how hard it's been? How stressful? And to top it off, this damn storm . . ."

"Nothing's funny," Maggie said. "Father John, he's great." She pictured nothing but strangers clad in various ensembles, none of them morose enough for Brynn's taste—*cry harder*; a bunch of people Brynn never knew or gave a shit about filling up pews and pretending to care while Florence brought a cyclone down atop the church, tearing off its roof, sending the steeple careening into the earth like the devil's arrow. Maybe if Florence made landfall at just the right time, the service wouldn't be so bad.

Maggie's phone vibrated in her messenger bag. Another text from Dillon, no doubt. Hell, if Arlen was fine with inviting strangers to the funeral, Maggie should have invited Dillon to tag along. It would have made it easy to wriggle out of staying at the house, at least. Aunt Maggie shacking up in her old room with a random guy? Not a snowflake's chance in Georgia.

A defunct gas station came up on the right, an old black Cadillac facing the highway parked out front. A FOR SALE sign sat propped against the inside of the windshield, so sun-bleached it was hardly readable anymore. It was a giant boat of a vehicle. Brynn would have loved it: a dead man's hearse.

"What about her friends?" Maggie asked, looking back to her sister.

Arlen scoffed—a reflex—then corrected herself with a long sigh, as if realizing how insensitive her initial reaction was. "There's going to be an obituary. It's not like I know who those people are, Maggie."

Those people. That's what their mom used to call them. Maggie recalled their mother's face when Brynn had brought Simon, her first boyfriend, over for the first time. Clad in all black, and with an unspiked Mohawk lying dormant atop an otherwise shaven head, he was immediately deemed one of *those people.* If you asked Stella Olsen, it was a damn tragedy to have someone like Simon wandering around her pristine estate. Maggie caught her snorting at his discarded combat boots next to the front door, limp and unlaced, scuffed and well-loved. *Disgusting,* she had snarled, not once stopping to consider that he could have just left them on his feet—that he'd taken them off to be courteous, and all his thoughtfulness got him was an ugly behind-the-back jab. But those types of things hardly blipped on Mrs. Olsen's radar, just as they failed to register on Arlen's now.

"Isn't her phone upstairs?" Maggie asked.

"Mom!" A whine from the backseat, cutting through the conversation, momentarily obliterating the electronic calliope of educational apps that were nothing more than glorified video games. *F is for Friend, Family, Fun . . .*

"Her what?" Arlen asked, ignoring Hayden's outburst.

"Her cell phone," Maggie said. "Isn't it upstairs in her room?"

"Mo-om!" *G is for Girl, Game, Ghost . . .*

Maggie closed her eyes against the sound. She took a breath, trying to keep her agitation in check.

Arlen shook her head, not getting Maggie's point. "I guess . . . ? I don't know. I was only in there for a second."

"Because if it is, we could call—"

"You think I'd stay in there for longer than a second?" Arlen asked, cutting Maggie off. "Do you really think that's something I would have wanted to do?"

"Mom-*eeeee*!!"

"Jesus, Hay, *cool it*!" Arlen snapped, and for half a second Maggie was overtaken by the sudden urge to vomit into the footwell of the front seat. In Arlen's flash of impatience, her voice sounded exactly like their mom's, as though the woman had clawed her way out of the grave, having risen from the dead. *H is for . . .*

"But I'm hungr-*eeeeee*," Hayden squealed. "I want Donald's!"

"Yeah, can we go to McDonald's?" Hope chimed in, jumping to her little sister's aid. "Mom? Can we? I'm hungry, too. I can't remember the last time I ate. Can we?"

"I wanna see the Ronalds!" Hayden.

"No." Refusal. Flat. Unaffected by the abrupt onset of backseat famine.

"But I'm *starving*!" Hope. "It's still forever till home!"

"I want chickens!" Hayden.

"Mom?" Harry, even-toned and leaning between the two front seats like some sort of child trauma mediator; channeling Sally Struthers, imploring Arlen to please remember the children.

"I want catch-ups!" Hayden's tone was reaching optimum pitch. "I wanna play in the jungle!"

"Oh my God." Maggie, but a mere whisper. Suddenly, replying to texts didn't seem half bad. She reached into her bag.

"Stop *yelling*, Hay!" Hope roared at her sister. "It's not gonna help!"

Phone out.

"You're going to cause an accident," Arlen announced, as if subtly threatening the lives of her offspring would somehow calm them down.

Screen on.

"You're gonna cause an accident!" Hope yelled while Hayden continued to screech. "And you're bugging Auntie Magdalene!"

"You aren't bugging me—" Maggie said, unsure of why she was about to deny such a self-evident truth. But nobody was listening anyway. She blasted out a message. *I is for . . .*

I'VE MADE A HUGE MISTAKE.

"*Hope.*" Arlen. An edge of warning in her tone.

"There," Harry said, pointing to an off-ramp, a highway sign announcing food, gas, and a creepy motel only child-smugglers would have used ahead.

Maggie bit her bottom lip, almost afraid to look in Arlen's direction, imagining her sister's face replaced by their mother's sallow skin, her distant bag-eyed stare.

"I want French eyes!" Hayden exploded in a fit of three-year-old insistence, tired of being silenced, refusing to be ignored. "I want *French eyes!*" she screamed, her legs kicking in a torrent of fury, as though kicking hard enough would send her Lecter-like child restraints flying from the car seat, allowing her to murder every person in that minivan for denying her the one thing, the *only* thing, she'd ever asked for in her whole entire life. "*I want French eyes!*" The rampage continued. Hope's quiet murmur of *jeez* was but a soft underscore to her little sister's blind outrage.

Maggie couldn't help herself. She laughed. Because Arlen's life was nuts.

SAVE ME! Fingers flying over the QWERTY keyboard.

"Mom?" Harry, staring pointedly at the quickly oncoming turn-off, his expression that of stoic desperation. *Take the easy way out*, it said. *Make it stop*.

WHAT? WHAT'S GOING ON? Dillon responding.

Maggie opened her mouth, about to offer to cover the cost, ready to admit that she was a little hungry herself even though queasiness was still clinging to the back of her throat like thin plastic film, like a wet tarp freshly pulled from a pool. But Arlen jerked the wheel to the right before Maggie could speak. The Chrysler hit the off-ramp way too fast. For a flash of a second, Maggie imagined the car flying off the road and into an embankment of trees, the branches hissing with summer cicadas and slumbering fireflies, the car slamming into an immovable trunk of an ancient oak, leaves and insects and birds exploding out and away from the tree like green fireworks. The Olsens' final hurrah. One last tragedy to wipe the entire brood out for good. And it would be Maggie's fault, because had she not required a ride from the airport, Arlen wouldn't have been pushed to the brink. *M is for Mommy, Madness, Massacre . . .*

Arlen eased off the gas, her expression taut, her eyes narrowed, angry at herself for giving in. The minivan cruised up a slight in-cline and came to a full stop. A road sign pointed them right. Arlen breathed in and out. In and out. Just like how they taught her in yoga class, no doubt. Trying to keep her cool.

In the minivan's stunned silence, Maggie's phone buzzed in her hand.

MAGS?

"Mom?" Hayden, calm, as though sensing her mother's bubbling rage. "I'm gonna have Donald's now?"

Arlen didn't answer. Instead, she spoke toward the steering wheel, as if speaking to herself. "I'm glad you're here, Maggie," she said. "Because *this*?" She lifted a hand, made a sweeping gesture toward the backseat. "My plate is full."

Maggie wasn't sure how to respond.

"Brynn knew that," Arlen said. "But she did it anyway, didn't she? She saved herself and left us to pick up the pieces, because in the end, everything is always about her."

Maggie swallowed against the lump that had formed in her throat. She couldn't deny that Arlen was speaking the truth. Brynn always did have a penchant for theatrics. Maggie suspected it was why she had refused to relinquish her share of the house. Not because Brynn *wanted* to live there, but because not selling was histrionic. A standoff. Something to keep her occupied because she didn't have all that much going on in her life. But Arlen resenting Brynn for committing suicide? That was cold.

Maggie furrowed her eyebrows, searching for something to say. *You shouldn't hold it against her* or *Where the hell were you when she needed help?* Except that finger was pointing right back at her, because where was Maggie, after all? In Wilmington. Refusing to come home no matter how many times Brynn had asked. Maggie looked down to her lap, frowning at her phone and the fraying knees of her jeans.

I'M FINE. She shot out the text and shoved her phone back into her bag, the sting of tears suddenly threatening to breach the stoicism and strength she was so desperately trying to keep intact. But just as she was sure she'd start bawling right there, another distraction came from over her shoulder.

Hope slid her skinny arms between the two front seats and coiled them around Maggie's left limb. And then, pressing her cheek against Maggie's shoulder, she gazed up at her aunt and echoed her mother's words. "I'm glad you're here."

THREE

WHEN MAGGIE SHOWED Dillon a picture of her childhood home, he called her crazy for giving up her share of the seven-thousand-square-foot pie. But the beauty of that white colonial was as false a front as Maggie's steady nerves. Sitting in Arlen's van, she found herself staring out the windshield at the place where she grew up, its banistered wraparound porch dotted with hanging ferns that now swung in the wind, three dormer windows protruding like sentries from a high-sloping roof. It sat lazily on its three-acre plot, beating the Georgia heat beneath a sweeping canopy of oak branches and swaths of old man's beard.

Maggie swallowed against the ball of nerves that had wormed its way up her windpipe, her right hand involuntarily rising to rub at the back of her neck. Her left continued to clutch her cell phone—a security blanket, her only tether to the life she'd created outside this place.

She didn't make a move to exit the vehicle, but no one else shared in her hesitation. Harry and Hope noisily climbed out of the car while Arlen struggled with the buckle of Hayden's car seat, all the kids now tangy with the scent of ketchup and fryer grease. With Hayden finally released from her restraints, she ran after her siblings across a pristine, freshly mowed lawn. Not mowed by Howie, of course, but by a service. That was, after all, the upper-crust Southern way.

Arlen lingered in the backseat while Maggie stared ahead, unsure of how to proceed. The place was appealing with its lovely dark-painted window shutters and white rocking chairs on the front porch—the grouping of rockers once referred to by their still-sober mother as the South Savannah Chapter of the Porch Sitters Union. All of it innocuous. Inviting. All of it a lie.

She nearly jumped when Arlen sighed, then spoke from behind her. "Look," she said. "I'm sorry. I know I'm being a bitch about all of this, but I'm just so angry."

Maggie looked away from the house and to the tree that had once been home to a swing. After their father's accident, Maggie had locked herself in her room, sitting cross-legged on the floor, staring down at an object Brynn had insisted had been nothing but a game. Brynn, on the other hand, spent a lot of time outside. She'd sat out there on that swing, completely clad in black, for hours at a time. One afternoon, she had pumped her legs hard, pushed herself as fast and high as she could, the branch overhead groaning against the strain. And then, at the apex of that arc, one of the ropes unraveled. Years of humidity, rain, and heat had Brynn flying toward the lawn with a garbled scream. Maggie, who happened to have been spying on her sister through her open bedroom window, watched Brynn soar through the air before landing hard against the ground. She twisted her ankle and dislocated her left shoulder attempting to catch herself on the grass. But it could have been worse. She'd hit the ground less than a few inches away from one of their mother's many flowerbeds, the concrete garden edging jutting upward in anticipation of lethal contact. It could have ended her right then, seven years ago.

"I guess it's just . . . despite all of her ridiculous death stuff, I never thought she'd take it this far," Arlen said. "How was I supposed to know that she was depressed even *more* than usual?" She paused, as though considering her own words, searching for their truth. But she was right. Maggie couldn't remember a time when Brynn hadn't prided herself on being weird and impossible to decipher. After Dad was gone, Brynn's black band T-shirts and slashed-up jeans graduated to caked-on makeup and pale contact lenses. And what had once been their mother's outright horror over her daughter's goth phase then shifted from quips and nags to radio silence. Maggie, on the other hand, had nearly lost touch with her lifelong love for the ocean. The fact that she had been out on Hilton Head Island when the accident had happened, that she'd been enjoying a sunset while looking out onto an endless expanse of water while her father— less than an hour away—was living out the last few moments of his life . . . it had nearly been too much to bear. And as for their mom? Once Dad was out of the picture, all three of the girls became invisible, as though they had perished right along with him. Alive, but dead. Ghosts unto themselves.

Maggie pulled her gaze away from where that swing used to be, nothing left but a piece of jute tied high up on the bough, like someone had hanged a body there, cut it down, and not bothered to cover their tracks.

"You're going to blame me for this, aren't you?" Arlen said. "I mean, we weren't close . . . but Brynn wasn't close with anyone, you know? You of all people know that she'd always been that way. She never liked me to begin with . . . so just how was I supposed to influence her, *help* her? What could I have possibly done?"

"It's not your fault," Maggie finally spoke, half expecting Arlen to breathe a sigh of relief. It wasn't Arlen's fault because Maggie was the one to blame. But rather than soothing her big sister's nerves, Maggie's attempt at compassion seemed only to ignite Arlen's anger.

"Well, of *course* it's not my fault!" She huffed, sweeping crumbs out of the cracks of Hayden's car seat with the palm of her hand. "I invited her to join us for dinner every night, Maggie. *Every night*, at least up until a few months ago."

"What happened a few months ago?" Maggie rubbed her phone screen against a patch of her jeans, cleaning off the smudges, if only to give herself something to do.

"She stopped coming down. I'd make enough for everyone, and her plate would go cold on the table. So I stopped offering. A waste of food. You try not to take offense, but . . ."

"Did you ask her what was going on?"

"No," Arlen murmured. "I figured it was just Brynn being Brynn."

Maggie winced. *Brynn being Brynn.* Their mother's words, but rather than a drunken slur, they were annunciated with a distinct Southern drawl.

"You two talked every now and again, isn't that right?" Arlen asked. "Did she strike *you* as upset about something? Did she *say* anything?"

That was the problem with Brynn. Suicide had always been the hazy overlay of every conversation, a fashionably subtle suggestion coloring her every word. Maggie couldn't count the times her middle sister had thrown herself down onto the couch or into an armchair like a distressed damsel, exhaling an exasperated *I'm going to kill myself* or *I wish I were dead*. Brynn being Brynn. And Brynn was always upset about something. Lately, it had been about Maggie's refusal to come home. About politics. About the fact that Arlen was a staunch conservative and had almost certainly voted Republican. *You know she did, Mags. Ugh, I could just die!* But that was Brynn's typical stagecraft. Suggesting that she was *genuinely* suicidal? Maggie shook her head. "No." At least not that she had known.

"You're sure?" Arlen said, pressing. Maggie shifted her weight in the front seat to meet her big sister's gaze, but as soon as she did, Arlen looked away. She plucked Hayden's sippy cup off the backseat. "I'm just glad the kids were asleep when it happened. I mean . . ." Her words trailed off, but it was too late; Maggie couldn't help but imagine it.

Harry and Hope decked out in their swim gear. Hayden toddling behind them, her floaties forcing her arms outward like the straw arms of a cornfield scarecrow. And there, between the house and the pool, Auntie Bee. Neck broken. Arms and legs ragdoll akimbo. Shattered glass catching the light like jagged diamonds in the sun. Music slithering out the broken window and up into a pristine summer sky. She pictured Hope and Harry parting just in time for Hayden to catch sight of the body, a toddler's laughing face skipping like a record, flickering like bad reception, hesitating before finally twisting into a mask of fear. A scream bubbling up her esophagus—one her siblings would hear faint traces of for the rest of their lives. *T is for Trauma . . .*

"No, you're right," Maggie said, pushing the thought away. "It wasn't right of her to do it the way she did." Brynn had done it after dark, but Harry could have gone downstairs for a glass of water. He could have seen. Yet if it hadn't been the pool at midnight, it would have been Brynn's room some other time—a place where she might not have been discovered for days. Maybe one of the kids would have found themselves wondering where their aunt was, knocking on her door, pushing it open to discover . . .

"I suppose it's silly to expect someone to consider such things at a time like that," Arlen mused. "I'm just sorry that I couldn't have . . ." A pause. A frown. "Anyway." She discarded her own remorse. "Don't sit out here all afternoon."

"Len . . ." The old nickname came tumbling past Maggie's lips before she could stop it. Arlen paused midretreat, palms against the seat and half out of the car, waiting for Maggie to speak. "I don't know if I can go in there."

Arlen pulled in a breath, as if preparing for a record-setting deep-sea dive. Maggie chewed the inside of her bottom lip, waiting for Arlen to spout off reason after definitive reason as to why Maggie would not be allowed to waver. The funeral. Arlen's need of assistance in dealing with this whole crazy screwed-up thing. No, this time there would be no ducking out. But rather than launching into a laundry list of why-nots, she exhaled the air she'd drawn in so deeply in a smooth and steady stream. "I'll see you inside," she said, and slipped out of the car.

Maggie listened to the sliding door of the minivan hiss closed, then watched her sister make a brisk line through the whipping wind toward the open garage door. Inside that garage, two bikes were propped against one of the walls. Not Harry and Hope's, but Maggie and Brynn's. Childhood relics their dad had wanted to keep, that their mom hadn't bothered to get rid of, and that Arlen was too busy to bother with. Streamers of black and silver hung from Brynn's handlebars. Maggie could still vividly remember how they fluttered as she rode, streamers that Maggie used to stare at as she trailed her sister—onward, to the cemetery gates.

FOUR

THE FIRST TIME Brynn had ushered Maggie to the neighborhood cemetery, Maggie had been nine years old. She had pedaled ferociously behind her older sister in hopes of keeping up. When they arrived at the gates, Maggie only blinked at the massive wrought ironwork before riding through its wide-open leaves. The overhead arc was adorned with the name of the graveyard in coiling, intricate script: FRIENDSHIP PARK.

"Do you know why they call this place Friendship Park?" Brynn asked after they snaked along the gravel paths, eventually reaching a particularly shady corner of the lot. When Maggie didn't respond, Brynn jumped off her bike and let it fall on its side with a crash. "Because all of these ghosts wanna be your friend. It's lonely as heck being dead."

It was warm in the sunshine, but Maggie's bare arms sprouted goose bumps under the branches of a grouping of oaks. Brynn motioned for Maggie to follow, and Maggie did—leaving her bike next to her big sister's, though she propped hers against a tree. Maggie liked her bike too much to let it lie on the ground like that.

Brynn's steps came to a stop when she reached a peculiar set of plots. Her knee-high purple-and-black-striped socks and new boots—a pair of Dr. Martens she'd been pining over for months, finally purchased by their father as an early birthday gift—looked spooky next to the headstones. Each marker had a little fence around it, not more than a foot or two high. Some were made of wood: tiny picket fences for fairy gardens made up of plastic flowers and occasional sun-bleached toys. Most, however, were made of wrought iron like the main gate the girls had passed through only minutes before.

But there was one grave site that was different from the rest—not a headstone, but a tomb with the name and date worn away, the epitaph nothing more than a faint impression of what it had once been. The top was cracked and slightly caving in, seemingly as ancient as the trees that surrounded it. And there, atop the waist-height stone box that held death inside, was a doll. It didn't look particularly antiquated; the doll's frilly white dress and matching bonnet looked clean, in perfect shape. But that didn't make the doll's pallid and expressionless face any less creepy. Its eyes were wide-open, staring out at anyone who dared to meet its gaze.

"You know who's the loneliest after they die?" Brynn asked, not swayed by her younger sister's backward shimmy away from the vault before her. "Kids. Because most people who die are old and boring. *Really* old, like that cranky guy down the street who gives us dirty looks when we ride by his house." The neighbor in question always seemed to be watering his lawn, bent over at a painful angle, one hand clamped down on the trigger of the hose nozzle, the other at the small of his back. And his looks *were* dirty. Glares, really. Anytime Maggie and Brynn rode by his place—which they did often—Maggie pedaled as hard as she could.

"And you know what old people hate?" Brynn continued.

"Grass?" Maggie was distracted by the doll atop that tomb. Perhaps the old guy wasn't watering his lawn to make it grow. Maybe he did it so often because he was trying to drown it instead.

"What? No, dummy. *Kids.*" Brynn delivered the news matter-of-factly, as though anyone who knew anything knew that single detail to be true.

"Really?" Maggie squinted at her big sister. "But what about Gram and Gramps?"

"Gram and Gramps don't count," Brynn explained. "Besides, even if they liked kids while they're alive, they're gonna hate 'em after they're dead. You know why?"

Maggie blinked away from that strange sarcophagus just beyond Brynn's shoulder. She imagined Brynn jumping on top of it, causing that fractured slab of limestone to collapse in on itself. And what would be inside? A coffin, or just the skeleton of what had once been a little girl? Maggie stared at her sister, finally managing to shake her head no in reply to Brynn's question, holding fast to her silence.

"Because dead kids remind dead adults of what it used to be like to be young, and they don't wanna remember that stuff. It makes 'em mad. That's why even alive adults bury kids in the corners of graveyards, like they did here." Brynn turned, motioning to the plots of smaller-than-usual headstones and tiny fenced-in rectangles of land like a fancy lady presenting the Showcase Showdown. Their gram loved *The Price Is Right.* "All of these are kids, see? And they're way back here to keep all the adult ghosts happy. Except . . . you know what?"

"What?" Maggie asked, looking back to that doll. It seemed impossible for it to have been sitting there for long, undisturbed. Wouldn't someone have taken it? Wouldn't the rain and wind have knocked it over? Wouldn't it have been moldy and rotten and falling apart by now?

"Dead kids are *never* happy because nobody wants to play with 'em. And *this* kid in particular?" Brynn kicked the box with the toe of her boot. "Just look at her grave, rotting away. You can't even read her name. Nobody wants to take care of her now, just like nobody wanted to play with her when she was alive."

"Why?" Maggie asked, though she wasn't sure she really wanted to know. Regardless, Brynn would tell her anyway. That was Brynn's way; if she had a story to tell, Maggie was going to hear it whether she wanted to or not.

"Because she was *evil*." Brynn's mouth curled up in a smile. "Born bad. She ended up killing her little sister—"

"Oh, *shut up*, Bee! What a load of baloney!"

"Baloney? You wanna bet?"

"Yeah!" Maggie scoffed. "You're just trying to freak me out again."

But Brynn's smile shifted to something far more serious—stern enough to give Maggie pause. "I'm not lyin', Mags. She killed her little sister. Poisoned her dead."

"With what?" If Maggie was going to be forced to listen to this dumb story, she wasn't going to make it easy to tell.

"With old-timey stuff in a bottle, like a potion."

"A potion." Maggie rolled her eyes. "That's the dumbest."

"Yeah, dummy, like cyanide. Betcha never heard of *that* stuff before."

Maggie shrugged. What did it matter if she had or hadn't? Brynn was still making it up. But Brynn wasn't swayed by her kid sister's skepticism. She never was.

"So, she poisoned her little sister, and then her mom found out about it, and you know what *she* did?"

"Probably called the cops? Duh!" Maggie was trying her damnedest to play it off. She wasn't scared of some stupid story. Brynn was full of them, every day something new. But that doll? Maggie couldn't keep her eyes off it.

"Cops?" Brynn snorted. "There weren't any cops back then, dork. This was olden days, remember? They had, like, a sheriff and that was it. Nah, her mom found out, and she snuck into the little girl's room late at night, and *then* do you know what she did?"

Maggie's mouth was starting to go dry. She shook her head again, her eyes still fixed upon the porcelain doll's face.

"She tied the girl to her bed and lit the sheets on fire. She left her daughter there, screaming." Brynn widened her eyes for effect. "Crying." She bleated out a wail, like one that could have possibly eked out of a dying girl. "Burning up!" She lurched at Maggie, her arms extended, her fingers twisted up like spooky five-legged spiders. Maggie squeaked and shuffled back. "And because the girl was so evil, the adults put her in a big limestone box so she'd be trapped forever. Except she *wasn't* trapped forever. She was way too powerful for that."

Maggie glanced back to her bike, suddenly sure it wouldn't be there anymore—magically vanished, made invisible by the demon child of Brynn's own making.

"One day, a girl came here to visit her gram at the cemetery all by herself. I can show you the grave if you want, since you probably don't believe me. It's just down there." Brynn motioned to some faraway plot, waiting to be challenged, but Maggie didn't dare. She knew it would be there. Brynn was meticulous about details, always prepared to be called out, to prove that what she was saying was true.

Once, at the dinner table, Brynn had muttered something about having a dream about their great-grandmother writhing in pain in a large canopy bed. Their mother had gone positively white, but had said nothing to prove or disprove her middle child's claims. Another time, Brynn had pointed to a spot along the highway while she and Maggie rode in the backseat to do some shopping in Savannah's downtown. *A boy and his family died there*, Brynn had said, only to be chastised for making up such a gruesome thing. Not a week later, a small cross had been erected in that very place, prompting their mom to pull the car over and demand the girls stay in the backseat. They watched her march up the soft shoulder, then stoop over the marker for what seemed like an awfully long time. She came back pale and silent. Maggie didn't know how Brynn did it, but there was truth to her stories. And this one right now, she could only assume, was no different.

"So, this girl who was visiting her gram, she heard weeping coming from this corner, right where we're standing now." Brynn whimpered, pulling her face into a mask of despair. "And the kid, feeling sorry for the weeping ghost, brought the dead girl a gift. A doll." Brynn looked back to the tomb, as did Maggie. "And now, that doll is the dead girl's only friend. And anyone who touches it is doomed to be cursed."

Maggie peeked back at the creepy glass-faced toy. The more she looked at it, the more that doll seemed strangely familiar—like maybe she'd seen it somewhere before. But Brynn wasn't done. Reaching out to grab Maggie's hand, she tightened her grip and took a few forward steps, forcing Maggie to creep closer to the crypt despite having backpedaled from that blank glass-eyed stare.

"Hey, cut it out, Bee!" Maggie tried to free herself from her sister's grasp, but she didn't have a chance, especially when Brynn used her free hand to give Maggie a forward shove. Maggie's bare knees hit the side of the tomb. The tips of her sneakers kicked its rough stone side. The doll stared ahead.

"See that thing?" Brynn asked.

"I'm gonna tell Mom," Maggie whined, trying to wriggle away.

"It's evil, too," Brynn hissed into her ear. "Just like the dead girl."

Evil. The word twisted around inside Maggie's head like a snake.

"I came here by myself yesterday," Brynn said. "And she threatened me . . . so I made her a promise."

Maggie stood frozen. Speechless. Her muscles tensed. The thudding of her heart insisted she look somewhere else, anywhere else but into that wicked marionette's eyes.

"I promised her that I'd bring her a friend, so she'd never be lonely again. I hope you both like one another." And then, all at once, Brynn spun around and fell into a full sprint across a headstone-dotted lawn with a gleeful laugh.

Maggie's mind screamed, *Turn around, stupid! You're being abandoned!* She could hear Brynn running toward her bike. But she couldn't stop staring at the effigy poised atop that box. The idea of that doll being wicked had her mind reeling at the possibilities.

The doll sliding off that tomb.

Finding its way out of Friendship Park, down the street, into the house through a window or unlocked door.

Climbing the stairs in the dead of night, its fluttery dress whispering across each riser.

Little laced-up boots tap-tap-tapping across the hardwood floor.

The fingers of a tiny hand slipping through the crack of Maggie's door.

"Mags!"

Maggie started when Brynn yelled her name. She veered around, spotted her big sister on her bike, already a good distance away. Twelve-year-old Brynn's sandy-brown hair shone in the sunshine, Jack Skellington smiling out from the center of her T-shirt, her stripy socks and heavy boots looking ridiculous with the purple shorts she wore.

"It's gonna get you!" Brynn bellowed. "Stand there long enough and it's gonna follow you home!" Her sister laughed and pedaled toward the front of the cemetery.

It was then that Maggie bolted toward her own bike, unable to help glancing over her shoulder . . . just once, to make sure she wasn't being chased.

And yet, despite being thoroughly spooked by her sister's story, Maggie followed Brynn back to Friendship Park only days later. They wandered the stones, read the names, and tried to calculate how old the skeletons beneath their feet were by counting on their fingers rather than inside their heads. Sometimes, Brynn would purposefully walk right on the graves, as if daring the dead to punch their hands through the soil and chase her away. She'd crawl up onto the headstones in her clomping boots, then leap off them and onto the grass. Maggie wasn't brave enough to do those things. Their dad said that stepping on a grave meant upsetting the person who owned it, and the last thing Maggie wanted was to draw attention to herself, especially with the promise Brynn had supposedly made to the girl in the limestone tomb.

That summer was boring, and so they continued to visit Friendship Park for a couple of weeks, Brynn's story refusing to fade from the forefront of Maggie's thoughts. She hated the idea of her loyalty being promised to that evil girl, but she was pretty sure *that* part of Brynn's story was a load of bull. That, however, didn't negate the idea of dead kids being lonely and abandoned—it was the one detail Maggie couldn't manage to shake. And so, while Brynn hopscotched across grave sites, Maggie collected bouquets of fading silk flowers from the grown-up plots and arranged them on the burial sites of those sad, forsaken kids. Maggie even went so far as to create such a bouquet for her mother, which, to Brynn's glee, had sent their mom reeling. *Oh my God, Brynn!* Their mother positively glowered at her middle daughter. *You take your sister to that cemetery one more time, and you'll find yourself spending a heck of a lot more time there yourself, and not because you want to, you understand?*

Oddly, their mother's threat was enough to persuade Brynn to lose interest; there was only so much fun you could have in a grave-yard, after all, even for a girl like her. Soon enough, Brynn was sucked into some TV show. Unable to shake the routine so easily, Maggie was left to sneak into the garage, climb onto her bike, and ride to Friendship Park alone. And the more she visited, the more that doll beckoned her. Eventually, all of Maggie's gathered flowers were for the stone mausoleum and what sat upon its top.

It was an offering: *Please don't be sad or angry.*

It was also, in a sense, a proposal, despite Maggie thinking bet-ter of it. Sitting next to the tomb, hiding from the sun, she picked dan-delions from the grass and murmured an impromptu promise. "I don't care what Brynn says. As long as you promise to be nice, I *can* be your friend."

FIVE

MAGGIE CONTINUED TO visit Friendship Park despite Brynn's loss of interest, because not visiting made her feel guilty. That, and she had never been one for hours in front of the TV. Beyond splashing around in her father's backyard pool and reading books about dolphins and sharks, she resolved to keep up her fake-flower ritual—gathering plastic blooms from the adult graves and passing them on to the kids, equally distributed, with one extra for the dolly that sat upon that ill-boding tomb.

After a few weeks, the effectiveness of Brynn's story had started to dissipate, and Maggie was no longer afraid, especially after she had put two and two together. That doll didn't look like an antique because it wasn't old. With Brynn downstairs, Maggie had snuck into her big sister's room to snoop around, and there they were at the back of her closet: a trio of porcelain dolls nearly identical to the one in Friendship Park, all of them propped up on their metal doll stands. Brynn had put the doll in the cemetery herself: merely a prop for her ghost story. She'd left it there because—not one for girly things—she had never liked the dolls Gram kept giving her for Christmas. At least one of them could be put to a good and creepy use.

And yet, despite the story losing its resonance, Maggie didn't dare tell her sister about her secret sojourns. She stopped by the grave site every day except for when the weather was bad, and those were the days when Maggie felt the worst. Because, even though she knew the doll was Brynn's, Maggie associated it with the little girl locked away in that ominous box. Two blocks from home, Dolly was sitting out in the wind and rain. Something about that felt wrong, especially when Maggie was safely tucked inside her home. Friends took care of one another, and Dolly deserved better. Leaving her out there like that—it just wasn't right.

It was during one of those very storms that Maggie's dad paused his channel surfing on the forecast, and Maggie overhead the newscaster talking about a storm called Katrina. A hurricane was coming, and while it was predicted to miss Georgia, the newscaster urged caution.

Always one for blowing things out of proportion, Maggie's mom was already freaking out, squawking about how they needed to go to the grocery store, how it was probably already being ransacked, how she needed bread and milk and eggs, and what if the electricity went out? They should have bought that generator they'd been talking about, regardless of its cost. What about her freshly cleaned windows? She'd just spent a fortune on a cleaning service, not to mention all the landscaping she had done. What about the oak trees in the yard? They were ancient. They'd never make it. She had to call Gram and Gramps, who lived out in Florida. They were still reeling from the effects of Hurricane Dennis. "They should have never moved out there," Maggie's mother exclaimed, all but weeping at the thought of her parents sitting out in their mega-fancy mobile home park. Maggie loved it out in Pensacola. Gramps let her drive his golf cart. They had a tennis court and everything.

Brynn, who was lazily curled up in an armchair with a Neil Gaiman novel in her hands, frowned at their mother's growing panic while Maggie stood frozen in the center of the living room, too young to decipher whether abject terror was the correct response.

"Time to batten down the hatches!" Maggie's dad announced. "Brynn, honey, get the shutters. I have to close up the pool."

"Peter, *please*, you need to come with me." Maggie's mother exhaled an exasperated sigh. "I have to call my mother!"

"You go, Stella," he said. "The sooner the better. I'll call."

"Go *alone*?" Maggie couldn't decide whether the suggestion to go to the supermarket had left her mom stunned or just plain annoyed. "You heard Chuck." Chuck was the weatherman; their mother was on a first-name basis with the guy, as though he came over for cookouts and beer rather than predicted the weather for the entire Georgia coast. "The parking lot will be a *nightmare*."

"You'll be fine." Dad.

"The lines are going to be backed up to the milk coolers. God, I need to call Arlen." She stomped off toward the foyer to gather her purse. "She and Howie should come over. They have Harrison to worry about. If their power goes out . . ."

"Dad?" Maggie frowned, tugging on her father's pants pocket as she watched her mother shuffle toward the door that led out to the garage. Peter Olsen turned his attention to his youngest. "What about me?" she asked. "What should *I* do?"

He smiled. "You? How about making sure you and your sister's bikes are safe and sound? You don't want to lose your wheels, do you?"

Lose her bike? That would have been a nightmare. Maggie shook her head in the negative, only to receive a get-going swat on the back from her father. A moment later, he was making a beeline for the backyard.

Maggie remained still for a moment, listening to Brynn hop up the stairs, taking them two by two in those clunky boots while Chuck continued on about the danger. *Severe threat. Possible category five. Unpredictable path.* Only when Maggie was sure that Brynn was out of sight did she skitter off to the garage.

The garage door was wide-open—Mom had a bad habit of leaving it gaping whenever she left the house. The oaks in the front yard were already groaning and bending against the growing wind. Leaves were tearing free of their branches. Sometimes, the storms were bad enough to strip those trees half-naked. This time, Maggie wondered if all their foliage would be gone, like an old man losing his hair. Twisting where she stood, she located her bicycle, safe and sound, propped against the wall next to Brynn's.

Brynn didn't ride much anymore. Sometimes she'd pedal a few blocks with Maggie to get a snowball covered in electric-green sour apple syrup. Maggie liked blue raspberry, because it reminded her of the ocean. Every now and again, their mom would send Brynn to the little convenience store a mile away, or to the garden center down the road to grab bottles of magic pellets that turned her blue hydrangeas pink. Sometimes, Maggie would tag along, especially to the store. York Peppermint Patties were her favorite, and that place sold them two for a buck. But otherwise, Brynn's bike sat around unused, collecting dust.

Maggie, on the other hand, rode almost every day despite Brynn's homebody ways, and she'd gotten fast. She could do a loop from here to Friendship Park in less than a few minutes, no joke. She'd timed herself on her dad's stopwatch one day. One minute, forty-five seconds. She'd almost collapsed from the effort, but it was a new record. Taking that into consideration, if it was safe enough for her mom to go to Publix on her own, it was certainly safe enough for a ride. She'd make it quick.

She shot a look over her shoulder, as if to ask the old oaks their opinion. The leaves kept tearing free, but most of them were holding fast. *It's not so bad.* Before Maggie could change her mind, she grabbed her bike by the handlebars and threw her leg over the frame.

Because friends didn't let friends suffer through hurricanes alone. Friends didn't let big sisters spook them out of lending a little kindness. Dolly had no one—all alone out there, abandoned and scared. There was nothing evil about that girl, and nothing wicked about that doll. It couldn't do anything to her because it was just a toy. And even if there had been an inkling of truth to Brynn's tale, even if by some chance Maggie was wrong and Brynn *hadn't* left that doll out there to creep her out, why would it hurt her? Maggie was being a friend. She was just being nice.

· · ·

By the time Maggie returned from Friendship Park, the wind was so fierce she was hardly able to pedal against it. She careened into the garage, for once letting her bicycle carelessly fall against the floor rather than leaning it up against the wall. Her mother's car was still gone—she was still at the Publix, probably fighting local neighborhood ladies for the last gallon of sweet tea. That was good. It meant Maggie only had to dodge two people rather than three. She tucked the doll beneath her arm, then reconsidered, cramming the toy beneath the thin cotton of her Georgia Aquarium T-shirt.

With half the doll's skirt and booted feet hanging out from beneath her shirt, she dashed through the kitchen and into the hall, throwing herself onto the stairs that would lead her up to her room. She took them two by two, her anxiety growing sevenfold as she neared Brynn's room. If Brynn spotted what Maggie was doing, she'd be pissed. Not only was Maggie screwing up her spooky story, but she was taking possession of something that didn't belong to her.

It was Brynn's doll—a gift from Gram. If Brynn wanted to leave it out in the cemetery to get destroyed by the rain, that was none of her kid sister's business. Those were the rules.

But the thing was, that doll was no longer Brynn's. Her sister had given it to the dead girl in Friendship Park, and it was up to Maggie to keep it from getting ruined by the storm. The doll went beneath Maggie's bed. Maggie's guilt was filed away under *what Brynn doesn't know won't hurt her*. Besides, what difference did it make? Honestly, why would Brynn care?

That night, the storm raged. Their electricity went out, and their mom was losing it, unable to get through to Gram and Gramps's place in Pensacola. She was nearly inconsolable, which was why their father shooed both Brynn and Maggie upstairs.

"Time for bed," he told them.

"But the storm!" Maggie protested.

"It's just rain here," Dad said. "And your mom needs some space."

Brynn didn't argue—she'd spend the rest of the night on her phone until the battery died. But Maggie didn't have a phone, and the inability to flip on the light at any given moment freaked her out.

"What about Gram and Gramps?" She was near tears when her father folded back the sheets for her to slide into bed. "How come Mom can't get them on the phone?"

"Because Gram and Gramps only have a landline, Crazy," Dad explained. "The lines are down. Their power is out, too."

"But what if it's really, really bad this time?" She crawled onto her mattress and stuffed her legs beneath the covers.

"Then they'll go to the elementary school, remember?" Maggie did. Gramps had explained it to Maggie's mom, once. *If the storms hit hard, they evacuate us into the gym. It's not a block from the house and it's at a higher elevation. We'll be fine.* Maggie had found the idea of it pretty funny: her grandma and grandpa shooting hoops with a bunch of old folks, their orthopedic shoes squeaking on the court, waiting for the hurricane to pass.

"Are you sure they're gonna be okay?" Maggie asked, still skeptical. "How will they get there if it's really bad, Dad? Gram's walker . . ." Gram recently had had both of her hips replaced. She couldn't walk on her own if the pain got too bad. And Gramps would never leave her. Not on his life.

"They have that zippy golf cart, remember? I promise, they're going to be okay. Now, try to get some sleep, would you? I need to deal with your mother."

"Is *Mom* gonna be okay?" Maggie blinked at her father. He gave her a goofy look, like, *Mom is too nuts to ever be okay.* Maggie couldn't help it; she cracked a smile. "Wait, *wait!*" She stopped her dad as soon as he turned to go. "What about the lights?" On the way upstairs, her dad had brought two emergency candles along—one for Brynn's room, and one for Maggie.

"Can't help you there, kiddo," he said. "You're just going to have to act your age. You're twenty-seven, right?"

"Da-ad." Maggie huffed.

"Sorry." He held up his hands. "You don't look a day over twenty-four."

"I'm almost *ten!*" She was pretty sure her father knew that, but she couldn't help stressing that fact. Sure, she wasn't a baby anymore, but the wind was howling. What if the windows exploded? Didn't stuff like that happen during really bad hurricanes? She'd seen it happen in movies, so . . .

"Yeah, almost ten," he said. "Which, really, it's kind of embarrassing. I'm surprised you allowed yourself to get so old." Maggie was trying not to crack up again. Her dad had the art of making her feel at ease down to a science. Brynn was a tougher audience, but he could make her laugh, too, if he really tried. "Now, seriously, Crazy. Sleep. Or at least try to."

But she couldn't. Whether it was the hurricane—which the Olsens dealt with by shuttering the windows, making sure they had plenty of batteries for flashlights, and buying up half the Publix canned soup aisle—the idea of her grandparents cowering in a corner of their house out in Florida while their windows blew up around them like bombs, or the marionette that was looming beneath her mattress, she didn't know. But she was scared, which was dumb. After all, her dad was a native Savannahian. He knew how to handle the weather, and the same went for Gramps. Heck, *he* used to be in the marines, which meant he wasn't afraid of anything.

And that thing beneath her bed? Maggie knew it was innocuous, just a fancy toy. But Maggie couldn't help but wonder exactly why Brynn had hidden the remaining dolls toward the back of her closet like that. Did she just not like them, or was there some other reason for their exile?

Don't be stupid, she thought. *If dolls like that were really evil, they would have killed her by now.* She chuckled to herself at the idea of it. Brynn, being chopped up by tiny knives held by tiny doll hands. But her amusement was insincere. The more she thought about those things being able to come to life, the more creeped out she felt.

Eventually losing her nerve, she slid out of bed and dragged the blank-eyed girl out from beneath her mattress by the leg, carrying her to her own closet instead. Once there, she paused. She *could* set up Dolly outside of Brynn's room, pretend she had risen up and walked herself to the Olsen place under her own "evil" power. Brynn would positively freak out. But however fun it would be to prank her big sis, using the doll as the butt of a joke felt off. Brynn deserved it, sure, but Dolly didn't.

She cleared a space amid an array of stuffed animals and placed the doll among them. "There," she whispered. "You'll be safe in here." That, and Maggie would feel safer with a door between them. She shut it tight, and eventually the howl of the wind lulled her to sleep.

．　　．　　．

Katrina brought heavy wind and rain to Savannah, but the Olsens escaped relatively unscathed. One of Maggie's mother's favorite oaks went down in the front yard, and tree branches littered the property. Men with chain saws arrived a few days later to haul the mess away. Mom finally got through to Gram and Gramps. Pensacola had gotten clobbered, and their house was under half an inch of water—the entire mobile home park was. But Gramps wouldn't hear of abandoning ship. They had insurance, and he was determined to get started on the cleanup as soon as possible. Mom flew down a few weeks after the storm to survey the damage and help make her parents' temporary home at an extended-stay motel more comfortable.

And by the time all of that happened, the school year was in full swing. Maggie intended to take Dolly back to her rightful spot but there was always something—homework, a TV show, the occasional fight with Brynn—that kept her from making the trek back to those cemetery gates. Besides, leaving Dolly on top of that tomb felt like a betrayal. And so the doll stayed in Maggie's closet, tucked away among her other toys.

By the second month of school, Maggie was head over heels for her new friend, Cheryl Polley. Cheryl had moved to Savannah from Atlanta, and they had struck up a conversation over one of Maggie's Georgia Aquarium T-shirts. "I've been there," Cheryl had said. "Like, a ton of times. The starfish are my favorite." That's all it took. Maggie was smitten.

Theirs was an obsessive devotion. They ate lunch together,

spent weekends at each other's houses whenever they could, even ended up buying matching necklaces with a few bucks they pooled together during a trip to the mall; BEST FRIENDS was stamped across both pieces of a bisected silver heart. Maggie cast a glance out toward Friendship Park every time she passed it on the bus, but its allure had faded. She was busy with homework and trying to master the art of tetherball. Then there was the pipe dream: rumor had it Kelly Clarkson was going on tour, and Atlanta would be one of her stops. Maggie and Cheryl spent weekends plotting how to talk Cheryl's mom into driving them to the city, and how the heck they'd be able to afford it if their mothers refused to buy them the tickets.

Meanwhile, somewhere in the back of her closet, buried beneath dirty laundry that missed the hamper, was Brynn's doll. Maggie didn't bother returning it to the cemetery. With Cheryl in the picture, it seemed far less pressing than before.

SIX

THE MOMENT MAGGIE stepped inside her childhood home, she instinctively reached for her phone, ready to text Dillon about how coming back was too much, how staying in her old place was beyond her limit. But before she could type out a message, she was shot through with that familiar twinge of pain. Not sadness or nostalgia for her lost parents or dearly departed sister, but literal pain.

The agony Maggie had felt in her neck and shoulders had led to thousands of dollars' worth of chiropractor visits, hundreds of spinal adjustments, and hours of physical therapy. Year after year, she closed her eyes while doctors cracked her neck, wiggling her toes after each pop of vertebrae, making sure she still could. The possibility of a freak accident had never been far from her thoughts: paralysis by way of a professional. And yet nothing alleviated the crippling knot rooted deep at the base of her skull.

Now, standing in the open front door of the home her mother had designed to reflect an issue of *Southern Living*, Maggie reached around to the back of her neck, pressed her fingers against the bumps in her spine, and sucked air in through her teeth. She hadn't felt that pain in so long, and yet there it was, that all-too-familiar tension collecting at the top of her spine. Strange, but she supposed it was befitting of the circumstance. It was all the stress. Besides, she deserved the discomfort. After her dad had passed, she had grown numb. After her mother's death, the emotional part of her brain had, for the most part, closed up shop. And now, with Brynn gone, Maggie *wanted* to cry, *wanted* to mourn the loss of the person she had been closest to in life, and yet the tears refused to come. At least the pain that was settling into the muscles of her upper back was just that: suffering, a cheap stand-in for the biting anguish she couldn't manage to feel.

She dropped her duffel bag in the foyer next to the stairs, hesitated at the base step, and finally allowed herself to meander down the house's main hall. A gallery of photographs lined the area, ending at double French doors. Those pictures had once been of her, Arlen, and Brynn, but were now replaced by Harrison, Hayden, and Hope. She stopped just shy of the French doors, her fingers flexing and relaxing at her sides like twin hearts. Had it not been so overcast, the watery iridescence of the swimming pool beyond the doors would have splashed dancing light onto the ceiling overhead. But now, it simply looked like an angry ocean, disturbed by the intensifying wind. She thought about going out there, daring to graze the flagstones with the soles of her shoes. But why? To remember the awful night Uncle Leon had roused her from sleep during what should have been a fun summer adventure at Hilton Head with her cousins? To recall the drive back to an empty house, the pool cover torn away from its rails? To see if Brynn's shadow was lying there, like a stain refusing to come clean, so much like her father that it was as though history were repeating itself? She turned away, moved toward the kitchen, and stepped into the room with a wince.

"You're still having trouble with that neck?" Arlen glanced up from a laptop upon the kitchen island. A large digital SLR camera sat next to it. Next to that, Arlen's phone, the same one she'd used to call Maggie two days before. *There's been an accident. You have to come home.*

"I didn't think so, but . . ." Maggie continued to rub, but the more she jabbed her fingers into the tight muscle, the more it hurt. "Stress, I guess."

It occurred to her that she hadn't texted Dillon back. She would, though, just as soon as she settled in.

"Or the plane. They'll do that," Arlen said. "Those neck dough-nuts look ridiculous, but they're worth the humiliation. You don't have one, do you?" She jabbed the enter key on the keyboard, giving flight to a freshly composed email.

Maggie tried to shake her head, but only managed another cringe.

"You should know better," Arlen said. "The last thing you need is another picture-perfect CT scan. Even with insurance, it'll cost you a small fortune."

The scan, along with a spinal tap, had been done when Maggie was just shy of fifteen. It had been the chiropractor's idea—one that had triggered the strangest emotional response from their mother. Stella Olsen, a woman who approached child rearing with what could only be described as a lackadaisical hand, was positively horror-struck at the mere mention of such a test, let alone the idea of there being something genuinely wrong with her youngest child. She started throwing around theories as fast as a coked-up med school dropout. WebMD became her obsession, and by the time Maggie's appointment for the scan arrived, her mother was sure of her arm-chair diagnosis: brain cancer, maybe spinal meningitis, possibly both. But Maggie's tests came up clean.

"Anyway, I've got some photos I need to edit or the client is going to lose her damn mind." Arlen raised a hand, waved it over her head like an injured bird. "Total bridezilla. Absolute nightmare."

"You're working?" Maggie looked to the computer. A photo stared out at her from the screen. The bridezilla in question was wearing a crazy-eyed expression, trying to hold a near-manic smile. *I'm so very happy right now!*

Maggie hadn't managed to complete more than a quarter of her exam the morning she had received Arlen's call; the questions she *had* answered, she'd probably flubbed. With her head down and her shoulders slumped, she had walked her test to the front of the lecture hall—all eyes on her because she was the first—and slipped it onto her professor's desk without a word. She managed to make it to the restroom before bursting into tears. Maybe she had been weeping for Brynn, but at that moment, it had felt more like frustration than grief.

"I don't have a *choice*, Maggie." Arlen exhaled a dramatic sigh, falling short of a full explanation. Maggie didn't need one. Ask a wedding photographer about the worst possible time of year for sibling suicide, and each one would scream: *Wedding season!* "Brynn's car is in the garage," Arlen said, sliding over a bundle of keys. "I don't know if it's filled up, and I don't know what she left in there, so proceed with caution. Maybe you can clean it out if it's full of junk. I don't know what we're going to do with it; probably get the title changed over and sell it . . . unless *you* want to drive it up to Wilmington."

Maggie shook her head that she didn't. She already had a car. Having two made no sense.

Arlen yanked open a kitchen drawer, tossed out a Post-it pad, and scribbled a name and address. "This is the mortuary we're using." It was the same one they had used for both parents. "And this is Father John's number. You can call him anytime. He remembers you." Odd, considering Maggie only remembered Father John from officiating Olsen family funerals. Even after all that death,

Maggie never was one for praising the Lord or shouting *Amen*. Science had overridden her faith. "I've taken care of most of the details, but just swing by, okay?" Arlen gave Maggie a pleading look.

"Swing by?" Maggie offered Arlen a blank stare.

"The mortuary," Arlen clarified. Yes, *that* place, where men in snappy suits attempted to look sympathetic while trying to upsell caskets that cost as much as Cadillacs. Nothing quite says *I love you* like satin lining and high-gloss veneer.

"Can't you come with me?" There was something about that place—the pressure, the options, the memory of their mother sitting zombielike and unblinking as the funeral director turned his attention from the unresponsive adult to her three children, searching their faces for signs of life. Arlen, who had been twenty-two at the time, scribbled her signature where their mother's should have gone. She'd handled their mom's funeral, too. And here she was again, at death number three.

"No, Maggie, I can't. That's why I needed you here, to help me deal with this. We talked about this . . ."

"But I don't even know the budget," Maggie protested, and that was true. Hours after she had bombed her test and regained her composure, she had called Arlen to ask about arrangements. She had offered to pay for some of the expenses, but Arlen had declined the help. *Just get here*, she had said. *That's all I ask.* And so Maggie had paid a small fortune for a next-day flight and come home, despite it being the last thing in the world she had wanted to do.

"They have the budget," Arlen assured her. "And if you really need me, I've got my cell."

Another zing of pain. Another wince. Maggie hissed through her teeth as she leaned against the island, jabbing her fingers against muscle and bone. Arlen pulled open another kitchen drawer and placed a bottle of Tylenol onto the counter in an unspoken admonishment. *I don't have time for this.*

"Should I take the kids?" That was desperation talking. The last thing Maggie wanted was to shuttle a trio of children around town for any reason, for any amount of time. But at least she wouldn't be alone in a room full of empty coffins, wondering which one Brynn would have hated the least.

". . . to the *mortuary*?" Arlen widened her eyes, as though the mere suggestion was as good as a slap across the face.

"Right," Maggie murmured. "Dumb idea."

"There are fresh towels in the upstairs bathroom, as well as some shampoo and stuff I picked up at the store, in case you want a shower before you go."

Maggie watched her sister from across the island, Arlen's eyes fixed on her computer screen, her maternal instincts so strong she no longer had to think about the things that came out of her mouth as she spoke them. Autopilot mothering, an inherited trait.

She wondered how Brynn had felt about losing a maternal figure only to have another one immediately take her place. Brynn would have been happier if she had moved out; God knows Arlen had asked her to do so more than half a dozen times. *I mean, honestly,* Arlen had complained. *I have kids, a family. Brynn continuing to live with us, it's just . . . weird.* The money would have been good for her: the girl who couldn't keep a steady job to save her life, claiming she didn't like humanity enough to cope with a nine-to-five; the girl who had to wear all black all the time as though any other color would result in her breaking out in an aggressive form of hives. She could have taken the cash, moved out of Savannah—a town where she had never fit in, would *never* fit in. Unfit to be a country-club debutante sipping mimosas with her girlfriends every weekday afternoon. Hell, unfit to be the girl *serving* the mimosas. Where they came from—unless Starbucks or McDonald's was looking for help—Brynn Olsen was virtually unhireable, and her doom-and-gloom outlook didn't help. Not around these parts.

And yet, even with Arlen's harping and Maggie's gentle suggestions of leaving the place behind, Brynn had stayed. *I can't*, she had said. *I just . . . I can't*. Maggie couldn't grasp her sister's motive. Brynn, it seemed, was as determined to remain in their childhood home as Maggie was committed to never return. But after years of fighting, it seemed that Brynn's refusal wasn't something for Maggie to understand. If Brynn wanted Maggie to get it, she would have surely explained—something she never got the chance to do.

Pulling Brynn's keys into her hand, Maggie stepped back into the foyer and paused at the base of the stairs.

ARLEN IS SENDING ME OUT TO BUY A COFFIN. Send.

ARE YOU SERIOUS? Immediate response.

DEAD SERIOUS. Send. And then a follow-up emoji—the one that was laughing so hard it was in tears.

NOT FUNNY! Dillon, always the serious one. Maggie cracked a smile at her screen, slid her phone into her back pocket, and grabbed the strap of her duffel bag before hefting it onto her shoulder.

. . . but she didn't make it up the stairs. Hesitating for yet another beat, she paused to gaze at the doors that led out to the pool for a second time. Her heart fluttered to a standstill, her eyes catching what looked to be something running across the flagstones and out of sight. Were the girls out there? Maggie looked back to the kitchen, considered asking Arlen if that wasn't a bit morbid. Unsafe. Kids around an open pool. The wind. Inevitable rain. And then, was there a stain on the stonework where Brynn had fallen? Who had scrubbed it clean if it was gone? How could Arlen ever allow her kids out there again, and why had they ever been allowed out there at all?

She couldn't bring herself to approach the doors. But she also couldn't, in good conscience, not let Arlen know that her kids were out there on their own. Because what if one of them fell in? How would Maggie forgive herself for that?

"Len?" Maggie started to move back toward the kitchen, but she paused when she heard both Hayden and Hope charging down the upstairs hallway.

But . . . Her attention shifted to the double doors once more. *Maybe I should* . . . No. She looked away with a shudder, readjusted her grip on her bag, and slowly began to ascend the stairs to her old room.

She knew: it was still here. That thing still lurked within those rooms.

SEVEN

T WAS STRANGE to hear laughter echo down the upstairs hallway. It felt sacrilegious—something that would anger Brynn's spirit if only she could hear. But mourning wasn't meant for children. It was doubtful that Maggie's gleefully squealing three-year-old niece knew what death was, or understood that after the ambulance that had parked outside the house had driven away, she'd never see her Auntie Bee again. But that was Hayden. Hope, on the other hand, appeared to understand that Aunt Brynn was forever gone; she simply didn't seem to care.

With laughter continuing to reverberate through the stairwell, Maggie found herself staring at Brynn's closed bedroom door. Her duffel bag hung heavy off her left shoulder as her fingers extended toward the knob, both wanting and dreading to see the mess that her sister had left. It had been a few days, and while it was possible that Arlen had replaced the shattered window to keep the house secure, it was doubtful there had been time to fix the carpet. It was almost certain that there would be spatter, if not dried pools of rust dotting the rug.

Maggie jerked her hand away from the knob when Hayden came barreling down the hall in a flurry of giggles. She was a burst of sparkles and bright green tulle, swinging a ribbon-adorned Tinker Bell wand back and forth like a hatchet without a blade. Chased by Hope—who was still decked out in her dance leotard—little Hayden was blinded by the joy of her big sister's pursuit. She didn't seem to notice Maggie standing there. The toddler ran by in a rush—still smelling of French eyes and chickens—and let out a gleeful twitter at the end of the hall, then disappeared through an open door that must have led into her room.

Hope, however, was more observant. Her laughter stalled and her smile faded as soon as her aunt Maggie came into view. Slowing her steps, Hope approached her aunt with a mixture of hesitation and suspicion. She paused a few feet from Maggie before allowing her brown eyes to flick to Brynn's closed bedroom door.

"Are you going in there, Aunt Magdalene?" Hope's question felt ominous, as though the answer should have been a resounding *no*. And yet Maggie slowly nodded in the affirmative. "Uh-oh," Hope said, responding to Maggie's gesture.

"What?" Maggie asked.

"Mom said to stay out." The girl shifted her weight from one ballet shoe to the other, back and forth in a half-hearted temps lié.

That meant Maggie was correct in her assumption, however dark: there were still signs of suicide in there. But she posed the question anyway. "Did your mom say why?"

Then again, maybe it *had* been cleaned up. Perhaps Arlen had warned the kids to stay away simply to keep them from rifling through Brynn's stuff. It was a matter of respect. But there was something in Hope's expression that suggested otherwise, something that assured Maggie that stories had been told, the kind of dark tales Brynn used to tell at the dinner table, about bad guys and boogeymen, of shadows and phantoms.

"You shouldn't play in there." Hope twisted her fingers in front of her, as though trying to wrench them free of her hands. "Bad things are inside. It's why Auntie Bee got sick."

Maggie furrowed her eyebrows. "Sick?"

"Yuh-huh."

"Sick how?" Maggie asked. It was only then that she caught a whiff of something strange: smoke, or a freshly extinguished candlewick—faint but undeniably there. It smelled like Brynn's room, but out in the hall.

Hope shrugged. "I dunno."

"What—is something burning?" Maggie's gaze roved the hall, searching for the source of the scent. But she was distracted a moment later.

"I gotta go watch Hay," Hope said.

"Hold on—" Maggie reached out to her niece, but Hope skittered away, too quick to catch. "Hope, *wait* . . ."

But Hope disappeared into the same room Hayden had. A beat later, the door slammed shut behind both kids, assuring Aunt Maggie that their conversation was over. No grown-ups allowed.

From downstairs, an aggravated yell. "No slamming!"

Maggie looked back to Brynn's door. Arlen hadn't mentioned anything about Brynn being sick. And during their phone conversations, neither had Brynn. Maybe *sick* had been the only way Arlen knew how to explain suicide to such young kids. Because didn't you have to be heartsick to take your own life?

But for Arlen to tell them that bad things were in there was a total Brynn move. Bad things, like contagious depression, like a communicable alternative lifestyle. Maggie couldn't help it. She snorted, imagining Arlen's reaction if, years from now, Harrison came home with dyed-purple hair, or Hope showed up from college with a ring through her nose and a combat-boot-wearing boyfriend at her elbow.

She reached out to Brynn's door again, gave it a few light taps. *Knock knock.* "Did you hear that, Bee?" she murmured into the empty hallway. "Bad things—" She stopped midsentence, her attention diverted to where her own room used to be. And while the hallway was empty, she could swear she'd seen something skitter across the backdrop of the farthest wall. "What . . . ?"

And then, a *tap tap tap* resounded from inside Brynn's locked-up room.

Maggie staggered backward. She gawked at the door before her. Had she really just heard that, or was this house playing tricks on her already? *Just a loose screw, Crazy.*

"Shit." She whispered the word to herself, though it was unclear whether she was cursing the possibility of her imagination running wild or the fact that the house was still what it used to be: visited. "Shit, shit, *shit.*"

She turned away from Brynn's door and fled, just as the girls had, walking just a little too quickly to where her bedroom had once been.

• • • •

With her nerves rattled, Maggie was more than happy to leave the house, even if it was to visit the mortuary. For the third time in her life, she found herself surrounded by caskets. A tall, sad-looking twig of a man in a three-piece suit ushered her into the showroom at the back of the funeral home, every other footfall accented by the softest squeak of his leather shoes. "I'll give you some time," he said, not once raising his voice above a hushed murmur. He smelled like coffee and the faintest twinge of cigarettes. When he tried to smile, it made him look pained, like he had a bad stomachache. Finally, he gave up on niceties and left her alone in the showroom of the dead.

The room was mood-lit, which felt both fitting and grossly inappropriate all at once. In the dimness that was probably meant to be soothing but simply came off as bizarre, coffins were lined up in perfect rows of two. In the center, upon raised and dramatically illuminated platforms, the showpieces: funerary boxes gleaming with lacquer and silver-plated finishings, propped open to boast quilted velvet interiors, matching pillows, and memorial plaques. There should have been a sign: SHOW THE DECEASED YOU LOVE THEM! SHOW THEM (WITH YOUR WALLET) THAT THEY WILL BE FOREVER MISSED!

There was a backlit display case with urns of all shapes and materials centered upon the back wall: hardwood boxes carved with praying hands and crosses; brass lidded canisters featuring doves and flowers, one sporting an eagle flying across an etched American flag. Brynn would have *loved* that one. Patriotism at its best. All the display pieces were spotless and free of fingerprints. The room was so silent, so torpid, it might as well have been six feet beneath the ground.

If it had been up to Maggie, Brynn would have been cremated. Her ashes would have been placed in a simple wooden box until half of them could be spread in Bonaventure Cemetery, while the remainder would be sprinkled beneath the oaks of Forsyth Park—two of Brynn's favorite places in their hometown. But Arlen had taken it upon herself to make the arrangements, and because Maggie wasn't bearing any of the financial burden, it felt wrong to put up a fight. Burying a sibling was hard enough as it was. Disagreement would only make it worse. Maggie refused to make this any harder, and so she selected a simple black casket with white satin trim. Elegant and understated, unlike the pink-and-gold nightmare she'd now spotted at the far end of the room. Brynn would have been gleeful had she seen it. Hell, she would have climbed in and taken a selfie.

After Maggie placed a signature on the solemn man's clipboard, and after he'd expressed his whispered condolences another half dozen times, she stepped out of the building and slipped into

Brynn's black Toyota Camry. She sat motionless in the driver's seat
for a long while, staring at the selection of pendants that hung from
the rearview mirror: a cameo of a skeleton bride and a tiny bird skull
attached to wooden rosary beads. The dash was swathed in a black
velvet cover—a custom job Brynn had commissioned on Etsy, if
Maggie had to guess. Vinyl stickers of bands, most of which Maggie
had never heard of, decorated the back window. She'd only noticed
the bumper sticker after she'd pulled into the mortuary's parking lot.
MY OTHER CAR IS A HEARSE. It would have been funny had the
circumstances been different, but now, all it made Maggie want to
do was cry.

Distraction came in the form of a soft chime from the depths
of her messenger bag. A text. Maggie let her head fall back against
the headrest and closed her eyes. Dillon. Oh God, she still hadn't
responded to any of his countless messages. She was an asshole, and
she owed him an apology. Hopefully, he'd say it wasn't a big deal.
There would be tension, but neither one of them would dare bring
it up. She breathed out into the windswept heat of the car. Despite
Florence crawling toward the coast, it was still in the midnineties.
These summer storms rarely brought relief. Jutting her arm into her
bag, she fished out her cell.

But it wasn't Dillon. It was Cheryl.

ARE YOU STANDING ME UP?

It would be nice to see her again. Maggie only wished the occasion hadn't been so sad. A wedding. A random Wilmington encoun-
ter. Hell, even an awkward run-in at a high school reunion would
have been better, as if Maggie would ever attend such an event.
Brynn, though? She'd been patiently awaiting her ten-year home-
coming, looking forward to walking the halls, busting into her old
locker, graffitiing the bathroom stalls, and making up her crazy stories around the punch bowl she'd just spiked.

Me? Brynn had said. *I can't wait to see all those losers again. Prim little bitches, empty-headed jocks—they'll all believe me when I tell them I've founded my own chapter of the Church of Satan.*

Right, Maggie had replied; it had been during one of their last calls. *Because that's totally plausible.*

Yeah, you may be right. I'll go more subtle, draining cadavers of their juices at the morgue or heading a hazmat crew that removes dead bodies from, like, those houses on Hoarders *or something.*

Proceed with caution, Maggie had warned. *People love that show.*

Yeah. You're right. Digging bodies out of piles of their own garbage will probably get me voted onto reunion prom court. Back to the drawing board.

Or maybe you want *to be on prom court. Like Carrie.*

There had been a long silence on the line, and then, after a beat: *Would it be weird if I brought my own bucket of pig's blood?* And then, both girls had cackled together like a tiny coven of witches.

Brynn would miss it, now. There would be no *Carrie* reenactment at their old high school. And Maggie would miss Brynn.

"I'm sorry, Bee," she whispered. "I should have come home like you'd asked." The tears started to well up. She squinted them away, her phone blipping in her hand.

CAN'T STAY LONG, JUST SO YOU KNOW.

She texted Cheryl back.

ON MY WAY NOW.

She didn't text Dillon, but she would. Later. After she met with Cheryl, after she got some things off her chest.

• • • •

Impresso Espresso had once been one of Maggie's favorite places, with an old fireplace in the corner that crackled with the burning of real pine logs during winters that were never actually cold. She had spent countless afternoons upon the cushions of those cozy couches and armchairs—sometimes laughing with friends; sometimes alone and upset, lamenting. That fireplace was currently dormant, and while the doors were typically propped open in the summer, the wind was too vicious for that now. Some storms passed quickly, but Florence refused to let up.

When Maggie pulled the door open to step inside, Cheryl Polley's ruddy brown hair blew across the curve of a bare shoulder like something out of a shampoo commercial. But she looked nervous, unhappy to be there, as though meeting up with her former best friend for the first time in years was the last thing she wanted to do. It was disappointing to so readily recognize Cheryl's lack of enthusiasm, but Maggie understood the source of her old friend's frown. What happened in the house hadn't just destroyed Maggie's family. It had mauled her most cherished friendship as well.

"Cher?" Maggie paused next to the little table Cheryl had selected, close to a window and away from the line of coffee drinkers who came and went despite Florence's onslaught.

"Hey." Cheryl rose from her seat and gave Maggie a slightly awkward hug. Cheryl's white tank top—faded from one too many washes—sported a cross in front of a row of stylized pines. SAINT MICHAEL'S YOUTH CAMP was scrawled around the design. Cheryl had been into religion when they had been younger, but she'd really gone gung ho after the two had fallen out. Now, she was a full-time camp counselor when she wasn't taking classes at the seminary. Maggie wondered if Brynn knew what path Cheryl had taken in life, and whether, when she had learned it, her eyes had rolled right out of her head.

"You look great," Maggie said, taking a backward step when Cheryl released her from their embrace "How are you?" She knew the answer to that question before Cheryl had a chance to retake her seat.

"I *was* fine." Blunt. To the point. "Until you called."

She deserved that, but it still stung to hear it.

Sitting down, Maggie peered at the scarred tabletop, unsure of what to say. "I'm sorry," was the only thing that came out.

"Are you?"

"Yes, I am, Cher." Maggie tipped her chin upward to meet her old friend's eyes. She liked to think that the strength of their former bond couldn't altogether fade, but Cheryl was making it clear: that was a long time ago. She had moved on.

"Anyway . . ." Cheryl looked away. "This is just a lot to handle. I don't really know what to say other than *I'm sorry for your loss*, but I know how much you love that."

This was true. After Maggie's dad had his accident, all that free-flowing sympathy had desensitized her. After her mom went, the condolences just felt flat-out strange. But Brynn—well . . . both Maggie and Cher had grown up hearing the whispers. People were almost certainly saying suicide was no surprise. If anything, they were likely shocked that Brynn had waited as long as she had.

"How did you find out?" Maggie finally asked. Were their inner circles already talking? Was Brynn's demise starring local gossip, too hot to keep quiet?

"Arlen was the source," Cher said. "She spoke to Father John about the funeral, Father John mentioned it to someone at the rectory, that someone else told someone else. It got back to me, since I'm working at the camp and people know we were close." *Were.* "You know how things go around here." She shifted her weight in her seat, narrowed her eyes at the sweating plastic cup of iced coffee next to her elbow. "But I suppose it's better that you hear it from me than from someone else."

"Hear what from you?" Maggie's attention shifted from Cheryl's hands to her face. "That my sister is dead? Or that you finally believe me?" A moment later, she was glaring at the tabletop again. What kind of family had so much tragedy? Three deaths in less than a decade, all under the same roof. It was unheard of, like one of Brynn's weird stories brought to life. Had what Maggie done been so bad? Had she incited something unthinkable?

Cheryl's fingers snaked across the table, catching Maggie's hand. "No," she said. "You know that's crazy, Maggie." *Just a loose screw . . .*

"Then why are you so pissed at me?" Maggie pulled her hand away. "If you think it's all bullshit, why did I practically have to beg you to meet me here?"

"Because I know what you want to talk about," Cheryl fired back. "And I don't want to talk about it. What's wrong with that?"

"You're scared," Maggie said flatly. Cheryl belted out a laugh, setting Maggie's already frayed nerves on a razor's edge. "What? Why is that funny?"

"Because it's nonsense," Cheryl said. "We've been through this before. First with your dad, then with—"

"Yeah, thanks for the recap, Cher. *I know.*"

Their friendship had deteriorated more than a year before Maggie's father had died, but to Cheryl's credit, when she had heard the news, she had come running. Maggie had bawled her eyes out on Cheryl's shoulder; she had blubbered about how it had been her fault, how if she hadn't gone to the beach with her cousins, maybe she could have saved her father from such a tragic fate. *It told me not to go, but I went, and now . . .* Back then, at thirteen, Cheryl hadn't been of the mind to rebuke Maggie's belief that she had somehow cursed her father. By the time Maggie came back to Savannah for her mother's funeral, Cheryl had firmly placed one foot upon the neck of logical explanation and the other in the hands of God.

"Look." Cheryl breathed out a sigh, then leaned back in her seat. "I don't want to come off as unfeeling or anything, but Brynn had issues. She always did. When I said *hear it from me*, what I meant was that people *are* talking. And they're saying some crazy stuff."

Maggie glanced up again. Cheryl's cinnamon-colored hair was glowing in the sunshine. For a blip of a second, Maggie saw the girl she used to love more fiercely than anyone in the world. Her closest friend—the one who used to help her catch lightning bugs in empty pickle jars; the girl she used to walk with along the train tracks, placing pennies upon the rails; the companion who had allowed Maggie to place a stupid board across her knees, who had put her hands upon a planchette, not knowing what the future would hold; the friend who, after what had happened in Maggie's room, refused to ever come over again. The one who had torn her side of their best-friend necklace from her neck and thrown it onto Maggie's carpet so many years before.

"Like what?" Maggie asked.

"Just crazy stuff." Cheryl rolled her eyes. "Like how Brynn had been into witchcraft and voodoo. Personally, I think that's ridiculous. There's a rumor that she was a Satanist or whatever . . ."

Maggie would have laughed had she not been on the verge of throwing up, if Cheryl herself hadn't once suggested that Brynn was into *weird stuff* because she didn't look like everyone else. Or maybe Brynn had gone through with the Church of Satan story after all, and all of Bible-thumping Savannah had bought the lie.

"But someone said they saw her hanging out at Friendship Park in the middle of the night just a few days before all of this happened, lingering next to the kids' graves," Cheryl continued. "Just like she used to when we were kids."

Maggie tensed. Okay, Brynn hadn't mentioned anything about Friendship Park in years. After their dad's accident, she hadn't breathed the word *ghost* in Maggie's presence, as though afraid of waking a slumbering beast, and she certainly hadn't gone to the graveyard unless it was with the family, in broad daylight, to place flowers onto their father's headstone.

"That particular detail," Cher said, looking down to her hands. "Well, it's a little hard to rebuff, you know?"

"She was probably just visiting our parents," Maggie protested.

"Okay, I'll give you that. But then she showed up at Saint Michael's . . ."

"Wait, *what*?" Now this was making no sense. The idea of Brynn attending church was ludicrous—unless, of course, she had gone there to burn it to the ground.

"I know, right?" Cher gave Maggie a look: *Yeah, weird.* "I wasn't there. Camp has been nuts this year. We've got, like, fifty kids running around. But my gran never misses a service. She saw Brynn sitting in the last pew . . . and Maggie, she said that Brynn looked *bad*."

"Bad how?"

"Sad, exhausted . . . sick, I guess."

Sick.

"And less than a week after my gran brings up Brynn Olsen, I get a call from her little sister, as though you had somehow overheard Gran ask, *How* is *that friend Maggie of yours, anyhow?*"

Maggie's stomach pitched. She stared down at her lap, the buzz of people coming and going nothing but muffled cotton in her ears. It didn't make sense. Why hadn't Arlen mentioned Brynn being sick? Maybe Arlen hadn't noticed it with how scarce Brynn had made herself in the end, but that theory was blown apart by Hope's warning Maggie to stay out of Brynn's room. If the *kids* knew that Brynn had been ill, Arlen did, too. She should have at least texted Maggie to let her know. Or at least brought it up on their drive from the airport.

And then there was the church. The *church*. Why in the world would Brynn have—

"Sanctuary." Maggie whispered the word beneath the noise of the café, the revelation lighting up each and every nerve.

It's the only thing churches are good for, Mags, Brynn had explained during one of their cemetery visits. *If you're scared, you go to church and the evil can't get you, because evil things can't go inside there.*

How come? Maggie had asked.

Because evil is superstitious, Brynn had said. *It's like walking under a ladder or breaking a mirror. You know nothing bad is gonna happen, but you aren't gonna go out of your way to do those things, either. Evil stuff doesn't believe in God. But it's not gonna go marching into a church to find out if God is real, either. Evil stuff is a coward. So, if you're ever really* scared, *you go to church.*

Brynn had been running from something. She was seeking protection.

"She was scared," Maggie said. "It's why she kept asking me to come home, but I didn't. I could have, but I—"

"Maggie." Cheryl reached out again, placing her hand on top of Maggie's own. "I wish you'd stop this," she said softly, her words muddled by the hiss of an espresso machine, the whir of a burr grinder. "You *have* to stop this. You're going to drive yourself insane."

"So, how do I stop it?" Maggie asked, genuinely wanting to know the solution. Because as far as she was concerned, there was no way. This was her life. It was her fault. It was who she'd become.

"I don't know, I just . . . I wish there was some way to prove . . ." Cheryl paused, then straightened in her seat.

Maggie looked up at her friend. "What?"

Cheryl's expression went dark. Her features shifted from soft to determined. "You know I'm training to become ordained," she said. "I'm not official yet, but maybe if I was there, with my knowledge. I don't know. Maybe it would help."

"Where's *there*? Help with what?" Maggie shook her head. "What are you talking about?"

"Let's just do it again."

"Do it again . . ." Maggie swallowed against the lump that had lodged itself in her throat, dry like a pill. It was pointless to play dumb. Neither one of them had forgotten their final night together, the evening they had started to grow apart. "But you said—"

"I know what I said. But my beliefs don't have any influence over yours, right? You aren't just going to believe me if I say *it's not real*. But if I can *show* you . . . I think it would help."

Help. Hearing that word come out of Cheryl's mouth made Maggie want to jump out of her seat and march across the parking lot toward Brynn's car, just get in and haul ass out of there. *What would Jesus do?* Brynn would have thrown her head back and howled: *Run, Forrest! Run for your life!*

Maggie pulled away from Cheryl's touch. "I don't know . . ."

"Look, you're studying oceanography, right?" Cheryl asked. "That's what I've heard, anyway. Forget me and all the religious stuff. You're a scientist. If you believe in logic over old wives' tales, it doesn't make *sense* for you to have any issues. So, let's just do it. *Nothing* will happen," she pressed. "And when we find ourselves sitting there like a couple of idiots, it'll prove that this has all been in your head."

Except Cheryl didn't know the whole story. Nobody did. After Dad, there was no way in the world Maggie dared breathe a word of it to anyone.

Don't go.

She'd promised to be a friend to whatever was living inside her house.

Don't go.

She'd spent countless nights with that board—the same device that had destroyed her and Cheryl's friendship—but, rather than Cheryl sitting across from her, there was no one. Not even Brynn.

Don't go.

It was Maggie's fault, all of it; it had been her reality for so long.

If Cheryl was right, though . . . if she somehow proved that Maggie's role in the deaths of her parents was nonexistent? How would that feel? Who would she become, then? If this tragedy wasn't of her making, who did that make her? Who was she?

Maggie's bottom lip trembled.

"Maggie." Cheryl's tone was steady. "I know we've gone our separate ways. Things aren't the way they used to be. That's just life, you know? But I just . . . I'm sorry how things turned out between us. I feel bad. I've *felt* bad. I owe you this."

"I don't know . . ." She echoed her doubt, barely a whisper this time around.

"Hey, I don't really want to do this, either. I don't know what they'd say if they found out at seminary. But I just . . ." She hesitated. "Maybe I want to make sure, too. Maybe it's something that's been bothering me, that question of *what if.* I mean, you said it wasn't you, right? That night, when we . . ."

Maggie shook her head. No, it hadn't been her. She hadn't spelled out those words. Her fingers had been on the planchette, but her hands had been guided by an invisible force.

"So, let's just do this," Cheryl said, making the decision for them both. "If only to prove to us both that this has nothing to do with you. Okay?"

Maggie squeezed her eyes shut, but she managed a nod. "Okay," she whispered. Because at least Cheryl *wanted* to help. Beyond that, she was on her own.

EIGHT

BRYNN'S INFLUENCE OVER her youngest sister came into its own on Maggie's twelfth birthday. Armed with a pocket full of celebratory cash, Maggie wandered the aisles of the local Toys R Us without adult supervision. Her mom was next door at the Barnes & Noble, having a coffee and thumbing through magazines. No matter, though. That birthday cash was burning a hole in Maggie's pocket, begging to be spent.

She didn't know what she was going to buy, but despite officially being a tween, she couldn't quite shake the childish need to leave the store with *something*. The Barbies were immediately passed up; Maggie never was into those, and besides, Arlen had left boxes upon boxes of them up in the attic when she moved out. Maggie considered the stuffed animals, but decided against them—too babyish and boring as far as she was concerned. A selection of art supplies was perused. Maggie loved art, but her desk drawers and half her closet were stuffed full of Crayola markers, sticker books, reams of construction paper, and tubes of glitter glue. Anything she bought would just be a repeat of what she already had. A new bike would have been nice—hers was starting to show some wear and tear, and she didn't even have streamers like Brynn's for her handlebars—but she only had forty bucks. Sure, she could buy streamers now, but putting them on her beat-up old bike seemed lame, and a brand-new bike was way out of her league. Maybe she'd get lucky next year, for her big one-three.

But for now, she aimed herself toward the board games at the back of the store. If she couldn't find something that she'd enjoy on her own, she could at least pick up a game that she and Cheryl could play during their upcoming sleepover. Heck, if she got something good, perhaps Brynn would skip out on talking to her boyfriend all night and want to play, too.

The selection was vast. Floor-to-ceiling game boxes had turned an entire wall of the store into a colorful checkerboard. But none of them sparked Maggie's imagination. That was, until she spied something simpler and far less vibrant than the rest. Tucked into the corner of a shelf like an exile among its more dazzling brethren was a white box bearing a picture of two pairs of hands. They were candlelit, basking in the glow of mystery. One of the pairs bore heavy rings—a fortune-teller gazing not into a crystal ball, but into an off-white plastic heart with a hole in its center; some sort of wooden board lying beneath it, decorated by a smiling sun and discontented moon.

OUIJA, the box announced. MYSTIFYING ORACLE.

Maggie took a step closer, pulled it from the shelf, and flipped it over to see what the game was all about. Except the back of the box was blank—nothing but white cardboard, as if to suggest that what rested inside defied explanation. It was, after all, mystifying. Only the oracle could accurately illustrate its power.

Maggie vacillated over the decision for a few minutes. The Mouse Trap game *did* look fun, and she'd lost a lot of her plastic Hungry Hungry Hippos balls when she had overturned the box in the attic, white marbles spilling everywhere, lost forever among Gram and her mother's useless old junk.

There was, of course, the grown-up option: buy nothing and save the money. But it was her *birthday*. Spending her cash on a game she knew nothing about was risky, but the idea of going home empty-handed was too lame for words. Besides, those glowing hands were alluring, beckoning her to dare. She glanced over her shoulder. Was a dawdling store employee watching her from behind the shelves, wondering if she had the guts? She didn't see anyone as she tucked the box beneath her arm. If it was awful, she could always return it. At least, if she could get her mom to drive her down here again.

Maggie's mom was waiting for her next door at the bookstore. Sipping a latte from the B&N café and reading a freshly purchased copy of *Southern Living*, she never saw her daughter's purchase or asked for specifics. Stella Olsen wasn't one to pry. Besides, what could Toys R Us possibly stock that Maggie wouldn't be allowed to have?

"Got what you wanted?" was the only question she posed, tossing her paper coffee cup into the trash bin as they walked out to the car. Beyond the magazine, she was clutching a new Nora Roberts novel, more than likely itching to get home, grab a glass of Riesling, and read.

"Yep." Maggie held the bagged board game close to her chest, an anxious tingle assuring her that she was getting away with something she shouldn't have, that she was somehow getting in way over her head. Those mysterious hands on the box didn't seem like they were meant for kids, and there was something ominous about those rings, something foreboding about the blankness of that white cardboard back. Even the cashier, who looked like she was about Brynn's age, had eyeballed Maggie's selection, as if considering warning the twelve-year-old against taking it home. And yet there it had been, next to Operation and Apples to Apples. That in itself was proof enough: she had nothing to worry about, and she couldn't wait to show her sister.

Brynn regarded her little sister's birthday purchase with more skepticism than Maggie had expected.

The fifteen-year-old high-school sophomore peered at the box as she stood in the center of her room, the walls plastered with posters of bands their dad found infinitely amusing—Depeche Mode, the Cure, the Smiths, and a group that called themselves the Police. Maggie thought that was a pretty peculiar name, because who the heck named a band after cops? When Maggie had posed the question a while back, Brynn had shrugged and showed Maggie an old record their dad had given her by the same group. *I guess he grew up listening to them, too*, she had said, wearing the faintest shadow of distaste. It was never cool to be into your old man's music, but that record had somehow found its way onto Brynn's wall—a keystone to a menagerie of glossy paper, all of it radiating outward from a black record sleeve with bright red digital gibberish at its center: GHOST IN THE MACHINE.

"You don't think it's cool?" Maggie asked, disappointed in her sister's nonreaction to the game box Brynn now held in her hands.

"No," Brynn said, flipping the box over for the umpteenth time, as if not believing that it was completely blank. "I've seen these before. They're just a bunch of crap. Too bad, too, because it's not like Mom is gonna drive you all the way back there to return it."

"Well, what's it supposed to do anyway?" Maggie asked.

Brynn gave her kid sister an *Are you serious?* look.

"I mean, it doesn't *say* anything," Maggie reminded her. "The back is blank. I couldn't just open it to see . . ."

"It's supposed to let you talk to the dead," Brynn said.

Maggie felt her eyes widen, big as her mother's fancy teacup saucers—the ones she only used on special occasions, and sometimes not even then. *I don't want the girls damaging them, Peter. They're heirlooms, for heaven's sake.*

"I told you, it's fake," Brynn said. "It's for, like, parties and stuff."

"Oh." Maggie's wide eyes narrowed with subtle disappointment. This impulse purchase was clearly a mistake. "Have *you* played before?"

Brynn shrugged, not committing to an answer.

"Well, can we try it anyway?" Maggie asked. "Since I spent my birthday money?"

"Not now." Brynn dropped the box to her feet and casually toed it beneath her bed.

"Why not?" Maggie asked, looking to the bed skirt that was obscuring her birthday gift from view. "It's my birthday. If it's a party game, let's have a party. And how come it's going under *your* bed and not mine?"

"Because you can't have a proper séance in the middle of the day, dummy," Brynn said. "And because if Mom catches you with that thing, you're gonna have a lot of explaining to do, and you totally suck at excuses. I'm surprised she didn't see it when you bought it."

That was because Maggie had a sneaking suspicion her mother would make her take it back, and now Brynn was confirming her wariness. She didn't ask Brynn why getting caught in possession of the board would have been bad, but the thought of getting in trouble for playing that thing only made her want to try it out more.

"Can we do it tonight?" she asked.

Brynn shrugged, seemingly uninterested. That in itself was weird, because here it was, a chance to speak to spirits beyond the grave, and Brynn was acting like it was the most boring suggestion ever.

Brynn, the girl who couldn't stop telling ghost stories to save her life. Brynn, who once fashioned broken-down cardboard boxes she had painted black around her bed to make it look like a coffin. Brynn, the girl who couldn't stop watching horror movies and claimed one of her favorite songs was a tune by the Smiths called "Pretty Girls Make Graves."

"But Brynn, it's my *birthday*!" Maggie couldn't help it: she whined. Because it wasn't fair. Birthdays only came once a year.

"Fine," Brynn said, relenting. "Whatever. But don't blame me if—" She cut herself off.

"If what?" Maggie asked.

"Nothing," Brynn said, then gave her sister an impatient look. "I'll see you later." That was code for *get out*.

"Okay, see you later," Maggie echoed, too excited by the prospect of an honest-to-goodness birthday séance to complain.

. . .

That night, Maggie wolfed down her birthday dinner—meat loaf and mashed potatoes, which her mom insisted was Maggie's favorite but wasn't (*You* love *my meat loaf, Maggie*)—and hurriedly cleared the table of plates and glasses. "Where's the fire?" her dad asked, and for the first time in as long as she could remember, Maggie flat-out lied.

"Brynn and I are gonna watch a movie in her room."

"What movie?" Dad asked. "And what about the cake?"

"I don't remember the title," she told him, a pang of guilt twisting up her insides for half a breath, but it wasn't enough to keep her from covering her tracks. She turned away from her father and continued loading the dishwasher. "Besides, I'm too full for cake. Can't we wait a little?"

"Maybe because you devoured your food like a bear," Dad said.

"We can wait," Maggie's mother chimed in. "But it's ice cream cake. Brynn, you're going to have to remember to pull it out of the freezer and let it sit for a while when Maggie is ready."

Brynn didn't respond. She was too busy messing with her flip phone, probably playing Snake or Tetris. Maggie wondered if she'd ever have a phone as cool as her sister's. Maybe she'd ask for one next year, when she'd be thirteen. Then again, what she really wanted was her own computer. Now, she had to use AOL on her dad's machine in his home office downstairs. She wasn't even allowed to have her own screen name, unlike Brynn, who had spent a whole week thinking up the perfect username.

"I was looking forward to that cake," Dad murmured. "I guess I'll wait it out while watching a movie, too. Want to guess what it's called?"

Maggie rolled her eyes. "Da-ad . . ."

"I'll take what's behind door number one, Monty," Brynn said, not looking up. "Oh, that's the *only* door? Such options. I do declare."

"It's a little something called *Die Hard*," their dad announced, always triumphant at the mention of his most beloved film. "Maybe you've heard of it?"

"*Yippee-ki-yay, mother—*"

"Brynn!" Mom.

"*I'm just a fly in the ointment,*" Brynn quoted, then snapped closed her phone, got up from the table, and ducked out of the room.

Just a monkey in the wrench. Maggie couldn't count how many times her dad had watched that film. Probably at least a hundred thousand, maybe even more. She was convinced her father wanted to be like that cop guy, John McClane. He probably had dreams of crawling through ventilation systems and dodging bullets and everything. Boys were such wackos.

But *Die Hard* would earn Maggie and Brynn a good two-hour

window. Their dad would be absorbed, and their mom had that new novel to pore over. She was a sucker for romance. Her bookshelves were chock-full of the stuff.

When Maggie finally made it up to Brynn's room, the place smelled of melted wax. She wasn't sure where Brynn had gotten all those candles, but there were at least a dozen of them casting odd shadows across the walls. Brynn was playing another one of Simon's borrowed CDs. Last time, it had been a band called Echo and the Bunnymen, which Maggie had thought was cute. This time, it was a soundtrack to a movie called *The Lost Boys*. A guy was singing about crying for his little sister. There was a choir of kids harmonizing something that sounded like the commandments behind him. It gave Maggie the creeps.

"It's like a fire in here," Maggie said, distracting herself from Brynn's music selection.

"Hurry up, get in." Brynn motioned her forward. "Shut the door, before Mom smells it."

"She's reading in Dad's office." Maggie paused, suddenly nervous at the sight of the unboxed board lying on her big sister's bed. It almost looked as though it were glowing, beckoning her toward it, urging her to give in to its mystery, its potential for magic.

"This is *your* idea, you know," Brynn said. "I don't even want to do this . . ."

But Maggie wasn't going to chicken out. There was nothing to fear anyway, right? Brynn had said it was fake. Nothing but a party game. A big fat hoax.

"Sit." Brynn pointed to the rug on her floor, then turned down the music. "Cross your legs pretzel-style." Maggie did as she was told, and Brynn placed the board between them so that it balanced upon their knees. "Now, if you want this to work, don't screw around. No laughing."

Maggie nodded again and dropped her fingers on the planchette.

"Lightly," Brynn said. "Barely touching it. Like this." She gingerly held her hands above the pointer, as though invisible wires were holding up her wrists.

Maggie lifted her fingers a little, trying to mimic her sister's position. This was more complicated than she had thought.

"Who do you want to talk to?" Brynn asked, which was surprising; Brynn hardly ever asked Maggie her opinion on anything. Perhaps it was because it was Maggie's board or her birthday—whatever the reason, Brynn's graciousness left Maggie blank-brained.

"Umm . . ." She blinked, trying to think above the song slithering from the speakers. Brynn had set that creepy song to repeat. Finally, Maggie blurted out the first dead person she could think of. "Elvis."

"Oh *God*." Brynn's head fell backward, as though the agony of having a kid sister was suddenly too much to bear.

"What? Gram *loves* Elvis," Maggie insisted.

"Gram also loves Grape Nuts. If we're going to talk to a dead guy, we may as well talk to someone cool, like Kurt Cobain."

"Who's that?" Maggie asked.

Brynn's head rolled forward again. She looked serious, and a little disgusted. Maggie glanced down to the board, then back to her sister.

"Okay," Maggie said. "Kirk Cobain."

"*Kurt.*"

"Whatever. So, what do we do?"

"You have to call him to the board," Brynn said. "Say his name, and then say, *I call upon thee.*"

Maggie sucked her lips into her mouth and looked to the heart-shaped pointer between them, the flickering candlelight casting dancing shadows across the plastic.

"How come you don't just do it?" Maggie asked. If Brynn knew how to play, why was she making Maggie run the game?

"Because it's your birthday, remember?" Brynn flashed one of her fake smiles—the kind their dad referred to as *the teenage sneer*. Those smiles drove their mom up the wall. *Why does she have to smile at me like that? Arlen never smiled at me like that!*

"Um, Mr. Kirk Cobain . . ." Did Maggie *really* want to do this?

"Kurt," Brynn corrected for the second time. "It's *Kurt*."

"Jeez, okay. Sorry! *Kurt* Cobain, I call . . . What was it again?"

Brynn groaned. "I call upon thee," she said.

"Oh. Oh yeah." Maggie squared her shoulders. "Mr. Kurt, I call upon thee!"

The planchette stayed where it was, unmoving. Maggie looked up at her sister. "Did I say it right? Are we supposed to move it or something?"

"Shhh!" Brynn hissed, then shut her eyes and breathed in deep. "I'm calling upon the spirit of Kurt Cobain." A pause. "Of Nirvana." Another pause as she peeked at her sister. "Which is a band, for those who are way too lame to know. Probably one of the best bands *ever*, in case you were wondering. Except for Depeche Mode, because Depeche Mode is *the* greatest band of all time."

Maggie rolled her eyes. This was dumb.

"Hey." Brynn narrowed her eyes. "I told you, be *serious*."

"Sorry," Maggie murmured. "I thought it was supposed to be fake, anyway."

"Is there *anyone* here?" Brynn asked, apparently giving up on Kurt. "We call upon the spirits that live inside this house."

". . . Why would there be spirits living inside this house?" Maggie whispered. Nobody had died there, had they? "I thought Mom and Dad built this place from scratch."

"I don't know, Mags!" Brynn huffed. "Maybe if we actually waited for an answer . . ."

"Maybe the house is built on a graveyard," Maggie offered, gaping at her own suggestion. "Like that one movie we watched about the girl and the TV static. Remember? The one where they put real dead bodies in the swimming pool? That was *so gross!*"

"Ugh, you know what?" Brynn pushed the board off her knees. "I've got stuff to do."

Maggie frowned. "Awh, come on, Bee. Let's try again. I'll be serious this time, I swear."

"I don't feel like it anymore. Besides, I still have homework. And I want to call Simon." Brynn moved to the stereo, popped the CD out of the player, and grabbed her old standby: *Violator. The greatest.*

The mention of Simon sealed the deal. Maggie sighed, because Brynn was *obsessed* with Simon, and if she was thinking about a call, Maggie's quality time with her older sister was officially up, birthday or not.

Maggie reluctantly rose to her feet, then pulled the board game box off the bed and opened it up. "You really think this *never* works?" Maggie asked, placing the board in its rightful spot. "Even if you're super serious and don't laugh or anything? What if you played it at a cemetery? Wouldn't something have to happen then?"

Brynn grabbed the top of the box off her comforter. "See this?" she asked, tapping a chipped fingernail next to a name. "These guys make toys, Mags. Like Nerf and Sorry! It's meant for entertainment purposes."

"Then why'd you set all this up?" Maggie motioned to the candles, to the ambience of the place. Even the song had been spooky. It seemed like an awful lot of effort if Brynn didn't believe the board could work.

Brynn hesitated for a second, then shrugged. "Because it's your birthday." Her answer rang hollow, not quite right. "I don't know, whatever. Forget I even bothered, okay? Just go."

Maggie frowned down at the board again. Leave it to her to screw it all up.

"But leave the board," Brynn said.

"Huh?"

"Just leave it." She paused, as if considering her own reasoning. "It's safer in here." Except that didn't make sense. If it was just from the toy store, what danger was there? "In case Mom looks," Brynn said, clarifying.

"I'll just hide it," Maggie said. "She won't find it."

That only seemed to irk Brynn even more. "Fine, whatever." She was suddenly hostile. "Just get out, already."

Maggie didn't take offense to Brynn's mood swing. They were standard procedure. *Teen angst* is what their dad liked to say. It paired well with her teenage sneer. But that didn't mean Maggie was happy with being kicked out of Brynn's room so fast. She stared down at the box in her hands, the smell of fire crawling up her nose. The fortune-teller's fancy rings were still calling to her, still convincing her that, had Brynn only been more patient, something *would* have happened. If Maggie only had faith in the power of the oracle, it was sure to work. Because that was the thing about magic. You had to believe.

An hour before bedtime, Maggie was called down for birthday cake. Brynn didn't come down, too busy yammering with her boyfriend.

"What happened to watching a movie with your sister?" her dad asked. He'd cut a massive piece of ice cream cake for himself and was happily eating it while watching the tail end of his film.

Maggie shrugged, half-heartedly stabbing at her own piece with the tines of her fork. Her mom had bought vanilla. Maggie didn't even like vanilla, just like she'd never been nuts about meat loaf. Everyone knew her favorite was cookies and cream, but her mom never did make a big deal out of that kind of stuff.

"Simon," Maggie murmured.

"Ah." Dad nodded, as if that name explained everything. "Well, you can finish watching this with me, right?"

Another shrug. She didn't much feel like *Die Hard* tonight. "I'm just gonna go upstairs and read," she said.

"You sure, Crazy?" Dad asked.

"Yeah." She'd take her cake with her. Maybe she really would read, or maybe she'd do something else.

Once upstairs, she shut her door behind her and, despite the rule of no locked doors, twisted the lock button to engage the bolt. She abandoned her cake plate atop her desk. It would melt there, nothing but a pool of cream and soggy cake until her mom found it in the morning. Maggie didn't have any candles like Brynn, so she turned on the closet light instead, leaving the door open a crack while the rest of the room was left dark. It was there, in the glowing long rectangle of light, that Maggie took a seat upon her floor, placed the board upon her knees, and rested her fingers upon the planchette the way Brynn had shown her.

"I call upon thee," she whispered. "Is there anybody here?"

She waited. Chewed her bottom lip. Her nerves roiled around her stomach. But nothing happened. She began to slide the pointer's three felt-covered feet around to spell out random things. MAGS. BIRTHDAY. SIMON. DUMB. And then, just as she was about to give up and place the board back in its box, the planchette jerked toward the upper-left-hand side of the board.

YES.

Startled, Maggie pulled her hands away. A second later, she was shoving the board, the empty box, and the pointer beneath her bed before crawling onto her mattress, spooked. "Whatever," she whispered, coiling her arms around her knees. "It's just for parties," she told herself. "It's a hoax, like Bee said."

Except that didn't feel true.

And the soft rustling that came from her closet later that night only convinced her more.

NINE

THE LAST TIME Maggie had come home—three years ago—her bedroom had been untouched since she had left. Her mother, as though in unspoken apology, had left it just as it had looked the day Maggie had left Savannah. But what Arlen had referred to as Maggie's room was now unrecognizable; its only familiarity was its location—still at the end of the hall, on the right, across from the bathroom that Maggie and Brynn had fought over while growing up.

She hadn't bothered taking a good look around before heading off to the mortuary, but now she was faced with the full impact of her room's transformation. The walls, which had once been painted a vibrant ocean blue, were now a pedestrian beige. The gallery wall she had created with a mishmash of wildlife posters, framed photographs, and water-themed watercolors was gone. In its place was a mirror flanked by a trio of small canvases—black-and-white landscapes that Maggie had seen at a Wilmington Target while shopping for apartment essentials. Surprisingly, her furniture remained, albeit unrecognizable beneath a face-lift of white paint.

Maggie slid her hands into the back pockets of her jeans and spun around, her gaze falling onto the closed closet door. She'd left a lot of stuff in there when she'd taken off for college. Arlen hadn't called to ask about whether Maggie wanted to keep any of the clothes she'd left behind, or asked if she wanted the novels she had alphabetically organized along her bookshelves, either. Those books, now missing, had been replaced by bric-a-brac that gave the room a staged Pottery Barn feel. "Probably tossed it all up into the attic," she muttered, imagining a tower of disorganized boxes awaiting her return among both her mother's and grandmother's things. Poor Gram. She had passed away due to complications after yet another surgery. Gramps had followed her shortly after. *Probably for the better*, Maggie thought. It would have been hard for them to deal with their daughter's passing, but the death of a grandchild? Impossible.

She took a tentative step toward the closet, a door that had been a constant source of anxiety, one that never seemed to want to stay closed, that emanated weird noises from within. Scratching, like there might have been a mouse in the walls. Stuff falling off hangers and shelves. Things that, when she complained about them to her parents, had been written off with perfectly logical explanations. *It's just your imagination, kiddo.* Her father's insistence failed to help her sleep at night. She had loathed that closet up until her very last day in that house. But now, with the room redone, it felt safer to approach.

She expected to see nothing but emptiness—maybe a couple of towels thrown over the bar, some hangers for guests. But when she pulled open the door, she was taken aback. Arlen might have tossed some of Maggie's stuff upstairs, but it looked as though she'd tried to cram the majority of it right here into the walk-in. Confronted with the things of her past, Maggie's initial reaction was to recoil. She didn't want to dredge up the unease with which she'd lived for so long. It's why she had left, why she did everything in her power not to come back. The heavy burden of responsibility was too much to bear, here. At least out in Wilmington, she could distract herself with Dillon, with school.

But again, a sense of calm pulled at the corners of her heart.

It's just stuff. Something to keep her occupied while she was here. Because if she had no interest in keeping any of it, she could at least do Arlen a favor and liquidate the stuff. It was something to keep Maggie busy, to keep her from sitting in the hall across from Brynn's bedroom door, staring at the knob, willing her still-to-be-interred sister to pull it open and give her that signature teenage sneer she'd never quite shaken off. *Hey, dummy.*

Maggie moved the stack of book boxes out of the closet to make space, then confronted the racks of clothes she hadn't worn in years. That, paired with all of her abandoned shoes, would fill up at least a half dozen trash bags. They'd be tumbled down the stairs, tossed into the back of Brynn's Camry, and driven to the Salvation Army before Maggie's return flight three days from now. All that stuff had been left behind because her apartment in Wilmington was small—less than six hundred square feet with two tiny closets; at least, that's what she had told herself while packing hardly anything for her first semester away. But part of Maggie had been glad to get rid of the possessions that had made her who she had been in the past. The whole point of going to Wilmington was to get out of town, to start over, to forget all the bullshit with her mom, to erase what had happened with that goddamn board.

She jutted an arm between a couple of hanging shirts and shoved them aside before surveying her shoes. A perfectly decent pair of runners sat among a menagerie of otherwise worn-out sneakers. She'd stuff those into her duffel bag. Running along The Loop always helped clear her head. Now, after what happened to Brynn, Maggie might very well have to pound the pavement every morning to keep herself from going mad.

She plucked up the sneakers to place them aside, then glanced to the overhead shelf. It was stacked with plastic tubs full of more clothes. Various shoe boxes were stockpiled in the upper corner, stuffed with pictures and high school memories. But there was an oddity as well. Just behind those boxes, there was an old sweater—not folded or hung like the rest, but thrown, as if in an attempt to hide something from view.

Maggie furrowed her eyebrows, tossed the sneakers onto the bed behind her, and rose up on her tiptoes to snag the sweater by its hem. But she hesitated as soon as her fingers touched the cording.

Tap tap tap. The sound came from behind her.

Maggie's pulse skipped like a needle on a dusty record.

Standing among the things that had made up her previous life, her right arm still held aloft, she felt something brush up against her; something waist-height and featherlight, just enough to electrify the skin. The light in the room shifted, as though someone—or something—had snuck up behind her.

Maggie didn't move. Didn't breathe. She squeezed her eyes shut and waited for that all-too-familiar sense of not being alone to pass, as it always had; to pass, but to never quite leave her, because it was always there. Always radiating from shadowed corners. Stopping her in her tracks as she walked through the house, warm one second, cold the next. *Drafts*, her dad had explained. *Brynn's stories*, her mother had scoffed. *Maybe a little of both*, Maggie had told herself, purposefully forgetting the fact that Brynn's stories consistently held a strange sort of truth.

But now, rather than that feeling of not being alone fading, she felt small fingers coil around her left hand instead.

She jumped at the sensation, her right arm jackknifing away from the closet's upper shelf. Still clinging to the hem of that discarded sweater, she inadvertently yanked it down from its resting place. Something heavy tumbled along with it, hitting the carpet with a hard thud.

"Jeezy creezy, Auntie M!"

Maggie exhaled a yelp, both hands fluttering protectively to her chest. She stared at Hope, who had somehow soundlessly snuck into the room.

Hope squinted her eyes as she studied her aunt, much the way a kid would inspect an interesting insect—perhaps just before tearing off its wings. "Are you *okay?*"

"Yeah," Maggie said, trying to play it off. "Yeah, I'm fine. You just scared me, that's all. What's up?"

And what the hell was that smell? It was the second time she'd caught a whiff of smoke since coming home. It must have been Hope—the scent was coming from her clothes, as though she'd stood in front of a charcoal barbeque a few days prior. Dillon smelled like that often. *It's manly*, he said in his best-but-still-terrible Dexter Morgan impersonation. *It smells like testosterone and red meat. Like Cro-Magnon.* Perhaps Howie had been grilling something for dinner a few days past? Maggie remembered from her own childhood, the scent of burning charcoal could take days to fade if you didn't wash the clothes.

"I just wanted to see if you want an Otter Pop. We've got a bunch in the—hey." Hope's attention wavered. She furrowed her eyebrows, then pushed down against the billowing tulle of her tutu to look at the sweater that lay between them both. "What's this?" She leaned down, plucked up the woolen fabric, and moved it aside.

And there, lying faceup, was porcelain-faced Dolly.

Maggie's heart launched itself into her throat. She was suddenly scrambling out of the closet, pushing Hope along with her before slamming the door shut.

"It's nothing," she said. "Just some old junk. Let's go get that Otter Pop."

Hope peered at her aunt's peculiar reaction. "That's not—"

"Downstairs." Maggie's tone was clipped, more forceful. She needed to get out of that room. Her hand fell upon Hope's shoulder, guiding the girl toward the open door. "I hope you have cherry," she said. "That's the only kind of Otter Pop I'll eat."

Small talk. Optimism that she'd be able to steady her trembling breath by the time they reached the kitchen. Because, while that doll had in fact been Brynn's, Maggie could swear that Dolly's face had changed.

What had once been a blank expression was now more of a smile. As though welcoming Maggie home.

. . .

"Shit!" An involuntary curse tumbled from Maggie's throat and into the gale. A trash bag fell from her fingers and into the garbage bin along the curb. Her hands groped at her shoulders and neck, as though touch alone could exorcise her worsening pain. But countless sick days, a handful of hospital stays, CT scans and X-rays, a spinal tap, and an MRI had long extinguished that sort of wishful thinking. By Maggie's senior year, four different doctors had been left stumped, all four exhaling sighs of exasperation and declaring that her phantom pain was spawned by grief.

It may be psychological, one had suggested.

Might just be that you're still growing, another had murmured around the cap of his pen.

If this was the old days, you'd be put in a mental ward as a hysteric, Brynn had joked, but Maggie hadn't found it funny, probably because it was true.

She jabbed her fingers into the meat of her shoulders and glared at the bag inside the bin. Hope had been mistaken about the Otter Pops. There hadn't been any in the freezer, and so Maggie had gone upstairs to take care of . . . that thing. Hidden among an assortment of threadbare T-shirts and items that weren't suitable for donation, and wrapped in that old sweater like a mummy twirled in gauze, was the doll. She couldn't stand looking at it. It reminded her too much of the visits to Friendship Park, both with and without Brynn. It coaxed the memory of sleepless nights to the forefront of her mind, all those evenings she'd slept on the couch even as a teen, only to be teased by Brynn for being afraid of the dark.

Pivoting on the soles of her sneakers, she tried to fend off what felt like a million pounds pressing down onto her bones. *It may be psychological.* That doll wasn't the problem. It never had been. It was this house. It was making her sick, too laden with sorrow and guilt, with memories too terrible to recall.

"Auntie Magdalene!"

Maggie started at the sound of Hope's squeaky little-girl voice carried upon the wind, exhaling a soft mew when the motion sent an electric jolt of pain down the side of her neck. The kid positively refused to leave her alone. It was as though the house had assigned Maggie a watcher, and Hope had been selected for the job.

Hope stopped in her tracks upon the driveway, as if spooked by her aunt's suffering. Her hair whipped across her face as she held a bright red Otter Pop in her right hand. "Auntie Magdalene?"

"Can you call me Maggie?" she asked.

"But I like *Magdalene*," Hope protested. "It's like the lady from the Bible."

That was precisely why Maggie *didn't* like her full name. A once-possessed woman who had watched Jesus die, who'd gained her sainthood by way of repentance. If all of this was somehow supposed to turn Maggie into a martyr, she wasn't sure how much more lamentation she could take.

"They were in the garage fridge, not the kitchen one." Hope thrust the Otter Pop in Maggie's direction. "What were you throwing away? And what's wrong with your neck?"

"Just cleaning out my old room," Maggie said, "and I'm fine. I just pulled a muscle. You shouldn't be out here . . ."

"You mean the stuff in the closet?" Hope glared at the trash can, looking awfully serious for someone her age.

"Yeah." Maggie plucked the ice pop from Hope's fingers and motioned for the girl to follow her up the front porch steps. Florence's roiling clouds weren't letting up anytime soon. Maggie had lived through some lengthy storms, but this one was taking the cake.

"Come on," she told the girl. "Let's get back inside. It's going to pour."

Hope turned to follow her aunt up to the house, latching on to her arm as they both hit the porch. "But why are you cleaning out your room when you're going to stay?" Hope asked. "Now that Auntie Bee is gone, you *gotta* stay. Isn't that why you came back?"

Maggie froze upon the porch planks. She slowly turned her head to look at her elder niece. Save for the dance wear, it was like looking through a wormhole twenty years deep. Grown-up Maggie on one side. Young Maggie just a foot away.

"What were you throwing away, Auntie Magdalene?" Hope asked again, but this time something dark flickered across her face. Something knowing, as though she'd seen what Maggie had done with the doll. Maggie pulled her arm free of Hope's grasp.

"Nothing," she said. "Just trash." She took a single step away from the child.

Hope's gaze narrowed faintly, as if reading the lie. "The lady from the Bible," she said, "had seven devils inside her, Auntie M. I learned that at Sunday school. You don't want devils crawling inside your stomach, do you, Auntie M? If you tell fibs, the devils can get inside."

And then, as if to punctuate the kid's point, pain shot through Maggie's neck once again. Maggie hissed through her teeth, her hand clamping down against the ache.

"You should always stretch before dancing," Hope continued.

"My teacher says muscles are like rubber bands. You can hurt yourself real bad if you don't."

Arlen stepped outside through the open front door. "Maggie? What are you two doing out here? It's positively hideous. Hope: inside, now. Go play with your sister." Hope exhaled a huff and stomped her bare feet as she disappeared into the foyer, exiled to watch over a boisterous toddler who could be heard from somewhere deep inside the house.

"Sorry." Arlen issued the apology only when Hope was out of earshot. Arlen's attention paused upon the cherry ice pop in Maggie's grasp, then trailed back to her sister's face. "She's a bit of a hanger-on. When she heard you were coming, she got really excited."

"Kind of weird, don't you think?" Maggie asked. Arlen shook her head, not understanding what could possibly be weird about a niece being clingy and enthralled by a woman she knew nothing about. Then again, kids were strange. Indecipherable. Precisely why Maggie didn't want one of her own.

"Did you take that Tylenol?" Arlen asked, changing the subject.

"I forgot," Maggie murmured. "Hey, Len? Why didn't you tell me Bee was sick?"

"What?" Arlen tried to feign innocence, but Maggie wasn't about to let her off that easily. She shifted the ice pop from one hand to the other, using the coldness of her empty palm to at least somewhat soothe the ache.

"Hope told me not to go inside Bee's room because it's what made her sick."

Arlen tipped her head toward the slowly rotating porch fan overhead—off, but pushed by the wind. "Oh Lord," she murmured.

"I thought that maybe that's how you had explained her depression to them," Maggie continued. "*Sick*, because depression is an illness. You wouldn't have been wrong. But then I met Cheryl for coffee—"

"Cheryl Polley?"

"—and she said the same thing. That Brynn had looked sick. That her grandmother had mentioned it after she saw Bee at Saint Michael's. She was at church, Len. Brynn. *At church.*"

Arlen lifted a hand to rub between her eyebrows, avoiding eye contact, staring at the floorboards, her perfectly pedicured toenails peeking out of her strappy sandals. Arlen had been keeping secrets, and now she'd been found out.

"Why didn't you tell me?" Maggie asked, her own hand still working the painful knot that had stiffened the muscles of her neck. "You could have called or texted. I could have asked her what was wrong." Maybe a single simple question would have changed everything: *Brynn, how do you feel? Brynn, are you okay?* Perhaps that tiny inquiry would have meant the difference between life and death. If Maggie had just chosen the right words, had told her sister she loved her before hanging up, perhaps things would have been different. If she had only invited Brynn to hang out in North Carolina, to get away from Arlen and the kids, or had finally caved and revealed her secret: she'd played that board alone. She'd played it for years, up until the day their father had died. *It's my fault. My fault . . .* Had Maggie done that, maybe Brynn would still be here now.

"And what would that have accomplished?" Arlen's attention shifted to Maggie's face. "Don't stand here and suggest that knowing all the details of what went on here would have somehow changed what Brynn decided to do, okay?"

"I just—"

"You just want to blame someone," Arlen said coolly. "But the truth of it is that you haven't been home, Maggie. Not for the holidays, not for birthdays, not at all. But you would have been her savior, right? You would have made it better if you had only known."

Maggie was stung by her sister's implication that she couldn't have helped. It was a hurtful, ugly thing to say. She wanted to yell,

This isn't my fault, but that would have let the devils in, according to Hope. "Why was she at church, Len? Can you at least tell me that?"

Arlen squared her shoulders, staring defiantly into her little sister's face. "Why does anyone go to church, Maggie? She was looking for answers."

Maggie shook her head. Yes, people filled up pews in the hope of basking in some sort of soul-affirming confirmation. They were desperate to know that this wasn't it, that this thing called life wasn't all that they had to work with. They wanted to find God. But Brynn wasn't people. Arlen had said so herself, Brynn was Brynn, a girl who had never been scared of death, had never voiced the need for some far-fetched assurance that there was a heaven or that her sins would be forgiven. Those ideals were as bizarre to Brynn Olsen as her outward appearance had been strange.

"She was scared," Maggie said.

"Scared of *what*?" Arlen asked.

"Of what's here," Maggie said, nearly inaudible. Something had happened—something Brynn hadn't mentioned during their phone calls, something that had her asking Maggie even more urgently than before to *please come home. I need to see you. What will it take?* What Brynn didn't know, however, was that fear was exactly what was keeping Maggie away.

"Maggie?"

With cold fingers pressed across her mouth, Maggie stared at her big sister. "Something's wrong, Len," she said. "Something's *been* wrong ever since Dad . . ."

Arlen's gaze slingshotted away, as though the mere mention of their father was a slap across the face.

"You can't live here." The words slithered from Maggie's throat— secret thoughts she hadn't dared bring up finally finding their voice. "It's not safe. It hasn't been safe for years."

When she looked back to her sister's face, Arlen was peering at her with incredulous alarm. But it wasn't a look of worry. Rather, her expression was tense with a concern Maggie had only seen her wear once before—the day she had spent all afternoon on the phone with receptionists and doctors, desperate to pull their mother out of her hole. Now, that anxiousness was pointed squarely in Maggie's direction.

"Mags . . . I think that maybe you should . . ." Hesitation. "I'm sorry, but you need help."

Bullshit, she wanted to say. If this was all in her head, why the hell had Brynn sought sanctuary? If Arlen didn't suspect anything, why were her kids going to Sunday school? The Olsens had never been religious, and yet there was Hope, telling Maggie who Mary Magdalene had been. Talking about devils.

"She was scared, Len." Perhaps if she repeated it, Arlen would come to the same realization Maggie had: this wasn't Maggie's imagination. It wasn't just unshakable guilt. This was real.

But rather than being overtaken by revelation, Arlen shut her eyes instead. She looked ready to speak, but rather than responding, she reached out and placed her hand upon Maggie's left shoulder. And then, as though at a loss for words, she gave that shoulder a squeeze before turning and stepping into the foyer, just as Hope had done.

Maggie was left staring at the open door, Arlen's touch tingling upon her skin. She swallowed against the desert of her mouth, breathed heavy, the familiar twist of anxiety snarling up her guts.

Her phone buzzed in the back pocket of her jeans.

Dillon.

She began to reach for it, only to stop short.

Because wafting from inside and drifting upon the wind was that familiar scent. Smoke. The smolder of a candlewick, blown out by a nonexistent breath.

TEN

A RLEN WAS LESS than pleased when the doorbell chimed, but she stopped short of asking Cheryl Polley to leave. Maggie had forgotten to mention Cheryl's visit. The thing about Brynn going to church still had her reeling. And then there was the doll.

By the time Cheryl arrived, Maggie was ready to call it a day and forget the whole thing. But Cheryl had made the drive, and it would have been rude to send her away, almost as rude as not telling Arlen they were going to have company. And for that, she felt like an ass, but what was done was done. All she could do was murmur a soft-spoken *sorry* and give her sister an imploring look—*please don't hold it against me*—as she ushered Cheryl through the living room. Arlen and Howie watched from the couch, their viewing of *The Blacklist* interrupted as the two old friends shuffled upstairs.

The kids were already in their rooms, the girls most likely sleeping while their older brother was reading comic books or playing video games.

"She's pissed at me," Maggie told Cheryl as they began their climb. "I questioned her about Bee."

"Grief is hard," was all Cheryl said, but Maggie could tell she wanted to say more. Only a few seconds downstairs, and Cheryl had caught the off-putting vibe. Arlen was keeping things eerily normal. There was hardly any talk of Brynn. The kids didn't seem to be bothered by the passing of their live-in aunt. And when Howie had come home from work, he had given Maggie a *How the hell are ya?* as though she were visiting for visitation's sake. Just dropping in. No big deal.

All the normalcy was jarring. But then again, Maggie hadn't bawled her eyes out when Brynn had found their mother dead in the bathroom, either—pills strewn everywhere, the tub overflowing, their mom's temple caved in from crashing against the edge of the sink, pink water making a slow creep beneath the door. Even Maggie's freshman-year roommate, Anessa, had found her lack of reaction odd. Anessa—a psych major—had been a fixer just like Dillon. *Are you* sure *you're all right?* She asked that same question over and over, as if waiting for Maggie's calm exterior to crack, for the ugly emotions of realizing herself an orphan to turn her into a weeping, inconsolable mess; almost eager for it to happen, if only to be given the chance to tinker with an anguish-stricken mind. Is that why Dillon was texting so often? Was he waiting for her to fall apart? Was he *needing* her to lose it so that he could put her back together again?

The collapse hadn't happened after Maggie's mom died. And the tears weren't flowing in regard to Brynn's death, either. Maggie could only muster the profound sadness of having lost both Brynn and her mother years before they were truly gone. With her mom's funeral, Maggie had spent the days leading up to her trip home looking through the handful of old photographs she had brought with her to school. All of them featured her dad. The Olsens: one big happy family untouched by calamity, alcohol, pills, or pain. In them, Maggie's mom was always cheerful, her smile as constant as Brynn's black clothes and perturbed *I hate taking pictures* scowl.

Losing her mother wasn't something that had happened without a wrenching of the heart, but their final blowup had left Maggie bruised. The way she had jerked Maggie backward by the arm just after Maggie had flushed her meds; the ear-splitting way she had screamed before shoving her youngest daughter against the wall, hissing declarations of what a mistake it had been to have her. *I should have stopped with Arlen!* And then there was the slap, so hard it made Maggie see stars. Stella Olsen's diamond ring had been rotated with the stone facing her palm—a habit she had adopted to keep that princess cut from getting caught on jambs. That afternoon, it caught Maggie's left cheek, leaving a jagged cut nearly two inches long in its wake. Maggie's dad had given her that ring. Maggie had been at the jewelry store with him when he'd bought it. *I don't know about this stuff, Crazy. You pick it out. You know what she'll like.*

Only a few hours after that ring had slashed across her face, Maggie started packing for Wilmington, thanking her lucky stars that she hadn't caved to her mother's insistence that she go to school across the river. The Skidaway Institute of Oceanography was so close, Maggie could have lived at home for four more years. But now, Maggie was sure she'd be happy to never see her mother's sloppy, drugged-out face again. She'd wished it before, when the fights had started to get bad: *It should have been her, not Dad.* But now—

"Maggie?" Cheryl gave her an encouraging smile. "That's what we're here to do, right? Deal with grief?"

"Shit." Maggie paused in front of her bedroom door. "The board. I don't even know where it is." She'd meant to look for it, but the doll, and then Hope . . .

Cheryl looked dubious. It was a convenient hiccup, one that would keep them from doing what Maggie had, earlier that afternoon, somehow convinced herself was a good idea. The only way out. *Repent.* But now, with Cheryl here, she couldn't rightfully throw up her hands and declare it a bust. Not without at least *appearing* as though she was giving it a shot.

"Arlen tossed a lot of my crap into the closet, but I didn't see it there," Maggie explained. "There's probably more up in the attic."

"Then I guess that's where we'll start." Cheryl shrugged, as though the task couldn't possibly be that difficult to tackle. After all, how much stuff had Maggie left behind?

Apparently, a lot. The girls searched the attic for a better part of half an hour before returning to what had once been Maggie's room. Together, they went through the remainder of the bedroom closet, but there was no sign of the board.

"Maybe Arlen found it and threw it away," Maggie suggested. Perhaps, for once, this was a bit of good luck. Not finding the board meant no séance, and quite frankly, that was the last thing Maggie felt like doing tonight.

Except, back in the furthest reaches of her mind, she was still that mystified kid. Despite everything that she knew, there was an inexplicable pull. *Because what if you can talk to Brynn?* a little voice whispered. *You can ask her about the fear, about why she was so afraid.* And if Maggie could contact Brynn, she could also reach out to her dad. *Dad.* She missed him. She'd have done just about anything to hear one of his silly jokes again.

"Earth to Maggie." Cheryl raised an eyebrow. "You okay?"

"Yeah, sorry," Maggie said. "Maybe we missed it. I'll look in Brynn's room." They hadn't missed it, but Brynn's bedroom was one place Maggie had yet to look, and it was certainly a place she wanted to go alone. "Just give me a minute."

And yet, as soon as she moved down the hall toward Brynn's room, Maggie was certain that a minute wouldn't nearly be enough.

Brynn's room had always been dark, all deep purples and hazy grays. But in the three years that Maggie hadn't been home, that room had taken a turn from darkly benign toward . . . something else. Perhaps it was the new plum-colored wallpaper, its damask pattern reminiscent of haunted Victorian homes. Maybe it was all of that fabric—velvet tapestries so heavy they were bending the curtain rod beneath the bulk of their weight, pooled upon the floor. But more than likely, it was the menagerie of bedsheets that had been thrown over every reflective surface in the room, and there were many.

She could make out a mirrored chest of drawers against one of the walls, its silver exterior gleaming just beneath the skewed hem of a thin white sheet. A wall of mirrors of all different shapes and sizes had been carefully arranged into a mysterious gallery upon the bedroom's farthest wall. Those same white sheets hung limp across their frames, like a gallery of mounted ghosts. Only one was left exposed.

Maggie's breath caught in her throat. She pawed at the wall, searching for the light switch, which, when flipped, caused an ornate chandelier to blaze overhead. Shards of fractured light bounced throughout the room like a sea spray of stars. That light brought attention to another sheet, almost certainly having been pulled away from that single uncovered mirror. The sheet, puddled upon the floor, had seemed harmless until Maggie caught a glimpse of what it obscured: broken glass. The carpet hadn't been replaced. And while Maggie couldn't see behind that thick velvet curtain, she was sure it was hiding a plywood board nailed to the windowsill. It would be a wonder if Florence didn't blow it into the room by morning.

She struggled to swallow as she took in the view. Maybe this was why Arlen had warned her children against venturing inside. Those sheets captured the essence of a morgue without a body. She rubbed a palm against her arm, trying to snuff out the goose bumps that were breaking out across her skin. She didn't want to shrink back, didn't want to be one of the people Brynn would have snorted at—*you're just like the rest*—but the eeriness of that wall of mirrors, the hidden window, the tiny glass shards catching the light like snowflakes . . . it was nearly too much to bear. These were the things Brynn had seen in the last few seconds of her life. These were the walls she had stared at as her timeline ticked down to nothing. These were the images she had been so desperate to shut out that she'd done the unthinkable: an act she herself had once deemed as cowardly, selfish, and weak. But why? What had she been looking for at Saint Michael's? Why hadn't she simply told Maggie that she was afraid?

Maggie's gaze darted to the massive four-poster bed, to what looked like etchings upon one of the posts as crude as school-desk graffiti. She faltered, almost afraid to move. *Don't, don't, don't.* The air felt thick, alive with a static charge. "Brynn?" The name was a mere whisper, just enough to break the tension of that taut, unnerving silence. If her sister's spirit were still there, perhaps she'd give Maggie a sign. But Maggie couldn't stand there forever. Cheryl was waiting. She pushed past her reluctance and stepped farther inside.

The carvings on the bedpost looked like they had been made with the tip of a knife or, more likely in Brynn's case, a nail file. The possible culprit lay atop a sheeted dresser, next to a few bottles of nail polish, hair spray, and Brynn's makeup bag. Maggie approached the rough engravings with measured steps, her chest tight, the feeling of not belonging in that room sweeping over her in a rush of newfound anxiety. And still, those crude symbols coaxed her forward, inviting her to discover what it was that had truly pushed her sister over the edge. The entire post was covered in those crooked ciphers, creating a spiral pattern that was as beautiful as it was unsettling: a mad-woman's epitaph.

Except those letters didn't form Brynn's last words. Maggie's steps hitched and stalled, bringing her to petrified stillness. Her mouth fell open in soundless disbelief. Her heart pounded hard enough to send a rush of heat to her face. And then, there was that scent again—the redolence of a just-snuffed-out wick, the lingering aura of soot.

Paralyzed, all Maggie could do was stare, her gaze fixed on the letters that coiled upward in a whorl of alphabet. A B C D . . . on it went. X Y Z. And then three solitary, disjointed words that made Maggie want to scream.

YES. NO. GOOD-BYE.

Tears stung her eyes. The ache of her neck intensified, like bony fingers pressing hard into flesh. And then, as if wanting to see the terror that had inevitably come to rest upon her own face, her attention snapped to the uncovered mirror beside her. Something shifted in its reflection; a darkness darted away from her, as if something had been standing behind her, grinning as Maggie discovered Brynn's terrible secret. An involuntary gasp tumbled from Maggie's throat as she spun around to look behind her. And there, in the corner of the room, was a blot of darkness, half obscured by a velvet panel that flanked the window of Brynn's last leap.

Don't, don't, don't.

And yet, against all reason, Maggie forced herself forward. With arms extended, she shoved aside the curtain, only to find herself stumbling backward. That shadow failed to disappear the way she expected it to, the way it always had when she'd been brave enough to approach it as a child. This time, it didn't vanish, didn't reassure her that her dad was right—that all of this was just her imagination spawned by her middle sister's love of horror movies and Edgar Allan Poe. This time, the chimera slithered across the wall, slow at first, before blasting past her in a rush, leaving a burning stink behind it, scorching Brynn's wallpaper with an arcing scar of black.

She tried to cry out, but found herself unable to breathe. What the fuck was *that*? What had she just seen? She couldn't seem to take her eyes off the singed trail that now decorated the wall—at least, not until she heard that noise. *Tap, tap, tap.* Her attention jumped across the room, only to fix itself upon the sheet on the floor. Because it was no longer lying flat, hiding the bloodstains her sister had left behind. There was a shape beneath it. A body. *Brynn.*

Finally, her fear knocked her free of her stasis. A cry tore itself free of her throat as she barreled out of the room, leaving Brynn's door wide-open in her wake. Throwing herself into the guest room that had once been her personal space, she found it impossible to squelch her own trembling. Half swallowed by the closet, Cheryl started at Maggie's sudden reappearance.

"Whoa!" Cheryl began to rise from the floor. ". . . Are you— Maggie, what happened?"

"Brynn." She couldn't stop shaking. "*Brynn.*" She knew it was impossible, and yet she'd seen the lump beneath that sheet with her own eyes. And that shadow. She'd lived with those strange shifts of light since she'd been twelve years old, but she'd never seen it up close before. Not like that. *Never* like that.

"Brynn what?" Cheryl was standing now, her hands lightly clasped around Maggie's arms.

"I . . ." *I saw her.* Impossible. *Just a loose screw, Crazy.* "I did this," she whispered. "All of this is my fault." And then she started to bawl.

Cheryl pulled Maggie in for a hug.

"I'm fine," Maggie whispered into Cheryl's shoulder, but her words rang hollow. "I'll be fine."

"Maggie?" Arlen appeared in the hall, having been alerted by her outcry. Now, clad in a pair of yoga pants and a loose-fitting top, she looked in on Maggie and Cheryl as they embraced. "What's going on?"

"Nothing." Maggie shook her head, unable to meet her sister's gaze. She'd left Brynn's door wide-open. Surely Arlen had looked inside before pulling it shut. She'd mention the wallpaper, the way it was burned.

"It's just hitting her, I think. She needs some time," Cheryl said. "She'll be okay."

Maggie continued to hide against her former best friend's side, waiting for Arlen to ask: *What happened to the wall? What were you doing in there?* But, nothing. *Because it's gone*, Maggie thought. *If it was ever there at all.* She finally heard Arlen sigh and wander out of the room.

"Wait." Cheryl took a backward step, giving Maggie a stern once-over. "You'd gone in there before now, right? Into Brynn's room?"

Maggie slowly shook her head in the negative.

". . . Oh God, Maggie . . ."

"Forget it," she said, wiping at her eyes. "Really, it's fine. I'm just freaking out." The anguish had arrived. Brynn was forever gone.

"Are you sure? Do you want me to leave?" Cheryl asked.

"No, no . . ." It was good to have Cheryl here. She didn't want to be alone.

"Okay, because . . ." Cheryl took a few steps toward the closet behind them, reached inside, and held up the board for Maggie to see.

Maggie was dumbfounded. Save for looking through the clothes, she'd gone through everything in that closet. The majority of the boxes were stacked against the bedroom wall now. There were no hiding spots, no place to miss something as conspicuous as a board game box.

"I guess you were right," Cheryl said. "We must have missed it the first time."

No, they hadn't. The damn thing hadn't been there when she had looked on her own, let alone when she and Cheryl had investigated together. And yet there it was in Cheryl's hands. A whisper of a voice told her to calm herself, to take a seat, to open the box and place it across her knees. *Reach out to Brynn. Reach out to Dad.*

"But it's probably not a good time," Cheryl said. "Maybe we should just talk?"

Talk about what, the fact that Maggie had just seen a twisting shadow lurking in Brynn's room? That Brynn had carved up her bedpost, as though that board had infected her blood? That Maggie hadn't listened to whatever existed inside that board when it had told her not to go, and the next thing she knew, her father was dead?

"No." *Repent.* "Let's just get this over with."

She sank to the floor, sitting just like Brynn had taught her—legs crisscrossed—while Cheryl towered over her, box in hand, looking unsure. Eventually, Cheryl joined her on the carpet. She gave Maggie an attempt at a reassuring smile, and then pulled open the lid.

"Let's prove this isn't what you think it is," Cheryl said.

Maggie didn't look up, but she wanted to ask, *Prove what? That what I just saw wasn't real?*

Cheryl placed the board between them both. "This"—she tapped the board—"has no power, Maggie. None of this is your fault. Only God has that kind of power, and He protects us. He does no harm."

But all Maggie could think of at that moment was that she didn't feel safe. That this didn't feel right. She was afraid and, like Brynn, needed sanctuary. Because this was the last place in the world she should have been. The pain in her shoulders was back, biting, drilling hard into her muscles. And that smell of smoke? It was strong again. Either it had followed her in, or she had followed it here.

ELEVEN

DESPITE CHERYL'S INSISTENCE that she wanted to help, Maggie could tell her old friend was less than comfortable being back in Maggie's old room. She could almost see the memories flooding Cheryl's thoughts, her eyes darting from wall to wall, searching for signs of what had once been.

After their falling-out, it had taken a couple of weeks for Cheryl to talk to Maggie again, let alone sit with her in the cafeteria. It was there that Maggie started to share stories of the scratching in the walls, the strange sensation of being watched, and the oppressive heaviness she felt every time she opened her closet door. *So, your house is haunted now?* Cheryl had asked. *I guess I better not go over, then.* As if she had been planning on going over ever again. Maggie knew what she meant, and it hurt.

She supposed that was part of why she hadn't told Cheryl the whole truth; why she had left out the part that, despite the knocks, Maggie had pulled the board out of its hiding place and placed it across her knees. She knew it was freaky, knew it didn't make sense, knew that after what happened with Cheryl, she should have been terrified to ever touch that thing again. Any other kid would have stuffed it in the trash, pronto. Off to the dump, out of her life forever.

And yet she found herself compelled to place it across her lap as her loneliness caught up to her. Because Cheryl had abandoned Maggie, but the board was always there.

And then there was the betrayal. Despite Maggie telling Cheryl her stories in confidence, Cher told her mom *everything*. Mrs. Polley was quick to blame it on the devils that must have been residing in the Olsen home. She even called Maggie's mom to complain. *You really should keep a closer eye on your kids, Stella. I'm sorry, but that older girl of yours? I've seen her in the cemetery.* Everyone's *seen her, hanging around with that boy* . . .

Their mother got angry, though it was unclear whether she was raging against Brynn or Claire Polley, who from that day forward was regarded as Pissy Mrs. Prissy. In turn, Cheryl became Little Miss Priss, and Maggie's mom began to insist that Maggie was better off without friends like her.

And yet, despite her mother's opinion, Maggie kept trying to win Cheryl back. But after what felt like months of failure, Maggie's despondency began to fade. Perhaps, just as her mom kept saying, it was better that Cheryl was gone. Maybe Maggie didn't need her. Perhaps all she needed was what she had upstairs, hiding beneath her bed. Because whenever she played alone, she felt better, as though she and that little girl from the cemetery really had become friends.

But now, years later, Maggie found herself staring at the board upon Cheryl's lap, and a sense of unease unspooled in the pit of her stomach like a coiled snake shedding its skin. Protest was on the tip of her tongue; she vividly remembered how Cheryl had rolled her eyes at the tales Maggie had told over lunch-line tater tots and applesauce cups. *You're such a freak.* The knocking. The scratching. Cheryl had discarded it all as nonsense, regardless of how hurtful that shirking had been. She hadn't been an ally, which is why, over ten years later, Maggie already knew what Cheryl would say if she mentioned the tapping that was most certainly back, if she brought up the shadow that had darted across Brynn's room: *There's a logical explanation for everything.* And the board having been missing, only to magically reappear? A simple oversight, like searching for a pair of glasses when they were right there, poised upon the tip of your nose.

But Maggie couldn't allow past bitterness to interfere with the fact that Cheryl was here now, wanting to help, and that perhaps she was right. Maybe facing her fear was exactly what Maggie needed to break out of this vicious cycle of guilt. She could spend the rest of her life believing that she was responsible for the deaths of her parents and sister, or she could get over this ridiculous theory once and for all. Ghosts? Curses? Please.

And yet, sitting across from her former best friend, mimicking the actions that had come just before their relationship had collapsed, was reassurance that no matter what Maggie tried to convince herself of, she would never escape the truth. Reality—no matter how insurmountable—would be heeded, just as the pulsating pain in her neck and shoulders would not be ignored.

Maggie rubbed at the knot of muscle at the top of her spine. Every minute that passed, the pain was getting worse.

"I can't," she finally said. Her anxiety, her sorrow over Brynn, the sadness that had crept back into her heart just seeing Cheryl in her old room again—all of it was perched upon her shoulders like a thirty-pound weight. "I'm sorry, this all just feels . . . off."

"Maggie . . ."

"You're right," Maggie cut in. "This needs to end. But this—"The board, repeating the past. "It won't fix anything."

"How can you know that?" Cheryl asked. "Look, I'm not comfortable doing this, either. Trust me, after that night . . ." Her words tapered off, but she didn't have to finish. The memory had scarred them both.

Regardless, Maggie kept her eyes fixed upon the board between them, her stomach churning, every muscle tense. Eventually, Cheryl exhaled in what sounded like defeat, and for half a second Maggie let herself relax. But rather than pulling the board from their knees, Cheryl spoke again, giving the whole idea one last try.

"I'm worried about you." Cheryl rubbed her hands against the knees of her jeans. "I guess, up until your phone call, I had hoped that you were happy, wherever you were." She plucked the planchette up off the board, flipped it over, idly inspecting the seemingly harmless piece of plastic. "I wish we could go back, you know? Erase that cemetery girl from our lives. Make that night vanish. Have stayed best friends."

All at once, Maggie could smell it—the scent of electricity, a static charge primed to ignite. The hairs on her arms rose on end. A chill scurried up her spine and into the base of her ponytail. She could see it on Cheryl's face—Cher was feeling it, too.

And then, before either one could acknowledge the disturbance in the atmosphere around them, a scream sounded from down the hall.

Maggie instinctively leapt to her feet. "What . . . ?!" The board tumbled to the carpet as she abandoned Cheryl, rushing for the bedroom door. Yanking it open, she could already hear footsteps bounding up the stairs—either Howie or Arlen dashing to their little girl's aid.

"Hope? *Hope!*" Arlen's voice was panicked, already on the verge of a breakdown.

Maggie skidded to a stop when she hit the upstairs hall, not because Arlen was already halfway up the stairs, but because something dodged into Hope's bedroom just as Maggie turned her attention to her niece's open door. It was *that thing*. The darkness that she swore had scorched Brynn's bedroom wall.

"Hope?!" Arlen beat Howie up the stairs. Howie followed shortly, pausing to regard Maggie with a glance. There was something dark in his gaze, as though Arlen had told him about all the tragedy in their past, as if she had said the words so plainly that they had been undeniable: *This is Maggie's doing. She's behind it all.* Howie ducked into Hope's room a second later, and Maggie found herself moving toward her niece's bedroom despite that nasty look. Some deep-seated maternal instinct was pushing her to make sure everything was fine. What if that shadow really was in there? What if, finally, someone besides her would be there to see it? But her trajectory was thrown off by another yell, this one from behind her, from inside the room that had once been her own.

"Cher?" Maggie veered around and rushed back from where she had come. The two collided as they both came to the door at once— Maggie running in to see what was wrong, Cheryl wide-eyed and determined to leave the room as quickly as she could. Cheryl's right hand—which had been clasped across her neck—was jostled free, revealing what looked to be a bleeding abrasion just above her collarbone that hadn't been there ten seconds before. It nearly looked like the shape of half a heart. "Oh my God, what—"

"I have to go." Cheryl's words were clipped, breathless. Politeness be damned, she shoved Maggie aside and moved fast down the hall.

"Wait, what happened?" Maggie pursued her, bounding down the stairs, beating Cheryl to the front door. "Cher, tell me," she demanded, blocking the exit, but Cheryl wasn't having it.

"Get out of my way, Maggie," she said, trying to yank Maggie away from the door's handle. "I shouldn't have ever come here." Her voice warbled. She was on the verge of panic, ready to burst into hysterical sobs. "I should have known better. Goddammit, I should have followed my gut."

"Please, just tell me. Cher, I need to know." But Cheryl overpowered her, pushed Maggie aside, and pulled open the door to rush across the covered porch. She nearly tripped down the front steps as she went.

Maggie bolted after her. "Stop! Cheryl, *please!*"

Cheryl unlocked her car with a push of a button on her key fob and quickly ducked inside. Maggie found herself holding the top edge of her old friend's door, keeping it from slamming closed, stopping Cheryl from screeching away. "Just wait, okay? What—"

But Cheryl's expression brought her to a midsentence halt. It was a look of undiluted terror. Everything Cheryl had come to believe had—in the few seconds Maggie had left her alone in that room—been challenged. Or threatened. Or both.

Cheryl had seen something. She'd been attacked by it.

That thing, it remembered exactly who Cheryl was.

Maggie swallowed against the sudden dryness of her throat, seeing herself reflected in Cheryl's twisted expression of dread. Her, just after learning of her father's death; her, learning of her mother's death, despite the bitterness she still felt; her, the night Arlen had called, the storm howling outside her apartment, that broken shutter slamming against the exterior wall in warning: *It's happening again. All over again. It's real. This is all so very real.*

She took a backward step and let her hand fall from Cheryl's door. But rather than speeding away, Cheryl gave Maggie an imploring look. "You shouldn't be here," she said. "You need to get out. Now."

Maggie then watched her drive off. She waited for the red glow of Cheryl's taillights to disappear down the street before she turned back toward that house—the windows warm with yellow light, the board and batten gleaming in the moonlight, everything about it simultaneously perfect and wrong. Suddenly, Maggie wasn't sure whether she'd be able to go back inside. And yet, a moment later, she was locking the front door behind her—locking herself in—and climbing the stairs to the second floor.

She stopped at Hope's door. Howie was missing—probably checking in on either Harry or Hay—but Arlen was sitting upon her eldest daughter's bed. "What happened?" Arlen asked. "Was that Cheryl who was screaming?"

Maggie faintly shook her head, unsure of her own response. Was she saying *no* because she was in denial, or because she didn't want to talk about it? "Is Hope okay?" was all she could manage.

"Just a nightmare," Arlen said. "She gets them every now and again, especially these past few days. But everything is fine." She brushed a strand of hair from Hope's small round face and gave her kid a smile.

"Did your friend leave, Auntie Magdalene?" Hope asked. "Did I scare her away?"

"Yeah." Maggie tried to suppress the wince that now accompanied her every move. "I mean, no, you . . . I—"

"Good," Hope said flatly, cutting Maggie off. "I didn't like her."

Maggie stared at her niece.

"*Excuse* me." Arlen's words were sharp. "I don't think that's a very nice thing to say, do you?"

Hope gave her mother a grievous look. "She's not really Aunt Maggie's friend, Mom. Right, Aunt Magdalene? The only friend that lady's got is *God*." The five-year-old rolled her eyes, leaving both her mother and aunt stunned.

Arlen gaped.

Maggie opened her mouth to speak, but no words came. And so, instead of responding, she simply turned and went back to her room.

Quietly shutting her door behind her, she leaned against it and closed her eyes. It was only when she reopened them a moment later that she saw the planchette on the floor, its tip pointing at her. *You.*

And there, where Cheryl had sat only minutes ago, was Dolly. Blank-eyed but smiling.

A real friend.

Hello.

TWELVE

AFTER THAT PLANCHETTE had pointed to YES, it took Maggie days to find the nerve to touch it again.

She had stashed it under her bed, sure it would stay hidden there forever. Whether the Ouija was meant for parties or not, it had done a heck of a job creeping her out. Yet, during a particularly drab sleepover, when all the Chex Mix had been eaten, Kelly Clarkson's latest CD had been karaoked to, and hours of *Gilmore Girls* had been watched, Cheryl issued a dramatic sigh as she sprawled out across Maggie's bedroom carpet.

"I'm *so* bored," she mused. "And I'm totally not even tired yet. I wish we had more stuff to do. Did you hear? Jenny got a new puppy. She showed me a picture and it's *so* cute. I just wanna squeeze its face." Jenny was Cheryl's friend, not Maggie's. And while Maggie supposed she could be a friend to them both, there was something about Jenny that turned Maggie off. Firstly, Jenny had made it clear that she thought ocean stuff was lame. *Sharks? Gross.* And second, Maggie got the sneaking suspicion that Jenny wanted Cheryl to be *her* best friend exclusively, a feeling that Jenny didn't want Maggie around. "Next time," Cheryl said, "we should sleep over at her place instead."

"We can find stuff to do," Maggie protested. "Wanna go swim?"

"Swim again? In the middle of the night?" Cheryl looked dubious, and it was true, Maggie *would* get in trouble for swimming without an adult to keep an eye out. But it was the first thing that came to mind. "I don't really feel like swimming, Mags. It makes me smell gross," Cheryl said. "Besides, there's mosquitoes."

"Should we look up Justin's concert stuff again?" Maggie didn't have her own computer yet, but her dad let her use his laptop anytime she wanted, just as long as she didn't download anything or take it off his desk. That, and they never did talk their mothers into driving them up to Atlanta for that Kelly Clarkson concert. But that was okay, because they were into Justin Timberlake now. Brynn had a car, and Maggie had a plan. She and Cher just had to find the money.

"What's the point? I bet the tickets are all sold out by now, anyway. We're just wasting our time."

"Well, um . . . we can go hunting for junk in the attic?" Maggie was running out of options. "Arlen put all kinds of things up there when she moved out. I bet there's loads of cool stuff."

"Yeah." Cheryl sighed again. "Or loads of hairy spiders with gigantic fangs. No way."

Maggie chewed her bottom lip as she looked around her room, searching for a solution to Cheryl's waning interest. She wasn't making it easy. What the heck was left?

"Hey, wanna see something scary?"

"Scary?" Cheryl finally twisted her head around to make eye contact. "Scary like what?"

This was probably a bad idea, but it was too late to back out now. Maggie slid off her bed and reached under the bed skirt, drawing the board and its planchette out into the open. She'd sworn to herself that she would never use it again, not after how the pointer had jerked away from her touch. But this was important. If Cheryl grew bored of Maggie, where would that leave her? Forgotten: a lonely girl abandoned by her best friend.

"What the heck is that?" Cheryl asked, giving the board a once-over.

"Sit." Maggie patted the carpet. Both girls took up the position— legs folded, the board balanced between them. "Want to talk to some ghosts?"

And rather than recoiling or looking at Maggie as though she'd lost her ever-loving mind, Cheryl simply shrugged her shoulders and said "I guess?" like it was the most arbitrary question in all the world.

"Okay." Maggie placed the planchette in the center of the Ouija. "You gotta put your fingers on this, real light-like. You can't press down, otherwise it can't slide."

Cheryl did as she was told, but almost immediately pulled her hands away. "Wait," she said. "Maybe this isn't a good idea. I mean, can't some ghosts be bad?"

Maggie considered this, but ended up dismissing the idea. "Sure, but only the ghosts you actually call to the board will show up. As long as you don't call anyone bad, it's okay. At least that's what Brynn said." Except Brynn had said no such thing.

Cheryl hesitated, but eventually bought Maggie's explanation. She returned her hands to the planchette. "Have you done this before?" she asked.

"Sure," Maggie said.

"And it worked?" Again, Cheryl was skeptical.

Maggie stared down at the YES at the corner of the board. "Nah," she said. "Brynn says it's just for parties, but it's fun. Who should we talk to?" When Cheryl did nothing but shrug with indifference, Maggie slumped where she sat and peered at the plastic pointer—silly to think such a thing could be used to communicate between worlds. And to think she'd been sure this dumb pointer had moved on its own. More than likely, she'd just bumped the board with her knee.

"Brynn would know," Maggie said. "We should see if she wants to play."

Cheryl shifted her weight almost uncomfortably, then gave Maggie an unsure glance. "No way, Mags. She'd for sure talk to someone bad."

"What is *that* supposed to mean?"

Another shrug. Clearly, Cheryl didn't want to take responsibility for the gossip that was going around about Maggie's sister, but Maggie had heard it, too. Brynn was always seen hanging out with combat-booted, Mohawk-spiked, Misfits-jacket-wearing Simon, always messing around with her new group of high school friends. Rumor had it they believed themselves to be real-life vampires. Some kids said that sometimes Brynn's group would wander around Friendship Park after dark and do devil stuff. These stories eventually reached their mother, and were brought up at the dinner table in exasperated tones.

Do you know what they're saying, Brynn? Do you have any idea? It's embarrassing. I can't go anywhere without people looking at me like . . . like I've raised a monster.

Oh, for God's sake, Stella. Their father dropped his fork onto his plate and tossed his napkin onto the table. *If they're looking at you like that, then maybe you should stop filling those spaces.*

Filling spaces? she asked. *You mean, stop going to the salon? The Publix? Perhaps next you'll suggest that we stop eating, is that it? Should I stop buying groceries? Feeding the family?*

She's just a kid, their dad insisted. *If your hairdresser is too dense to understand that, you should find a new one before your hair goes up in flames.*

Brynn took their father's defense as an invitation to up the ante. She spent less time at home because, as she once told Maggie, *I'd rather kill myself than spend another second anywhere near that bitch.* Their mother had no desire to accept Brynn for who she was and, in turn, Brynn hated her for it.

"I don't think she'd talk to someone bad," Maggie told Cheryl, defending her sister, determined to not follow in her mother's judgmental footsteps. "Those stories are lies. Brynn's just different."

"Yeah, but she and her friends go to the cemetery, right?" Cheryl asked. "Why would you do something creepy like that if you aren't doing something weird? My mom says that unless you're going to the graveyard to pray for someone, you've got no business being there."

"Well, I've gone there a bunch of times, and I wasn't praying," Maggie confessed. "Does that mean that *I* was doing something wrong?" Granted, some would frown upon Maggie robbing graves of their fake flowers, but that wasn't a crime, was it? She wasn't stealing them, just spreading them around so nobody would feel left out. And yeah, she'd grabbed Dolly off that old tomb, but it was Brynn's, and she'd only done it to protect it from getting ruined in the storm. Dolly was still hidden away in the closet. She needed to return her to her rightful spot . . . if she didn't forget.

"You went to the graveyard with Brynn and her friends?" Cheryl didn't buy it. Boys like Simon didn't hang out with tweens like them.

Maggie shook her head no. "Just with Bee, and it was a long time ago." A pause. "She told me this dumb story." She got up, moved to the closet, and dug through the various miscellany upon her closet floor until she located the porcelain doll that had sat out in the graveyard for weeks. "She left this to freak me out."

Cheryl frowned, clearly not liking the look of that thing. "You should have left it there."

"I couldn't. A storm was coming."

"So? She was the one who put it there. Who cares if it got ruined?"

Maggie looked at the toy in her hands. *She* had cared. The idea of the doll getting ruined, regardless of whether it was a prank, had bothered her too much to let it happen.

272 *Ania Ahlborn*

"Besides, *that's* creepy, too," Cheryl said, staring at the doll. "What if they did something to it, like hexed it or something?"

"Hexed it?"

"Yeah, why not?"

"Because that's stupid," Maggie said. "So, Brynn's a witch now?" She gave the doll a final glance before returning it to the closet, making sure to shut the door tightly behind her.

"Maybe not Brynn, but her friends might be. Or maybe she is, because she got sucked into it. That's how people in cults get other people to join. I watched a documentary about it."

Maggie frowned at that.

"You know what it says in the Bible, don't you?"

Maggie nearly rolled her eyes. It was always the Bible these days. Heck, as far as Maggie was concerned, it was Cheryl who was going to turn out weird, judging by how often she went to church. Maggie, on the other hand, went two or three times a year.

"It says that you don't have to be bad if you're hanging out with bad people. Those bad people can bring the devil into your life. You could be the nicest person, but hanging out with bad people is contagious. Like a disease."

Maggie didn't want to believe that. Brynn's friends were definitely strange, but she'd met Simon a couple of times, and he had seemed nice, more interested in Maggie than Brynn ever was. And sure, maybe he was just being polite to his girlfriend's kid sister, asking questions like what television shows Maggie liked and whether she listened to a lot of music—she didn't dare bring up Justin or Kelly to a guy like him—but Maggie liked to think that he was genuine, a sincerely cool guy who just happened to have a crazy haircut.

"You know what we should do? Talk to someone from the graveyard," Cheryl suggested.

Maggie retook her seat upon the floor. "Why?"

"Because if Brynn is doing something creepy, they'd know about it."

Cheryl had a point. There were hundreds of ghosts lying in wait in Friendship Park. If Maggie wanted to clear up the rumors about her sister, what better way than to go to the source?

"But we'd have to know who to ask, I guess," Cheryl said. "We'd have to go over there and get a name or something. Off one of the gravestones. And I'm not going out there, *especially* not in the middle of the night. You'd have to pay me a million bucks."

That wouldn't be necessary. Maggie inhaled a steady breath and spoke. "I know someone. A little girl . . ." She didn't know the girl's name; the limestone atop that fractured tomb was far too weathered to make out. But Maggie was confident she could summon her. After all, she'd visited so many times. She placed her hands on the planchette and spoke in a low voice: "Little girl from Friendship Park, the one with the dolly on top of the box . . . are you there?"

"You mean Brynn's doll?" Cheryl asked, but Maggie shushed her, focusing on the planchette beneath their fingertips, waiting for it to do something wild. Spin around in circles. Levitate. Spontaneously combust. But it did nothing.

"Dolly?" Maggie said. "Remember me?"

Nothing.

"Maybe you're doing it wrong," Cheryl said.

"Shhh!" Maggie hissed just as Brynn had. "We've got to concentrate or it won't work. Don't talk!"

"Jeez, sorry!" Cheryl looked a little perturbed, not appreciating being snapped at. But she had a point—Maggie was doing it wrong. She was forgetting the most important part.

"Little girl of Friendship Park, I call you . . ."

No. That wasn't right.

"I call onto you . . ."

Nothing. Cheryl shifted her weight, growing impatient.

"Crap, umm, I call upon you . . . ?"

"Ugh." Cheryl rolled her eyes.

"I *call upon thee*!" That was it.

"Magic words?" Cheryl asked, unimpressed. "*There's no place like h*—"

The planchette moved.

Both girls yelped and jerked their hands away.

"Mags!" Cheryl yelled.

"I didn't do it!"

"Yeah right!"

"I swear, I didn't . . ."

"You're such a liar. You're just as weird as Brynn, I swear," Cheryl said, quite serious. "I keep telling my mom she's wrong, but maybe not."

"Your mom's a jerk," Maggie said.

"She is not! Take it back."

But all Maggie managed was a muttered "I'm not weird."

Except, now, Maggie was wondering if her fate truly was sealed. What if she grew up to be just like Brynn and, in the end, her own mother hated her? She pushed the board away. It thunked against the ground, still half propped up against one of Cheryl's knees.

"I'm *not* weird," she whispered again. Except . . . who was the girl who kept sneaking off to the cemetery despite Brynn having lost interest long ago? Who was the girl who had bought a Ouija board with her birthday money and had requested a séance instead of a party? Who was sitting with that board next to her feet right now? Was this her destiny, to follow in her sister's footsteps? Would she argue with her mom the way Brynn did now?

"Hey." Cheryl frowned. "*Hey*, don't get upset, Mags. I didn't mean it. Let's not fight, okay? Here." Cheryl placed the board back on Maggie's legs. "I'll be serious, okay?"

Maggie sucked in her bottom lip, but eventually relented. She didn't want to fight, either, regardless of whether Cheryl's last comment had hurt her feelings. She *did* want to know what Brynn was up to, because she missed the way she and her sister had once been: inseparable, almost best friends. An answer from the board wouldn't just be useful in stopping all those nasty rumors; it would also help Maggie get close to Brynn again.

"Hey, Dolly?" Cheryl, this time. "We have a question."

No movement.

Maggie shook her head. "We probably scared her away."

"Scared a *ghost*? That's a laugh. Dolly . . . if you're here, do you know Maggie's sister Brynn?"

"Let's just forget it, Cher," Maggie murmured. "I'm kinda tired anyw—"

The planchette began to crawl.

Both girls gaped at each other again.

"Are you—" Cheryl.

Maggie shook her head. *No.*

It stopped.

"Ghost!" Cheryl's eyes were wide, glittering with a newfound sense of excitement. "Hey, ghost, do you know Brynn?"

One second. Two. Five seconds.

The planchette reversed direction.

Again, bewildered stares from both girls.

H.

Maggie watched the pointer swirl across the board, her own fingers hardly touching it at all.

I.

"Oh my gosh," Cheryl whispered despite herself.

M.

"*Him*?" Maggie asked. "Him who? Simon?"

"Who's Simon?" Cheryl asked.

"Brynn's boyfriend."

"That weird guy? It's gotta be," Cheryl said, her excitement continuing to grow. "The ghost is talking about Simon!"

A.

G.

It stopped there.

"*Him A G.*" Cheryl wrinkled her nose, not getting it.

"Who's A G?" Maggie asked the board. Arlen's name started with *A*. But *G*?

U.

"This is weird," she said softly. "I don't feel right, Cher. Maybe we shouldn't be . . ."

"Oh, don't be such a drag, Mags."

Their wrists started to bend, the planchette slowly spinning in place rather than weaving across the letters.

"*Him A G U,*" Cheryl said. "How is anyone supposed to understand this thing without a dumb decoder pin?"

"Brynn said it doesn't work, remember?" Maggie murmured. "She said it's just a game." But when she looked up, Cheryl was staring at her with a disturbed look across her face. "What? What's wrong?"

"It's not *Him A G U*," Cheryl said. "It's *Hi, Mag. You.*"

Maggie blinked, then looked down at the board. And that's when she saw in what position the planchette had stopped. The tip of the plastic pointer was aimed right at her.

"I don't want to play anymore," Maggie said, and shoved the board away, once again hiding it beneath her bed.

"But don't you want to know about what Brynn's up to?" Cheryl asked. Maggie did, very much so. But it seemed to her that Cheryl was the one who was really intrigued now. Maggie, on the other hand, was nothing short of reluctant.

Cheryl wasn't deterred by Maggie's change of heart. She jutted her arm beneath Maggie's bed and retrieved the board, repositioning it upon their laps. "Hands," Cheryl said, nodding at the pointer, her own fingers already in place.

"Cher . . ."

"Hands!"

If Maggie didn't do it, Cheryl always had Jenny. And sure, Maggie had other friends at school, too, but she and Cheryl shared a special bond. It was less than a year before they would both be eighth graders. After that, they'd be at a new school, changing classes every hour, learning how to navigate the halls, trying not to be outcasts amid all the cool kids in some massive cafeteria. Brynn would be there, but Brynn didn't ever want to hang out anymore. For all Maggie knew, by the time she was a freshman, Brynn—who would be a senior—would pretend they were strangers. *Maggie? Maggie who?* Sulking, Maggie dropped her fingers onto the planchette. Because she didn't want to lose Cheryl, not to something as stupid as this.

This time, the planchette didn't hesitate. It began to trace circles across the center of the board before settling upon an H, and then an I.

"It's talking to you," Cheryl said. "Say *hi* back, Mags."

"Hi," Maggie said softly, frightened. "Do you remember me? From the . . ." *The cemetery.* She didn't want to say the word, didn't want to remind the little girl speaking to them through the board that she wasn't the same as they were, that she was dead. Because if Brynn was right, that would make Dolly's owner angry. It would make her rage.

The planchette circled, then stopped on YES.

"Do you remember Brynn?" Cheryl asked.

YES.

Maggie didn't want to do this anymore. But she forced herself to keep her fingers on the pointer. She needed to prove herself. She didn't want to be the boring fraidy-cat friend.

"Do you know what she does out there with her weirdo friends? Is she doing creepy stuff?" Cheryl was really getting into it now.

NO.

"See?" Maggie whispered across the board at her friend. "Let's stop, now."

"You *made* it say no," Cheryl suggested. "You're pushing the thing around."

"I'm not pushing anything around," Maggie said. "How am I supposed to know *you're* not pushing it?"

Cheryl narrowed her eyes, annoyed by the insinuation. "Because *I'm* not. I already told you. And if I *was* pushing it, I'd have made it say *yes*."

The planchette circled.

NO.

"Whatever." Maggie frowned. This wasn't fun anymore.

L.

I.

"You're making it mad." Cheryl.

K.

E.

"I thought you said I was just pushing it around." Maggie.

NO.

"Well, you probably *are*."

LIKE.

"Hey, ghost." Cheryl. "Prove that you're real."

The planchette increased speed.

"Do something. Slam a door. Push something over. Make a sound. Pull Maggie's hair."

"Pull my—*hey*." That hadn't been nice.

NO LIKE.

"*No like*—no like what?" Cheryl asked.

"Cher, let's stop, okay?"

NO LIKE.

It spelled it out again.

NO LIKE.

"I don't want to stop," Cheryl insisted. "We're having fun, right?"

And then, it settled upon a single letter.

NO LIKE U.

Maggie slowly looked up at Cheryl, and when their eyes met, Cheryl lost her nerve. She lifted her fingers from the pointer. "Yeah, okay, fine," she said. "Whatever. Let's do something else. Something *boring*." Leaning back on her hands, she exhaled a sigh, trying to play off her rattled nerves as casually as she could. "I guess we can watch *American Idol*."

But Maggie couldn't get her hands off the planchette. She tried to lift them, but they were cemented there.

"Maggie, come *on*," Cheryl whined, impatient. "I thought you didn't want to play this stupid thing anymore."

The planchette glided across the board.

FRIEND.

MAG.

YES.

"I'll just call my mom, then," she murmured. "Since *you're* the one being creepy."

FRIEND.

MAG.

YES.

Maggie could feel the words at the back of her throat, but they were getting stuck there, like water held back by a dam. *I'm not doing this. Cher, it isn't me.*

FRIEND.

Over and over, like a mantra.

FRIEND.

Cheryl rolled her eyes. "*Weird*," she said. "Like you-know-who."

CHER.

"Um, *yeah*?" Cheryl arched both eyebrows, as if unsure whether to be annoyed or amused.

BITCH.

Maggie's mouth dropped open.

HATE.

She shook her head. No, this wasn't her. No, no, *no*.

"... What?" Cheryl blinked in disbelief. "*What?*" But rather than storming out, she snatched up the pointer, tearing it away from Maggie's hands. "You think that's *funny*?!"

"Cher ..." Maggie's voice returned, as though that planchette had temporarily stolen her ability to speak. Her right hand leapt to her collarbone, pressing against her half of their mutual best-friend necklace.

Cheryl threw the plastic pointer across the room. It hit the wall with a crack.

"It wasn't me," Maggie said weakly, knowing how ridiculous it sounded. "Cher, I promise, it ..."

"Forget it!" Cheryl was crying now, gathering up her stuff. "You know what? It doesn't matter. I don't even care."

"But ..."

"But nothing." She veered around, giving Maggie a hard glare. "You know what, Maggie? *You're* the bitch!" The curse made Maggie wince, but Cheryl wasn't deterred. "You should go hang out in the graveyard with your sicko sister," she spit out. "Go join a devil cult, Mags. Then you can talk to the dead people *all* the time! And, and ..." She noticed the placement of Maggie's hand, then reached up to her own necklace and tore it free of her neck. "You can keep this. Find someone else." She threw the necklace down onto the carpet and stormed out, leaving Maggie alone with the board across her lap.

. . . .

Maggie was devastated. She tried calling Cheryl the next day, but Cheryl's mom insisted she wasn't home. When she called the day after that, Cheryl happened to be out with her dad. After a week of trying, Maggie's mom rested a hand upon her youngest daughter's shoulder and gave her kid a sad sort of smile. "Honey, Cheryl doesn't feel like talking. Let's stop calling her house, okay?"

That afternoon, Maggie sat down with her school pencils and stationery set and began to write a note of apology—*Dear Cheri, I'm so sorry*—but she couldn't think beyond the light tapping on her bedroom window. At first, her heart soared at the sound. Maybe Cheryl was outside, tossing pebbles at the glass. That seemed like a Cheryl sort of thing to do, something they'd both laugh at because it was hokey and lame. But when Maggie abandoned her desk chair and pushed the curtains aside—her heart thudding in her ears with eager anticipation to see her best friend standing on the lawn—there was no one in the yard, and with no tree branches anywhere near the window, it was impossible to decipher where the noise originated.

Squirrels, she thought. *Squirrels on the roof.* They drove Maggie's mom crazy. Surely that's where the tapping was coming from.

That night, with her note only half-finished—*I promise on our whole friendship, it wasn't me*—the tapping on the window graduated to a knock.

Squirrels? Not unless they were inside the walls, banging on two-by-fours with their tiny fists. She hit pause on the DVD she was watching—*Panic Room*, borrowed from Brynn, and most certainly not approved by their mother—and followed the knocking to a spot behind her bed.

Tap. Tap. Tap.

Maybe a mouse skittering behind the plaster? But when she put her ear up to the wall, the knock seemed to come from the back of the headboard, as though an invisible hand were reaching out from beneath the mattress and rapping its knuckles against the wood.

"What the heck?" She went downstairs and reported the knocking to her father, who—a few minutes later—came into her room with a ratchet set to tighten the bolts of Maggie's frame.

"What're you watching, Crazy?" He peered at the TV. "It looks scary."

"It's not," Maggie said.

"Oh yeah?" Dad gave his youngest daughter a look. "Doesn't look like it's Mom Approved, and it sure as heck looks like it might make a little girl hallucinate some strange knocks in her poorly lit room."

"I'm not *hallucinating.*" Maggie crossed her arms over her chest. "And I'm not a little girl," she muttered beneath her breath.

Dad didn't bother to counter her argument. He checked the headboard. "Loose screws," he said, tapping Maggie's forehead with a finger. "Get it together. Either that, or stop watching scary movies." Maggie stuck her tongue out at him, but she couldn't stay mad for long. Besides, he was right; it *was* nuts. There was no such thing as ghosts. Just her imagination. Her newfound resolve, however, didn't keep her from tossing that Ouija board into the steamer trunk at the foot of her bed and latching it tight.

In case the knocking came back. Which it did.

Tap. Tap. Tap.

Always in threes.

Tap. Tap. Tap.

Now, from inside the trunk.

As if to say:

Let. Me. Out.

THIRTEEN

MAGGIE FOUND HERSELF sitting next to Brynn on the couch, waiting for Simon to arrive. It was New Year's Eve, and their parents had gotten snazzed up to attend some sort of fancy gala downtown.

"Hey, Bee?" Maggie squinted at the TV.

"Hey, what?"

"I don't get it," she said. "You know how you said that board doesn't work?"

"Oh my God, are you *still* going on about that?"

"I just want to know something," Maggie said, trying to come off as casual.

"Fine. What?"

"Well, if it *doesn't* work, then how does the pointer move and stuff? How do the words appear the way they do?"

Brynn looked up from her phone with a raised eyebrow. "You think they just *appear*?" she asked. "Like, a ghost is really doing it, huh?"

Maggie lifted her shoulders up to her ears.

"Like, ghosts just sit around waiting for dipshits to break out their stupid Ouija boards that they bought at Toys R Us so they can spell out stupid crap like *I like big boobs* and *Let's order pizza*?" Brynn paused, suddenly looking thoughtful. "I should have ordered pizza."

"Or bad stuff," Maggie said, only to immediately regret it. Because now her sister was looking at her with flat-out suspicion.

"*Bad* stuff? Are you screwing around with that thing?"

"No!"

"Bullshit, yes, you are."

"No, I mean, not anymore." Maggie frowned. Another lie. Before the board had been around, she hadn't had to cover her tracks. But since she'd brought it home, she'd lied to her dad on her birthday, and now she was lying to Brynn. "But I played with Cheryl—"

"Little Miss Priss."

"—and it spelled out awful stuff, Brynn. Stuff I'd never say to Cheri, like, ever. And that's why she left and hasn't come back. That's why she doesn't want to be my friend anymore."

Brynn appeared to consider this. She sat silent and motionless for a time, as if thinking something over. Then again, she might have been back to thinking about pizza. There was still time. Their dad had given them twenty bucks before heading out the door.

"And now there's knocks in my room," Maggie added, albeit quietly.

"Knocks," Brynn echoed.

"Yeah, and scratchy sounds."

Brynn gave her sister a look. *You're bullshitting me*, it said.

"You've got to believe me, Bee," Maggie pleaded with her sister. "Are you *sure* the board really doesn't work?"

"I guess it *could*," she murmured. "But . . ."

"But what?"

"You ever heard of the subconscious?"

Maggie shrugged.

"It's, like, stuff you do or say without knowing you're doing or saying them. It's your mind acting out on your innermost thoughts."

"Yeah?"

"So, maybe you actually *did* want to say those things to Little Miss Priss, but you couldn't bring yourself to do it, so you had the board do it instead."

"No." Maggie shook her head, vehemently denying the possibility. That was ridiculous. Maggie was hurt, sure. And she'd been jealous of Cheryl and Jenny's budding friendship. Maggie had felt left out because Cheryl had changed. She'd become more distant, distracted. But for Maggie to call her a bitch? "No way," she said. "Cher's my best friend. Or . . ." She frowned, realizing the inaccuracy of her word choice. ". . . was . . ."

"Yeah, well . . ." Brynn lifted a single shoulder up toward her ear. "Sometimes best friends suck a big one, so get used to it."

But Maggie couldn't bring herself to believe it. Because even if it had been her unconscious mind, why hadn't she been able to stand up, to throw the board off her knees and chuck the pointer across the room? None of it made sense.

"But—"

The doorbell chimed.

"But nothing," Brynn said, leaping off the couch to answer the door. "Don't be a drag, okay?" She shot a look over her shoulder, as if to say: *Do* not *embarrass me in front of Simon.*

Maggie bit her bottom lip and moved to her father's armchair. A few minutes later, she was happy she had. Brynn and Simon were cozying up on the couch, neither one of them able to stop touching each other for more than half a second. It was gross, which was why Maggie decided to focus all her attention on the movie Simon had brought with him. The opening credits began to roll, and all three of them immediately began gorging themselves on Orville Redenbacher's buttered popcorn, Diet Cokes, and red Twizzlers that Maggie didn't much like but couldn't seem to stop eating.

The movie was boring at first, something about an archeologist and a mysterious artifact—*Indiana Jones* without the rolling boulders and monkey soup. She considered ditching out and going upstairs to watch *Dick Clark's New Year's Rockin' Eve* on her own TV, same as the Olsens usually did as a family every year. Or maybe she'd pull the board out again. It might be fun to ring in the new year by talking to the undead. It sure as heck would trump Simon's taste in films.

Except, by the time Maggie had gathered up the nerve to excuse herself, the film cut away from the archeologist to the story of a little girl instead. And when that little girl's mother discovered a Ouija board in the basement? Well, Maggie was riveted. And absolutely terrified.

A handful of scenes later, that same little girl peed herself during a party in front of all her mother's fancy friends. At that point, Maggie pressed a decorative pillow to her chest and gaped. Because what the hell *was* this? What had Simon brought into their home?

"Gross." Brynn pelted popcorn at the TV screen. She and Simon couldn't manage to keep quiet for more than a few minutes at a time, laying down witty quips after what seemed like every line of dialogue. But Maggie's attention was fixed, her eyes glued to the tube, and by the time Regan MacNeil was thrashing in her bed, Maggie was struggling to keep her own scream at bay. Stuffing a corner of that pillow into her mouth, she kept herself from revealing just how scared she was, worried that maybe Brynn would make her go upstairs or turn off the movie completely, which Maggie both wanted to happen and knew she would challenge if it did. Because she *had* to know how it ended. She had to know what her own future held.

Every now and again, her eyes would dart toward the staircase leading up to the second floor. There was a sensation of something standing at the top of the stairs, just out of view, like a kid hiding out, watching the TV through the slats of the balustrade. Except the feeling coming from upstairs wasn't curiosity; it wasn't a sense of inclusion. It was heavy. Black. Swirling with menace. And the more Regan transformed into a snarling demon on screen, the more Maggie wanted to run from room to room, flipping on every light.

Even Brynn and Simon fell silent when the flick went off the rails. The story spiraled toward madness, and Maggie could tell that they, too, were disturbed by the things they saw. Brynn was probably regretting having shut off all the lights; she was more than likely considering another movie right after this one—something funny to break the tension. That was Maggie's go-to technique whenever Brynn scared her just before bed. Cartoons, or the Farrelly brothers. *Dumb and Dumber* was one of her favorites. She couldn't count the times Lloyd Christmas and Harry Dunne had put her at ease with their snorts of laughter, assuring her that the world was stupid and hilarious rather than a terrible, festering wound.

When this movie ended, though, Maggie wasn't sure she could move. Her body had petrified within its protective pillow-clinging huddle. The anxiety that had grown inside her chest was coiled up tight, promising to rouse with the slightest of shifts, to suffocate her beneath its crushing weight.

Brynn and Simon fell back into their usual teasing. Simon collapsed against the couch like a tired prince, his black T-shirt and jeans nothing more than pronounced shadows against the beige upholstery. He began to convulse while Brynn laughed next to him. Then he fake-vomited all over the floor before attacking Brynn, pretending to puke into her mouth and onto her hair. She parried him with flailing hands and uncontrollable laughter.

Meanwhile, Maggie sat motionless, staring at the TV as the credits rolled and that creepy music played, waiting for something evil to crawl out of the screen. It was only after a few seconds of goofing off that Brynn realized her little sister was too quiet, too still.

"Mags?" she asked. "Hey. Oh man. Are you totally freaking out?"

Maggie didn't respond. She continued to hug that oversized pillow to her chest like a soul shield. There was a terrible feeling in the room—one that neither Simon nor Brynn seemed to register. Whatever had been lurking at the top of the stairs had now descended—backward and in reverse, having crab-walked down the risers just as Regan had. Maggie was certain it was standing directly behind her, leering. She could feel electricity upon her skin. She could smell it. Something was burning. Going up in smoke.

"Shit, Maggie?" Brynn sounded concerned this time. "Dude, if you're freaking out, you better not say anything to Mom." Because if Maggie did, Brynn would be in a world of trouble. Maggie wasn't even sure Simon was allowed to be there. Brynn would be grounded for life, and Maggie would never hear the end of it from her disgruntled sister.

Maggie managed to blink out of her stupor, but rather than releasing the pillow, she only clung to it more. "I'm okay," she whispered. "I'm okay." An echo, as though saying it over and over would make a falsehood true.

"Hey, didn't you say you guys have a board?" Simon's question made the hairs on the back of Maggie's neck stand on end.

No. She wanted to scream it at him. *No, no, NO.*

"Yeah, Mags does . . ." Brynn said, still watching her kid sister.

"Well, bring it out!" Simon said, beaming, pushing his fingers through that floppy black Mohawk. "Let's talk to some fuckin' demons."

"Ehhh, probably not the best idea right now," Brynn said.

Simon sat up from his sprawl across the couch and raised both eyebrows at Maggie. Secretly, she found him painfully pretty, like one of the all-black-wearing bad guys in an anime movie. But now,

in the darkness, his pale face and odd expression made him look dis-
concerting, like a ventriloquist's dummy. If he made like he was going
to come after her, she was sure she'd burst into tears.

"You afraid something's gonna steal your soul, little sister?" he
asked. "That stuff really happens, you know. There are documented
cases . . ."

Maggie held her breath. Those tears were coming, their sting
creeping across the backs of her eyes.

"This movie, it's based on a true story, you know. There's even
a book written about it. And it's not just people they can get into,
either," Simon continued. "It's *things*, too."

"Hey, Si, don't," Brynn said, taking a seat next to Maggie. And yet,
when the cushion of the armchair compressed beneath her weight,
rather than being comforted by her big sister's presence, Maggie
jumped up and off the furniture like a startled cat. Brynn stared at
her with surprise. "What the hell, Mags?"

"Nothing!" The word came out as a yell, though she didn't know
why. She looked down to the pillow she was now wrenching with
both hands. It felt like the only pure thing in that room, so she hugged
it again, refusing to release it from her grasp.

"Dude, okay, now you're freaking me out!" Brynn yelled back,
then got up to cross the distance between the couch and the wall.
She flipped a light switch. A small table lamp burst to life, cutting
through the malicious darkness of the living room. But the shadow
the light should have blotted out stayed exactly where it wanted to
be, cemented in the material world. She imagined it swirling. Huddled. Clinging to the walls. The furniture. Grinning. *Grinning . . .*

"I'm going to bed," Maggie whispered into the fringe of the pillow. She didn't want to go upstairs by herself, but she couldn't beg
Brynn to go upstairs with her while Simon was there. And she certainly didn't want to stay downstairs, where that shadow lurked.

"But it's not even midnight," Brynn protested.

"You're gonna miss the ball drop," Simon said.

Who cared about the dumb ball drop? To all the people who froze their butts off out in Times Square, the new year meant new possibilities, a fresh start, a clean slate. The night felt exciting, full of mystery and potential. But not to Maggie. Not now. Not after what she'd just sat through. Not with how twisted up she felt.

Now, the future felt nothing but ominous.

Bad things lingered on the horizon, she was sure of it. Very bad things.

. . .

That night, Maggie couldn't sleep. Even with the desk lamp on and the TV muted, every time she shut her eyes, the same sensation swept over her like a fog: the feeling of someone sneaking up on her, tiptoeing through her bedroom in that high-stepping cartoonish sort of way. Demons flashed against the backs of her eyes—perfect replicas of the awful monster the movie had invoked. Pulling her blankets up beneath her chin, she buried her face in her pillow. If she managed to fall asleep, she was sure her apprehension would wane. But sleep seemed next to impossible. The knocking that was coming from the back of her headboard wouldn't stop—a light *tap, tap, tap*, always in threes. *Just a loose screw, Crazy.* Yeah, right. There was no way she was imagining it this time.

Her heart thudded to a stop when she heard the opening and closing of a door—*What was that?*—only to realize it was her mom and dad, back from their party. They were talking downstairs. She could hear the jingle of her father's car keys. Her mother laughed, then laughed again, but more quietly the second time around. Maggie imagined that they were both a little drunk. At least, that's how couples in the movies came home after a long night of fancy parties.

Despite her shot nerves, the fact that her parents were home gave Maggie more confidence to keep her eyes closed. Nothing bad could happen when they were home, right? That, and the repetitive nature of that tapping eventually lulled her in a trance.

Tap, tap, tap.

She squeezed her eyes shut. *Just don't look.* If she didn't see the shadow, she could pretend it didn't exist.

It might have been an hour, or a minute, or just a few seconds of slipping away, but it felt like she'd been sleeping for days when her unconsciousness started to lighten around its otherwise dark edges. She shifted her weight, unable to feel the bed beneath her. She groped for the mattress, for her blankets, but there was nothing but air. In her mind—in real life?—she was floating, equidistantly suspended between the mattress and the ceiling, her hair cascading down toward the floor as hungry, twitching figures filled every corner of her room.

Maggie struggled against that still-clinging sleep, fighting to open her eyes. *It's coming!* Somehow, she was sure that the moment they blinked open, she'd hit the mattress with a heavy thump. But that was impossible. It was that movie, that scary levitation scene. Things like that were nothing but Hollywood. They couldn't happen in real life.

But her skepticism offered no comfort. *Wake up!* She bolted upright, miraculously seated upon her bed. With heaving breaths, she searched the walls of her room, pausing to stare into corners that were a little too dark despite the lamplight. The shadows felt alive, and the longer she gazed at them, the more it seemed like they were biding their time, waiting for her to look away.

The television threw out reassuring images that the world was as she had left it. Normal. Clearly lacking in the demonic department. But that closet door . . . she was sure there was something behind it. That wicked, lurking thing. The creature that smelled like smoke.

Go get Dad, she thought. But her mother would be annoyed. It would only prove that Brynn had been up to her usual tricks again, and that would inevitably lead to trouble. Maggie didn't want that to happen. After all, it was Simon who had brought over that awful film. Bee had just wanted to impress him. She had protected Maggie when Simon had wanted to bring out the board.

With her teeth clenched, Maggie lay back down and tried to force herself to sleep, but it kept happening. Every time she managed to drift off, she was overcome by a sensation of rising upward like a helium balloon. Each time, she gasped awake, only to find the room just the way she'd left it. Untouched by the supernatural. Except for that light tapping. Incessant. Never wavering. *Loose screw.*

She could go sleep on the couch. Except that would give away her fear just the same. Their mom would know. Brynn would be held responsible.

And then, the mattress rumbled beneath her.

Her fingers dug into the sheets. She tried to scream, but the yell got stuck in her throat—nothing but an air bubble of panic as she scrambled off the bed. Except, when she hit the floor, she came to discover that it wasn't the bed frame that was moving. It was her. She was shaking, as though in the midst of an epileptic fit. Maggie lifted a hand to look at it, crying out when she couldn't get it to stop jerking back and forth. The tremors kept her from standing upright. A whimper escaped her as she began to crawl toward her bedroom door, unable to keep herself from picturing it: a long arm reaching out from beneath her bed, catching her ankle, and yanking her into the abyss.

GO GET DAD!

She wormed down the upstairs hallway to her parents' bedroom door. And yet, even though she was trembling, she paused just before pushing it open, struck by the very real childhood fear of rousing her parents from their sleep. Her mom would demand to know what was going on, why Maggie was so scared. She'd find out about the movie, about Simon coming over. There was no doubt Brynn would be barred from seeing him for the rest of winter break, and Brynn would positively *hate* Maggie for ruining her life.

But Maggie couldn't remain in the hall. The shock of not being able to walk was freaking her out. What if, somehow, she'd become paralyzed? What if she really *was* possessed? She had to go to the hospital. Or to a church, where the demons couldn't get her, just like Brynn had said.

Maggie pushed her parents' bedroom door open and crawled into darkness. She made it to her dad's side of the bed, hesitated, and eventually placed her trembling hand on her father's exposed arm.

"Dad," she whispered, not wanting to wake her mother. Maybe if she was quiet, her dad would keep a secret. "*Dad.*" But it was her mother who stirred, then opened her eyes and gasped. For half a second, Maggie was sure her own face was no longer there, replaced by the bloated and cracking visage of the devil himself. It was why her mom looked so afraid.

"Oh my God, *what are you doing*?" Maggie's mom hissed, clearly startled by the fact that there, in her nearly pitch-black room, her daughter was writhing around on the floor.

"I can't . . ." Maggie lifted a hand to illustrate what she was about to say. "I can't stop shaking." And then, the fear that had built up inside her became too much to bear. She began to cry. "There's something in my room. My bed . . . I . . . I keep floating . . . I can't—"

"Oh Jesus *Christ.*" Stella Olsen threw the sheets off herself, marched around the bed, and caught her daughter by the arm before yanking her up to her feet—pissed, but determined to be quiet. "Hush!" she whispered. "You're going to wake your father."

And just like that, Maggie was escorted out of her parents' bedroom and back down the hall. There was no mention of her tremors, as though her mother hadn't noticed she was in the middle of a seizure, and there certainly was no regard given to Maggie's claims that her room was haunted.

"Back in bed," her mom commanded. "*Now.*"

"But . . ."

"Enough," she snapped. "I've had it with this stuff, Magdalene." She stomped across the room and turned off the TV.

"No!" Maggie whimpered. "*Please.*"

Her mother gave her a stern look—*You're too old for this*—but jammed her finger against the television's power button regardless. The TV screen came back on.

"I'll expect an explanation in the morning," she said. "You better start working on it now, young lady, because I expect it to be good." And then, she left Maggie alone in her room.

Somehow, her mother's unadulterated annoyance wiped out Maggie's fear. Whatever that shadow was, it was gone now, no match for the ferociousness of Stella Olsen, furious over being roused from her sleep.

The next time Maggie woke, it was morning, and the only terror she felt was for the retribution that would inevitably be handed down, the thousands of questions she knew she'd have to answer, all before breakfast.

•

When Maggie finally came downstairs, Brynn and their dad were sitting at the kitchen table while Maggie's mother banged pots and pans next to the sink. When Maggie stepped inside, the air was sucked out of the room, as though she had been the subject of intense discussion and now that conversation had come to a screeching halt. Dad

raised a curious eyebrow, as though already having heard the tale of
the incredible crawling girl, weeping about seizures and paralysis and
floating above her bed. The cookware settled into silence as Maggie's
mother turned to give her youngest daughter a pointed stare. Brynn—
her hair a rat's nest of tangled black—glared at Maggie from behind a
plate of half-eaten pancakes. It was a look Maggie knew well. Brynn
had been interrogated and was, perhaps, being handed her conviction.

Their father broke the tension. "Happy New Year, kiddo. You
hungry?"

"Happy New Year, Dad." Maggie shuffled toward the breakfast
table with her head down and took her regular seat.

"So, what's your excuse for last night?" Maggie's mother leaned
against the kitchen counter, awaiting a sufficient answer as to why
she'd been woken.

Rather than making eye contact with anyone in the room, Maggie swallowed and focused her attention on the half-empty carafe of
orange juice in the center of the table. She reached over, caught it by
its tapered neck, and poured herself a tumblerful. Maybe if she acted
normal, her mom would huff and get tired of being mad.

But it seemed that, at times, Stella Olsen thrived off anger, and
this morning was one of those times. "Your sister believes she can
convince us that nothing stupid went on while she was in charge,"
she said. "Though why I trusted such an immature child with the task
of babysitting you, I can't fathom. An immature child who's *supposed*
to be a young woman, by the way."

Maggie's eyes inched their way toward her unhappy sister.
When their mom was fuming, she'd pelt them with endless underhanded comments, all of them actively suggesting that the child she
was discussing was nowhere within earshot.

"Well?" Mom gave Maggie an expectant look. "Out with it, or
you'll *both* be grounded."

That was it, then. Brynn had been sentenced.

Maggie swallowed a mouthful of juice. Her attention shifted to her dad, searching for backup. He wasn't offering any. This time, she was on her own.

"I just . . ." Maggie hesitated, her fingers working the hem of her sleep shirt. She could tell them everything, and maybe they'd believe her. Except, at this point, Maggie wasn't sure what *she* believed. Had she been floating above her bed, or was it just her imagination? Had she *really* been shaking so terribly that she couldn't manage to walk? The memory of crawling down the hall was vivid, and yet, as soon as her mom threw back the sheets and grabbed her by the arm, Maggie had miraculously recovered the use of her legs. Didn't that prove it was all in her head; that it was, as Brynn would have insisted, her subconscious?

"You just what?" Mom was losing her patience. When she asked questions, she wanted answers, and fast.

Maggie glanced back to Brynn, who was now frozen in midchew. Brynn stared back at her with a look that transcended spoken words. *Keep your stupid mouth shut.* If Maggie spilled about Simon, Brynn wouldn't just be grounded; she'd be dead and buried.

"I just didn't feel good," Maggie said. "I think I ate too much junk food."

Brynn looked down to her plate. After a beat, she continued her breakfast.

"That'll do it," Dad chimed in. "My grandma always used to tell me, if you eat a bunch of crap before bed—"

"*Gross*, Dad," Brynn cut in.

"Okay, we've heard it," Mom said at the same time.

"—you'll wake up with bugs in your butt," Dad finished.

Maggie couldn't help herself. She smiled, then chuckled, loving that nonsense belief. Her dad grinned back at her, then reached across the separating distance to ruffle her hair. That's when Maggie decided that, no, none of that stuff last night had been real. It couldn't have been. That movie had scared the hell out of her, but that was all it had been.

Except Maggie's smile faded as she looked down to her empty plate. Because she could feel it again, that presence. The thing that had lingered in her room last night had now slipped into a sunny corner of their kitchen. The scent she had assumed was nothing more than a burnt pancake now smelled sharper, more pronounced, despite the stove being off and all the pans soaking in the sink.

And when she glanced over to her mother, she saw it. Nothing more than a blip of darkness, ducking around a door jamb to hide itself just as Maggie looked its way.

FOURTEEN

MAGGIE'S PHONE KEPT buzzing in her hand.

I'M GOING TO TALK TO YOUR PROF TOMORROW.

HOPE YOU DON'T MIND.

I KNOW YOU'RE UPSET.

TEXT ME WHEN YOU CAN, OKAY?

Dillon.

But she didn't feel like talking. Not after what she'd seen in Brynn's room.

She closed her fingers over her phone and pressed it to her chest as she lay in bed, unsure of why she was still in that house, of why in the world she would close herself up in that room again. Maybe it was an honest attempt at reliving the past, of getting back to a time when things had been okay. *Repent.* But all it got her was the inability to close her eyes the very same way she hadn't been able to as a girl.

Lying on her side, she stared into the corner nearest to the closet door—the corner that had always seemed darkest, that *still* felt dangerous despite the time that had passed and all the renovations that had been made.

That doll, the way it had appeared back in her room after she'd tossed it out. She had heard the garbage truck rumble up the street, unless it had been the storm. She had been certain it was gone, and yet . . .

It was just the storm.

It was a prank. Someone was screwing with her. It had to have been Hope. She had asked what Maggie was throwing away, had snuck out there before the truck had come, dragged the trash bag out of the bin, and then brought that doll back into the house.

But what about that shadow? And that fucking *board*, the way Cheryl had found it in the closet despite Maggie having gone through all the junk before Cheryl had arrived? Was it possible that Maggie really hadn't seen it?

"No way," she whispered to herself.

Those letters carved into Brynn's bedpost. The mirrors, all shielded but one. A white sheet on the carpet. The glitter of glass. The remains of her sister's lifeblood nothing but a stain waiting to be torn out and incinerated. No, the board *hadn't* been in the closet. She was nearly certain that Brynn had, at one point, found it and taken it with her down the hall. Maybe that's what Arlen had meant when she said that Brynn had been sick; perhaps that's why Brynn had stopped going downstairs for meals. She'd been holed up like a hermit, her fingers upon that planchette, watching that plastic pointer glide over a board. She had been doing exactly what Maggie had done. It had become an addiction. A calling. An all-encompassing desire that could not be denied.

And now, it was starting all over again—boards vanishing and reappearing out of nowhere; the doll, tossed in the trash, only to be back in its place. All repeat performances of when she was a kid: pencils, school notebooks, once her entire backpack full of homework gone without a trace. She'd spend hours looking for them, eventually blaming Brynn for playing her dumb tricks. Their mother would yell. Their father would give Brynn the look: *Be a grown-up*. Brynn would scream: *What do you want me to do, pull it out of thin air? I didn't take it!* Maggie would cry, in a panic because she hadn't finished her assignments and there was a quiz on her missing notes the next day. Sometimes, during the drama, Maggie's mom would burst into Brynn's room with the intention of finding the missing items, only to discover them in Maggie's room instead, exactly where they should have been. Those were the days Maggie got in serious trouble. And while the grounding was bad, her big sister's resentment was worse.

Then there was that closet door, having a penchant for not staying latched. Maggie *never* left it open; she was afraid to, always making sure it was closed by pulling on the handle thrice before going to bed. And yet she'd wake to it wide-open. That, or she'd leave her room only to return to the closet door ajar. She'd complained to her dad about that the same as she had about the tapping, and there went her father with one of his tools, with his sound logic. *Just a bad latch*, he'd say. *No monsters. Just a big chicken sitting on her bed.*

That shadow, though? She'd never told her dad about that. It felt off-limits, like maybe, if she told him that much, he'd genuinely start to worry; like maybe, if he thought she was seeing ghosts, she'd get sent away. She'd watched enough scary movies to know that sometimes, when kids were crazy enough, they had to go to big hospitals out in the middle of nowhere. And those hospitals? Those places were even more haunted than her house.

That shadow continued to creep into her periphery. Reflections in the bathroom mirror, in the giant wood-framed heirloom in the hallway; sometimes the mere reflection in the turned-off television screen. There was something lingering beyond those twin images, something deeper than reality. Back then, she'd been sure it had all been an illusion, that constant buzz of nerves playing tricks on her. *Just a loose screw . . .*

But now . . .

Maggie sat up.

Had Brynn felt that same sensation? Was *that* why she had so many reflective surfaces in her room?

She shoved the sheets aside.

Had Brynn's initial fascination turned into terror? Was that why she had covered the mirrors, why she had sought sanctuary within a church?

About to swing her feet over the edge of the mattress, Maggie was suddenly gripped by childish fear. Her eyes darted back to the closet door. Still closed, but refusing to offer solace. The moment her toes brushed across the carpet, that shadow would grab her ankles. It would drag her down, lurching into the room from inside that closet to finally swallow her whole.

She nearly shrieked when her cell phone vibrated against the palm of her hand. The screen lit up, illuminating the darkness in an eerie blue glow. *Goddammit!* Couldn't he leave her alone for a few hours, at least? She flipped the phone over and squinted against the glare of the LCD screen, ready to ask Dillon to give her some space.

Except . . .

Maggie stared wide-eyed at the phone, her head registering miniscule shakes of denial.

No.

Her breath escaping in tiny gasps.

No.

Brynn's raccoon eyes and purple-smeared mouth smirking at her, as if amused. The teenage sneer.

No.

HI MAGGIE HI, it said.

MAGGIE HI. Again.

FRIEND WELCOME HOME.

She threw the phone onto the mattress, leapt off the bed, and darted toward the door before stumbling into an equally dark hallway—one that felt far longer than it should have. And as she stood there, swathed by night, she wondered what, exactly, she intended to do now that she was out of that room. Leave? Abandon her sister, her sister's children, in the house that was haunted by her own doing?

She shot a look back through her open bedroom door, her throat clicking dryly as she swallowed against the lump that had formed there. Her phone was buzzing every few seconds, phantom messages blipping onto the screen.

And there, across the room, the closet door was slowly creeping open.

She couldn't see it, but she knew it was there. A shadow in the darkness, darker than the night that surrounded it. Watching her. Waiting.

An ever-present nightmare.

Her inescapable, preordained, self-prophesized truth.

.   .   .   .

Screaming.

Someone was screaming.

Maggie's muscles spasmed, jerking her into full consciousness. She'd been up all night, wide-eyed and curled into the corner of the sofa. But as soon as the sun started to rise, exhaustion hit her hard. She'd drifted in and out of wakefulness all morning, but now, sleep was stripped away with the roughness of a Band-Aid pull. A zing of pain speared through the base of her skull. Her heart clamored up her windpipe. For a moment, she couldn't remember where the hell she was. All she knew was that she had fled the terror she felt last night, turned on the living room lights, and hunkered down on the couch like a terrified child, and now, someone was screaming the way she had wanted to just hours before.

"I don't want appo, I want *oh-ange!*"

Maggie blinked at her surroundings. Her mother's living room, but not her mother's things. One of Arlen's Pottery Barn pillows was crushed against her chest. She winced as she pushed herself up to sit, the vertebrae in her neck feeling as though they'd fused together overnight. The pain was worse than ever now. Yeah, the couch—that had been a *splendid* idea.

A whimper tripped across her tongue. She grabbed at her neck in a feeble attempt at relief. But this wasn't just a crick from sleeping in a fear-induced huddle. This was the very agony that had kept her out of school and landed her in doctors' offices, a pain that had hit her head-on after speeding home from what was supposed to be a fun-filled week on the beach.

Don't go. Friend, don't go.

Another scream. High-pitched. A tiny soprano. "I want oh-ange! Not this juice! Momma, *noooo!*"

"*Hayden!*" Arlen's tone snapped like a rubber band. Even from clear across the house, her aggravation was clear. It had seemed odd that Arlen wasn't mourning, that she hadn't processed the fact that Brynn was gone, but now, Maggie could hardly blame her. Because who in the world could think, let alone grieve, with a three-year-old screaming into your goddamn ear all day?

Maggie squeezed her eyes shut, rubbed at the bridge of her nose. "Jesus fucking Christ," she whispered, trying her best to ease the tension that was now quite literally making her neck pop every time she moved.

She had two more days in Savannah. Today, all details for Brynn had to be in order. Tomorrow, the funeral. That was, if Florence allowed it to happen at all. And at this rate, Maggie doubted she'd be able to make it without an emergency chiropractor adjustment, if she could even find a place that was open in the middle of a god-damn storm. But she was quickly inching up to her threshold; once she crossed it, moving around—let alone thinking straight—would become next to impossible. And leaving Savannah? How was she supposed to leave now, after what had happened last night?

"Did you sleep down here?"

Startled, Maggie blinked her eyes open, then dropped her hands to her lap. Hope stood not three feet from her, her hair a tornado of golden candy floss. The Caribbean blue of her pajamas was bright enough to force Maggie into a squint. Elsa the Snow Queen smiled at her from the center of Hope's sleep shirt. Its bottom hem was snagged on the pink tulle of her tutu. Hope lifted a piece of Nutella-smeared toast to her mouth and took a giant bite, leaving chocolate track marks across both cheeks like a clown's gruesomely wide smile.

"Hey, Hope." Maggie needed a drink, and not just juice. A screw-driver. But judging by Hayden's skin-flaying screech, they were fresh out of OJ. A crying shame.

Maggie tried to roll her neck, winced, and stopped midway.

"Did you hurt yourself again?" Hope asked, her chocolate breath cutting through the distance, twisting Maggie's already knotted stomach into a tighter snare.

"Just sore," she murmured. "Why's Hay screaming her head off?"

"Oh." Hope's attention shifted in the direction of the kitchen, then returned to her aunt a moment later. "She always does this."

Maybe this is why Brynn killed herself. Maggie considered the pos-sibility, then immediately hated herself for such a nasty thought.

"I heard what you said," Hope announced.

"What I said?" Maggie asked.

"Yeah. You shouldn't use the Lord's name in vain." Hope spoke around a mouthful of bread and hazelnut spread. "And you shouldn't curse. Especially the F-word. *Especially* if you're a girl. My mom says."

"Sorry." Maggie detached herself from Arlen's now misshapen throw pillow. She propped it against the arm of the couch, not bothering to fluff it back into shape. That would drive Arlen nuts, no doubt. She needed a shower. The scorch of hot water would at least ease some of that stiffness from her shoulders. Her phone was still upstairs.

Hi, Maggie, hi.

Instant nausea.

She had to show Cheryl the messages that had come in from Brynn's number; maybe *then* Cheryl would understand how much Maggie needed help. Or maybe Maggie would finally crack and call Dillon, tell him everything, ask him what she was supposed to do. *See a psychiatrist*, he'd probably say, because this sort of narrative didn't fit into Dillon's scientific world. Back in Wilmington, she and Dillon believed in logic and reason. Here in Savannah, none of that seemed to exist.

Another wince as she got to her feet.

"I told you not to go in there," Hope said, her tone flat, stopping Maggie in her tracks.

She stared at her niece—five years old but somehow ancient. Somehow *knowing*. Maggie felt her throat constrict, as if threatening to close up in anaphylactic shock.

"Hey, Hope?" The words felt gooey, coated in phlegm. Any second now, she'd be tripping over herself to get to the bathroom. The queasiness was getting worse the longer she stood there, as if standing so close to her niece was intensifying the sensation. "Do you remember how I threw something in the trash yesterday, when the bin was out by the curb?"

Hope furrowed her eyebrows as she chewed, but she didn't respond.

"Did you take out what I put in there?" Maggie asked.

Her niece continued to devour her toast. Hope looked completely unconcerned, and her nonchalance only made Maggie that much more anxious. Had the kid gone cagey, the answer would have been clear: yes, she'd gone digging through the garbage; don't tell her mom, don't get her in trouble. But the way she stood there, so lackadaisical in her tutu and pajamas, so utterly torpid—it made Maggie want to join Hayden's screaming fit.

"Hope?" Maggie swallowed, watching the kid. "Can you answer me?" With the last bite of toast packed into her cheek, Hope's gaze slowly drifted upward to meet her aunt's eyes. "Did you bring that trash back inside?"

The inquiry caused Hope's eyes to darken a shade, but Maggie refused to be deterred.

"Maybe I should ask your mom, then," Maggie suggested. "Since you don't want to tell me yourself."

Hope pursed her chocolate-smeared mouth, then took a step forward to lessen the distance between herself and her aunt. The scratchy edging of her tutu brushed across Maggie's bare knees. Being so close was the last thing Maggie wanted, but being afraid of a five-year-old, of her *family* . . . it was beyond ridiculous. And so she stood her ground.

"You aren't always very nice, Auntie Magdalene," Hope said.

"What? How am I not nice?" Maggie straightened to her full height.

"You call your friends bad names. And you curse. And you throw away stuff that doesn't belong to you," Hope said. "That's like stealing. That doll isn't yours, and you know it."

Another scream, as though little Hayden were somehow personifying the wails trapped inside Maggie's head.

"But I won't tell my mom," she said. "Because I love you." Flat.

Affectless. "No matter what." And then, with a few backward steps, she wandered off, leaving Maggie frozen in front of the couch, tumbling toward panic.

You call your friends awful names.

Hope was talking about Cheryl. About something that happened a decade before. As if Hope had somehow been there to see it happen herself.

FIFTEEN

MAGGIE SLAMMED THE trunk of Brynn's Camry closed and climbed into the driver's seat. With all the windows rolled down and the wind whipping through the interior, she blasted the stereo in the driveway. It was a feeble attempt at soothing her rattled nerves, but at least it brought her back to the days when Brynn would do this very thing—sit in the car when she was particularly pissed, listening to darkwave and smoking clove cigarettes while Maggie spied on her from the upstairs window.

By then, the fights between Brynn and their mother were out of control. Their mom was hardly ever sober, and when she *did* have momentary blips of lucidity, they were brought on not by a clear mind but by the rare lulls in her seemingly permanent high. That respite, however, was always accompanied by an emergency doctor's appointment, another prescription, their mother's tires squealing down the road as she booked it to the pharmacy. By then, sobriety would have meant full-blown withdrawal. Dangerous depression. Anger and constant crying. A complete mental break.

Both Maggie and Brynn had tried to help, lending encouragement while Arlen attempted to get their mother to see a shrink. *I already have a therapist*, was their mom's go-to response. And she was right, she did indeed have one. Unfortunately, that quack—along with Mom's collection of other doctors—continued to prescribe the very drugs that were robbing the girls of their remaining parent.

Eventually, even typically coolheaded Arlen reached her breaking point. Rifling through their mother's things and calling the numbers she found on every orange pill bottle she discovered, Arlen demanded to talk to each prescribing physician while Maggie and Brynn watched on in muted fascination. Naturally, none of the doctors would breathe a word about their patient without power of attorney. Arlen yelled a menagerie of colorful swears into the phone that afternoon. *Fucking drug dealer!* and *Soul-sucking asshole!* had been among her favorite insults. After eight attempts, Arlen had all but thrown her cell phone across the room. It was the first time Maggie had seen her eldest sister get so emotional. And yet she couldn't quite pinpoint the source of Arlen's anger. Was it their mother's downward spiral, or was Arlen pissed because she wasn't used to being denied her way?

Regardless, the girls' efforts got them nowhere. Their mother continued visiting the same doctors who kept giving her the addictive snake oil. Pills came from a variety of places around town—each doctor having their own designated go-to spot because Stella was smart. The pharmacists on duty couldn't be allowed to catch on. She paid cash rather than relying on insurance to foot the bill, and no one was the wiser. No one but her daughters, who frequently found ATM receipts on the kitchen island for hundreds of dollars' worth of withdrawals. But they couldn't do a goddamn thing about it because it was Stella Olsen's money. Their mother was an adult.

Maggie had been out the afternoon Brynn's first panicked call came in, sitting on the floor at her Advanced Placement English teacher's house, working on her graduation speech, with a calico cat curled up in her lap. She ignored the ringing of her cell phone from the depths of her backpack, but when it rang for the third time in less than two minutes, Mrs. Miller gave Maggie a stern yet thoughtful look. *It might be an emergency.* And so Maggie answered the call.

You have to get over here! Brynn had nearly screamed the words, and that's what had scared Maggie the most—her sister's tone. The panic in her voice. Maggie sat cemented in place as she listened to Brynn cry on the line. She sounded as though she were on a boat, or in a swimming pool, or at the lake they used to visit with their father when the Georgia heat got too oppressive to stand. Water sloshing. Heavy thuds against something hard. Wet limbs hitting porcelain and tile.

During Maggie's rush home, an ambulance blasted past her, lights on, siren blaring. She pulled over as it passed, watching its re-flection in her rearview as it turned onto a street a few blocks down, pointing itself toward the closest hospital. When her attention fi-nally drifted from the mirror to the world outside her car window, she found herself parked in front of a wrought iron fence, the head-stones of Friendship Park just beyond.

Stella Olsen didn't die that afternoon. Oh, hell no. She had her stomach pumped and was back on the couch, popping pills like candy less than twenty-four hours later.

It's what pushed Maggie over the edge.

With her arms loaded up with prescription bottles, Maggie marched to the downstairs guest bathroom. Bottle caps bounced against the floor. A rainbow of colorful pills splashed into the toilet bowl. Every bottle she emptied was chucked across the room and against the wall—an angry *fuck you* directed at every opiate, every depressant, every doctor who undeniably knew Mom had a problem. The bottles ricocheted against the sink counter, the mirror, the open bathroom door.

Brynn had materialized during this spectacle, watching, incred-ulous, knowing that the repercussions would be severe. She called

Arlen. *Um, you might want to come over*, she suggested. *I think Mags may have just started World War III.*

An understatement, to be sure. A few minutes later, Brynn was pressing a dish towel to Maggie's wounded cheek, both girls weeping, their life pure and utter chaos. Arlen arrived after the attack. She drove Maggie to the hospital for stitches. Before she left that night, she looked her little sister in the eyes and sighed. *It's good that you're leaving*, she said. *Just get out of here. She's toxic. Make a better life somewhere else.*

The scar on Maggie's cheek had all but faded when, a few months later, Stella Olsen performed an encore, this time with a permanent end.

And for her first few hours as an orphan, Maggie couldn't help feeling nothing but anger. Their mom had broken beneath the weight of tragedy. She had loved their dad so deeply that she had been destroyed by his loss. *Surely*, people had more than likely thought, *the girls must understand how terribly sad that is.* And yes, it was. But the real tragedy wasn't that she had suffocated on her own mourning, but that the love she claimed to have had for her children hadn't been enough to convince her to live.

Maggie now looked up from Brynn's steering wheel and toward the house they'd all grown up in, and a twinge of resentment tightened into a calcified stone at the very center of her chest. Perhaps if Stella Olsen had possessed any decency, she would have spared her children years of pain. Maybe, had the girls not grown up under the thumb of an addict, Brynn's life wouldn't have ended this way.

Or maybe Maggie was just kidding herself. Perhaps fate really was at play, and she herself had set it into motion—a stupid kid with too much curiosity, a girl who hadn't known when to quit. It was easy to blame their mother, but the truth of it was, none of this would have happened if it hadn't been for what Maggie had done.

She pulled out of the driveway and guided the car down the road. The oaks were ragged from their endless beating. They waved their ancient and now mostly leafless limbs at her as she passed, as though trying to warn her to stay back.

But Maggie didn't stop until she rolled up to Friendship Park. Only then did she hit the brakes, and rather than regarding the headstones with sympathy, she glared at them instead. It hadn't crossed her mind to visit their father's plot during her visit, because buried right next to him was their mom. And somewhere, apart from them, would be Brynn.

Maggie pictured her favorite sister placed in the children's section of the graveyard—no room for her next to their parents. Brynn, twenty-five yet still a child.

Dead kids are never happy because nobody wants to play with them.

Except the Olsen girls had been unhappy long before any of them had died.

Maggie guided the Camry through the cemetery gates faster than she should have. Gravel popped beneath the tires as she rolled toward the corner of the graveyard she hadn't dared visit in a decade. Brynn's rosary beads and tiny bird skull bounced along as she went.

Thunder rumbled in the distance. Florence was getting ready to finally make landfall, to ravage all of Savannah with wind and heavy rain, but Maggie didn't let the danger of it keep her away.

Slamming on the brakes when that all-too-familiar stone sarcophagus came into view, she threw the car into park, shoved the driver's door open, and marched around to the back.

There, in the trunk, was that goddamn doll. This time, she'd get rid of it for good. She'd put it back in its place, where it should have stayed. But Simon's warning rang in her ears: *It's not just people they can get into . . . It's things, too.* Yes, the doll had started out as belonging to Brynn, but it had ceased being hers the moment she had left it on that tomb. And stupid Maggie had brought it home. Stupid, gullible Maggie had offered to be its friend.

She grabbed the doll by one booted foot, slammed the trunk closed, and marched toward the grave site she'd rescued it from so long ago. And as she approached the tomb, she felt herself grow that much more vengeful. Her father. Her mother. Now Brynn. With whom would this end?

Her fingers tightened around the doll's leg, and rather than carefully placing it upon the grave where she had found it, she tossed it instead. The doll swept through the air in a wide arc, landing hard against the top of the limestone box. There was a crack, like the pop of a lightbulb. One of its small porcelain hands exploded against the monument's top, mimicking the shards of broken glass hidden beneath a sheet upon her sister's floor.

"There," she said. "Have it back." Perhaps this was all that was needed—the relinquishment of something she should have never taken, a half-hearted apology to make amends.

She marched back to the car, slammed the door shut, and peeled out of there with narrowed eyes and a tightened grip. When she reached the front gate, her foot twitched against the gas pedal, ready to drive away without a final glance. No more Friendship Park. Never again. But rather than careening onto the road, she found herself robbed of breath.

Because there, half a block ahead and pedaling toward the open cemetery gates, was a little girl on a bike. For a moment, Maggie was certain she was hallucinating, seeing herself over a decade in the past. Maggie, the little girl who would visit the dead on sunny afternoons. Maggie, who had once collected a bouquet of silk flowers for her mother, only to watch her recoil from them as though they had been covered in blood. Maggie, rushing toward the graveyard with Katrina at her back.

She closed her eyes, then opened them again, hoping that the action would clear her vision and make the little girl she was sure wasn't there disappear. But rather than vanishing, the girl became that much more vivid. Not a figment. She was, in fact, very real.

As Maggie rolled past—her foot barely grazing the gas—the little girl looked up from her furious into-the-wind pedaling. And through that gale-whipped veil of hair, Maggie recognized her.

Hope.

She was headed to Friendship Park.

Alone. On Maggie's bike.

. . .

Maggie put her niece in the rearview mirror. Too stunned to think straight, she didn't stop the car or offer to drive Hope back home. But rather than booking it back to the house, she found herself in Impresso Espresso's parking lot, staring over the curve of the steering wheel, her mouth dry, her stomach twisted into a fist, her fingers coiled tight against her lips.

Don't go.

She'd promised she'd be back. But she had broken her promise.

She had left, first to go to the beach. As punishment, her father was taken.

Maggie left to go to college, and her mother wound up dead.

She came home for the service, left again to go back to Wilmington . . . and Brynn had started to grow distant, eventually pleading for Maggie's return. And, as if in retribution for Maggie's refusal, she had killed herself.

And now, what would happen after tomorrow? When Maggie got on the plane to fly back to North Carolina, what would happen to Arlen and the kids? What would happen to Hope?

Her cell buzzed against the side of the car's cup holder. She hadn't paid attention to it all morning, afraid to look at her received texts, not wanting to see more of them coming from Brynn's phone. But now, something compelled Maggie to reach out and snatch that cell up. Part of her hoped it was whatever had been sending messages the night before—an affirmation that it was time to do something drastic, that all of this had to end. Now.

But it was Dillon, offering nothing short of a promise that things were going to be okay.

TALKED TO YOUR PROF YOU HAVE A RETEST NEXT WEEK! CALL ME!

Dillon, doing everything he could to make Maggie's life a little easier. He was straining to prove himself, to be a good boyfriend. If only the message had come a day or even an hour earlier; if only she hadn't seen Hope out there, riding through the wind on Maggie's old bike toward those lonely graves.

. . .

Arlen looked surprised when Maggie rushed back into the house. She almost yelped when Maggie grabbed her by the arm and pulled her down to sit on the living room couch.

"I have to tell you something." Maggie spit out the words before she could think better of it. Exhaling, she let her hands fall to her knees. "I did something bad."

"What?" Arlen shook her head, not understanding.

"When I was a kid," Maggie clarified. "When we were all still living here together. I mean, you were already living with Howie, but Mom and Dad and Brynn . . ." It suddenly hit her that, of the people she'd just mentioned, three were dead. Her entire family, on the brink of extinction.

Arlen said nothing. She only stared, a veil of bewilderment resting uneasily across her face.

"On my twelfth birthday, I brought home a Ouija board." Maggie felt Arlen tense beside her.

"What?"

"I kept it a secret. Mom didn't know. And Brynn kept saying that she'd be pissed, so I never said anything." That pain was back, biting at her neck. Involuntarily, her right hand flew back, trying to squelch the ache with her palm.

The wind was howling. Suddenly, a bang sounded from outside. A shutter flapped in the gust. All that was missing was Dillon, jumping at the noise.

"I . . ." Arlen faltered. Surely she'd been in Brynn's room after the suicide. She had to have seen the letters carved into Brynn's bedpost. Brynn's death was connected to that board, whether she had sworn the Ouija was a bunch of bullshit or not. But if she had been a skeptic, all signs pointed to Brynn having become a believer in the end.

Arlen rose from the couch and rushed across the room to the window in question. "This damn shutter," she complained, yanking the window open. *You want feex, you feex.* Maggie watched her from a distance, sickened by a thought: an endless loop of torment, that's what this was. History was repeating itself. The shutter. The storm. The bike ride to Friendship Park.

"I know why Brynn didn't want to move out," Maggie said. "There's something living in this house." She almost whispered the words—like the beginnings of a spooky story that would have thrilled Brynn to bits. "I've seen it. It's been here since I was a kid. And she was . . . she was protecting you . . ."

"Maggie, I swear." Arlen rolled her eyes as she returned. "Florence is about to barrel headlong into this house, Howie's still out there because he's an idiot who doesn't know when to say when at work, I've got the kids to deal with, the funeral is tomorrow, and you're telling me crazy stories? I don't have time for this, okay?" She was about to walk by, dismiss the whole thing as nonsense, but Maggie caught her by the arm and yanked her down. "Jesus, Maggie, what—"

"You *have* to have time for this. I've tried to convince myself that it's all been in my head, but . . ." But the phone. "I got texts, Len. Texts from Brynn. Last night."

Arlen opened her mouth to speak, but all she did was gape.

"Except it wasn't her. How *could* it be her? Don't you get it? It was . . ." What, the shadow? The little girl from Friendship Park? The doll? She knew she sounded insane, and to top it off, she had no proof, having left her phone in the car.

Arlen stared at her, mystified. Could it be that mental illness ran in their family? Maybe Brynn hadn't been the only crazy one. Perhaps Maggie was right there with her.

"I know it sounds nuts, Len. At one point, even Brynn didn't believe. When I brought that board home, she said it was bullshit."

"That's because it *is* bullshit," Arlen said, wrenching her arm free of Maggie's grasp. But Maggie could hear the hesitancy in her sister's voice. If it was powerful enough to lead Brynn down a path of lunacy, that thing was imperious. There was no telling what it could make someone do.

"But she never really believed it didn't work," Maggie said. "She tried to keep it in her room so that I wouldn't mess around with it. She told me that if Mom found it, I'd get into a ton of trouble. But I think she wanted to keep it because she was drawn to it, just like I was." Even at twelve years old, Maggie had seen something in Brynn's eyes—a morose sort of hunger for the afterlife.

"And I *know* it works, Len," Maggie continued. "Because I played it with Cheryl and she stopped coming over. I played it myself for months. And then . . ." She paused, casting a glance her big sister's way. She could read the warning across Arlen's face. *Don't tell me what I think you're going to tell me. Don't you even dare.*

Back then, playing alone hadn't seemed like that big of a deal. Making a promise to something invisible seemed harmless. But after that New Year's Eve with Simon and Brynn, Maggie started to understand: the human mind was vulnerable; a *child's* mind was only that much more volatile. If there ever was a perfect scenario for a spirit to use someone as a portal to the living, it was a solitary kid screwing around with a spirit board, oblivious to the dangers. Because it was just a little bit of spooky fun, right?

"And then that shadow thing showed up."

Maggie waited for Arlen to recoil, to act as though Maggie were infected with some deadly contagion. But rather than pulling away, Arlen simply frowned. "Oh, come on. There *is* no shadow thing, Maggie. I've been living here for years—"

Out of the corner of her eye, a shift of light. Maggie's attention snapped to look down the hall toward the kitchen. Something was slithering along the wall, too quick to make out. Lingering. *I'm here.*

"—and I have yet to dodge flying plates, hear moaning ghouls, or see a goddamn ghost, okay?"

"But the wallpaper in Brynn's room," Maggie said. "Didn't you see it?"

"See what?"

So the scorch mark was gone, then. Maggie shut her eyes and squeezed the bridge of her nose. Was she really losing it?

"Maggie, see—"

"Then what about Cheryl?" Maggie asked, deciding to forget the wallpaper. Pressing the point would only make her look like a lunatic. She let her hand fall to her lap and looked back to her sister's face. "Cheryl, last night, she stormed out of here . . ."

Arlen had no response. She hadn't seen what had happened, had no idea what they'd been doing in Maggie's room when Cheryl had screamed. She hadn't seen the abrasion on Cheryl's chest.

"She was scared, Len. I followed her out to the car, I tried to keep her from leaving. And you know what she told me?"

"To repent for your sins and join the Jesus camp?" *Repent.* Arlen snorted, but all that snide comment did was make Maggie miss Brynn all the more. "If you ask me, that girl has always been off. Little Miss Priss, wasn't it? Mom was right about her . . ."

"She told me that I needed to get out of here, that I shouldn't be here," Maggie said.

"Oh *God.*" Arlen waved a hand, casting aside those ridiculous notions. "Echoes of her nutcase mother, no doubt. That woman is an absolute *lunat*—"

"Just listen!" Maggie was on the verge of tears, now. Arlen had always thought herself smarter than everyone; she'd never been good at shutting up or sitting still. And then, as if to derail Maggie's story, that scent returned. "Do you smell that?"

Arlen raised her hands in surrender. "I *am* listening," she said. "But you have to admit, you sound—"

"It's smoke," Maggie said.

"I don't—"

"I keep smelling it."

"I don't smell anything," Arlen said.

"Len, listen . . ."

"Listen to *what?*"

"I started talking to this kid in the cemetery." Maggie looked down to her lap, then caught her bottom lip between her teeth. "I told her I'd be her friend. And then . . . that one summer . . ." Suddenly, she was regretting ever bringing it up. Because how was she supposed to admit to this? *It's your fault.* Her heart twisted inside her chest. *All your fault.*

"You mean, when Dad . . . ?" Arlen hesitated. She couldn't bear to say more.

Maggie mutely nodded. "It was my fault," she then whispered. "The girl, she begged me not to go, but I left anyway. She just kept saying, *Don't go, don't go.* But I didn't listen, because the board was a fake. I kept thinking about how Brynn had said it was just a game, how maybe it had been my subconscious. I should have never been playing it, I should have left it locked up, but it's like . . . it's like I couldn't stop. So, I told myself, *Go to the beach.* I told myself, *Have a good time. Forget the board. It's time to move on.* I made up all these excuses as to why it would be okay. Because it was fake. Brynn *swore* it was fake."

"Jesus, Maggie . . ."

"So, I shoved the board under my bed, and before I knew what was happening, Uncle Leon was driving me home. And then I got here, and the pool cover was pulled from its rails, and you showed up with Howie, and I . . ."

"*Maggie* . . ." Arlen squeezed Maggie's wrist, as if trying to snap her little sister out of it, but Maggie refused to give in to the temptation; she wouldn't clam up. Maybe if she purged herself of this poisonous secret, things would get better. Perhaps this was the way to break free of the curse.

"Brynn said it," Maggie confessed. "She *blamed* me. And then Mom . . ."

"Brynn was in shock," Arlen interrupted, her tone clipped and embittered. "Just like we all were. And Mom was a drug addict. We tried everything. *You* were the brave one, remember? You stood up to her the way no one else had. What happened to her was nobody's fault, *especially* not yours."

"But Brynn . . ."

"Brynn was clinically depressed, Maggie. Just like Mom was."

"And that's why they died?" Maggie asked. "That's why Mom took all those pills and Brynn jumped out her window? Because they were depressed? Not because of me?"

"*Yes.*" Arlen scooted a little closer. "Maggie, of *course* not because of you. Brynn idolized you. She thought you were the most incredible person on God's green earth."

Maggie's bottom lip began to tremble.

"When she was still coming down for dinner, she'd talk about you all the time. She would brag to the kids about their super-smart auntie working out on the coast, about how you were going to figure out how to clean up all the trash in the oceans and save the coral reefs. Hope was riveted. It's why she clings to you the way she does. Her favorite movie is *Finding Nemo*—not because she's crazy about Dory, but because of all the stories Brynn told her about *you.*"

Maggie pressed her hands to her face and breathed out a sob.

"Maggie, stop." Arlen rubbed a circle across Maggie's back. "Have you been blaming yourself all this time?"

A nod. Another staggered breath.

"Oh, Mags. None of this is your fault, okay? None of it is true."

"But Dad . . ." Maggie whimpered. "He could have swum across the ocean. How could he drown like that? How could the pool cover just—"

"It was an *accident*," Arlen assured her.

"Then where's Hope?" Maggie wept, a jab of pain stabbing her right between the shoulder blades.

"What? She's upstairs with Harry."

Maggie shook her head. "No." Because no matter how much Maggie wanted to believe she was free of responsibility, Arlen was wrong about it all. It *was* Maggie's fault, and what she had seen just that morning had been proof.

"She's not," Maggie said. "I saw her, Len. She was riding my bike."

Again, tension from her big sister. Suddenly, that comforting hand disappeared from Maggie's back. Arlen stiffened beside her, and when Maggie looked up, Arlen's expression had gone from comforting her baby sister to trying not to panic at the silly crap pouring out of Maggie's mouth.

"What are you talking about?" The question was clipped, no nonsense. "She's upstairs with her brother."

"Go check," Maggie whispered. The scent of smoke was nearly overwhelming now, but Arlen didn't seem to notice it. She was too busy scrambling off the couch, nearly tripping over the coffee table as she backed away.

"Where is she?" Arlen demanded. "Harry . . . !" The name came out as a startled bleat. A moment later, there were footsteps overhead.

"Yeah?" Harrison replied from upstairs, unseen. Maggie watched Arlen's face twist beneath the weight of startled realization. Again, a shift of light. Again, another blip of darkness too quick to catch. It was getting impatient.

"Where's your sister?" Arlen was moving fast across the room, stopping a few feet from the couch to look up at the boy Maggie couldn't see. "Where's Hope? You're supposed to be with her!"

Hesitation. ". . . I am?"

Arlen spun around, shooting Maggie a glare. "Where is she?!"

Maggie knew this would be the last real conversation they ever had, knew that this moment would seal their fates. They wouldn't speak again. Not as siblings. Not like this.

"Jesus, Maggie, what is *wrong* with you?" Arlen demanded. "Have you bothered to look outside? Do you know how *dangerous* it is out there? If you saw her, why didn't you *grab* her?"

"Because I was scared, okay?" Maggie said softly, then looked away from Arlen, unable to keep her sister's furious gaze. "I saw her riding to Friendship Park, just like I used to. Riding through the storm to the dead girl. *That's* how I know all of this is true."

SIXTEEN

WHEN ARLEN RUSHED out of the house to look for Hope, Maggie openly sobbed for the first time in years. She didn't bother hiding her emotions when she felt Harrison lingering just beyond her line of sight, not even when little Hayden toddled up and placed a sausage-fingered hand upon her knee.

"There, there," Hayden said, patting Maggie like one would pet a house cat, a child's attempt at comfort in a situation she couldn't possibly understand.

And yet, despite Maggie's momentary meltdown, she couldn't shake the knowledge that it would be a matter of minutes before Arlen came back, and Maggie didn't want to be there when the duo returned. There would be anger, barbed and demanding questions. If Arlen sentenced Maggie to an immediate silent treatment, the punishment would be peppered with accusatory glares; narrowed eyes reminiscent of Brynn's resentment, shot across the breakfast table when things went missing, when the innocent had been blamed.

Poor, weirdly beautiful Brynn. She hadn't just jumped out her bedroom window and onto the paving stones surrounding the very place their father had perished—she would have survived such a fall with a twisted ankle or a few broken bones. But Brynn had been dead by the time paramedics arrived. Dead, because she'd smashed her window with a desk chair, collected a shard of broken glass in the palm of her hand, and inexplicably stabbed that razored fragment not only into her neck and shoulders, but into her face, inflicting dozens of vicious cuts before finally leaping from the window's ledge. Her stereo had been blaring Dead Can Dance when Arlen had discovered the body, like a punch line to a morbid, self-deprecating joke. Meanwhile, a channel of blood did a snail's-crawl across the stonework into the water, dark red turning to swirls of diluted pink like an artist's paintbrush staining turpentine.

There had been no mention of the Ouija board during Maggie and Brynn's long-distance conversations, just as there had been no talk of avoiding Arlen's dinner table, or depression, or churches and seeking out safety from the unknown; no mention of carving letters into bedposts the way a scribe would have fashioned ancient runes into stone. But their phone calls had been punctuated with that same recurring question that Maggie was certain would haunt her forever: *When are you going to visit? Please, why don't you come home?* And Maggie's answer, steadfast: she was too busy with school, too involved with her internship, she and Dillon had something coming up, the timing was bad, she couldn't make it work.

Meanwhile, that shadow had been lurking in the background, listening all these years. It had heard every excuse; had grown tired, embittered, and rancorous, taking umbrage at every untruth. Each one of Maggie's refusals had brought deeper insult.

Maggie had broken her promise. She had left this place and refused to return.

Brynn was left to suffer for Maggie's sins.

And now, with Brynn gone, that darkness would turn its attention to someone Maggie wouldn't be able to so easily ignore.

Because Hope was innocent. Just a kid. A perfect victim for the evil Brynn had so casually described as a girl, that Maggie had been sure had just been another spooky story too far from the truth to heed.

It wouldn't be long now, and Arlen would be furious—an anger that would be too reminiscent of their mother's rage to bear. All Maggie wanted was to hurry and pack her bag, take Brynn's car to the airport, abandon it in short-term, and let the damn thing get impounded. Except all she'd do would be to sit there, staring out the airport windows as rain pelted the tarmac. If the shadow thing couldn't keep her here, Florence wouldn't let her leave.

Now that Auntie Bee is gone, you gotta stay.

For a second that felt like an hour, she couldn't find air. She pictured Arlen's van flying off the road—the kids in the back—all four wheels off the pavement as it sailed across an embankment and into a tree. A lake. The oncoming grille of a semitruck doing eighty on the freeway just outside of town. Vivid. So real she could hear the metal of Arlen's van buckle and twist. The boom of igniting gasoline. Arlen screaming as she tried to pry her seat belt out of the latch. All three children flailing against the orange lick of flames. The kids, wailing. Hayden's high-pitched toddler cry, undiluted innocence piercing through the chaos.

The yelling in her head turned real. Hayden was screaming again, but rather than being consumed by fire, she was in the throes of another tantrum somewhere down the hall. Her words were shrill and indecipherable, angered by the fact that life wasn't as simple as it should have been. No orange juice when you wanted it. The last of the French eyes devoured by a cantankerous sibling. Her mother, having fled the house in search of her older sister, leaving Hayden to battle her crippling emotions alone.

That tantrum was the fulcrum. It veered Maggie's own emotional state away from panic and toward response. She gave in to her instinct and ran out the door, leaving two underage children alone, just as she had abandoned Hope outside the cemetery gates. But staying would mean facing Arlen's wrath, and to save the last of her tribe, she had to avoid Arlen's demand for Maggie to pack up her shit and go. *Forget the funeral. I want you out!* Maggie had to fix this before she was forced to leave, before tragedy found them once again.

She climbed into Brynn's car and drove, stopping in front of Friendship Park to stare down its center lane. She tried to imagine what her sarcastic sister would tell her to do, what strange and dark suggestion Brynn would make to appease the ghost Maggie had released unto the world. *Just kick it in the ass, Mags. Exorcise that shit.*

Spotting movement, she found herself blinking at Arlen's van. A few more seconds and it would turn down that center road. Maggie shoved her foot against the gas and sped away.

Fuck it. She needed to find Cheryl. Perhaps if they held another séance, if she could just get through to whatever it was that was living in the corners of those walls, maybe *then* she could fix what she'd broken. If a broken promise could ever be repaired.

⋅ ⋅ ⋅

She knew Cheryl wouldn't meet up with her again—not after how she had fled from Maggie's house. When they were kids, Maggie had eventually backed off, dissuaded by Cheryl's fear. But that wasn't going to be enough for Maggie to stay away this time. Back then, it was a matter of hurt feelings. Now, Hope needed help.

She grabbed her phone off the passenger's seat and googled the number for Saint Michael's Church, then asked the receptionist where their youth camp counselor could be found. "It's an emergency," she explained. "I'm a friend of Father John." The woman on the line didn't question it. Instead, she handed over Cheryl's location and wished Maggie the best of luck.

If only luck could help me, she thought, then disconnected the call.

Hell, if only God could help me, maybe things would still be okay . . .

Perhaps Brynn hadn't been searching for a safe haven. Arlen had said it herself: Brynn had been seeking answers. Perhaps, then, *this* was the question she was looking to resolve: *How do I save my family? How do I stop this thing?* Could it have been that *that* was why Brynn had been so adamantly pleading with Maggie to come home? Had she been desperate for help, for someone to listen who would actually believe?

She found herself pushing eighty down a winding stretch of road just outside of town: Southern coastal lowcountry dotted with swamps, swallowed by the drooping branches of live oak heavy with long tangles of witch's hair. Florence snarled overhead—dark and angry, ready to crack open and re-create Noah's flood. Maggie slammed on the brakes at the last second, nearly missing the turn, and whipped the car onto a narrow and unpaved road that guided her through a rusted steel utility gate. PRIVATE PROPERTY. That sign shuddered in the wind, threatening to come off its screws. After a minute of bouncing down a washboard road, what looked to be a working farm came into view. There was a barn, the Saint Michael's Youth Camp logo fading against the wood. Long rows of picnic tables were lined up beneath a wide awning that jutted out from what looked to be a stable of some sort. Most of the tables were empty, but some still donned plastic tablecloths, which were held down by grapefruit-sized rocks, the vinyl flapping like ghosts struggling to get free.

In the distance, a handful of older kids were running around in a rush. Some carried buckets and gardening tools. Others were tending to animals, trying to herd them to the safety of a big red barn.

Cheryl wouldn't be happy to see her. At all. And talking about what had happened at the house would almost certainly have found a firm place on her list of conversations to avoid—especially right now, with her charges running around like a manic mob of sheep. No matter. Maggie stepped out of Brynn's Camry and made her way toward the barn, only to stop short when she heard her name spoken into the wind.

"Maggie . . . ?"

She turned and squinted against the gale. Cheryl had stepped out of the stable, embroiled in the struggle of keeping her hair at bay. "What are you doing here?" Maggie had half expected her to start screaming that her space was being invaded, that Maggie had to go. But rather than raging, Cheryl looked concerned.

"Cher, I . . ." What series of words would convince her old friend to come back home with her, to return to the place Cheryl had told Maggie to leave? She faltered, unsure of how to proceed.

"Oh. Wow. You took my advice," Cheryl said, derailing Maggie's spiraling thoughts. "You left." Maggie opened her mouth to speak, but no words came. "Um . . . hey, if you need a place to stay, just until after the funeral, there's a room in the rectory. It's tiny, but it's a bed."

"Cher, no." Maggie looked down at the tips of her sneakers, the bluster stealing away her words. A particularly heavy gust threw off her balance. Maggie braced herself against it with a few sideways steps. Cheryl watched her in silence, and Maggie could feel her mood shift from accepting to on guard. "Look, I already know what you're going to say—" Maggie began, but Cheryl cut in before she could continue.

"So, you didn't leave."

"No."

"Then don't ask. I told you, I'm done. I shouldn't have let myself get sucked into this stuff again."

More thunder overhead. Florence was no longer coming. She had officially arrived.

Maggie drew in a breath, ready to protest, but Cheryl beat her to the punch.

"I *know* it was my idea, Maggie. Nobody likes seeing a friend blame themselves for things beyond their control. Nobody with a conscience, at least."

"But now?" Maggie asked.

"Now . . . I think that maybe you're right. Maybe you've been right all this time."

Maggie's eyes paused upon the abrasion on Cheryl's collarbone. Its half-heart shape made her want to scream, *Can't you see what it looks like? The necklace* . . . A coincidence, no doubt. It had nothing to do with friendship, nothing to do with wiping out the competition, rendering Maggie lonely, pushing her toward that board day after day.

"Cher, *please*. I can't do this alone. I need your help."

"Why?" That single syllable fell flat, unrelenting. If Maggie couldn't come up with a good enough answer, the conversation was over.

"Because I think it's gotten to Hope," she said, shoving strands of loose hair behind her ears. "I think that if I leave—" She swallowed the spit that had collected at the back of her throat, the mere thought of something happening to her niece, the thought of it being Maggie's fault all over again . . . "Don't you get it? This is why Brynn wanted me to come home. She needed help, too. It's why she went to church. And now she's gone."

When she glanced back to Cheryl, Maggie noticed her gaze was distant, focused on the kids rushing around the barn a dozen yards away. She was a woman who didn't belong anywhere in Maggie's world, a girl who shouldn't have ever heard Brynn's weird stories or placed her fingers on Maggie's plastic planchette. A person who, now that Maggie was giving her a good hard look, wouldn't sacrifice any more of herself than she already had, not for a long-dormant friendship. At least not now, not after this.

"I need help, Cher," Maggie repeated. "I don't know what to do."

"I don't know what you should do, either," Cheryl said. "But I can't . . ." She hesitated, fumbling for the right words. "I'm sorry, Maggie, but I should have never gotten involved."

Maggie bit her bottom lip, nodded despite herself. Had she been in Cheryl's shoes, she wouldn't have wanted to be part of it, either. And the fact that Cheryl had experienced something malicious enough to have her running for her life—it meant that whatever Maggie had invited to live inside that house was able to reach out, to lay hands on anyone who dared get in the way of its ultimate goal. Like Cheryl had said once upon a time, it was contagious. It could infect, damage, destroy.

"All I know," Cheryl said, "is that whoever you've been talking to . . . I don't think it's who you think it is."

"The girl from the cemetery," Maggie said.

"Yeah, that. I don't think so." Cheryl frowned. "You know what the Bible says? *And no wonder, for Satan himself masquerades as an angel of light.* The most dangerous spirits disguise themselves as innocent. Why would a little girl do what's been done to you, Maggie?" Cheryl asked. "If what you say is true, if it's all linked, why would a *child* do those terrible things?"

Because she was evil, Brynn had said. *She was born bad.*

And then there was Maggie's broken promise. Children threw tantrums when they didn't get what they wanted. Hayden was perfect proof of that. This spirit, if it *was* a child, would have turned Arlen's house into a hub of poltergeist activity. It would have knocked over picture frames, slammed doors, pushed dishes off counters, and spilled glasses of milk.

But Maggie's ghost did none of those things. It worked in far darker shades.

Except that was crazy, wasn't it? More demented than Maggie believing that she was responsible for the deaths of her parents and big sister. No, Cheryl's theory was nuts; too left-field.

"I don't believe that," Maggie said. "It's not—"

"What, a demon? Are you sure about that?" Cheryl's fingers grazed the abrasion upon her skin.

Maggie's fingers trailed to her own chest, recalling the way Cheryl had torn her side of their best-friend necklace from around her neck. That hand drew backward to press into the knot of muscles that, for the first time since her return, seemed to have relaxed. That sense of being watched, the feeling of balancing upon the edge of calamity, she'd felt it again last night. And maybe she *was* going nuts, but it had felt stronger than before, as though Brynn's suicide had somehow lent it fortitude. But now, at the camp, it was gone.

Because it lives in the house, she thought. *It's waiting there, just as it always has. I have to go back.*

Cheryl looked away again, back toward the gaggle of kids in matching T-shirts, all of them scrambling, some laughing, others looking up at the sky, freaked out, because maybe this was it. The sky was falling. It was the end of the world.

"These types of things, they can attach to other people," Cheryl said. "I'm sorry about Brynn, Maggie. I really am. But I can't do this. There's just too much on the line." A pause, a searching glance. "I don't know," she finally said, giving up on the calculation. "I wanted to help, and now I . . ."

"I'm *begging* you." Maggie tried again, because if Cheryl wasn't going to help her, who would? "One friend to another. Please don't abandon me again, Cher. She's just a kid."

Cheryl's tense features softened, if only a little.

But Maggie wouldn't accept the refusal she knew was inevitably coming. First Arlen and now Cheryl—they were leaving her with no option but to give up, and how was she supposed to do that when she knew that Hope, Harrison, and Hayden were in harm's way? Didn't they understand that she was trying to make things right?

"You're part of this, now," Maggie said. "You invited yourself over. You wanted to try again, and now it feels like it's stronger. I trusted you, Cher."

Maggie's assertion sparked a change in Cheryl's expression. The muscles in her neck went rigid. Her lips pressed into a tight line. Another gust of wind blasted them both, each woman momentarily struggling to keep her footing.

"How do you know it hasn't already attached itself to you?" Maggie asked. "How do you know that this thing, whatever it is, isn't going to target you if I leave this undone?"

Cheryl's cool exterior began to crack, her face twisting into a mask of something between aggravation and fear. She glared at the kids in the distance. To Maggie, it was all about Hope; to Cheryl, those kids were what mattered. "You need to go now, Maggie," she said, her tone steady. "You can put the blame on me all you want, but you know better than anyone: *you* did this. This is *your* fault."

The response struck Maggie in the chest like a full-fisted punch. The night Maggie's father died; Brynn's accusation coming out of Cheryl's mouth.

But Cheryl was right. Whatever was lurking in the corners of Maggie's room, whatever it was that she'd pulled from the other side, Maggie was the one who had ushered it into the world of the living. And rather than dealing with it head-on, she had run away, allowing it to stay exactly where it wanted to be. And that's where it had festered. Where it had grown.

"I'm sorry," Cheryl said. "Please leave. Right now. And don't come back." She turned away, walking back toward the stable, adding finality to her demand.

Maggie struggled not to cry. She stared at Cheryl's back, hoping that maybe, at the last minute, she'd change her mind—maybe she'd turn and offer some parting words of encouragement. *It's going to be okay.* But Cheryl disappeared into the building, and Maggie was left standing in the wind, the first patters of hard rain like needles against her cheeks.

⋅ ⋅ ⋅

Maggie drove back into town, but she couldn't bring herself to return home. Lingering in Friendship Park, she disregarded the weather as she walked among the headstones, just as she had when she was a child. She nearly scooped up a bouquet of weather-beaten silk flowers from beside a grave, the petals soaked and drooping with rain, but resisted the temptation. It was one thing to retrace her steps, to try to gather her thoughts and figure out how to make this work. It was another to continue giving the dead the wrong impression. She was no longer the little girl inviting ghosts to her home. It was time to reject that part of her life . . . and she was certain that one spirit in particular would rage in response.

She stopped at the tomb she had visited just that morning. The shattered doll was gone. Because of course it was. It's why Hope had ridden Maggie's bike to the cemetery in the first place. Whatever it was hiding in the shadows wanted back what Brynn had gifted so long ago. Except Brynn hadn't just bestowed that doll upon it. No, she'd promised more, hadn't she?

She'd pledged her own little sister.

And, perhaps, at any other time, Maggie would have been angry with Brynn for doing such a stupid thing. Because this was just as much Brynn's fault as it was Maggie's. But Brynn was gone.

It was left up to Maggie now, and she had to take it full circle to where it had begun.

In her room. Alone. Just her and the darkness, and that board in between.

SEVENTEEN

PETER OLSEN HAD spent his high school career on the swim team, his senior year as captain, went to college on an athletic scholarship, and found his way onto the national team in the spring of 1986. But rather than attending the games in Seoul, he watched them on TV while bouncing baby Arlen on his knee. *That's just life*, he'd say when it came up. *You roll with the punches, and I love my girls more than I love being a fish.* Having kids did not, however, negate the man's love of water.

Having a pool in the backyard was Peter's only demand when he and Stella bought three acres of land and set off to build their dream home. Having hung up his swim cap in the name of family, he tossed aside his hopes of gold medals and busted his ass as a financial manager instead. That hard work earned him a swimming hole deep enough to dive into, measuring forty-one feet long from end to end—exactly a quarter of the length of the standard Olympic size. Maggie spent summers watching her dad butterfly back and forth, ticking off his laps in a little notebook and keeping time on a stopwatch like a pint-sized coach. Peter Olsen was skilled enough to have crossed the English Channel. He could have planned Alcatraz escapes.

And yet, somehow, he drowned.

It happened the summer before Maggie's freshman year of high school, on a day just like any other. Hot. Humid. Maggie had hidden from the mugginess of the outside world in her room, closed up behind a door that was locked more and more often. *Symptoms of becoming a teen*, her dad had diagnosed. Maggie's parents had, after all, gone through the very same thing with both Arlen and Brynn.

Except Maggie's lock wasn't turned out of anger or angst. It was turned out of necessity, to keep her secret from being revealed. That day had been just like any other. Maggie sat on her bed, legs pretzeled together, that board upon her knees.

"I'm going away for a few days," she said, compelled to explain her absence to an invisible presence that, it seemed, only she could feel. The board hadn't been happy.

Don't go.

"It's not going to be long."

Don't go.

"Well, I already told everyone that I was going, and I *want* to go. I haven't done anything fun all summer."

Friend. Don't go.

She rolled her eyes at herself. *What am I doing?* Explaining herself to something invisible, to something that, every now and again, she still questioned could really exist. *Just a loose screw. Subconscious. A hoax.*

"I'm losing it," she murmured, then tossed the board into the steamer trunk at the foot of her bed. Cheryl had been right, Maggie *had* gotten weird. She needed to disconnect from that thing, to find a new hobby. A trip to Hilton Head with her aunt, uncle, and cousins couldn't have come at a better time.

Brynn—forever the antisocial loner—had refused the invite and decided to stay home, listening to music and playing *World of Warcraft* in her room. *Yeah, because I need a tan like I need an asshole on my elbow*, she had scoffed. Typical Brynn. Flippant. Snide. Maggie had shrugged and left with her extended family that afternoon.

The drive hadn't been long, but after a stop for an early dinner and shopping with her aunt for a new bathing suit, Maggie had only gotten to see the beach for a few minutes before sunset. No big deal, though. She decided to wake up bright and early the next morning so she could spend the entire day basking on a towel and swimming in the surf. That, and she'd borrowed *The Perks of Being a Wallflower* from Brynn. She couldn't wait to read it.

But she never got the chance.

Maggie was nudged awake and ushered out of bed by her uncle Leon—a man of large girth but few words. He murmured for her to get her things, explained that he needed to drive her home. When Maggie questioned why they were leaving, why they had to drive back to Savannah at a little past two a.m., he only shook his head, his face pale against the glow of the dashboard, his fingers wrapped tight around the steering wheel.

The house was empty when they arrived. Maggie called her mom via the house phone, but she wasn't answering her cell. Brynn had left her own cell phone upstairs next to her computer, *World of Warcraft* logged out after a stretch of inactivity. Both of those things sent a shock wave of terror through Maggie's chest. Because Brynn never went anywhere without her phone, and she would have never left *World of Warcraft* running like that, not unless she'd been too distracted to log herself out.

Maggie stood at the double French doors leading out to the yard, staring at the pool cover that was now crumpled and floating in the water, wondering what could have caused it to have been torn from its tracks like that. Arlen was the one who finally showed up at the house, red-eyed as though she'd spent the night sobbing. Howie was with her, but Harrison—still just a baby—was not. Arlen looked startled to see their uncle sitting silently upon their couch; Maggie had told him he could leave, but Uncle Leon wouldn't hear of it. *I'll stay until someone comes,* he had said, and then paced the house, back and forth.

Arlen's bottom lip quivered as she spoke. "It's Dad." But that was all that she said.

Sitting in the backseat of Arlen's car—Uncle Leon following close behind in his own vehicle—Maggie expected to be driven to the hospital. It was clear there had been an accident. Maybe their father had caught his hand in the pool cover's motor. Was that why it had been torn from its rails? But instead of heading to the ER, Arlen turned down a familiar residential street and pulled into the driveway of a familiar house. Auntie CeeCee and Uncle Dee weren't really Maggie's aunt and uncle, but she'd regarded them as such for as long as she could remember. They lived in a hundred-year-old farmhouse that they'd spent what seemed like their entire lives renovating. Maggie loved it, from the massive carved newel post at the base of the stairs to the antique freestanding range Auntie CeeCee had custom-painted a beautiful pastel yellow to match her kitchen's decor. This visit, however, was less than cheerful.

Inside, sitting upon Aunt CeeCee's midcentury couch, Maggie's mother was weeping. Brynn sat next to her, stone-faced, her eyes fixed on Maggie as soon as she followed Arlen, Howie, and Uncle Leon inside. Brynn got up, marched across a '50s-inspired living room, and grabbed Maggie by the arm, escorting her to the darkened front yard.

"Ow, Brynn! What's going on?" Maggie asked as her sister shoved her along. "Where's Dad?" She hadn't seen him inside, but if he was at the hospital, why was everyone here?

"This is *your* fault," Brynn hissed, giving Maggie a shove. "*You* did this. I told you I didn't want to . . ."

Maggie stumbled backward, shaking her head, not understand-ing. "Didn't want to what? Brynn, *where's Dad*?"

"You got that board, and I . . ." Brynn's eyes were narrowed, her eyeliner smudged. "Admit it . . . you brought something into the house. You screwed around with that thing and you *invited* it. I should have taken it from you. I should have—"

Maggie blinked at her raccoon-eyed older sister. While Maggie had gone off to the beach, Brynn had gone toe-to-toe with some sort of grim reality, and reality had won with what looked to be a total knockout.

"Bee . . ." Maggie heaved the nickname onto the lawn between them, trying to keep her breathing steady, doing her best to keep her anxiety from spiraling out of control. "What are you talking about? I haven't used it since . . . since Cheryl stopped coming over last year."

Brynn didn't look at her, and Maggie was glad. If she had, she'd have read the lie.

"Please," she said, reaching for Brynn's hand. "Where's Dad, Brynn?" But she knew. "Why's Mom crying?" It had to be. "Why are we here?" There could only be one reason.

Brynn's countenance twisted up with more emotion than Maggie had ever seen rush across her sister's face. "Dad's dead, Mags," she said, jerking her hand away from Maggie's touch.

The world tilted on its axis.

". . . Wh-what . . . ?"

She'd suspected, but hearing those words spoken aloud made the ground shift, like tectonic plates during an earthquake.

"He's dead," Brynn repeated. "And I just . . ." She pressed her hands over her face. "I should have never let you . . ."

And then, the girl who never cried broke down and wept.

EIGHTEEN

MAGGIE SAT IN Brynn's car outside the cemetery until well after dark, hoping that if Arlen, Howie, and the kids hadn't been sleeping due to the storm, they'd at least all be gathered in a room together, waiting it out, and nobody would see Maggie arrive. Florence was rumbling loud enough to shake the windows, now. The rain was falling at an impossible horizontal angle, slamming itself into only one side of Brynn's old Camry. The lightning was a dangerously spectacular light show. Every few seconds, a flash of bright white caught the wrought iron curves of the cemetery gates, stenciling dark curlicues against the night sky. The storm had finally caught up to her, and it was one that she wasn't the least bit prepared to face.

Her phone, still lying on the passenger's seat, blinked with an unread message.

MAGGIE, I'M WORRIED. BAD NEWS ABOUT THE WEATHER. NOT TOO BAD HERE, BUT THEY SAY SAVANNAH IS GETTING HIT HARD. YOU OKAY?

Dillon. He deserved an answer. She grabbed up her cell, exhaled. I'M OKAY. Send.

WHY HAVEN'T YOU BEEN RESPONDING TO ME? DID YOU GET MY TEXT ABOUT YOUR RETEST?

YES. Send. BUT I HAVE TO STAY. I'M SORRY.

A moment later: STAY? WHAT? HOW LONG?!

He wouldn't get an answer to his question because Maggie hadn't a clue. If her plan worked, it would be only long enough to make sure that shadow figure was gone, long enough to wait out the storm. If the plan went awry, well . . .

It won't. It'll be okay. It has to be okay.

She pulled her hair back in a messy ponytail, slid Brynn's key into the ignition, and drove slowly through the deluge of rain.

The house was dark. No doubt the electricity was out. The storm shutters were closed up tight save for one—the one Arlen had to struggle with during Maggie's confession earlier that day. It flapped in the wind, mangled by the merciless beating it had taken throughout the day. The giant oak Brynn had swung from after their father's death was half destroyed. A massive, leafless branch lay upon the lawn, lengths of jute still tied around its middle, as if in reminder: *I wiped out your sister, I can wipe you out, too.*

Maggie parked along the curb. It was an instinctual move, one Brynn had taught her when Maggie had first started to drive. *Don't wake the witch.* Not wanting to rouse anyone with the sound of the engine or the slamming of a door, she only realized how ridiculous that was after she bailed out of the car. The storm was raging. It would have been impossible for any of the Olsens to have heard a thing.

The garage door didn't budge when she pushed the button on Brynn's key ring remote. The entry pad affixed to the house next to the garage didn't work, either. *No power, dummy.* She struggled with the door, which luckily rolled upward—Howie must have gotten home after the electricity had gone; he'd pulled the emergency latch and hadn't engaged it again. Arlen's van, Howie's sedan, and a pair of what she had thought had been long-abandoned bikes sat in the dark. Brynn and Maggie's bicycles leaned against the wall, side by side, their handlebars tangled together, as if forever bound, but her bike was unlike Brynn's. Just like in her own childhood, it was being used while Brynn's stood forgotten. Hope was reliving Maggie's past, and Maggie had to stop it. She ducked inside, out of the rain.

After Katrina, her father would stay up all night to make sure all was well anytime these storms hit Savannah; because out in Pensacola, Gram and Gramps had been okay, but things had gotten scary. Their place had flooded, and all the windows had been blown out. Gas stations' awnings had been torn to shreds, leaving twisted metal in the streets. There was talk of them moving back to Savannah, where the storms weren't quite as brutal, but they never did. Maggie wondered if Howie was the type to stay up the way her father had. Her fingers were crossed that the answer was no.

Inside the house, there was no movement, no flicker of emergency candles, no family huddled on the couch listening to the howl of the wind. It was dark—so dark that, had Maggie not known its layout by heart, she would have never found her way to the second floor. Upstairs, she closed her bedroom door and pressed her back against it, waiting for her eyes to adjust. And then she fixed her attention first on the dark inkblot of shadow beneath her bed and then onto the closed closet door. She wanted nothing more than to reach out her hand and slide it against the wall, to feel for the light switch and flip it upward—desperate for the safety offered by way of a blazing bulb. But even if she gave in to her fear, the light wouldn't come this time. Florence would make sure of that. This time, Maggie couldn't run from her fear.

Outside, the lightning lit up the world like a strobe; inside, only faint slashes of that brightness found their way through the shutter slats. Despite every nerve in Maggie's body attempting to revolt, she forced herself to slide down to the floor. Rain-wet palms pressed against the carpet. She rocked forward onto her knees.

Thunder rumbled as she crawled across the room in the very same way she had as a girl. But rather than shimmying away from her room as quickly as possible, she now inched toward the pitch-black shadow that lingered beneath her bed. It was impossible to not recall the shaking. The scratching. The soft tapping from behind the headboard. Her childhood nyctophobia hadn't been misguided, and it certainly wasn't unbefitting now. Because there was something inside that room with her. Something watching, reducing the confident young woman Maggie had become to the scared and shivering child she had once been.

She reached the edge of the bed, the shadows beneath it so dark they seemed to pulsate with every hitch of her breath. She trembled as she reached toward the darkness's edge, her fingers lighting up ghostly pale in another bright electric flash.

"It's a hoax," she whispered. "A party game." A stupid toy she'd bought because the box had been mysterious, those soothsayer's hands beckoning her to place her fingers on the planchette, to see what the mystifying oracle could predict.

Maggie's fingertips brushed the hem of the bed skirt, but she pulled away. The valance shivered in a breeze that didn't exist. She braced herself and shoved her hand beneath the bed, but felt nothing but carpet. The board was gone again, vanished from the spot it should have occupied, unregulated by reality's rules.

And then, the closet emitted a soft click.

The scent of smoke coiled around her as the air left the room.

With her eyes having adjusted to the darkness, Maggie could just make out the closet door swinging open ever so slowly. Her body vibrated with a scream that was desperate to wrench itself from her throat. But there was nothing but silence beneath the muffled sound of the storm.

Nothing but the wind, the rain, and the faint *tap, tap, tap* that, despite the downpour, she still managed to hear from behind the headboard just beyond her shoulder.

Oh yes, I'm here. I've waited for you so long.

Maggie didn't dare look away from the closet. The door was still creeping open, and there was something hiding beyond the threshold—something peeking through the blackness, obscured by the jamb. The sound of another lock clicking open had Maggie veering around. Her bedroom door slowly crept inward, allowing the faint whisper of music to drift in from the direction of Brynn's abandoned room. Hymnal. Archaic. Undoubtedly the same track that had been playing when Arlen had found their sister upon the flagstones downstairs.

Rising to her feet, she felt detached from her own movements. Certainly, she was controlling her limbs, and yet each step felt guided, forced by an invisible hand. Her eyes darted back to the closet, to the shadow she knew was waiting there, but that blot of darkness was gone. *Just a loose screw, Crazy.* Except, no. It had always been true. She had tried to deny its existence, so it reached out, as if taking up Cheryl's challenge: *Hey, ghost. Prove that you're real.*

Maggie moved through her open door and stopped in front of Brynn's room. The door was now wide-open despite being shut only minutes before. The familiar scent of melting wax invited her inside.

Stepping into that room was the last thing Maggie wanted to do. Its interior was pregnant with a static charge as strong as the lightning outside; a sense of pent-up energy, of wicked intent. Her attention snapped to the wall that had been singed by that thing—*What, a demon?*—but no longer held proof of what she had witnessed. Except there, just peeking out from beneath the sheet that had been tossed over broken glass and bloodstains, was the corner of the Ouija board that should have been in Maggie's room, but was now in Brynn's instead.

She faltered, unsure whether she could take another forward

step. A moment later, the step was taken for her. What felt like a child's hand pressed hard against the small of her back and pushed, forcing her to the edge of the sheet that kept the final traces of her big sister hidden from view.

"What do you want?" Maggie's words trembled, a mere whisper beneath the music nobody in the house but her seemed to be hearing. As if in response, a spike of pain skittered up her spine and settled between her shoulder blades. Her hands flew backward, palms clasping at her neck. She exhaled a muffled cry, only to feel it again, like claws biting into the flesh just above her collarbone. The intensity brought her crashing to her knees.

"Okay," she gasped. "*Okay.*" Reaching out, she pulled the board free of the sheet, drawing it to herself despite every fiber of her being telling her, *Don't, don't, don't.*

But this was not a matter of choice. She'd made that years ago.

Crossing her legs lotus-style, she placed the board upon her knees. "I–I call upon thee." She half wept the words. But before the planchette could move, Maggie found herself gasping at the onset of sudden, inexplicable silence.

The blare of the storm was gone.

No wind.

No rain.

It was a different sound now, a splashing from beyond Brynn's window. A sound so familiar it had Maggie pushing through the pain, shoving away the board, and scrambling to her feet. "Dad?"

She threw back Brynn's heavy drapes and discovered the window unboarded, unbroken, unshuttered. One story below, the pool shimmered with bright underwater lights. The wind was gone. The rain had ceased. Nothing but a figure—her father—swimming back and forth, executing a perfect fly, while a little girl sat on the edge of the shallow end, her bare feet kicking against the lapping waves.

"Dad . . ." The word left Maggie's throat in a breathless whisper. This was impossible. "Dad!" Louder, attempting to get her father's attention. But all it rendered was the upward snap of the small girl's head. Their eyes met.

That should be me.

But it wasn't Maggie, and it wasn't Hope. It was a different child altogether, donning a dress that looked nearly identical to that of the doll's; she was kicking her feet and grinning, but the smile wasn't friendly. It was forewarning.

Hi, Mags, hi.

Spinning away, Maggie ran for Brynn's open door and bolted for the stairs. If she could get to the pool, maybe she could see her father again. Perhaps, even if he was just an illusion, she could tell him she loved him. She missed him. She was sorry. *Please, forgive me . . .* But a scream brought her to a startled standstill, a repeat performance of the night before. But it wasn't Hope.

A voice called out: "Mom?"

Maggie felt herself go faint, her fingers clutching the newel post. "Oh my God, Mom?!"

That voice. It was Brynn.

The yelling was coming from beyond the master bedroom door. Brynn, discovering their mother's body, limp and bleeding upon the bathroom floor.

A wave of nausea hit Maggie head-on. For a second, she was sure she was about to fall headlong down the staircase: another tragedy at the Olsen house. Poor Maggie, neck broken only a few days after her sister had passed. But she somehow managed to change course, throwing herself toward her mother's old bedroom. Her destination was, however, denied again, by the sound of shattering glass coming from Brynn's room.

What's happening?

Maggie veered around, her breathing coming in uneven heaves. *What the hell is happening?!*

Not knowing where to look, she cried out when she noticed the tremors in her arms, reminded of the night she'd crawled down that very hall to the door she was standing at now. The scent of smoke grew heavy, almost suffocating as she tried to draw in breath. And as if determined to make that memory as vivid as possible, the thing that had been living in her closet all these years scurried out from her bedroom and into the hall on its hands and knees. Rather than being a blot of darkness, this time that thing had taken shape.

It was small. Black. Its skinny, spiderlike limbs feathering like burnt paper, like wood that had turned to coal. It ducked into Brynn's bedroom so quickly it seemed like nothing short of a hallucination, a blur.

Maggie stood petrified, unsure of how to continue or where to go. Her mouth worked against the air, trying to draw in enough breath to cry out. *Wake someone. Anyone.* Arlen or Howie, even one of the kids would have been better than the solitude that surrounded her. But something told her that they wouldn't hear her; something assured her that right then, she wasn't in the same house as them. It's why the rain was gone. Why the wind had stopped. She was somewhere else, somewhere beyond what should have been possible. In between worlds, where screaming wasn't allowed.

Not afforded a yell, she felt her breath stolen once again. Brynn's voice came from beyond her sister's open bedroom door.

"Why won't you come home, Maggie?"

Her heart tripped over itself.

"I miss you. Why won't you come home?"

That voice sent her into an involuntary forward stumble, desperate to see her beloved Brynn one last time. *Bee, I'm sorry.* But when she tripped into the room, Brynn wasn't there. But the spirit board she had abandoned moments before was surrounded by dozens of flickering candles, lit just as they had been on Maggie's twelfth birthday, the night Brynn had taught her little sister how to summon the dead.

The window, which had been unbroken, was now but a jagged glass-rimmed portal to the outside world. Maggie dashed across the room, remembering her father. Downstairs, the little girl was gone. Two figures, however, remained.

The wind returned, blasting into Maggie's face.

Another crack of lightning illuminated her father, half tangled in a tarp, floating facedown in the center of the pool.

The rain returned, nothing short of a torrent. Water crashed into the pool, turning that iridescent, glowing liquid into a raging sea.

And there was Brynn, unmoving upon the flagstones, like a shattered doll fallen from a shelf.

"Oh God." Maggie careened backward, searching for the thing she had seen scurry into the room mere seconds before. "Where are you?" She turned in circles, scanning the corners. "*Where the hell are you?*" Another vindictive response: the pain in her neck and shoulders gripping her like a vise.

Maggie's eyes went wide with surprise, shocked by its intensity, by its pitiless unrestraint. She stood motionless, paralyzed with both anguish and dismay, staring at the wall of mirrors Brynn had left behind, gaping as the sheets that covered them were all simultaneously torn away by the frenzied gale.

And there, in half a dozen identical reflections, perched atop Maggie's shoulders, was that *thing*. Charred and long-limbed with an almost oversized head attached to its frame, that skeletal figure. A *child*. Its blackened feet and bony fingers digging hard into Maggie's skin.

Maggie bellowed out a cry. Reflexively, her arms swung high, hands flying around her head and neck like trapped moths against a bell jar's curve. She screamed again, spinning like a top, stumbling into Brynn's cloth-covered dresser, which was stacked with makeup, hair brushes, blazing tea lights, and creams. The collection tumbled off the dresser's top and onto the floor. Candles splashed melted wax across the baseboard and the corner of an old afghan rug.

Maggie stood frozen in place for a moment, her arms stretched outward as if to keep herself steady on her own two feet. Maybe she'd scared it off. Maybe it was gone. She swallowed hard, afraid to look anywhere but at the sheet covering the top of Brynn's mirrored dresser. "I imagined it," she whispered. Perhaps if she spoke the words aloud, they'd somehow become the truth.

Except, no. As soon as that denial crossed her lips, the pain came back, this time more vicious than before. Maggie yowled and crumpled to the floor. "Stop!" She intended it to be a yell, but was too breathless to project the demand, too overcome to be strong-willed.

But you can't give in this time. You can't let it win.

Pushing through the anguish, she snatched Brynn's nail file off the floor.

Get up. She imagined Brynn making the command. Narrowed eyes. Looking mean. *Get the fuck up, Maggie. I tried to fix this for you, but—*

Maggie forced herself to her feet, back in front of the mirrors. Regardless of whether she wanted to see that thing again or not, this was her fight. She had started it. It had to end with her. If it was still perched on her shoulders, she'd stab at it over and over until it was gone. She'd kill it so it couldn't hurt anyone else. She'd kill herself before she let this madness continue.

Your fault.

Her arm trembled as she lifted it upward, that file pointed at her own face.

All your fault.

She shimmied sideways, just enough to see the curve of her shoulder, the slope of her neck.

You did this.

She squeezed her eyes shut and exhaled a muffled mew. She didn't want to see it. Didn't want to see it. Didn't want to see it sitting there, leering like a snake.

"I'm *sorry!*" She screamed the words as her eyes shot open and she took in her reflection—an apology to her sister, to her mother, her dad. Hell, to the thing that she'd just seen, singed and smoldering. *I'm sorry that I brought you into this world. I'm sorry that I didn't know how to put you back.* But it was gone, nothing but the reflection of a wild-eyed girl left in its wake. She hardly recognized herself—a woman on the brink of mania, clutching a weapon, ready to kill herself, to fight an invisible foe.

Had Maggie scared that spiderlike creature off, or was it merely hiding, lying in wait? No. That smoky scent was only growing stronger. Maggie coughed, twisted around again, searching the corners of Brynn's room for what felt like the thousandth time, only to be left gasping at a new discovery.

The bottom hem of Brynn's drapes was starting to smolder. A few of the candles she'd toppled were still alight, sending curlicues of smoke up from burning velvet. She fell to her hands and knees, grabbing a handful of white sheet from the floor, and began to choke the flames. But her attention snagged on what she'd uncovered: a massive stain the color of rust, so much bigger than she had imagined it to be. It was the spot where Brynn had stood and bled, broken glass cutting into the palm of her hand, wounds weeping blood from the damage she'd done to her face and neck—a result of what she'd undeniably seen in the single mirror that had been left exposed.

Brynn had seen that burnt figure.

It's why she'd covered all of those mirrors up.

It's why she had stabbed herself.

She had seen it, poised there upon her neck.

And now, Maggie was seeing it as well—not on her shoulders, but in the corner of the room. It hadn't rushed out to hide. Rather, it was curled up between a bedside table and a wall of framed baroque art, as though transfixed by the growing fire licking up the drapes and the wall.

It was afraid.

Her mom lit the sheets on fire and left her there, screaming . . .

Maggie found herself nearly choking, either on the smoke or on the sudden onset of realization. Because Brynn's story, however impossible, had been true.

I came here by myself yesterday and she threatened me, so I made her a promise.

Brynn and Maggie in Friendship Park. Brynn shoving Maggie toward that tomb.

I promised her that I'd bring her a friend, so she'd never be lonely again.

"Oh God," Maggie whispered, her gaze snapping to the board just shy of her sister's blood.

Why won't you come back, Mags? How many times do I have to ask?

"It used you to get me to come home."

That thing . . . Brynn's death had been by design. It had killed her, knowing that Maggie would rush home for the funeral. It had scared her to death, sure that the Olsen sister it *really* wanted would return.

Rage. It wasn't a spark but an explosion, right there in the center of Maggie's chest. All of this had been a test. A game. Maggie left to go to the beach; her father was taken from her. Maggie left to go to school; her mother was pushed to the brink. Maggie left Savannah again, refusing to let tragedy cement her in place, and the force she had released had decided the game had lasted long enough. Checkmate. Brynn had been its sacrificial queen.

"You son of a bitch." Maggie gritted her teeth, her eyes fixed on the board on the floor. "You think you're going to win this?" It was then that she grabbed a blazing candle in one hand and a fallen can of Brynn's hair spray in the other. If this thing was afraid of fire, she'd either scare it out of the house or burn the damn place to the ground.

With a flick of her thumb, she popped the top off the can. Her finger on the trigger, she glared at that goddamn ghost. "This is for my sister," she hissed through her teeth, and pressed down, releasing a rope of flame through the air. It ignited the board and the carpet around it within a blink. The cowering figure in the corner screeched as Maggie pointed her makeshift flamethrower its way. It dodged, leaving a fresh scar of soot across Brynn's wallpaper. A moment later, Brynn's four-poster bed was engulfed in flame.

Brynn had known all along: there was something wrong with this house. It's why she had stayed—not because she wanted to live in Savannah, not because she had some inexplicable connection to the place they had grown up, but to protect her nieces and nephew. But Arlen would never leave voluntarily, which was why it had to be destroyed.

"Fuck this place," Maggie murmured, tossing the can of hair spray to the floor.

This would leave her remaining sister with no choice. The Olsens would have to leave.

The flames were high, now, halfway to the ceiling. The heat was burning Maggie's cheeks, threatening to ignite her hair. Satisfied that there was far too much fire for Howie to extinguish in a bold attempt to save the place, she raced out of the room and down the hall.

Why isn't the fire alarm going off?

Because this was its last attempt.

It wanted them all.

If they all burned together, the Olsen family line would be no more.

Maggie banged on the walls as she flew down the hall, then threw open the master bedroom door and yelled, "Wake up! Fire! We have to go!" She found the entire family holed up in Arlen and Howie's bed. The adults scrambled to sit upright. And, as if seeing the shadow standing directly behind her aunt, Hayden's eyes went wide. A second later, she pealed out a scream.

. . .

In the time it took them all to get onto the front lawn, half the second floor had been consumed. Windows exploded one after the other, just like Maggie imagined they had at Gram and Gramps's place so many years ago. Harry looked on, dumbfounded, as fire trucks rolled onto the property. Hayden wailed for her favorite stuffed bear, which had been abandoned inside her parents' room. Arlen cried right along with her while Howie held them both, trying to comfort them during one final misfortune. Florence had no mercy. The wind continued to blow, fanning the flames, setting nearby trees alight, tossing fiery debris onto the rain-soaked lawn.

Hope stood motionless, staring at the burning monolith before her. Eventually, she turned to Maggie, and taking her aunt's hand in her own, she leaned in and whispered into Maggie's ear, "I'm scared, Auntie Magdalene. But at least you're here."

NINETEEN

BRYNN'S CAMRY SURVIVED the fire, having been parked along the curb.

Maggie sat in silence in the backseat as the car rolled toward the funeral home. It had been too late to postpone.

Howie drove while Arlen sat next to him with Hayden in her lap. Dazed and exhausted, they looked like a grouping of lunatics, everyone in their pajamas but Maggie, who was wearing the same thing she'd worn the day before. Aunt CeeCee would meet them in the parking lot with clothes bought at Target. Arlen hadn't argued. They had nothing left, so there hadn't been a point.

Sitting in the front seat, Arlen looked just as their mother had after their father had died. Her expression was blank, her eyes glazed over, a zombie personified. Howie directed the car without a word, more than likely stunned at the cruel irony that, not more than a handful of hours after losing it all, they were expected to mourn something different. But there was no avoiding it. Interments weren't events that could be easily put off. Brynn was waiting, and Florence would not be attending. The storm was over. It had left them behind.

And yet, despite the somberness of the morning and the joylessness that would follow them throughout the day, Maggie couldn't help but feel hopeful. For the first time during her visit, little Hayden wasn't screaming. With no car seat, she was fast asleep in Arlen's arms, as though sensing that the thing she'd grown up with had finally been expunged.

"Auntie Magdalene?" Hope now placed her small hand upon Maggie's own as they sat together in the backseat. Harrison pressed himself against the door, staring out the window, not speaking or listening, in his own world.

"Yeah, kid?" Maggie gave her niece a thoughtful glance.

"Does this mean that you aren't going to live with us after all, because the house is gone?"

Maggie frowned at Hope's expression. The little girl looked positively wrecked, as though the thought of losing her aunt was far worse than losing all of her things. "I'll stay for a little while," Maggie told her, drawing her close. "At least until everything gets sorted out, until you guys have a new place to go." Until she was sure it was over, that it was finally safe.

Hope nodded, seemingly satisfied with that answer. She went quiet for a bit, studying Maggie's hands before speaking again. "Don't you think that Auntie Bee should be burned instead of buried?" There was an audible intake of breath from both of Hope's parents. Maggie found herself stammering, unsure of how to respond. "It just seems like she should be burned," Hope said, either unaware of the sudden tension she'd created or simply not caring that she had. "Like the house. Like the girl in the graveyard," she said, looking to Maggie for approval.

"The girl . . . ?" Maggie suddenly felt sick. She needed to get out. She needed air.

"Yeah, like the girl in the graveyard," Hope repeated. "You know, the girl who's your friend."

Arlen slowly turned to look at Maggie from the front seat, her face nothing short of aghast.

Maggie said nothing. She looked out the window instead, trying not to scream.

. . .

When they pulled up to the mortuary, the double doors were open. A few people fiddled with umbrellas they no longer needed. There were still a few clouds overhead, but by afternoon, the sky would be a bright and pristine blue.

"Will you put this in the trunk?" Arlen asked, handing Maggie Hayden's blanket from the front seat, crumpled and smelling of smoke. "It stinks. I don't want to take it in."

Howie parked the car and the family climbed out. Maggie stayed behind, clutching Hayden's blanket to her chest as she peered at the clouds that were now a faint gray rather than an ominous black. Finally, she turned back to the car and moved around to the trunk, popping it open, only to stop short.

Because there was Brynn's old porcelain doll—one hand shattered, its glass faced cracked.

"Hey, you found it," Hope said, nearly making Maggie jump. "Sorry I said it didn't belong to you before, Auntie. I was wrong."

"Wrong?" Maggie choked on the word, her eyes never wavering from the doll that stared dead-eyed up at her from the trunk of the car.

"I said it wasn't yours. But the little girl told me the truth."

"The truth," Maggie whispered.

"Uh-huh."

"And . . . what's the truth?" Maggie asked, feeling the tremor in her hands start to quake, suppressing the shrieking that was inching its way up her throat.

"That it's always been yours to begin with," Hope said. "Ever since you brought it home with you. You promised, remember? You said you'd be her friend."

Hope ran away then, skipping across the parking lot as though her house hadn't just vanished, as though her aunt hadn't died.

It was then that Maggie felt it, the pain making its return. Except this time, the dull anguish in her neck was punctuated by something new, something sharp and digging in. Her gaze jumped to the side-view mirror of Brynn's old car. And then she saw it.

Soot-black.

Clawing into her shoulder's curve.

Five bony fingers, refusing to ever let her go.

AUTHOR'S NOTE

When I was a girl, about eleven years old, I walked into a Toys R Us with a twenty-dollar bill crushed into the palm of my hand. I found myself in front of a wall of board games, and out of all those games, I chose one that I would never forget; or, perhaps, the one that would never let me forget I chose it.

The real-life Ouija board that haunted me through my childhood is gone. I don't know where it went or how in the world it could have been misplaced. But the furniture of my childhood room, where I had used the board, remained long after the board had disappeared. Once I was ready to move on to something more adult in my teenage years, my mother decided not to get rid of my canopy bed or dresser, or even my desk or the white steamer trunk that sat at the foot of my bed. Instead, she transported it to a cabin my father had built in the woods, resolving to use it for guests whenever they might arrive. I loved that cabin, but I hated walking down that upstairs hallway. The room that held my old furniture was at the hallway's end, and there was always a feeling . . . like something was off. I stepped inside that room only once and immediately left. It felt cooler than the rest of the house, almost damp somehow. There was a smell, too; one I couldn't place.

That house burned down, engulfed in a fire that left much of the land surrounding it strangely untouched. The fire wasn't paranormal, and yet, despite knowing all the details, I still think back to that room, that furniture, the fact that its energy, post-board, had always felt dangerous somehow. I still think back to the ghost of my child-hood and wonder, had the board somehow made it up to the woods? Had it been in that room? Had I abandoned it, and was it angry? Is it possible to haunt yourself, and what would happen if you did?

I Call Upon Thee is a work of fiction, but it's the closest thing I'll get to an autobiography of how my "strangeness" came to be. The board was real. The cemetery, real. The night I watched *The Exorcist*, real as well. And the part where twelve-year-old Maggie suddenly realizes she's in over her head? Yeah, that too. Of course, there's em-bellishment and exaggeration, but it's cobbled together from true events, odd memories, and the occasional nightmare.

And that, my friends, is why I'll never contact the dead again.

ACKNOWLEDGMENTS

As there are lengthier acknowledgments at the end of the original publications of *The Pretty Ones* and *I Call Upon Thee*, there are only a few thank-yous I'd like to make here: To my agent, David Hale Smith, thank you for continuing to be awesome. To my editor, Ed Schlesinger, thank you for continuing to put up with me . . . and occasionally checking in to make sure I'm still alive. To my publisher, Gallery Books, and specifically to Jen Bergstrom, thank you so much for believing in me the way you do. You deserve all the chicken feet. And last, but never least, thanks to my readers, without whom I'd be little more than a figment of my own strange imagination.

ABOUT THE AUTHOR

ANIA AHLBORN is the bestselling author of the acclaimed horror thrillers *I Call Upon Thee*, *The Devil Crept In*, *Brother*, *The Pretty Ones*, *Within These Walls*, *The Bird Eater*, *The Shuddering*, *The Neighbors*, and *Seed*. Born in Ciechanów, Poland, she lives in South Carolina with her husband and their dog. Visit www.aniaahlborn.com or follow her on Facebook and Twitter.

9 781501 187537